If You Go Down in the Woods
A Wendlewulf Productions Book

ISBN: 9780473088507

PUBLISHING HISTORY
Published by Wendlewulf Productions 2015

Copyright GR Boxell 2015

Cover by John Clark

Printed by Amazon

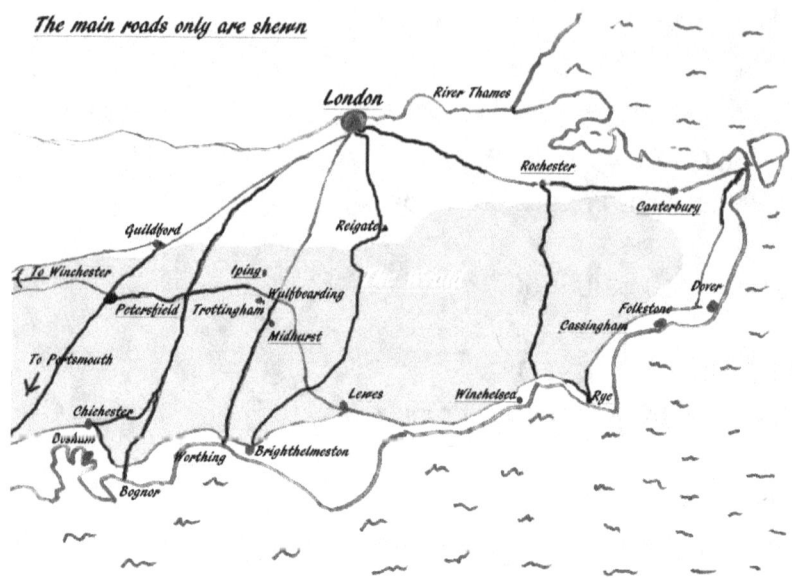

The main roads only are shewn

Dedicated to my younger twin brothers who died in my mother's womb.

Notes:

The use of italics indicates the speaker is doing so in one of the French dialects, of which there were many.

(see end of book for more notes)

Chapter 1: In the Greenwood

The summer sunlight filtered through the green leaves of the forest trees producing an unusual light that made the pale green of the two young men's shirts a deeper green where it hit their backs. The air hung humid and heavy, causing even the birds to still their calling. The slightly taller of the fair haired men looked to the other and signalled to him with eye and hand to move to the right. Silently his companion moved, constantly checking that he was where he was supposed to be. The taller man held up his hand, then, once the other had stopped moving, pulled an arrow with a hunting head carefully from behind his back, using his fingers to ease the barbs through his belt; he held the arrow up and nodded that the other should do similar. The two nocked their arrows at the same time. At a signal from the taller they both rose and loosed together. With thumps that were almost instantaneous the arrows struck the roe deer that had been browsing the grass in the small clearing; it staggered, tried to run, then collapsed, its back legs still trying to run.

Godfrey Wulfson, yeoman of the village of Iping, looked to his twin brother Thomas and smiled. 'Good shooting little brother.'

Thomas snorted in disgust; 'An hour between us and I am still "little brother" to you.'

'Someone has to be the eldest and wisest of the family.' Godfrey smiled at Thomas as the two archers unstrung their long elm bows.

'Right big brother, right'

The twins moved into the small clearing where the young buck had been grazing on soft succulent grass that had been refreshed by the previous night's rain. Thomas took out his knife, pulled the creature's head up by its small upright antlers and slit the deer's throat to end its misery. Godfrey used his long hunting knife to extract the arrows, placing them on the ground away from the deer to be retrieved later. The twins then turned the dead deer onto its back, slit the skin along its stomach and, whilst Godfrey eviscerated it, Thomas started to dig a hole with his own long blade to bury the guts. The two worked quickly and skilfully, displaying the abilities they had acquired from years working as beaters and huntsmen for their French speaking betters when they came to hunt the deer driven into the hunting hurst at Midhurst.

'As the eldest I nominate you to carry the deer back home Thomas.'

'Ah, but as the eldest, and therefore the biggest, it should be your honour brother.'

Godfrey grunted in amusement, for he was indeed half an inch taller. He pulled off his shirt, exposing his sweat gleamed white torso, then handed the shirt and his bow to Thomas. Grabbing the deer carcass, a pair of feet to each hand, Godfrey hoisted it onto his shoulders. 'Lead on little brother.'

'I hope you have a warrant for hunting in these here woods?'

Godfrey and Thomas stood dead still, both slowly edging their right hand towards their hunting knives.

'Don't try it, we have you covered. One move and you will find feathers growing out of your back,' added a second voice.

Thomas let out his held breath; 'Ganger Greenwood, you could not disguise your voice if you tried.'

Ganger and his mate and fellow forester, John Forest, burst out laughing.

Godfrey let the deer carcass slip from his shoulders and turned round shaking his fair haired head. 'You two will one day get hurt when one of us reacts before looking to see who it is challenging us. Anyway, we have a warrant to cull deer, it just hasn't arrived yet.'

'And,' added his twin, 'you may be foresters, but would you know what a warrant to hunt looks like?'

'Of course,' insisted John Greenwood the Ganger. 'It looks like this!' He fumbled in his script and produced a piece of parchment with an impressive wax seal on it.

'We used that to get us out of trouble when a Crowhurst forester found us in his patch with a couple of fallow deer the other week.'

'Where did you get it?' Godfrey asked, holding out his hand.

John Forest handed it over. 'It fell out of some Lordship's baggage at the last Midhurst hunt.'

'Fell out?' queried Thomas.

'With a bit of easing,' John confessed. The forester looked to Godfrey; 'Well, what does it say? You know I can't read. Is it a hunting warrant?'

Godfrey shook his head. 'No idea. I think it is written in French, or Latin – it is not in English.' He passed it to his twin, who also examined it.

Thomas pursed his lips. 'I had wondered if it might be in a form of English they speak elsewhere, you know, north of Watford or even further into barbarian lands, but then I would have recognised at least some of the words.' He gave it back to his brother.

5

Godfrey had another try at reading the words. 'Could the forester at Crowhurst read it?'

Ganger gave a snort. 'Nah. He squizzed it long enough and nodded his head as if in understanding a lot. I know enough of letters to know he had the thing upside down – see the seal is at the top, not the bottom like it is on most documents.'

'So why did he let you go?' chimed in Thomas, 'He should have taken you, and your "warrant" to someone who could read.'

Ganger nudged John Forest in the ribs. 'Do you think it was the fact that there was only one of him and six of us?'

'Maybe.'

Ganger took the warrant back, folded it carefully and tucked it back into his script. 'Mind you, we won't be off hunting over Crowhurst way again.'

'At least not for a while,' John agreed.

'Why don't you get your local priest to read it for you?' Godfrey asked.

Ganger shook his head slowly; 'And has him ask where I got it from?'

'John of Chichester is priest at Trottingham, ' Thomas informed Ganger. 'He is close enough family to us to ask no questions.'

'Maybe.'

'Anyway, Master Foresters, what brings you this way? We,' Thomas looked to Godfrey. 'We know you are not after catching honest yeomen taking the odd deer to supplement their food supply.'

'Not in these woods anyway,' Ganger confirmed.

'Not our patch,' John confirmed. 'But we were looking for you. We have a problem and think you two likely lads can help us.'

Godfrey scratched at a gnat bite on his shoulder; 'I am always nervous when people like you ask for help.'

'I wonder why?' Thomas completed the sentence.

'Any way,' continued Godfrey, a trickle of sweat running down from his face from his sweat darkened hair. 'How did you know where to find us?'

A small, delicately built youth with an almost feminine face, swarthy complexion and black hair appeared from behind John Forest's back, 'I told them where you might be,' the boy said in a slightly accented English.

Godfrey and Thomas both gave the slim boy a strong look. The boy smiled back; 'I said you were going to the clearing near the old iron forge for archery practice,' he gave a stage wink to acknowledge the lie.

Godfrey looked to his twin before addressing the boy; 'All right young Will Greenleaf, we will talk to you later about this.'

'And me too?' asked a white faced boy with dark brown hair who had appeared seemingly from nowhere.

'You too Sebastian.'

'So,' Godfrey gave his attention back to John Forest. 'So, what is the problem that made you seek us out?'

'It's Cedric of Steadham's swine.'

'They can be a problem,' Thomas agreed.

'It's not his swine that's the problem,' Ganger clarified. 'It's the French.'

'The French are always a problem, ever since Willie the Bastard arrived here uninvited.' Godfrey gave his shoulder another scratch. 'So what's new?'

'What's new,' stated John Forest. 'What's new is that some of them are stealing Cedric's swine, driving them down the road to the coast.'

'King's men?' questioned Godfrey, still paying more attention to his shoulder than to the Midhurst foresters.

'No, not King's men; real Frenchies.'

'There is a difference?'

'Ah,' Ganger came back into the discussion. 'You know our good King John …'

'A far better King than his brother Richard who knew only how to tax us poor English,' interrupted Thomas.

'As I was saying,' Ganger came back in a louder voice. 'Our good King John lost Normandy recently.'

'Lost it? It is a very big place to loose,' snorted Thomas. 'Did he look under his bed?'

'Look smart arse, you know what I mean, he lost his Lordship of Normandy, lost his castles, got kicked out by the French King, is no longer Duke of Normandy.' Ganger gave the twin an exasperated look and thrust his hands on his hips in a belligerent stance.

'Yeah, well,' Godfrey's voice was low pitched as he tried to ease the situation. 'He lost Normandy, what's that to us?'

John took over the conversation; 'It pissed off those of his baron's what had land there as well as here.'

'I heard something about that at the last hunt our own baron held.'

8

'And some of the barons have been up in arms against the King since.'

'The barons are always at each other's throat, even revolting against the King from time to time as I have heard said. Nothing new there.'

'Except,' said Ganger, tilting his head towards Godfrey rather than Thomas, who he had been staring down. 'Except the revolting barons ……..'

Thomas fought down the temptation to make a comment on all barons being revolting.

'…... have invited the French King's son ...'

'The dolphin,' John contributed. Thomas was tempted to say "Not Flounder?" but Ganger had gone back to staring at him.

'The Dauphin, Louis I think he is called, to come over and be King of England.'

'Over my dead body,' Thomas said, emphatically.

'Could happen Thomas, it could happen, 'cos he has already sent some of his men over to merry England and the bastards are in our woods stealing our swine.'

'Cedric's swine,' Godfrey corrected Ganger.

'Cedric's today, mine tomorrow and yours the day after.'

'So Ganger, what are we going to do about it?'

'That's why we came looking for you two.'

'We did indeed,' agreed John Forest. 'We are going to get Cedric's little piggie wiggies back for him.'

'So put down your ill-gotten ……..' Ganger started to say.

'And illegally killed,' reminded John.

9

'…… deer, leave your hunting arrows with the carcass, take these three war arrows each, and come with us.' Ganger continued as he waved the feathered shafts at the twins.

John Forest sidled up to Thomas and whispered; 'I'm sure you wouldn't like us to mention to your Lord, the Lady Maude, in your Manor Court that we had found you with a red hand, bloody shoulders and a freshly slaughtered deer at your feet, a deer that rightfully belongs to her.'

'The warrant is on its way,' Thomas protested.

'So is Christmas.' Ganger gave a wicked smile. 'Now hurry up, we have to meet with another Steadham man, Granfer Gilbert Green, back at the old disused iron kiln. He has gone home to get bows for him and Cedric.'

'Where is Cedric?' said Godfrey, as he placed his and Thomas' hunting arrows into the empty chest cavity of the roe deer.

'Tracking the Frenchies.' Ganger stuck six war arrows, four with leaf shaped heads and two with long bodkin needle heads into the dirt. 'I got these when I did forty days service in Normandy last year for King John.'

John patted his fellow forester on the shoulder 'You did well out of that trip Ganger, lots of plunder.'

'I did,' Ganger pulled back his hood and wiped the sweat off his balding head. 'Plunder and arrows that I forgot to give back. I also developed a distinct dislike of the French; smelly lot, no manners and unable to brew a decent ale.'

Godfrey pulled his three arrows out of the dirt and stuck then behind his back, through his belt. 'Why are you helping Cedric? He isn't of your kin is he.'

10

Ganger pulled his hood back on and settled it comfortably on his head. 'I don't like the French and, besides, if they get away with stealing Cedric's swine today, as I said before, it will be mine and yours soon after with maybe your plough oxen to give them variety in their diet.'

Thomas pulled his arrows through his belt, moving them around till they felt comfortable and did not restrict his movement. 'Good point Ganger, good point, so we had best be off to meet up with old Gilbert.'

Godfrey poured some water from his leathern bottle onto his shoulders and started scrubbing off the dried blood with a handful of grass. 'Will; Seb?'

The youngsters came over, eager to be part of whatever was going on.

'Take the deer back to Iping for us,' Thomas told them. 'And do it with discretion, don't parade it up and down the village letting everyone know what we have been doing this morning.'

'And don't lose the arrows,' Godfrey added, pulling his shirt back on.

The four green shirted men carefully approached the disused iron kiln, treading carefully, avoiding any fallen twigs.

'You make enough noise for a herd of kine,' a voice hissed from behind them.

The men halted and turned their heads, looking for the source of the voice. They saw nothing.

Ganger shook his head; 'All right Granfer Gilbert, we give up. Where are you?'

'You youngsters still have a lot to learn from this old yeoman, even you foresters that are supposed to be such experts in wood stealth.' Gilbert Green, a man in his late fifties, but still upright and unbent, unblended himself from a clump of tall bracken where his faded green hood and stained brown shirt had kept him hidden from even the sharpest eye. He moved slowly and quietly towards the others. 'Cedric is up by the road; the Frenchies have stopped to eat, and by the looks of it, they have settled down for a banquet.'

'Good.' Ganger passed Gilbert three war arrows for himself and three for Cedric. 'I will want them back, so don't lose any.'

Gilbert grunted.

'What's the plan Ganger?' John Forest asked before taking a swig from his water bottle.

'We talk to Cedric, see where the French are, then work out how best to shoot them. We need to make sure we kill them cleanly, they will have spears and swords, and we don't, so we want to avoid any close fighting.'

Godfrey tilted his head, as he often did when asking a difficult question, 'Kill?'

'We don't want any witnesses; I learnt that in Normandy fighting for our King John.'

'If you say so.' Thomas looked to his twin for confirmation, Godfrey nodded agreement.

'We won't have to worry about the Murthrum Fine, they are invaders, so not under the King's protection and I doubt the matter would ever be brought to the Sheriff's attention, not that I know which side he is on, of course.'

'Follow me,' Gilbert hissed. 'Don't speak except mouth to ear and do try and keep quiet as you move.'

The sound of laughter drifted from where the Frenchmen were eating and drinking their mid-day meal, three were sprawled on the sunken road whilst a fourth stood, watching the pigs as they nosed the brush and bracken along the wall of the sunken hard clay track, searching for treats.

'I hope they don't catch my scent, my dear little piggies,' Cedric whispered worriedly into Ganger's ear. 'For they do love me and if they know I am near, they will run to greet me so they can have their backs scratched.'

'Little piggies? Big fat overweight mobile dinners,' Ganger murmured to himself before he turned and whispered back; 'We are up wind, trust me, I hunt for a living, I know what we are doing. My concern is more about getting in the right place to take the French.'

'Just as long as my swine are not hit.'

'If we do get them back for you, you will owe us.'

'A suckling one at Yuletyde.'

'Each!'

'Each?'

'Shhhh, we will talk later.' Ganger beckoned the others over, and they gathered close, heads touching. 'Cedric and Gilbert move well to the right, to the big oak that has split. When I signal with a throstle bird's mating call mark your target then loose your arrows at the one standing. The twins; you can move well to the left to where the stunted beech is; keep close in to avoid being seen. Take

13

the man sitting on his own; same signal. John and I will take out the other two, left for you John, right hand man for me. Hoods down, cloth visors up. String your bows.' Ganger watched to make sure all had correctly braced the elm bows they carried and that were taller than their owners. 'Now go, smoothly and quietly.'

With barely a rustle the men carefully moved to their positions, stoop backed, keeping their strung bows close to their bodies. The members of the pairings warning each other of fallen branches and twigs by the hand movements they all used when hunting.

Ganger gave plenty of time for the others to have got into position before risking a good look to confirm the French were still more, or less, where they had been before. Satisfied he gave the throstle call.

The archers marked their targets, drew the bow strings to their ears then loosed their arrows with wooden twangs and, with muffled thumps, the arrows hit home on the targeted Frenchmen. The standing Frenchman staggered backwards then started to walk ponderously forward; two more arrows hit him and he collapsed to his knees.

'Quick lads,' Ganger broke cover and ran towards the kneeling man. 'Before he falls over and breaks the arrow shafts!'

The Frenchman gave Ganger a puzzled look as he and the other archers appeared as if by magic from the forest along the low bank of the sunken road. The man vaguely waved his hands in front of him around the arrows in his chest and gut. Ganger kept eye contact whilst John Forest went behind the man, drew his knife, grabbed the man's hair, pulled his head back and then slit his throat. The dying man slumped back against Forest's leg, his eyes

14

glazing and his blood spraying. Ganger waited till the blood spurt reduced to a low pump then cut the man's clothing so he could wriggle the arrows free. Ganger looked around and saw that the others had already dispatched their own targets and were retrieving the arrows.

'Well done lads, clean kills.' Ganger wiped the arrow heads clean of blood on his victim's shirt. 'Cedric, once you have cleaned the arrows get them tame pigs of yourn so you and Granfer Gilbert can get them well away before anyone finds this lot and starts asking questions.' Ganger stood up; 'Right, the arrows. Hang onto a bodkin head and a leaf head between you so you can get your local blacksmith to make more of the same, but I will want mine back soon.' He kicked the corpse of the nearest Frenchman. 'John and I can't hang around as we have a way to go to get home. We will take the purses; you twins can have whatever you want from these vermin, but I wouldn't take too long as they may have friends nearby wondering where their "pork" has got to.'

John Forest quickly cut a length of material from one of the Frenchmen's shirts into which John the Ganger dropped the purses he had cut from the dead Frenchmen's belts.

Cedric and Gilbert waved as they took the swine off the road and made a ragged way through bracken back towards Steadham, each of the pigs grunting happily to be back in their owner's company, understanding the calls made to them by Cedric in an almost silent whistle.

'Don't take too much time young Godfrey,' encouraged John. 'This isn't strictly legal, even less legal than visiting other people's hunting grounds and taking their deer.'

15

'The warrant is on its way,' insisted Thomas with a smirk that betrayed the lie.

'Hush,' Ganger hissed. 'I can hear horses. Run!'

At the trot seven horsemen, with three pack horses in tow, came up the rise of the road. Dappled sunlight glinted off the steel helmet and mael brinie of the lead rider, whilst behind him in pairs were lesser men who were less well armoured but all carrying spears and all wearing padded jackets and helmets of boiled leather.

'*Stand,*' yelled the maeled Sergeant in French of the Isle de Paris. '*Stand I say, stand!*'

'Run!' countered Ganger and he and John Forest went into the woods on the left leaving the twins to go to the right.

'*Run them down,*' the Sergeant commanded. Then, once he saw the density of the woods he changed his mind, realising the vulnerability of mounted men in a heavily wooded environment. '*Dismount. Dennis? Hold the horses.*' Getting off his own mount the Sergeant looked left and right then came to a decision. '*Let those others go, we will get the ones up there on the right, the woods are thinner and we have a better chance of catching them.*'

Six French men, spears left with the horses, chased after Godfrey and Thomas, following the trampled ferns that led back to the path the Englishman had come down.

They had not gone far when, unseen by them, two arrows thumped into the back of Dennis, who had been left as horse guard.

John Ganger Greenwood and John Forest edged out of the trees, looked around to ensure the other Frenchmen had gone. 'Looks like we have got ourselves some horses John.'

'Let's hope we can find a discreet way of selling them,' John commented as the two foresters set about securing the reins of the horses.

Ganger walked the three horses whose reins he held, 'We'll hobble this lot then set about seeing if we can help the Wulfson twins.'

Godfrey and Thomas ran, weaving through the thick brush, dodging round the mature trees, hugging their bows close to their bodies. Breathing hard, they found the path that lead to the old iron kiln, behind them they could hear the French men-at-arms pursuing them, crashing through the scrub. The path met others in a cross road, Thomas took the left arm, Godfrey the right; heart beats away the French arrived at the cross road.

'*Which way Sergeant?*' The lead man bent over breathing hard.

The Sergeant glanced at the paths, listened, frowned, then came to a decision; '*You two take the left path. You two the centre path. I'll take the right with Jean.*' He listened again; '*Yes, do it, we have all options covered.*'

The two Frenchmen taking the left hand path progressed at a jog and turned a bend before the first man staggered backwards with an arrow in his chest; he lay on the ground coughing blood. His companion stopped in a shuddering halt, looked at the trees in front of him, saw nothing, then bent to examine his companion. An arrow took him though the side of his throat causing blood to spray bright red into the air.

The Sergeant ran as fast as he could, his scabbarded sword jangling on his mael coat; *'Move it Jean, move it, I have one of them in sight!'*

Godfrey stopped, turned and loosed his only arrow. The Sergeant turned his head as the arrow flew past him and watched as the Frenchman named Jean crumpled with a groan as the arrow bit deep in his thigh.

'Bugger.' The Sergeant turned back and launched himself in a run towards the Englishman.

Godfrey ran, and ran, and ran, then tripped on a hole in the track and fell. He rolled over to see the Sergeant draw his sword and advance on him grinning.

'At last my friend, I have you,' the Frenchman patted his sword in the palm of his hand. 'How you want die?' he muttered in heavily accented English. 'One bit at a time? Hmm?' The Sergeant brought his blade back over his head, ready to swing at the now kneeling Godfrey. *'Which piece shall I hack off first Englishman?'* He pursed his lips as he gauged his distance and target area. A slight rustle behind him caused him to turn his head slightly, just in time to see the flash of sunlight on the woodsman's axe as it came down to sever his sword arm. Apart from a short gasp, the Sergeant made no reaction, which enabled the axeman to take off his left arm too. The Frenchman sagged at the knees and came down to kneel in front of a surprised Godfrey. In another flashing arc the Frenchman's head was severed and went flying into the nearby

18

bushes and his trunk dropped to the left, pumping blood across the path.

Godfrey blinked and looked up at his nephew, Garth, Robert's son, his sister Edith's eldest. The lad took to leaning on his blood covered axe. 'That was close Garth, too close.'

Garth gave a lopsided smile, 'I know it was close, but your head was never in danger Uncle; I do know what I am doing.'

'That wasn't what I meant young man, and well you know it.' Godfrey held out his hand and let Garth pull him up. 'I meant the timing. Not your accuracy with an axe.' Godfrey stood and brushed himself down. 'There is another Frenchman back there on the track.'

'Already taken care of and I think Mark, Jack and Uncle Thomas have sorted out the others.'

'Good.' Godfrey continued to dust himself down, trying to stop his trembling leg from being seen. 'Anyway, young Garth, what are you all doing this way, I thought you had work to do? No one invited you to join us on this escapade.'

'Those Frenchies that surprised you just now had visited Wulfbearding earlier this morning. They didn't leave it looking too good after they raided and plundered it.'

Godfrey looked hard into his nephew's eyes; 'You were there? Your family is unharmed?'

The young man half closed his eyes and gave a gentle nod. 'All is well, at least for us. We were all helping Edward Black and his family with the charcoal burning and didn't come home till it was all over. We were lucky, those in the hamlet when the French came visiting were less lucky.' He took a deep breath before

19

resuming. 'Most made it into the woods though, thank God. We lost two men and some of the women were ...... well I just thank God my mother and sister were with us at the charcoal clamp.' Garth knelt, pulled some grass from a clump by the side of the path and started to wipe the blood off his axe head and haft. 'We have spent the rest of the day tracking them.' The youngster looked up at his uncle, that lopsided smile back on his face. 'Just as well we caught up with them when we did eh?'

'Indeed.' Godfrey picked up the dead Sergeant's sword and started to clean it of the Frenchman's own blood. 'We had better get the bodies stripped; this one is wearing mael, albeit with damaged sleeves'. Garth smirked. Godfrey put the sword gently on the ground. 'Their swords and daggers will come in handy.'

Garth came over, held the decapitated body up in the air by its feet whilst his uncle started pulling off the mael brinie. 'What now?'

'What now?' Godfrey gave a hard tug causing the brinie to fall off the Frenchman's trunk, Garth pulled on the dead man's feet and dragged the corpse clear, allowing the mael coat to crumple into a shiny heap. 'Now, nephew, we go back home, through the woods and leave our winnings with John the Priest at Trottingham before going to Wulfbearding to give them back what was stolen. Then we can help the folk of Wulfbearding bury their dead. After that we should put things right to the buildings, and plot revenge against the French Prince and his men, that's what'.

Chapter 2: We Plough the Fields

Plough Monday had been and gone and Godfrey's head had still not settled after the excess of ale and dancing. Every foot fall as he followed the ox team that pulled the plough jarred through his body and settled just above the top of his head, or so it felt to him. Godfrey's mood had not been improved by the fact that two of the six oxen had been borrowed from Osbert Limp Leg of the neighbouring village of Wulfbearding. Not only would Godfrey and his twin, Thomas, have to return the favour by lending him their oxen, the man's beasts had shed their shoes not long after the ploughing had started. That had caused a long delay whilst Thomas and Edward Black from Wulfbearding had been sent for and the two oxen rolled to the ground so the shoes could be refitted. Godfrey lent forward and gave the rump of the rearmost beast a prod with his goad, not that the creature needed it, but purely from a desire to share his own discomfort.

'Hey Good Fellow Godfrey,' the slim swarthy youth leading the team at the front called. 'Don't make Hawk and Pheasant go no faster,' the boy's slight accent became heavier with his agitation. 'They be upsetting Pert and Lively which means I can't hold onto Quick and Nimble.'

Godfrey mumbled what may, or may not, have been an apology.

'I'll be glad when it's tomorrow,' Will Greenleaf muttered to himself. 'Thomas ploughs tomorrow – I can't wait.'

'What did you say boy?'

'I said maybe I should sing?'

'Sing?'

'Right you are then:

'Come all you jolly plough boys come listen to me lay,

And join with me in chorus, and I'll sing the plough boys praise.'

Godfrey gave a groan; 'I'll give you "praise" young Will.'

The young boy sniggered as he led the team onto and round the headland so they faced back the way they came. He gave a quick glance back and smiled to himself, watching Godfrey struggle to get the coulter and ploughshare clear of the ground before letting them down again to start ploughing the return furlong of the land allocated to both Godfrey and Thomas. The boy started to sing again in his pleasant high voice, this time choosing a different Plough Monday song:

'Come all you sweet charmers and give me choice.

There's nothing to compare with a plough boy's voice.

To hear the little plough boy singing so sweet,

Makes the hills and the valleys around us to meet.'

The oxen lowed in encouragement.

Godfrey gave another groan then a gasp as the plough bit the heavy clay of the fallow field, jolting his sore head.

'And it's hark! The little plough boy gets up in the morn.'

'Dragged out of bed more like,' Godfrey called out into the short break in the song – the calling causing him visible discomfort.

Will gave a short laugh;

'Move along. Jump along!' he continued before changing the song's pace.

'Here comes the plough boy with Spark and Beauty, Berry,

Goodluck, Speedwell, Cherry, and its walk along.

We are the lads that can keep along the plough.

We are the lads that can keep along the plough.'

Godfrey cautiously shook his head, 'They are not even our oxen.'
He risked raising his voice and called out; 'I said; "They are not
even our oxen" Will.'

Will answered by singing a second verse, only louder with the
oxen joining in, seemingly in rhythm;

'In the heat of the day what a little we can do.

We lay by the plough for an hour or two.

On the banks of sweet violets where we take our rest,

While the cool breezy winds blow around us so fast.'

'An hour or two you lazy little plough boy? Dreams are free!'

'And we still have the rest of the acre to plough,' Will said to
himself quietly in a mocking voice.

'What did you say?'

The boy ignored Godfrey and carried on singing. Despite the fact
that it was early January, the sun was out and the day warm though
the gentle breeze was cold when it blew. On completing the
furlong Godfrey decided to rest the team. He nodded to his plough
boy to lead the oxen to the small holt of box trees. The woods
would provide a wind break where they all would rest and eat.
Godfrey and Will had just unwrapped the cloth bundle that held
their bread, cheese and winter wrinkled apples when voices caught
their attention. Towards them came Thomas in the company of a
well-dressed man with light brown hair and a clipped beard,
following closely behind were two other men in good clothes, but
of a lesser quality to that of the man with Thomas. The two men
were wary and had hands that hovered near their long daggers;
their eyes moving constantly, visually checking their surroundings.

23

Will stood up and studied the approaching group. 'Hey Good Fellow Godfrey, maybe it is the Reeve responsible for the woods you often hunt in - whilst awaiting the appropriate warrant of course,' he added in a lower voice. 'Maybe the Reeve has come to have words with you.'

Godfrey stood too and looked; 'That's not him and, besides, he wouldn't be chasing after us, not unless he wants to forgo the haunch of venison he gets from each deer we take.' He squinted to observe the two rearmost men. 'And they are not the Foresters from there either.'

Will, who was short as well as very slim, stood on tip toe; 'Maybe it is the warrener from over Easbourne asking about his rabbits?'

'If he doesn't want his rabbits taken he should keep them in the warren and not let them wander the heath; anyway it is not him.' Godfrey took another hard look. 'I just don't recognise him at all, though Thomas seems to be happy chatting away to him.' Godfrey continued to watch the group come closer. 'Hmm, who knows what this is about young Will. In case of trouble it may be better if you go and check the oxen's bait in their nose bags and top them up if need be. If there is trouble run back to the village and get us help.'

The slim dark boy nodded his assent and went to the sacks of oats and chaff tucked behind one of the box trees.

'Oh,' Godfrey called after him. 'Don't give them too much of the oats; you know what it does to their guts and it is me that is walking behind them.'

Will smiled and waved, happy to be reminded of the joke he had played that morning before bringing the oxen out to be yoked up.

Thomas and his companions got closer, walking on the unploughed sod. As they passed where Will was topping up one of the oxen's nose bags the lad started to sing again, his voice fluctuating as he avoided the wet nose and curious tongue of the big creature:

'It was of two young brethren, two brethren bold,
It was of two young brethren bold,
One he was a shepherd and a tender of sheep,
The other a planter of corn.
We will rile it, we will tile it, through mud and through clay
…......'

The well-dressed man came smiling up to Godfrey; 'Is he singing about you and your twin brother here?'

Godfrey looked the man over, taking in not only his quality clothes, especially his squirrel fur lined cloak of heavy maroon dyed wool and silver clasps, but also the man's very neat appearance with well cut hair and neatly trimmed beard; the whole set off by a hunting cap of matching maroon wool set at a jaunty angle with a pheasant's tail feather set in the bright yellow banding around the low set crown. 'Not quite but almost …......'

'Oh I am sorry,' the well-dressed man said. 'How rude of me, I was so taken by the lad's singing I forgot my manners.' He held out a hand; 'I am William, squire of Cassingham in Kent.'

Godfrey took the hand and shook it. 'William. You are a long way from home as I understand it.'

'I am,' William agreed.

'You obviously know my brother Thomas and he would have given you my name,' Godfrey said, cautiously, still unsure about the man's friendliness.

William gave an even friendlier smile. 'Indeed you are Godfrey Wulfson, yeoman of Iping and these,' he indicated the two men who appeared to be standing point guard to the rear of Thomas, 'are my Reeve, Mark of Cassingham,' the shorter and stockier of the two men looked to Godfrey and inclined his head, 'and my senior Forester, John Little.' The very tall forester turned and nodded to Godfrey, his row of strong teeth shewing very white in his large brown beard. Both men returned to scanning the open field and the box trees of the holt.

William seemed to take his men's behaviour as normal and readdressed Godfrey, who now had Thomas at his side; 'So, which of you is the shepherd and which the ploughman?'

'Well,' Godfrey started.

'We are both.' Thomas completed.

'We share the plough and have four oxen.'

William looked at the team and young Will, who was patting the big lead oxen with its white and red hide, whispering in the creature's ear. 'Six oxen?'

'We borrow a pair and pay back by lending out ours.'

'But six? I am from Kent and there two are normal, though sometimes four.'

'The soil here,' said Godfrey.

'Heavy clay,' contributed Thomas.

'Ah. But the shepherd part?'

'The Lord of our manor is the Lady Maud.'

'Her husband, Richard of Amundville, has land to the south.'

'On the chalk downs.'

'Near Brightelmstone.'

'We, and in fact the other yeomen at Iping, do time looking after his sheep there.'

'As part payment of our rent.'

'Not that we should have ever had to pay rent, according to our granfer.'

'Who had it from his granfer.'

'They say our family owned Wulfbearding and has lease of Iping before the Normans came and even after.' Godfrey informed William.

'But they were swindled out of it.' Thomas clarified.

Godfrey tilted his head and looked at the Kentish man. 'You are not Norman are you? You don't sound it, though your accent is a mite funny.'

William gave a short barking laugh. 'Find me a squire in England who is at least not part Norman! No, I am not after taking your land off you and only a small part of me may have been involved in your family's misfortune. My accent? Well I am from Kent and we are the real English having arrived in England long before you South Saxons!' He chuckled to himself, very amused at having bested the twins. 'So, with the shepherding it is not unusual for you and others to be away from Iping and possibly the other villages and hamlets around here? No one would question absences?'

Thomas looked to Godfrey before answering. 'Possibly not.'

'And,' William continued, 'I understand you both work with the hunt when needed and know the woods around her, and even further into the Weald, quite well.'

Godfrey looked to Thomas; 'Possibly.'

'Hmm.' William indicated with his hand that he would like them and himself to sit. The twins assented and the three of them settled on the ground with William facing the Wulfsons; his two men continued to stand and scan. 'There has been some trouble around here with the French,' he stated. 'Foraging and the like,' he continued.

'Thomas and Godfrey looked at each other, eyebrows raised. 'So we have heard,' Thomas said for them.

William gave another chuckle and smiled beguilingly before continuing. 'I heard that a certain French foraging party was killed near here. I also have heard that French courier riders going from Sandwich to London rarely make it out of this part of the Weald.'

Thomas and Godfrey looked at each other, eyebrows raised. 'So we have heard.' Godfrey said for them as they turned back to return William's gaze.

'You will also have heard that the French have taken good King John's favourite castle at Odiham, just over the Hampshire border.'

Thomas eased his buttocks into a more comfortable position. 'Should that worry us?'

'It would mean more French in these parts,' William responded, stroking the short bristles of his trimmed muzzle beard. 'It would mean more patrols out foraging and that should worry you.'

'As long as they stay away from us.' Godfrey took the chance to eat a piece of the cheese he had brought for lunch.

'They didn't stay away from Wulfbearding did they,' William reminded him.

'You know of that happening?' asked Thomas.

The squire of Cassingham gave another smile. 'Not much happens in the Weald that I don't know of. I make it my habit to know what is going on. I may be from Kent and you may be in Sussex but we all live in the Weald and nature knows no boundaries.'

'So where is this leading?' Thomas questioned, leaving his brother to continue eating.

'Where do you stand Wulfsons? With King John or with Louis the Frenchman?'

Thomas looked to Godfrey before answering. 'Why do you want to know? We just want to live our lives unhindered. Our beloved King John is a better King than Richard was but he still causes us grief from time to time with his quarrels with both the Church and his barons and now he has caused the French to land on our shores.' Godfrey nodded his agreement, his mouth being full of rye bread.

William waited to reply whilst young Will came and took his share of the food before returning to the ox team. 'The boy does not look as if he belongs here. All in your village, and round abouts, are tall and either blond or fair of hair. He is small, swarthy and has black hair.'

Godfrey downed a mouthful of watered ale from his leathern bottle before replying. 'We found him.'

'In the woods,' Thomas clarified. 'Some years back.'

'Must be, what, six years ago?'

'About that,' Thomas agreed. 'He couldn't speak English then.'

'Only French of a sorts.'

'Since he learnt English, when we ask him where he is from or where his family are from, all he tells us is that he got lost in the woods.'

'I think that is because he likes it here and doesn't want to leave.'

'His French can come in handy at times.'

'Especially when dealing with unscrupulous traders or …'

'Our betters?'

'I understand some French.'

'As we all have to.'

'But we never let on.'

'We let Will act as translator.'

William continued stroking his beard, deep in thought, gazing after the boy who was now feeding some bread crust to the lead ox. 'He can be trusted? He wouldn't go over to the French?'

'Ah,' said Thomas as he realised what this meant. 'You don't like the French either?'

'No.'

'Ah,' added Godfrey. 'You are not investigating the disappearance of various Frenchmen on behalf of the Sheriff.'

'No; I am seeking out fellow Wealden men willing to make things difficult for the French as they make their way through the Wealden woods.'

'We might ….' Thomas started.

'…... be interested in helping,' Godfrey concluded, passing the bottle to Thomas, who took a swig of the contents before offering it to William of Cassingham.

William gulped down a mouthful or two before passing the bottle back to Godfrey. 'If I need you I will pass you word. The messenger will tell you that Willikin needs you and where to meet.'

'Willikin?' Godfrey drank some more ale.

William gave another of his warm smiles; 'It pays to use another name in these affairs. What names would you use?'

Thomas nudged Godfrey in the ribs; 'What's it to be brother? I guess Robin Good Fellow has already been taken?'

'Actually, no,' William informed him.

'It's mine!' Thomas announced. 'You can't have it Godfrey – I'm Robin Good Fellow! Ha – beaten you big brother.'

'All right "Robin". What name shall I have then? Wulfhere after the founder of our folk?'

'Too close to our real name brother.'

'How about Herla? He was a great hunter.' Godfrey looked to his brother.

'It needs more, just in case there is another of the same name.'

Godfrey looked around, and then behind him at the trees. 'Herla of the Boxholt!'

'That would do,' Thomas agreed.

'So Robin Goodfellow and Herla Boxholt when I need you I shall send word. Gather around you others who are hunters in the greenwood, others you can trust, and others who can shoot a bow.' William stood. 'Oh, and see if you can get hold of some swords, in case you need them, though it is always best to kill as far from your enemy as possible.'

'We already have some,' Thomas informed him.

'The couriers normally carry one.'

'The missing French couriers?' asked William, getting ready to joining John Little and Mark Reeve.

'If you say so,' the twins chorused.

Chapter 3: Back on the Road Again

Godfrey sat on an upturned round of wood and lent his back against the whitewashed wattle and daub outside wall of the cottage he and his brother Thomas shared. On another round of wood in front of him were a dozen leaf shaped arrow heads and a dozen long bodkin arrow heads that Edward Black, the Wulfbearding blacksmith, had made for him. The winter's day was starting to fade into its long twilight and Godfrey was awaiting his brother's return with Will Greenleaf and their four oxen. The oxen had been hired out to the unfree serfs of Iping who needed them so as they could plough Lady Maud's demesne land, one of the unpaid duties they owed the Lord of Iping. Godfrey looked lovingly at the arrow heads which had been made to Edward's usual high standard. A distant lowing caused him to raise his fair head and look down the village's only road and he managed to see in the distance Thomas, Will and the oxen; they were not alone, for with them was a man with a heavily laden ass. Godfrey groaned to himself and shook his head at Thomas' habit of meeting strangers and bringing them home to eat and drink their way through the twin's carefully hoarded winter supplies. 'And with an ass too,' he muttered to himself. He got up and went to open the byre doors at the end of the house in order for the animals to be brought in for the night. He turned and again watched the approaching group, Thomas, as usual, was laughing. He had obviously told a joke for Godfrey could also hear Will's silver bell giggle and the amused bray of the man with the ass. Steam came from the oxen's noses as they trudged up the slight hill, their heads swaying side to side all together at the same time with each other. Godfrey took a sideways glance so that he could see the sledge the team were drawing behind them over the ice hardened clay surface of the road. He took in the amount of straw and the bulk of the bags the sledge carried; calculating how much feed the oxen had eaten during their day's work.

'Hey big brother,' Thomas called out. 'We have a visitor!'

'Right,' Godfrey acknowledged, taking in the stranger's slender size and travel worn clothes. The ass raised its head and then shook. Godfrey noticed that the heavy baskets on either side made a slight chiming sound and guessed the man was selling metal cooking pots and the like.

Will gave Godfrey a smile and a wave as he halted the oxen and commenced undoing their yokes.

'Don't forget to rub them down Will.' The boy gave Thomas a look that shewed he felt hurt to think that he would not do so, for the boy was very fond of the animals, especially his favourite, Quick, the lead ox. 'All right Will, you already know to do that; force of habit. Our father always reminded us when he was around even though we had been doing it since we were young boys,' Thomas conceded.

Godfrey went back to the rounds of wood and quickly scooped up the arrow heads and dropped them into his script, hoping the pedlar hadn't seen them already. He looked up and saw the man watching. 'Hunting arrow heads, I've had them made for the Lady Maud.'

'I am sure you have,' replied the man with a wink. 'She needs war heads when going after deer.'

Godfrey edged his hand towards the long hunting knife he kept at the front of his leather belt.

The man again winked at him; 'No need for that Good Fellow Godfrey, I've just been telling your brother Good Fellow Thomas that I am Gamble Gold the pedlar and I have a message from Willikin for you to pass on to Herla Boxholt and Robin Goodfellow.' He inclined his head towards the stout wooden door of the cottage. 'Can we go inside?'

The twins ducked their heads under the lintel and followed Gamble Gold into their cottage. Thomas went over to the wall that separated their quarters from those of the animals and came back with a stool which he put down beside the two already round the hearth. The pedlar was looking round, assessing the neat and tidy appearance of the cottage. 'Your ladies are very house proud; you are lucky men.'

Thomas smiled and gave a short chuckle; 'He is talking about you there big brother!' Thomas turned to the pedlar. 'He is the tidy one and I the messy one. Ladies? In the future hopefully, but for now we are single and trying to improve our lot in the world.'

'The taxes that King Richard placed on the village and the extra yield demanded for his ransom hit us very hard.' Godfrey sat and stretched out his legs towards the embers in the central hearth.

'Fifteen years since he died and we are still not as well off as we had been in my father's time,' Thomas added.

'Milked us English like old Farmer Giles' milch cow,' insisted his twin.

Gamble nodded in agreement as he sat down on the three legged stool Thomas had brought him. 'So, do you think the French Dauphin would be better?'

'Bloody foreigner,' Thomas spat into the hearth and the spittle hissed on the hot grey wood ash.

'King John could be thought of as a foreigner,' Gamble insisted. 'He certainly speaks no English, unlike his father.'

Godfrey leant down and pulled some kindling twigs towards himself. 'He may be a foreigner, but at least he is our foreigner.' He cast the kindling onto the ash and embers.

Thomas picked up an iron and prodded the fire back into life. 'So, you know how we feel; now what is the message from Willikin?'

'There is a job for Herla Boxholt and Robin Goodfellow and as many others of their ilk that can be found. Woodsmen, archers, men who can be trusted, men who can keep their mouths shut.'

'Where and when?' Godfrey threw some more kindling on.

'You will be told, just make sure Herla and Robin gather some men. Word should be here within a week or two.'

'How will the word be told? By you?' Seeing small flames starting to bite into the twigs Thomas lent over and placed some slivers of oak there for them to catch.

'Not by me; I have more villages in the Weald to visit for Willikin.'

'If not you, then who?' Thomas continued to feed oak slivers onto the resurgent fire.

'I am not sure, but most likely Alan atte Slaed.'

'How will we know it is him?' Godfrey left the others in order to start preparing the evening meal.

'Oh, if it is him you won't mistake him. You do like singing I trust?'

The door swung open and admitted Will Greenleaf; 'Singing? Oh I love to sing. Would you like to hear me?'

The sharp sunlight of a frost blessed day made the bright motley beribboned clothes of the jongleur seem even brighter than they really were and hid the fact that much of his thick particoloured over-shirt was faded and that his hosen was patched at the knee. The man adjusted his jaunty squashed pie shaped hat with its row of dyed feathers poked into the hat band to a jauntier angle and gave a beaming smile to an audience that consisted of the small children of Iping. In a quick, smooth movement he brought round his lute from behind his back and stuck a chord that was almost in tune.

'I sing you a song of daring deeds.

A song of brave men and not of fleas.'

The children laughed and clapped their hands at the words.

'A song so bold

It should not be told.'

The jongleur stopped his strumming and placed an index finger on his lips.

'The blood, the guts, they should all be spilled,

If the end of this tale is to be fulfilled.'

The man's voice was a whisper and he contorted his face, rolled his eyes cocked his head at the angle of a hanged man and hung out his tongue.

Women rushed forward and pulled their children away.

'You should not be singing such to our youngsters.' Mildred Nearboxholt stood close to the singer's face and wagged a finger at him. 'That sort of song is for the menfolk, not childer.'

The jongleur gave what he hoped was a disarming smile. He gave his lute a discordant strum.

'To find such men who not be here,' he sang.

'One needs to sniff for the stench of beer?'

Mildred gave him another close faced finger wag. 'You will not find our men drinking.'

'Not yet, not till after they be finished with bow and arrow. There be a competition betwix local holdings,' Agnes Crosseye added, shoving her two children into the small thatched wattle and daub cottage they called home.

Mildred nodded her agreement. 'Go down to our church of The Lady St Mary. That's where the archery butts are.' She stepped out of the man's way. 'And keep your singing of songs of violence stilled till you get there.'

The jongleur waited till Mildred moved right out of his way and then performed a high jump followed by a forward roll, all the time strumming his lute. Wide eyed children gasped in amazement as they peeped out from behind their mother's backs and round the leather flaps that served as front doors for the hovels of the unfree serfs of Iping. The man continued on his way, playing his instrument whilst leaping and clicking his heels in mid-air adding in an occasional back flip, much to the delight of his young secret watchers. The women of the village came and stood in the middle of the road and shook their heads and communicated their distaste of the entertainer to each other with sour faces and pulled down lips. The bright clothed man wended his merry way past the more substantial dwellings of the village's freemen with their whitewashed walls and oak shingled rooves. Onward he went, now just strumming, his acrobatics on hold now he had no children to entertain. He went past the house of the lord of the manor with its two storeys and windows sealed with oiled linen. Onwards he went towards the stone church of St Mary with its squat Saxon tower and new Norman porch. Onward he continued till he saw a dozen or so men taking it in turn to shoot arrows with their birding blunt heads at a willow wand wrapped in white linen cloth that stood in front of a small earthen butt with its face overgrown with weeds.

Godfrey put down his leathern jack that was half filled with ale that was fast going flat and nudged his twin brother, Thomas, in the ribs. 'It looks like Willikin's singer is here.'

Thomas stopped his drinking and followed his brother's gaze. 'I just hope to God the man is less forthright with knowing just who Robin and Herla really are than his mate the tinker was.'

'So do I brother, so do I.'

Thomas half brought his own jack to his mouth before changing his mind. 'I know we have talked to those we trust about helping Willikin, but that is not all the village.'

'And even those we trust don't know our assumed names.'

'Keep everything close to the chest: that's the best way.' Thomas resumed drinking.

The jongleur walked past the watchers, through the line of six archers and stood in front of the wand. 'Greetings one and all I am Alan of the Slaed and I am here to sing for you.' The men all looked puzzled at the strange man's actions and his total disregard for safety by going in front of archers without warning. 'So, gather round so you may hear my song,' he winked, 'for it is of great import.'

Thomas looked to Godfrey; 'I think this may be how we find out what that Squire of the Kentish Weald wants us to do.'

Godfrey nursed his jack of ale. 'I think you are right, but let's hope he gives us the call with discretion.'

The twins moved forward to where the entertainer stood, encouraging the other men to do the same.

Alan of the Slaed strummed discordant chords and swung from one side to the other as he watched his audience gather round him. Once satisfied they were all close enough to hear him clearly he picked a simple tune on his lute with a plectrum that had appeared, almost by magic, in his right hand. Having set the mood he began singing in a pleasant, but rather high pitched voice:

'I will sing you a song of men so bold,

Who haunt the greenwood to steal French gold.'

39

He played the tune again as the Sunday afternoon archers all smiled and nudged each other in the ribs.

'Willie Woodwose and Cockeyed Deer,
Listen closely and lend me your ear.'

Alan dropped an octave.

'Grimma Goodfellow and Hugh Whitehand,
Gather around with your bold band.'

He moved back up an octave.

'Mild and Meek it is you we seek,
Don't let your fears cause you to freak.'

Again he played the tune before he resumed singing.

'Now Old Long Beard and Harold Wink,
Hurry along and leave your drink.'

This line caused those men snuggling jacks of ale to hold them closer to their chests and shake their heads in response.

'Herla and Robin of the Box Holt,
Gather your bows before the game bolt.'

Thomas went to say something but Godfrey stayed him by catching his elbow.

'Gaspar the Ghost and Michael the Mouse,
It is time for you to leave your house.
Beggar the Bear and Grendle the Goose,
Now is the time let your men loose.'

The tune was played again but this time at a slightly faster pace.

'Now listen one and listen all,
While I tell you how the Frenchies may fall.
If we all gather at the fire stricken oak,'

Alan struck the face of his lute with a resounding slap.

'We may yet make the French see our joke.
Tis need we all meet in three days hence,
Up against the deer hurst fence.'
The tune again, but very slow.
'Make sure - be there - just on the time,
Just as soon as – the -curfew – bell – do – chime.'
Alan the jongleur gave a rattling strum that worked up and down
the scale before stopping and giving a deep bow.'
'Is that it?' asked Sam Samuelson, ploughman and pender of
Wulfbearding.
'Strange sort of song if you ask me,' added Robert of Dumpford.
The rest nodded agreement.
Alan of the Slaed seemed non-plussed by the comments and even
less upset by the fact that no one gave him any coins for his
efforts. He smiled, did a back flip and then jumped and clicked his
heels. 'One last song before I wend my way elsewhere.
There was a young lady from Bosham,
Who took all her clothes off to wash 'em.'
'That's better!' shouted young Jack Samuelson, Sam's younger
brother, his face red from drinking more ale than a young lad
should.
Alan laughed as he got ready to repeat the first lines of his song.
Godfrey guided Thomas away from the others, much to his
brother's chagrin.
'Come on Thomas, we have plans to make, things to get and
shoulders to be tapped. Either young Will or nephew Garth will
bring back our bows and arrows.'

'But I haven't heard that song and', he gave a wicked grin to Godfrey, 'and I was wondering if that young lady from Bosham, her what took her clothes off, was the one you have been giving a nod and wink to.'

'Shut up.' Godfrey gripped his brother's elbow even harder causing him to wince.

'That entertainer, it was the messenger William, or should I say Willikin, said would tell us when and where to meet him.'

'Sometimes little brother your sharp intelligence dazzles me.'

'Yes but,' Thomas pulled his elbow free from Godfrey's hard grip, 'He called me Robin of the Box Holt not Robin Goodfellow, which is the name I chose.'

'Too many Goodfellows; we are all Good Fellow as all free women are Good Wife.'

'Yes but I wanted to be Robin Goodfellow, like the wood sprite.'

'You are starting to pout and look like a spoilt child.'

'I am not.'

'You are, now get used to it, you are now Robin Boxholt as I am Herla Boxholt.'

'But I don't want to be Robin Boxholt.'

'Spoilt brat.'

'Spoilt brat am I?' Thomas started to roll up his sleeves getting ready to start a fight.

'Greeting boys,' came a cheerful voice behind them. 'May God give you good cheer.'

'Oh.' The twins stopped glaring at each other and turned to face John of Chichester, priest of the nearby village of Trottingham.

'Greetings and may God also be with you,' said Thomas, rolling his sleeves down.

'And with your wife Rose also,' added the thoughtful Godfrey.

The plump blond woman with sparkling blue eyes and rose blushed cheeks gave an inclined head in acknowledgement.

Thomas gave the attractive woman a wink before turning his attention to her husband, John. 'I hope you are on the way back home Father.'

'We may need those "things" we left with you for safe keeping,' completed Godfrey.

'Certainly my sons.' The priest deliberately put a protective arm around his wife and gave Thomas a look that was both amused and a warning. 'My wife and I have finished visiting your own priest and are just going back to Trottingham.' His wife nudged him and whispered in his ear. 'Oh, yes. Rose has just reminded me to wait until you join us before removing the "things" from their hiding place. That lid on the old squires tomb is really too heavy for just me to move.'

In the thick holt of ash and oak trees that stood behind the fire struck oak by the deer hurst at Charwood the twins, with their nephew Garth, Will Greenleaf, Mark Archer and others from Wulfbearding, Iping and Trottingham hunkered down and watched, waiting to see who else was there. Against the hurst fence lounged a dozen or so men. Like the twins and their band the men wore clothes of forest colours; green in its many shades, various browns, pale yellows and even maroon red. Thomas touched Godfrey's arm and indicated with his head to further along the woods where shadows stirred amongst the bare trees, winter dead brambles and bracken. Godfrey turned to the others, finger on lips. The twins continued to watch as the shadows carefully emerged from cover and became archers, bows strung, arrows nocked. One of the fence loungers held up a hand in greeting, pulled back his hood, drew down his cloth visor and revealed himself as William of Cassingham; Willikin of the Weald. This time the squire's clothes were as time worn as those of the men coming from the woods. Seeing who it was, the twins stood as one and beckoned the others in their band forward. As they too emerged from the treeline they saw why Willikin had been unconcerned about the other archers approaching with bows and arrows for, hidden behind the hurst fence, visible only as they made slight movements, were some of Willikin's own archers with their own bows strung and arrows nocked standing in the woods the other side of the deer run.

Willikin wore his usual benign smile; 'Greetings Michael the Mouse,' he called to the leader of the other band before looking across and waving to the twins. 'And to you Herla and Robin. A good day for hunting?'

Michael Mouse, with his small build and sharp features turned his dark brown bead like eyes on William. 'Greetings Willikin.' He stepped forward to the hurst fence to look over and jumped back when the bulk of John Little, William of Cassingham's reeve, loomed up from behind the fence. When Michael put his hand to his chest the big man gave a chortle and sat down again, sniggering to himself. The diminutive Michael took a deep breath and expelled it through rounded lips. 'Bugger me, that giant of yorn gave me a fright.' Standing on tip toe he took a careful look over the fence. 'Hmm, Willikin, I don't know quite what you have in mind but I hope there are more of us than this.'

Willikin gestured for Michael and the twins to step away from the others, once they were out of ear shot he addressed them in a half whisper. 'There are more, yes, but they have already been sent on.' Michael and the twins all looked at each other. 'The time, before the curfew bell?'

'Alan's song changed from village to village; we can't have too many people meeting all at once – we mustn't attract too much attention, we are taking a lot of risk as it is,' Willikin replied.

'Are there more to arrive here?' Godfrey's voice matched Willikin's in volume.

'Grimma Goodfellow and Hugh Whitehand with their bands.' Thomas raised an eyebrow.

Willikin sighed; 'No, not their real names, Robin.'

'The games we play,' Godfrey commented.

'Indeed.' Willikin looked to where the others were standing around, some talking, some drinking from their costrels, others just standing. He looked back to the twins and Michael; 'We are going to ambush a French supply train. They have landed at Southampton and some have moved to Winchester, where they have been doing a bit of plundering. Now they are on the road to London, where most of the French are based. We will take them near Four Marks, where the road narrows.' He looked at the three men. 'You know it?' They nodded agreement. 'Good. Now I want you to settle down to the south; one of my men will shew you where. Cut bracken and bury yourselves in it. Be near the road but

45

not at the edge. Have your bows strung and arrows ready.' He looked at the side of each man to ensure they all carried at least half a dozen arrows tucked into their belts at their backs; satisfied he continued. 'If you have swords make sure they either are in a scabbard or hid well under the bracken, there must be no risk of shiny metal being seen.'

Thomas snorted. 'Shiny? Have you seen how dull...' Godfrey gave his brother such a hard look his twin shut up straight away.

The squire of Cassingham drew breath and tutted before resuming to speak. 'Grimma and Hugh will be the other side of the road to where you will be. When it comes to the fighting just make sure you don't shoot each other!'

'Willie Woodwose and Cockeyed Deer?' asked Thomas.

'Mild and Meek?' Godfrey added.

Willikin stroked his beard, which was not as neat and trim as when the twins had met him before. 'They will be to the north. The plan is for their bands to attack the vanguard and close the road. My men will then harass the flanks just behind the vanguard. Hopefully this will cause panic and bring about a retreat. That is where you,' he indicated the three around him,' will come in. Let them get right on you then volley shoot. My man will give the call. There will be no more than six volleys, if that, then fall back, melt into the woods, don't hang around. Meet back here. You have the easy job being this side of the road. Grimma and Whitehand will have a longer trek back.'

Thomas grinned; 'Lucky them.'

'Indeed,' Godfrey confirmed.

'Right.' Willikin looked over at the bands gathered by the fence. 'Get your men and move, but do it quietly. Imagine you are poaching deer and the local forester knows you are about.'

'Not that we would know of such things,' Michael the Mouse insisted as he pulled his cloth visor up and his hood down.

'I want to sneeze.' Thomas whispered into his brother's ear.

'You dare, for your sneezes are such as they would hear you in London, let alone Winchester,' Godfrey whispered back.

'Its this dry fern; it's full of dust.'

'And insects that should be asleep this time of year but don't know any better.'

'And my feet are so cold they feel as if they have bands around each of the toes.'

'Mine are no better, so stop whinging.'

A shadow of light and dark brown silently crept along the small humps of dead bracken bending its head to each hump and giving a muffled hissing sound. It came to where two of the humps conjoined and hissed into the twin's ears. 'Keep the noise down.' The shadow raised its head, listened, sniffed and then lowered its head and whispered again. 'At the sound of my hunting horn stand with an arrow nocked. At the second blast loose. Target men on wagons if they are in your sight or, if there are mounted men, take down the horses. Don't shoot oxen pulling the wagons.' Mark the Miller of Cassingham, now revelling in the name of Little Midge, moved on to the next hump.

'Wake me when it's about to start big brother.' Thomas moved his head away from Godfrey's ear, pulled up his visor and brought it close around his nose to try and keep dust and insects out.

The cold damp of a winter's afternoon was starting to cause the hidden archer's muscles to cramp when the harsh blast of a hunting horn split the air. On both sides of the road murky shapes emerged from the undergrowth with arrows nocked. On the road to their front was a mess of men running with mounted men-at-arms trying to force their way through the pack. The archer's waited the second blast of the horn, their eyes picking their targets. When the second horn blast came they drew and loosed their arrows.

'NOCK,' Midge called. The archers pulled an arrow through from their belts, all the time looking for a new target amongst the crowd of men on the road. 'DRAW!' The archers pulled their bow strings back to their ears. 'LOOSE!' A cloud of arrows hummed through the air hitting men and horses.

'NOCK - DRAW - LOOSE.'

It was then that a low sided wagon, drawn by a pair of horses rather than oxen came round the slight bend in the road running down all before it till it came to a halt behind a stopped ox drawn wagon. Mounted on the sacks of grain in the horse drawn wagon's bed were half a dozen crossbowmen.

'NOCK,' but the rest of the command did not come as Little Midge spun round with a crossbow bolt in his arm. The archers carried on as if Midge was still giving the call, but the volley was ragged. The crossbowmen returned shot and men went down, but another two volleys by the archers cleared the wagon of men.

48

Godfrey looked at the chaos on the road with injured and panicked horses and men crashing into each other as they raced down the road back towards Winchester, abandoned wagons clogging their way. Godfrey took over the shoot. 'NOCK, DRAW, LOOSE.' Two more rounds hit the French. Godfrey was just looking to see how many of the archers still had arrows when he saw men in forest clothing, some with swords and bucklers, others with a sword in one hand and a bow in the other coming from the forest hacking at any Frenchmen near them.

One thrust his sword into his belt and pulled himself up onto the now abandoned horse wagon. He pulled back his hood. 'Willikin of the Weald bids his Mouse to move it, Herla to hurry away and Robin to run.' William of Cassingham pulled his hood back down over his head, drew his sword and, standing of the edge of the wagon, slashed at anyone foolish enough to get close to him.

Godfrey and Thomas held Little Midge tight as Henry atte Trottingham, priest of Cassingham used his knife to widen the wound in the miller of Cassingham's arm where the crossbow bolt had hit him leaving the missile shewing both sides of the wound.

'This will hurt even more as I will have to now whittle the wood at the fletch end of the bolt so I can break it.' The Franciscan friar did not wait for a reply before starting to pare the wood. Midge strained against the twin's hold but, rather than cry out at the jolting, ground his teeth instead. Once the shaft had been reduced considerably the friar looked up and gave the twins a nod; they held the miller tighter and the black habited man snapped the shaft. 'Right; so far, so good.' He looked at the wound and the shaft, judging if the break in the bolt was clean of splinters; satisfied he put one hand at the short arrow's entry point in his patient's arm; the other went behind and grabbed the arrow head and pulled the shortened bolt through the arm.

This time Midge did make a sound; he gave a short gasp and then slumped in the twin's grip. Gently the two Iping men laid him on his side.

'He bore that well.' Henry Trottingham poured honey from an earthenware bottle into the wound. He then pulled out some mouldy bread from the large script he carried, added honey to it, made it into a sticky paste then indicated to Thomas to bring him the strip of worn linen lying on the ground nearby. Singing a psalm quietly to himself he gently and most carefully applied the poultice and bound the arm. 'God willing he will heal.'

'Which is more than can be said for the two others we brought back with us,' Godfrey looked across to where Michael the Mouse and his men were making hand sledges from cut saplings to take their dead friends home.

'Crossbows are nasty things,' Thomas added unnecessarily.

'The Pope would ban them.' Henry went and washed his sticky hand in the water in a wooden bucket that hung from one of the many wagons that Willikin had brought back from the ambush.

'I will remind the French of that next time we meet.' Godfrey joined the priest at the bucket and cleaned off the dried blood that bemired his hands.

'I will shoot the bastards first and then tell them.' Thomas lifted off a sack of grain from the wagon and then used it as a pillow for the now sleeping Midge. 'Anyway,' he asked the priest. 'What is to happen to this plunder?'

Henry atte Trottingham patted a sack. 'Our squire says that it is to go back to those the French took it from.'

'None for us?' Godfrey asked.

'Only if there is a surplus,' the black clad friar informed him.

The twins' nephew, Garth, joined them. 'Well, even if we get none of this,' he patted a grain sack, 'at least we will have plenty of horse meat to eat for the next few weeks.'

Willikin shook hands with the chief of archers from over Haslemere way, waved a hand to the rest of the man's band and walked over to where Godfrey and Thomas were sprawled on the ground with their own men. As he got closer Godfrey and Thomas stood, dusted their hands off and waited for their leader.

Willikin ran his hand down his beard in an attempt to restore it to it normal neat state then gave a grin. 'It was a good fight lads, well done one and all.'

Thomas returned his grin and let it break into a smile. 'It was, and thanks to your planning, a great success.'

Willikin let his grin also become a smile, 'Thank you Thomas. It is Thomas isn't it?' The Cassingham man looked at the twins to judge their height. 'Yes it is Thomas, or should I say '"Robin"?' He turned to Godfrey. 'And how say you Herla?'

'It was good, but we did take some casualties.'

'That, I regret to say, is war.'

'True.'

Thomas looked at Godfrey before adding, 'Though the casualties were low due to the good planning.'

'True,' Godfrey conceded he then looked to Willikin, 'and the information that lead to the planning?'

Willikin chuckled. 'That is the key. You should not act unless you can plan and you cannot plan if you don't have intelligence. This is especially true if you don't have a large band of regular troops and have to call small bands of men together. Even getting a force this size,' he indicated the thirty odd men still in the clearing, 'takes time to get together so not only do I need intelligence about when and where the French and, or, the rebel barons are, I need it as soon as it is gathered, if not before.'

'Gamble Gold and Alan of the Slaed?'

'But two of my sources. My main area of lack is London.'

The twins looked at each other; 'London?' they chorused.

'London,' Willikin confirmed. 'London is full of French, but that is not the problem, the fact that the City is against King John, that is the problem.'

'We can understand that,' Thomas' voice was a fraction ahead of Godfrey's.

Willikin nodded his head in agreement. 'Yes, the King is sometimes his own worst enemy. Still, he is the anointed King and, as such, London should obey him.'

Thomas gave a snort, 'That's not what I heard said by some of the rebels' men-at-arms down on the coast when I listened to them talking over their ale back before the French arrived. They say King John signed a charter ....'

'And,' Godfrey continued for his brother, 'that charter had some good stuff in it to stop the King from being so high and mighty.'

'It sounded like a good idea to us.' Thomas looked to Godfrey who nodded his agreement.

'True and, yes, the King reneged on it which is one reason why the barons invited the French over with the offer of kingship for the Dauphin.'

'Silly move Willikin,' Thomas ran his hand over his sweat darkened fair hair.

'I agree and,' Willikin held up his hand to stop Godfrey from interrupting, 'and our King John has made many mistakes but he is the anointed king and that is why I fight for him.'

'We fight because we don't like the French,' Thomas informed him. 'If they win we will lose land and rights again as we did back in the old days.'

'I assume you are talking about King William? Him they called the Conqueror?'

Godfrey coughed and spat on the ground. 'In my family we still refer to him as Willie the Bastard. We should be lords of Wulfbearding but got cheated out of it even though the lord at the time hadn't been in arms against the Normans.'

'Him only having a daughter,' Thomas clarified.

Willikin shook his head, 'So you have said before.'

'But,' Thomas said, 'King John is our true King ...'

'Seeing as his Father King Henry, the second of that name, was almost half English.'

'And his mother was of King Alfred's line being the daughter of Eadgar the Aetheling's sister.'

'Unlike Willie Bastard who had no claim and just came and stole the land.'

Willikin, tired of a tirade he had heard before from not just the twins but others who claimed to be of pure English blood, held his hand up and started to walk away shaking his head in disappointment that some of the old wounds still ran so deep.

'But,' Thomas called after him.

'London,' continued Godfrey.

Willikin turned back. 'What of it?'

'Information.'

'You said you needed information from London.'

Willikin sighed and walked back to the twins whose strange way of completing each others' sentences was starting to annoy him. 'What of it?'

'I think,' Thomas said.

'We can help you,' completed a smiling Godfrey. 'We may have a source that can help.'

Chapter 4: Here's Good Luck to the Brewer

Godfrey edged his tired nag over the single lane bridge that span the sparkling waters of the River Wandle at Wandsworth. He carefully persuaded the nervous creature that, although the wooden planking made an unsafe sound, it really wasn't going to collapse under them. Once on the other side he fondly patted the pony's neck and muttered gently endearments to it. It was not Godfrey's usual mount, in fact it wasn't even from his usual ostler. He had hired it because it was plain dark brown with no markings. The animal was neither too high nor too low for anyone to make note of it and it had no distinguishing habits. Godfrey himself wore nondescript home spun and country dyed shirt, breeks, hood and horse cloak. The pair had travelled along the Portsmouth-London Road with little more notice from others than the occasional stare always given a stranger passing through a village. The pony being now settled, Godfrey turned off the road and followed a path that ran along the banks of the Wandle before following the Thames. The path was above the tidal marshland of the mighty river's bank, but still the going was soft. Godfrey had been this way a few times in the past but he knew that to get to his destination he needed to travel the path at low tide in order to ford the Falcon Brook and use the causeway on the other side in order to reach Edwin's Isle in the Battersea marshes.

The sun shone and the midges bit. The pony swung its tail to help keep the insects at bay but Godfrey's attempts to keep them off with his free hand were proving useless. At last they came to the brook and forded it up-stream of the ponding that fed the water mill that stood near where the Falcon met the Thames. Riding onto the island Godfrey was surprised to see that the building he was aiming for was now resplendent in a blood red wash rather than the dirty white he remembered. As he rode to the hitching post in front of the building's main door Godfrey noticed that the bundle of brush wood, that was the normal sign of an inn, was missing.

A man wearing clothes that had once been quality, but were now somewhat worn and bore some interesting stains, came out to greet him; 'Greetings sir, greetings. Welcome to The Red Barn. How may we accommodate you?'

Godfrey dismounted and tied his nag to the post, adjusted his cloak and looked carefully about. 'This is now The Red Barn?'

'Oh yes sir; The Red Barn. The finest bath house south of the river, discretion guaranteed.' The man looked past Godfrey. 'We provide the usual family and friends bathing facilities, of course, but I see you are on your own. There is no need to be lonely.' The man winked. 'We can provide company for you,' he coughed, 'of whatever sort fits your need.'

'The Red Barn is a stew?'

'Well we prefer the title "Bath House", seeing as we do in fact provide facilities for all folk but, yes, if you want to call it a "stew" you may and, yes, we can provide the sort of services you would associate with that name.'

Godfrey looked long and hard at the man before responding. 'I am looking for Godwin.'

'Ah, not the name of any of our young boys sir. Can I, perchance, interest you in Romana? An Italian boy, golden velvet skin, buttocks like a peach and eyes that are pools of desire. What he can do with a wet turnip leaf, well ......'

'Godwin is my cousin.'

The man looked offended. 'We only have people work here who do so of their own choice and there is no Godwin here. I am happy for you to talk to all the boys and satisfy yourself we do not have your cousin working here.'

'Godwin is a brewer, not a molly boy.'

'Oh,' the man's eyes opened wide and he smiled his relief, shewing yellow ragged-edged teeth in the process. 'You are a cousin of Godwin Wulf the brewer!'

'Yes.'

'He sold up and moved his brewing operation a few years back. His new place is where the Portsmouth Road crosses the Falcon. You will need to go back to Wandsworth then ride up the East Hill. You can't miss seeing his inn once you reach the top.' The man stopped talking for a moment to think. 'You could just ride along the Falcon back towards its source, but it can get quite tricky with marsh and bog and all that.'

Godfrey went back to his pony. 'Thank you, I think it is the Wandsworth way for me.'

'I'd get moving,' the man advised. 'Before the tide turns.'

Godfrey mounted, nodded acknowledgement to the man and set off back towards the dank earthy smell of the causeway.

Despite it only being the start of spring the day was warm and Godfrey made the most of the pony's gentle ambling gait to let go of the reins, carefully remove his dun coloured cloak and hang it over the animal's withers. As they reached the top of the hill he clicked his tongue and the pony moved into a trot allowing a cooling breeze to flow over them. The road was firm and there was even some dust that had been raised by previous riders hanging in the air so Godfrey pulled up his cloth visor to fully cover his nose. As they came down the hill Godfrey could see the bright glint of the Falcon Brook's water and stood in the saddle and at last saw, by the brook's bridge, a small collection of buildings within a hedged garth. He sat back down and let his mount carry him down towards his destination.

The enclosure had an entrance that could be closed by a gate made of wood that had furze woven into it. Godfrey rode in and two young boys ran out of a building that displayed the brewer's bush and an illustrated and worded sign that proclaimed it to be The Falcon Inn. The boys held his horse whilst he dismounted and took the tired animal away towards a water trough.

Another boy came over; the lad was just a mite shorter than Godfrey and had the facial shape, fair hair colouring and pale skin that marked him as family. 'Where is Godwin? I am his cousin, Godfrey from Sussex.'

'I have heard my father mention you and your brother cousin.' The youth indicated with his head towards a building from which an odorous mist emerged. 'You will find him in the brewing shed. We will take care of your horse. Coming so far I take it you will be staying, at least for the night.'

'I will.'

'Then I had best tell mother so she can prepare a room for you and put some more food in the pot.'

'Thank you...?'

'Godbert.'

'Thank you Godbert. We have met before but the last time I saw you, you would not have reached my knees!' Godfrey looked at the brewing shed, which now emitted a cough of steam. 'Over there you say?'

'Yes cousin Godfrey.'

The Sussex man walked to the shed, gradually letting his senses get used to the strong malty smell that was getting stronger the closer he got. The shed was open on one side and Godfrey looked at the back of a man who, apart from the fact he was a little shorter and had hair that contained much silver, could have been his own twin Thomas. 'You should be banned from the area for making such a stench!'

Godwin Wulf, brewer of Battersea, owner of The Falcon Inn, slowly reached for a long wooden paddle that still dripped liqueur and slowly turned round, easing the paddle in his hands so that he could easily swing it at the owner of the voice. 'We are a mile from any village so if you think you can come here complaining about this delicious smell....' he completed his turn to face his visitor. 'Godfrey!' he looked harder at the other's face. 'Or is it Thomas? I never can tell.'

'Godfrey.'

'And where is your twin?'

'At home, changing from his clothes to mine and then back again, several times a day and trying to remember what name he has when in which outfit.'

'You twins were always doing that when kids, or so you old dad used to tell me when he came up this way.'

'Now though it has a purpose. I can go away without anyone knowing that I have "gone away". Or at least that's what outsiders will think.'

Godwin nodded his affirmation then gave a lopsided grin; 'It's been a while since I have seen you cuz.'

'Too long, I didn't even know you had moved.'

'Ah.' Godwin held up a hand to stay his distant cousin then disappeared for a short time. When he reappeared he carried two leather jacks in one hand and a large jug which, by the thick creamy foam head that crept over the jug's edge at each step as the brewer walked, contained one of his famous barrel matured brews. With great skill the brewer filled the two jacks and held one out for his cousin.

Godfrey thanked his distant relative and sat down with his leather jack of foaming ale on the smooth wood of the bench at the back of the brewing shed. 'Foam?'

'Barrel matured with a good dose of honey for secondary fermentation – it is quite the fashion these days amongst the nobility.'

Godfrey took an appreciative sip before wiping foam from his top lip. 'Business has improved since the move from Edwin's Isle?'

Godwin Wulf smiled with the twisted lips smile that people knew him by. 'Oh yes, greatly. The old site on that Thameside island stuck in a big patch of bog was not the best of places, even if it did mean we avoided too much attention from inquisitive King's men when it came to tax collecting time.' He lifted his own jack and sipped off some of the foam. 'Ahhhhh, one of my best brews yet, if I say so myself; matured in an oak barrel with a drop of clover honey; it has to be clover honey to give it that special sparkle.' He looked to Godfrey for his reaction.

'Oh yes cuz,' Godfrey closed his eyes in pleasure and held the jack to his nose so that he could appreciate the full bouquet of the dark ale. One of your best brews yet.'

60

'You should visit more often, then you would be better able to judge if it is one of my best brews cuz.' Godwin seated himself on the bench and gently placed the earthen jug on the ground by his feet. 'I am happy you like it Godfrey, the water is purer here, the Falcon Brook gets a more muddy taint the nearer it gets to the Thames.'

Godfrey took another slip of the ale. 'So, business?'

'Good, really good. We no longer have to supply others for most of our income now. With the high road running past our door and being sat by the narrow bridge over the Falcon Brook, we get more than enough trade. In fact the wife and I,' Godwin looked past his cousin and smiled at the comfortably built woman in the garth supervising her young sons in their unloading of barley sacks from a wain, its pair of draught oxen patiently waiting, their heads lowered, their tails swishing. 'The wife and I, we are thinking of adding more space to The Falcon, putting on some more rooms for those coming up from Portsmouth and wanting to take a rest and refresh themselves before heading to Southwark and crossing the bridge into London.'

'This really is good ale Godwin; I wish we had such a good brewer down in Sussex.'

'Water; that is a large part of it. Where you live the water is too hard. Your brews, even with a brewer as good as myself, would never be more than "drinkable".'

'I should take some back with me, Thomas appreciates a good ale; will it travel though?'

'Yes, but you would need to let it stand for a week or so, especially seeing as your nag is hardly a quality piece of horse flesh and as like as not will give the ale a good shake on your way back home.'

Ah, but she ambles nicely; she doesn't shake the bones ....'

'Or the ale?'

'Or the ale,' Godfrey agreed. 'And in these troubled times it does not pay to have a quality mount.'

'True.' Godwin looked hard at Godfrey; 'Much trouble from the French? London is crawling with them.'

'Some trouble, though they seem cautious at present.'

'Cautious?'

'You have heard of Willikin of the Weald?'

'English wolf's head who is causing the French grief?'

'The same.'

Godwin gave a quiet chuckle. 'Just like in the old days?'

'You also remember the tales old Alfred, your dad, used to tell us about our mutual ancestor, Wulf the Brewer?'

'Oh yes, gave me nightmares they did. Wulf the wolf's head: he killed them here...'

'He killed them there,' Godfrey added.

'He killed them Normans everywhere!'

'Do you think the stories were true?'

'My old dad said they were and my granfer, Edric, he told the same tales.'

'Exactly the same, word for word, as you dad told them?'

'Exactly the same only with a higher body count. He told a gruesome tale did my granfer, when he were sober, which wasn't often.'

'I never met him. Did he brew a good ale?'

'Oh yes, but not as good as mine: the water you see, him brewing on Edwin's Isle and all that. Of course that's where old Wulf settled down when his Norman killing days were over.'

'Old Wulf the Brewer slayed many an enemy of the folk.'

Godwin emptied his jack and topped it up with more ale, carefully pouring it into his leathern vessel to keep the frothy head down. He gently shook his head, remembering dark winter's nights listening to his father telling the old tales and frightening his children whilst mother tried to get the youngest ones to bed before Alfred got to the really gruesome bits. 'Wulf the Norman slayer - Normans yesterday: French today?'

Godfrey held his jack up in a toast: 'Though these days, although the Normans are still all bastards, at least they are our bastards!'

Godwin touched his jack to his relative's jack in response to the toast. 'Though I don't say no to their money when they stop at The Falcon.'

'Which is as it should be: take money from them that took our lands.'

'Indeed.' Godwin took a mouthful of his ale, rolled it round his mouth and gave a sigh of delight at the taste.

'Do you remember how old Wulf got information on his foes?' Godfrey's voice took on a more serious tone.

Godwin closed his eyes and thought. 'Ah, yes, he used a travelling salt monger.'

'That's it.'

'Yes; no one questioned that man and his family travelling around, and everyone was happy to gossip to him when he sat and drank with him; sharing the news, or so they thought.'

'They did indeed.'

Godwin looked at Godfrey. 'I would think Willikin would be very interested in hearing some of the things that are said at The Falcon.'

'By Frenchmen?'

'And some of our so called "English" Normans.'

'They don't know you understand French do they?' Godfrey asked.

'It is not something I bandy about; it's best that way, especially as I tend to charge them more than I do my fellow English.'

'A shrug and a mouthful of local dialect, using your strongest accent, in response?'

'And they then tend to shrug themselves, give up and pay up.'

'Old Wulf the Brewer would be proud of you.'

Godwin smiled to himself with pride. 'It runs in the family cuz.'

'And so does gathering information?'

'As I say: "It runs in the family".'

'Not that I know Willikin, of course.'

'Of course, him being a Kentish man and all that.'

Godfrey drained his ale and reached for the earthenware jug that held more of the delicious dark brew. 'Do you deliver to Kent?'

'No off site sales since we moved from Edwin's Isle, but it is a thought.'

'I know some villages in Kent that could do with a regular supply of your produce.'

'My eldest son, Gilbert, is a terrible gossip and has a strong ear for other people's gossip. I could get him to do the deliveries.'

'What a splendid idea!'

'Indeed.'

'Mind, there must be more gossip in London than hereabouts.'

'I used to sell most of my ale into the City when I was based at Edwin's Isle. I needed to be in the London Brewers' Guild for that. I still belong so, maybe, I could attend more Guild meetings – the other brewers do love a chin wag.' Godwin gave another twisted lip smile. 'I used to supply the garrison at The Tower of London in those days.' Godwin nodded at the thought. 'They still ask me at times for some of my honey ale.'

'The best in Wessex,' Godfrey said, with a tilt of his head.

'The best in England,' Godwin insisted. 'No, maybe I should also offer them some of my dark ale too, seeing as I tend to brew the honey ale only in summer. The Tower Butler, who does the ordering, is a terrible one for saying things to me that perhaps he shouldn't, especially after a few pints of my triple brewed lanted rosemary ale.'

Godwin Wulf and Godfrey Wulfson drank a deep draught of ale and leant back on the bench, backs to the wall and they both smiled knowingly.

Chapter 5: A Shot in the Dark

'So, who is your friend?' Godfrey asked Gamble Gold as he passed him a lump of bread.

Gamble the pedlar took the bread and held out his hand for some cheese, which Thomas passed to him. 'Meet Harold the Harefoot.'

Thomas looked at the stranger with his light gold hair and dead honey brown eyes. 'I have heard of that name from my old granfer.'

Gamble gave a chuckle as he put the cheese into his lap and broke the bread. 'It won't be this one.'

The golden haired Harold turned his snake eyes on Thomas; 'I'm English.'

'Yes, and my granfer said Harefoot was at least half English.' Thomas studied Harold. 'I trust you are not his shadow walker.'

'Dreag,' Godfrey clarified.

'Them that are dead but still walk,' Thomas added before popping a lump of cheese into his mouth and enthusiastically chewing it.

'I'm English,' Harold repeated.

Thomas swallowed his cheese and then turned to Gamble; 'He's English.'

The pedlar nodded his head. 'He sure is and,' he passed a twist of bread to Harold, 'he is very much alive.'

Godfrey held his piece of cheese to his nose and sniffed it. 'Are you sure Master Gold?'

'I'm English,' Harold repeated.

'Oh yes,' Gamble passed another piece of bread to Harold, 'he's alive alright and he has a job to do.'

Thomas delved his hand into a wide mouthed earthen jar and fished out a pickled onion. 'So what is that to us?'

Godfrey held out a hand to his brother for the onion. 'We all have jobs to do.'

'Ah,' Gamble passed a piece of cheese to the Harefoot, 'his job is special and it is one he will need help to do.'

66

Thomas fished again in the pot and pulled out an onion for himself. 'Why us?'

The pedlar watched his charge as Harold put the cheese into his mouth and slowly chewed on it. 'You are familiar with Bosham and its area.'

Godfrey almost choked on his pickled onion and went into a fit of coughing that only stopped after he had taken several sips of ale from the leather jack Thomas handed him. 'Who says we know Bosham?' he managed between coughs.

'Willikin.' Gamble informed him as he passed more cheese to Harold.

'And,' Thomas started, 'how does he know about our connection with Bosham?'

Gamble Gold the tinker, tapped the side of his nose with an index finger.

'Henry the priest!' Godfrew stifled a cough and took another sip of watered ale.

Thomas nodded in agreement, 'He is from Trottingham originally.'

'So he would know our mother was from there.'

'Now he is the priest at Cassingham.'

'And sort of family to us.'

'On Dad's side.'

Gamble Gold held out a hand for more bread. 'Maybe.' He looked particularly at Godfrey. 'There is, of course, also the young lady who took off her clothes to wash 'em.'

Godfrey choked on his ale and Thomas had to slap him on his back repeatedly. Leaving his twin to breathe deep and wipe his eyes, Thomas gave the pedlar a quizzical look; 'How does Willikin know about her?'

Again Gamble Gold tapped the side of his nose with an index finger, this time from the other hand.

'Bugger,' Godfrey managed to say in between coughs.

'Seems your secret is out big brother.'

Godfrey nodded his head and returned to gently sipping ale.

Thomas gave his attention back to the two visitors. 'So we, Godfrey in particular, know Bosham. What of it Gamble?'

'Harold has a job to do there.'

'What sort of job?'

'A discrete one.' The pedlar took the cheese Godfrey held out, broke some off, which he placed in his lap, and passed the rest to Harold.

'I'm English,' Harold said as he took the proffered food.

'You see,' Gamble continued, 'the French are patrolling the roads now with parties of twenty.'

Thomas fished for another onion. 'Not round here.'

'No,' Gamble agreed, 'not round here but on the Winchester Road. Now Willikin does not want to stop them; he has his reasons, but he does want them lead by men less capable than the current captain, a certain Marc Le Pouf, called by us Mark the Strongman.'

'He's strong?' Godfrey managed to ask, his coughing now more, or less, under control.

'Too strong and far too efficient in his job.'

'So what has this to do with us?' Thomas put an onion between his front teeth and bit, spraying vinegar as he did so.

68

Gamble Gold wiped some of the liquid off his brown woollen cloak. 'We need someone to get Harold into Bosham where he will need a clear view of the south side of the manor house.'

Godfrey stood and walked to a shelf attached to the far wall and took down two rough pottery cups. 'And then?' He passed a cup to the pedlar and offered the other to Harold.

'And then Harold does his job and you all get out quick smart.'

'I'm English,' Harold said as he took his cup.

'The job?' Thomas asked as he filled the cups with watered ale.

'Mark Strongman.'

'Mark Strongman?' Godfrey sat down again and the leather seat of his stool gave a creaking groan.

'Mark Strongman,' Gamble confirmed. 'He dies.'

Thomas looked to his brother before asking the obvious question; 'How'

'Shot.'

'Shot?' the twins said together.

'Shot,' Gamble confirmed. 'Harold is a marksman but,' he fondly patted his companion's back, 'he is not the brightest star in the night sky.'

'I would never have guessed.' Thomas topped up his jack with ale.

'No, not the brightest, but' Gamble continued, 'one of England's finest archers.'

'I'm English,' Harold said, this time smiling and thus shewing emotion for the first time since the twins had first seen him.

'Our French friend has a "thing" going with the lady of the manor.'

'Her husband?' Thomas inquired.

'Is with the rebel barons.'

'But,' Godfrey interrupted, 'Bosham belongs to William the Marshal, and he is for the King.'

'And William Marshal is in Ireland avoiding King John who has made some interesting accusations against the Marshal.' Gamble downed his watered ale and held out his cup for more. 'Not that he says they are true, naturally.'

'The ways of our betters are beyond our understanding.' Thomas filled the pedlar's cup.

'Though,' Godfrey indicated to his brother that he should also refill Harold's drinking vessel, 'I have heard that William Marshal is an honourable man.'

Gamble downed his drink and held the cup out for yet more. 'None finer they say; very loyal.'

'So, the local squire is in rebellion not only against both his lord and the king, he is being cuckolded as well.'

'So it seems.' This time Gamble only drank half the contents of the cup.

'Not many trees,' said Thomas.

'For cover,' Godfrey completed

'And he is bound to have an escort, this Mark Strongman, so, how many men do we need?'

'You two and perhaps one other.'

Thomas pursed his lips. 'Not enough if he has his twenty men with him.'

'Or even ten.'

The pedlar finished off his drink and placed the empty cup down near the hearth with is glowing embers. 'Willikin wants just Strongman taken; he does not want a full war band operation. Now,' he leaned forward towards the twins, 'Strongman does come alone, with just a falconer by his side. They go into the spinney near the manor house, this during the day. Come evening her Ladyship, if the coast is clear, opens a window and hangs out a lantern. Strongman comes in, leaving his falconer with the horses. Once inside he opens the window and brings in the lantern.'

'Every time?' asked Thomas. 'That's a bit silly.'

'Same routine,' Godfrey concluded.

'A man of habit is our Captain Strongman. Now, when he leans out to take in the lantern that's when Harold gets him.'

Thomas topped up his brother's jack. He went to refill Harold's cup, but it was still full. 'Why not shoot him before?'

'Whilst he is in the woods.'

'Willikin wants him dead in the manor house: it will cause more scandal and,' Gamble Gold nudged Harold and nodded his head towards the cup the man held, encouraging him to drink, 'if he dies in the woods the people of Bosham may get the blame. By doing it this way the French will know it is Willikin of the Weald's doing.'

Harold drained his cup of watered ale. 'I'm English,' he said.

Huddling in the shelter of a hedgerow of mature trees Godfrey and Thomas peered at Bosham's manor house that sat to the north east of Holy Trinity church through a cloud of light drizzle.

Thomas wiped rain off the end of his nose with the back of his hand. 'Two days ago this Strongman was supposed to be here. If he isn't here by tomorrow I think we should call it quits and go home.'

Godfrey continued to watch the manor house. 'It is sister Edith's young Garth stuck out in the salt marsh up that creek waiting for us that concerns me.' He changed his view to that of the small spinney of hazel and aspen trees to the manor's west. 'At least we have somewhere dry to stay when not standing watch, all he has is that small rowing boat and a canvas cover to stay under.'

'I worry that he may get bored and risk slipping into the village.'

'Birds; he likes watching birds. There are lots of birds for him to watch on the saltings.'

'For two days?'

'Hopefully.' Godfrey pulled his oiled linen cape tighter round his neck to stop the persistent fine rain from sneaking in. 'Oh well, I'm off. You are welcome to your shift of watching.'

'I hope you enjoy your deep meaningful conversations with the witty Harold whilst drying out in the church's death house.'

'I thought I'd take a walk down by the quay first.'

'Oh, that's it; hoping to catch a view of that long legged Rose, the fisherman's daughter, her what takes off her clothes to wash 'em.'

'That was only once, and it was an accident that I saw her.'

'Of course it was.' Thomas moved into the watching position that Godfrey had just vacated. 'I bet she doesn't smell of fish either!'

Godfrey walked off, but not before pulling the hood of Thomas' cape from his brother's head, cascading drips of water down his twin's neck.

'He's here.' Thomas said as he entered the charnel crypt.

Godfrey stirred and eased himself off the pile of thigh bones he had made into a bed with the help of his and his brother's thick woollen cloaks. 'About time.'

'Rain's stopped too.'

'Good.' Godfrey looked across the narrow passage to the piled bones the other side and Harold the Harefoot; the tall blond man was sitting cross legged polishing his bow with a rag soaked in a mix of linseed oil and beeswax. Godfrey inclined his head to Thomas and then back to Harold. 'He's been doing that all afternoon.'

'He did the same this morning.'

'Didn't do it yesterday.'

'No, it was polishing the arrow heads then.'

Godfrey ran an appreciative eye over Harold's bow. 'Yew.'

Thomas sighed. 'I wish we could afford one of them, still,' he patted his own bow encased in its oiled lined cover, 'ash or elm are also a good wood for a bow.'

'Yes, but yew.' The twins gave a collective sigh and watched Harold enviously.

Harold looked up, seemingly aware of the brothers watching him. 'Target here?'

Thomas nodded. 'Yes this Mark the Strongman is in the woods so this evening....'

'With luck ...' Godfrey chipped in.

'... he will be visiting her Ladyship.' Thomas concluded.

'Good.' Harold gave his bow a final wipe. 'Now food and drink.'

'Has he eaten whilst you have been with him?' Thomas whispered.

'No,' Godfrey whispered back. 'Has he eaten whilst with you?'

'No, nothing today; nothing yesterday.'

'Nerves?'

'I doubt he has any.'

Godfrey went to where he had stashed the food and drink, selected some dried horse meat and some shelled hazel nuts, and handed them to Harold. Thomas handed over his leathern bottle, now only containing water rather than its usual small ale.

Harold took the proffered provision and promptly woofed them down. Wiping his mouth he stared at the twins before getting down from his ossuary perch. He turned and reclaimed his bow, found his arrows with their sharpened and shiny small swallow heads, grunted his satisfaction at his own work and headed for the stone stairs that would take them from the crypt into the newly built south aisle.

'Wait!' Godfrey hissed.

'We have to check the priest isn't about,' Thomas explained.

'Sext; that is due soon.'

Harold came to a sudden halt. 'Sex? Whores?' He licked his lips. 'I like that!'

'Sext!' insisted an exasperated Godfrey.

'It's a church service,' clarified Thomas, grabbing Harold's arm.

'I like church too,' Harold informed him.

'Yes, so do I,' Thomas replied.

'But,' added Godfrey, 'we must listen to it down here.'

'We have more food to eat whilst we wait,' Thomas added.

'Food?'

'Yes,' Thomas confirmed, 'food.'

'I like food.' Harold turned round and went and sat back on his pile of bones then stroked his bow whilst the twins went to get him the last of their food. 'I'm hungry.'

'That's funny,' Thomas whispered to Godfrey. 'I thought he said he was English?'

'Garth is ready?' Thomas used the toes of his right foot to adjust the position of the roll that contained his heavy wool cloak wrapped in his oilskin cape.

'He's ready,' Godfrey confirmed and also adjusted the position of his roll, but with his left foot.

'He didn't get bored watching the birds then?'

'He has caught crabs.'

'Has he now!' Thomas gave his twin a quizzical look.

'Not that kind stupid, he is not that sort of boy.'

Thomas sniggered. 'What's he done with the crabs then?'

'Got them in a wicker basket he "borrowed" from somewhere.'

'I hope its owner isn't out looking for it.'

'So do I.'

'Crabs?' Harold the archer asked.

'Crabs,' the twins both answered.

'I like crabs.' Harold licked his lips.

'I'm sure you do,' the twins replied.

'Light.'

'Light?' Thomas questioned.

Godfrey gave his brother a nudge in the ribs. 'There, look,' he pointed to the manor house where a window in the solar had had its shutter pushed open.

All three watched as a female figure with unbound hair leant out and hung a horn lantern on an unseen hook before closing the shutter again.

Thomas took his bow out of its linen bag and strung it before tying the bag around his waist. He pushed three arrows through the back of his belt. 'Now, we wait for his nibs to appear.'

Godfrey copied his brother before looking to see what Harold the Harefoot was doing. The marksman archer, with four arrows in his belt, was doing nothing but looking at the window. Godfrey was puzzled at the four arrows as Harold was said to never miss; he shrugged and followed the man's gaze, calculating the distance from the hedgerow they stood in, to the window.

'Fifty yards I'd guess,' Thomas whispered into his brother's ear.

Godfrey turned to Harold who was still staring at the window. 'Harold, do you want to get closer? There is that tree between us and the manor house; it would cut the range down to twenty yards.'

Harold made no move and he gave no acknowledgement that he had heard Godfrey.

Thomas lent to his brother's ear, 'Maybe he doesn't like the fact that the angle of his shot would be more difficult?'

'Maybe. I just wish he'd talk.'

'He does talk.'

'Yes, but not in the way normal people do; you know what I mean.'

'It is time.' The brothers started as Harold made his announcement. Harold pulled his hood back off his head exposing the golden gleam of his hair as the moonlight escaped from the broken clouds of the night sky. He took his yew longbow from its hardened leather case, kissed it and then strung it. He then returned to looking at the window. 'It is time,' he repeated.

Thomas and Godfrey also looked at the window. Thomas spoke quietly to his brother; 'I could hit the shutter easily from here, quite possibly anyone looking out of it, as long as they stood still for a while.'

'But a certain killing shot?' Godfrey asked him.

'That is the problem.'

'It is time,' Harold said again pulling an arrow from his belt and nocking it on his bow string, all without looking.

The twins also nocked arrows, ready to provide back-up if Harold missed.

'Me shoot.'

'Yes,' Godfrey confirmed. 'You shoot.'

'And,' Thomas added, 'if you miss, we shoot.'

'Me shoot.' Harold spared them a quick glance. 'I don't miss.'

'You don't miss?' Thomas asked ironically.

'He doesn't miss? Ever?' Godfrey contributed.

'I don't miss.' Harold was back watching the window. 'You put bows back in bags.'

The twins looked at each other, shrugged, unstrung their bows and put them back in their bags.

'I don't miss.' Harold put some tension on his bow and then relaxed it. He did this several times, warming up the wood. 'Then we run.'

'Then we run.' The twins went back to following Harold's watch on the now shuttered window.

Harold twitched an ear and stared at the window with even more intensity. 'Sssshhhhhh.' The archer moved his head slowly from side to side to give each ear an opportunity to assess the situation, all the time his eyes stayed fixed on the window. 'It is time.'

A gentle sound of male laughter drifted across the grass swathe as the wooden shutter partly opened. An indistinct female voice said something that sounded French. Again there was gentle laughter. The female voice said something that by its tone was teasing; more male laughter. The shutters gave a wooden groan as they were pushed fully open to reveal the naked torso of a big but well-muscled man. The female called out something which caused the man to turn and answer. All the time Harold just watched.

The man turned back to the window and leant out, reaching for the horn lamp on its hook. Harold drew and shot. An arrow hit the man between neck and collar bone leaving only the feather flights shewing. The man gasped and half pulled himself upright before Harold put another arrow into him that hit the heart.

'We run?' asked Godfrey, already half turned to flee.

'No.' Harold kept watching the window.

The man had slumped half hanging out of the window giving an occasional twitch. The owner of the female voice appeared and tried to pull him upright, all the time giving out a sound that was half moan and half subdued scream. Harold pulled an arrow from his belt and in a fluid movement shot the woman in the heart. As the woman fell forward he put in a second arrow, pinning her to her lover.

Harold turned to the twins; 'We run,' he said and took off at a very fast pace, bow in one hand and bow case in the other, through the trees, past the church, along the mill meadow and towards the salt marshes to the north of the village.

'He,' Thomas managed to gasp as the twins tried to keep pace with Harold, 'does ...'

'Run like a hare?' Godfrey gasped back.

All Thomas could give back was a short nod of his head as he needed all his breath to cope with the fast trot of Harold Harefoot.

The three killers stood on the muddy bank of the stream that cut across the saltings. Harold stood still, staring into the distance whilst the twins were slightly stooped, catching their breath.

Thomas was the first to recover sufficiently to stand upright. 'The boat is here somewhere I am sure of it.'

Godfrey, still stooped, cast his eyes along the creek bank. 'Somewhere here, please God it is somewhere here. I am not sure I can walk any further. First the run and now this cloying mud clinging to our feet.'

A hand tapped him on the back and a sibilant voice whispered in his ear; 'It is just round the bend of the creek, but you need to hurry. If you stay standing much longer you will all sink into the mud and never be found.'

Godfrey quickly dropped his bow and reached for his dagger.

'There is no need for that uncle,' Garth said in his normal melodious voice, and you had better pick your bow up before it too sinks into obscurity.'

Thomas turned and looked at Garth Robertson; 'One day young nephew your sense of humour will get you into trouble.'

'One day perhaps,' the lad replied.

Harold turned his dead eyes on the others. 'We go.'

The party started off, following in Garth's footsteps. Godfrey moved closer to his nephew, 'How come you managed to sneak up on us like that? Even old bats' ears Harold didn't hear you.'

The youngster chuckled. 'Well I knew you were on the way as you were making so much noise. With the clouds now cutting out the moonlight I wondered if you would find your way to the boat so I worked out which way you would come, and I have had three days to get to know the tracks around here, and set out towards your thunderous approach. I found this clump of sedge grass to wait in, out of sight and then, lo and behold, you stood in front of me.'

'We were supposed to let you know we were there by calling like a curlew.'

'So many curlew round here in winter time, I would never have picked if it was you or the birds.'

They reached the small rowing boat that Garth had pulled up into a large clump of sedge and helped him launch it into the narrow creek's brackish waters. Garth helped the others aboard before getting in himself. 'Your timing is good though, if it had been low rather than high tide, we would still be sitting around in the mud.'

The lad picked up an oar and pushed the craft out into the midstream and started rowing.

Harold sat in the bow, looking rearwards with a fixed stare, his feet resting on the basket of crabs whose nipping pincers he totally ignored.

Thomas and Godfrey sat in the stern watching Harold.

Godfrey lent towards his brother and whispered, 'I didn't like him killing the woman.'

'Nor I,' his brother replied.

'I wonder why he did it?'

'Ask him.'

Godfrey lifted his head and called to Harold; 'Why did you shoot the woman? We were told you were to kill this Mark the Strongman.'

Harold continued to stare back where they had come from, seemingly not having heard the question. After several oar strokes he deigned to glance down and stare at the twins. 'Willikin said kill both.' The archer then went back to watching the shore as the boat made it out of the side creek and into the waters of Chidham Creek proper.

Thomas looked to his brother, 'I suppose it makes sense. If only Strongman was killed the woman could have claimed he broke in, by killing both anyone finding their naked bodies nailed together, as it were, would know exactly what was going on. It might be enough to drive Bosham's squire from the rebel's side, knowing a Frenchie was bedding his wife behind his back.'

Godfrey nodded agreement then sighed. 'I still don't like the idea of killing women.'

'Talking of women,' Thomas brightened at the thought. 'What is this with you and Rosie of the Long Legs? I thought we agreed that we would look for wives together.'

Godfrey gave a smile as he replied. 'Then, little brother, you had better get a move on.'

Chapter 6: The Long & Winding Road

'I'm glad you are back,' Will Greenleaf said as he poured another cauldron of hot water into the wooden tun cask that had been cut in half. Normally it was used for fermenting barley for brewing ale but it also doubled as the village's communal bath. The twins hopped about, trying to mix the hot water with the tepid water the cask already contained. The movement caused a heady smell to arise from the wooden staves where the yeast from yesterday's brewing of ale had remained in the grain of the wood.

Finally happy about the temperature of the water Thomas gathered water in his hands and poured it over his head, shaking the drips out of his eyes. 'And we are glad to be back, if only for a bath.'

Godfrey rubbed his back against the half tun's wooden side to ease an itch. 'Seven days is long enough without a bath,' he said, reaching for a bar of lye soap balanced on the tun's edge. 'I need to get not just the smell of sweat off me but also the smell of old bones.'

Thomas laughed agreement and held out his hand for the soap whilst his brother used a pot to gather water to rinse the soap out of his hair. 'That and Harold's stale smile!'

'Err,' Will interrupted before the brothers could go off on another reflection and analysis of the previous week's activities. 'The reason I'm glad you are back ....'

'Is because you are tired of doing our work as well as your own?' suggested Thomas, trying to balance on one leg in order to wash his toes.

'No, it is because ...'

'You missed my cooking?' Godfrey chipped in.

'No, please, Good Fellows, let me finish,' Will's voice had a distinct edge to it.

'Go on then,' the twins replied.

'Well that jongleur was back here, singing.'

'As he does,' Thomas agreed.

'Badly and out of tune,' Godfrey added.

'Like his lute.'

Will looked around, found a part full bucket of cold water and proceeded to empty it over both the twins' heads. He waited till they had finished spluttering before he continued to talk. 'That jongleur was back here. His song was not quite the same. The names he used didn't alter but the meeting place was Cassingham.'

Thomas stopped the grabbing movement he was about to employ in the hopes of dragging Will into the bath. 'When is the meet?'

'His song said four days.'

'And,' Godfrey asked, 'when was he here?'

'Two days ago. I told him that Herla and Robin of the Boxholt were away. He seemed surprised and said he was told you would be back from your travel by the time he reached our village.'

Thomas started to get himself out of the tub. 'There is no trusting Frenchmen to keep to a schedule.' He heaved himself out and commenced dripping water on the brewhouse's beaten earthen floor. 'Come on big brother, we need to leave straight away if we are to get to this Kentish place in time.'

'Nuts,' Godfrey also levered himself out. 'I was looking forward to a comfortable night's sleep in my own bed.'

Thomas' voice was muffled as he rubbed his face and hair dry with a large piece of soft, worn, linen. 'Rather than Rosie Fish's?'

Godfrey yanked the linen away from his brother none too gently. 'I keep telling you – she is not that sort of girl.'

Before Thomas could continue baiting his brother, Will Greenleaf pushed him out of the way and removed the bung from the sawn tun cask to let the water out causing Godfrey to jump out of the way of the released stream of water. 'You need to get to Midhurst before the curfew bell. I have sent Seb ahead with word to the ostler that you will need fast mounts.'

'Talking of fast mounts: how was Rose when you last saw her?' Thomas ran, naked, towards the twin's cottage with an irate Godfrey in pursuit.

William, squire of Cassingham, looked over the men assembled in his great hall. He coughed loudly in order to get their attention. 'I'm sorry to have to bring you all here, especially as it is a great risk to have you all gathered together in one place, but what I plan for us to do next is bigger than the actions we have undertaken before and I need to ensure you are all fully briefed.' He cast his eyes around to ensure he had their full attention. 'Up till now we have, with the exception of taking out one reasonably sized convoy, been little more than a nuisance to the French.'

A beautifully dressed woman with nut brown hair contained in a gold snood net entered the hall accompanied by four young women in more sober clothes. William looked at her and smiled as she, and the maids, placed jugs of wine on a side table that groaned with plates of cold meats, dried fruit and bread. 'My wife,' he explained.

'So, if you be "Willikin of the Weald",' Ganger Greenwood called out, 'What do we call your Lady?'

'Mary?' William asked his wife.

The beautiful lady with the pleasantly rounded face smiled, shewing dimples in each cheek. 'Marion Freshwater, after our small lake.'

'Marion Freshwater it is my love.' William gave his attention back to his men, leaving the ladies to gather their skirts and leave the hall. 'As I was saying; we have been little more than a nuisance; killing their couriers, picking off foraging parties, harassing convoys. We gave them a shock on the Winchester road when we destroyed that convoy but they overcame that with highway patrols, checking for potential ambushes and the like. They were very effective and kept us on our toes as they were led by a very careful and cunning man, Mark the Strongman but, I am pleased to say, he has been removed from the scene.' Godfrey and Thomas nudged each other and smiled. William waited till the buzz from the men of West Sussex and South Hampshire, where Strongman's patrols had indeed cramped their style, had died down before he continued. 'The man now in charge is an English traitor, a certain William Atkins. He, fortunately for us, is not only rather stupid, he is also rather lazy and we shall use that to our advantage.'

'Excuse me Willikin,' Gilbert of the White Hand held up one of his habitually glove encased hands. 'If he is so stupid and lazy, why have they given him the role of running the highway patrols?'

William stroked his neat muzzle beard and smiled. 'They appointed him because he is very loyal and the French need the support of his Lord, to whom William owes his loyalty. It seems that Atkins was the Lord's fight trainer when a boy – he even calls him "Uncle Bill".' The men all laughed. 'So, we have "Uncle Bill" doing an incompetent job of checking the road and, without a strong man's hand on them, the rest of the men doing patrol work have also become lazy.' William eased his buttocks in the high chair and leaned his elbows on the table in front of him. 'The French are being pushed back everywhere in the south by King John and his loyal barons are containing the rebel barons to the north. If we can cut off their supply line from Southampton to London Dauphin Louis and his men based in London will be isolated and ineffective.'

'Then the French will go home?' Gasper the Ghost asked on behalf of the others, his deep bass sepulchral voice coming from within a deep hood that hid his face.

'All being well,' William agreed. 'There is, as always, good news and bad news.'

The men groaned, expecting the bad to be the dominant news. 'The bad news is that the men of Hampshire, whose share of the plunder from the Winchester Road convoy we took was to "look after" the oxen and wagons we took whose owners we could not identify, and thus get their property back to, will have to get those oxen to the heath at Blackmoor before the coming Sabbath.'

'Just the oxen?' a voice called from the back.

'Just the oxen,' William confirmed. 'Plus any cull kine you may still have after the winter.'

'We going to lose the animals then,' another voice called out.

'Hopefully no and if they are lost, all being well, the beasts will be replaced by others we take.'

There was much muttering amongst the men. William waited for the meeting to quieten down before rapping on the table in front of him with the pommel of his dagger and continuing. 'The good news is, we have a plan, one that we,' he indicated his henchmen John Little and Mark Reeve, 'have put a great deal of thought and effort into.' The assembled men cheered. 'Of course any plan can go wrong.' There was a low collective groan. 'But this one shouldn't.' The men brightened and smiled. 'Now, to make this plan work I need all the bands from Surrey, Hampshire, Sussex and Kent to gather. Once together what we will do is this. We will let the highway patrol go through, doing their now lazy and incompetent checking, we will let the vanguard pass bye, we will even let the convoy pass. We will then trap and wipe out their rearguard.' William could see the consternation this statement caused; he held up a hand to stop the meeting deteriorating into a huddle of talking men. Once order had been restored, mainly by men seeing his held hand and shutting their neighbour up, William continued. 'They have the numbers, we do not. So, what we do is cut them up into little groups where we do outnumber them. Remember, many of them are trained men of war, most of us are not; good archers,' the assembled men all cheered, 'but not men trained in warfare. I know many of you can use a staff as well as any man-at-arms can use a spear, and do so with the same deadly effect, and I know many of you have recently acquired swords.' Many of William's audience sniggered. 'But how many of the sword owners know how to use them; I mean use them effectively?' There was much nodding of heads. 'So, what we need to do is outnumber our foes, overwhelm them with an arrow storm and then, and only then, get stuck in and finish them off whilst they are still in a state of shock, for I do not want any, and I repeat any, survivors. This has to be an operation that is so devastating, so complete that the French will not want to use this supply route again. Once we have done this, the Hampshire and West Sussex men must, and I can't say this too strongly, must wipe out any French who dare to risk riding on that road, or anywhere near it. We need to create a region they will think twice about going into. Do I make myself clear?'

The men all cheered with some crying 'Yea!' and others 'OUT, OUT, OUT' as if they were King Harold's Huscarls at Hastings.

William stood, held up both hands for silence, and once he had got it, indicated the table with its food and drink. 'Pray, help yourselves. Then, after you have had your fill, go home, gather your men and await my call.' The men started to surge towards the provender. 'Just make sure you leave here in small groups,'

William called out over the now increasing sound as men elbowed each other for the best of the food and started calling out to their friends. 'We don't want to create too much attention.'

Thomas pulled back from the crowd; his hunting knife filled from tip to hilt with speared meat and joined Godfrey who had managed to acquire several rolls of manchet bread.

The twins divided the food between themselves so each had an equal share of the spoils.

Thomas held his knife up, ready to nibble the edge of a thick slice of smoked ham. 'Just what have we got ourselves into big brother?'

'Trouble,' Godfrey replied, splitting a roll and placing a slice of venison into it.

Will Greenleaf sat alongside Mark, the Reeve of Cassingham, and the twins. The youth was sipping from Godfrey's water bottle. Mark waited till the slim swarthy lad had finished before asking him for information. 'So,' the clean shaven man asked, 'what news on the highway patrol?'

Will removed the strands of black hair that had strayed into his eyes and looked at the Reeve. 'They have done two sweeps and have just started their third.'

'They didn't see you?'

'Oh yes, I borrowed some local swine and pretended to be looking after them as they foraged along the cleared section aside the road.' The boy smiled. 'The first time the Captain yelled at me in both French and English. The second time he just swore at me, in a mix of French and English and told me to get my hogs out of the way of his men; I pretended I only understood the English. The third time he told me, in English, to get gone as there was a big armed convoy on the way.'

Mark closed his eyes for a moment. 'He didn't seem suspicious?'

'Just bored.' Will took another sip of water. 'There was one really interesting thing.'

'Go on,' Thomas encouraged him.

'Well.' Will looked from Mark to Thomas; 'The Captain, he speaks English and French.'

'That we know,' Mark informed him.

Will looked back at the Cassingham reeve. 'Yes, but he speaks the funny old Norman French, like you hear here only in England.'

'Nothing unexpected there young man.'

'Ah, but his men, and there are about twenty of them, they speak a mix of pure Norman, Picard French, Paris French, and Burgundian French; there may be more types of French being spoken, but that was what I picked up.' Will wiped his mouth with the back of his hand. 'They are a very mixed bunch, possibly the dregs of their army.'

'So,' said Mark, his attention suddenly sharpened, 'they have problems understanding not only their Captain, but each other?'

Will gave a laugh that sounded like a tinkling bell, 'Oh yes, they get very confused at times. The fact that they don't seem very bright doesn't help them either.'

'The best news yet,' Mark tousled the youth's hair. 'Now young man, get yourself gone, as the Captain told you and get them hogs back to their owner before it gets too dangerous around here.'

The boy looked to the twins; 'Do I have to?'

90

The brothers answered together with an emphatic; 'Yes.'

Seeing Will's disappointment Thomas patted him on the shoulder. 'Later Will, when it is something smaller, but not this time.'

'Next time,' Godfrey confirmed. 'Now get them swine away from here as the smell of their shit is turning my stomach.'

The French rearguard kept a good distance between itself and the last of the ox wagons in a rather vain attempt to let the dust from the hundred or so wagons in front of them settle before they had to ride through it. Despite being April there had been few showers and although the road was frost hardened the top surface had turned to fine dust with the churning of wagon wheels and the iron shod horses and oxen of the convoy. Both the horses and the men of the rearguard drooped their heads as they plodded along at a slow pace, some riders had even dismounted and were walking alongside their mounts with their spears across the pommels of the horse's saddle. Having set out from Winchester early that morning they had already covered twelve miles and were still some five miles from where the earlier convoy had been ambushed. Even as they re-entered a wooded area from the heathland the men-at-arms had their attention more on the expected rest and refreshment they would get at Alton than the road ahead. Before them the front men could see where the trees had been cleared around the junction with the Gosport Road. Suddenly a herd of cattle, mostly big solid oxen, came out of the Gosport Road, swarming across in front of the rearguard. The French front rank ground to a halt and the dismounted men commenced to get back on their rouncies as they saw drovers appear on foot with their barking dogs trying to control the cattle beasts. The drovers appeared to be incompetent as their charges went both north and south on the Winchester Road, clogging it in both directions whilst the cattle dogs seemed out of control spooking both the cattle and the horses of the French men-at-arms. Soon anger and frustration replaced the Frenchmen's original alertness and suspicion.

The French noble leading the rearguard stood in his stirrups looking to see who was in charge of the cattle drove. Seeing a very tall man who seemed to be directing the other drovers by waving and flapping his arms he called out to him in the French of Paris; *'Man move those animals before we charge them down.'* Seeing he had the tall man's attention he yelled out louder. *'Get them off the road I said!'*

'Drop dead,' John Little, the squire of Cassingham's Head Forester, replied.

It was then that the massed archers that had been hidden on the road's north side stepped clear of the greening trees that had camouflaged them and loosed the first volley of arrows. Men and horses suddenly sprouted feathered shafts, though some of the arrows bounced off hardened leather helmets. Horses screamed, horses reared, many horses bolted looking to turn and race back down the road from whence they had come and safety. A second volley hit and added to the panic.

'Close the road!' John Little shouted above the din.

Some of the archers went to comply, but were held back by their fellows crying out 'Hold!' and 'Don't block the target!'

The road was closed, but it was by Mark Reeve and a select band that had been waiting for John's signal. They lined the road to the French rear three ranks deep. 'Loose in your own time,' Mark commanded and soon the escape route was closed to the French by dead and dying horses and their riders.

'Loose in your own time,' John the Forester called to the massed archers in the woods and now the men of the forest picked their own targets and brought them down.

Somehow the French noble in charge and his mount had escaped attention and he used the flat of his sword to stop some of the rout around him and gathered half a dozen men. Satisfied he had them under control the noble lead them in a charge into the woods away from the arrow shot. Neither he, nor his followers, has spotted the fine ropes that had been strung between the trees, some at a rider's height, some at a horse's chest height, others at a height that would cause horses to trip. The escape charge turned into a shambles of fallen men and beast. John Little and his incompetent drovers drew swords that had been concealed under their cloaks and proceeded to kill the fallen French noble and his men and put those of the horses that had broken their legs out of their misery.

Little Midge, Miller of Cassingham, his damaged arm well-padded by a bandage coloured a green that did not match the green of his shirt, led a band of men, made up of the elderly and the very young and started to round up the cattle and take them back down the Gosport Road.

Mark the Reeve brought up his own band of men, marksmen all, and started to clean up the few French still able to fight leaving John Little to stride up into the woods crying 'Hold! Hold!' and

93

causing the archers to cease their shooting now that their fellow English were mixed up with the remains of the French rearguard.

At last John Little was satisfied that the archers had at finally stopped shooting, for despite the cries of "Hold!" from himself and the various band leaders some of the less obedient, or more skilful, had continued to take a clear shot at their enemy and it had taken a few yells and clouts to bring everyone to heel. The forester blew a crude and short tune on his hunting horn and at the known signal the band leaders gathered round him. 'Right you lot,' he stopped for late comers. 'Right,' he began again, 'that was only the start of today's fun. Get your men moving to the north straight away, at the trot. Use the back path to Alton. Leave the arrows you have shot, we will collect them after we have finished here. There will be more arrows awaiting you along the way. I know there are a lot of you, and it must attract attention, but take no notice, just keep moving and don't stop for anything. Willikin is waiting for you and he will get word to you as to what he needs done next.'

'More bloody work,' Godfrey muttered to his twin.

'That's why Willikin didn't tell us all,' Thomas muttered back.

'Bastard.'

'Clever bastard.'

William of Cassingham sat on his short legged pony and watched the wagon park by the Alton butts. The wagons were drawn up in rows with their draught beasts who were working their way through their nose bags of food. The wagoners were sitting on the driving seats eating whatever food they had brought with them. In a separate part of the green were about thirty or so men-at-arms their spears and pole arms stacked in stooks whilst the crossbowmen amongst them had their weapons laid alongside them. Some of the men-at-arms had already eaten and drunk their fill and were catching some sleep before they were needed to march again alongside the wagons.

Cassingham moved his pony forward and his bodyguard of three men followed on their own mounts. The squire now had a clearer view of the butts and the green they stood on. He flicked his eyes towards Ackender Woods and caught the slight movement that indicated men slipping out towards the high hedge that surrounded the butts. William looked to one of his men, John of the Clear Sight. John took no notice of his leader and remained constantly scanning the hedge instead. Eventually he looked at William and nodded.

William of Cassingham gave the scene in front of him one more hard look. 'Now,' he said in an unhurried voice.

Nudging his pony forward of the other riders a man in an outfit that was completely scarlet, except for dark green trim around the bottom of his hood and shirt, held an exceptionally long hunting horn fitted with a metal mouthpiece. What could be seen of the man's face was covered in freckles and a wisp of copper hair escaped the confines of his hood. Looking round to get the squire's nod he turned to face Alton's butts and played a long haunting call followed by three short high notes.

Two things happened at once. A shower of arrows landed on the French men-at-arms and every other wagoner lent down, produced a blade and cut down the other wagoner sitting alongside him. More arrows then hit the men-at-arms and then more again before the hidden archers stared pouring through gaps they made in the hedge and started laying about with sword and knife, chasing those of the wagoners who had broken free and tried to make a break for freedom.

William rode up to the man with the hunting horn. 'It worked better than I expected Will Scathlock.'

The man in scarlet nodded his agreement. 'You said it was an old trick,' the man's Yorkshire accent was subtle.

'The founder of Kent, Hengest by name, arranged for the leader of the Britons to marry his daughter and bring his chief men with him for the celebrations. He sat each of these Welshmen alongside one of his English warriors. Once he had the Welsh drunk he cried "Op with tha seax!" and each Englishman bent down, pulled his fighting knife from the straw that covered the floor and killed his Welsh neighbour. We just made sure that each wagon had an Englishman sitting next to a Frenchman.'

'Aye Willikin, are you going to tell your English wagoners they were copying their ancestors?'

William of Cassingham gave a quiet chuckle. 'A waste of time: Hengest founded Kent, these wagoners are Hampshire men and I doubt they know the tale.'

Godfrey and Thomas were amongst the first of the archers from the first attack to arrive at Alton and lead their band down to the butts as directed by Willikin's men in Ackender Woods. As they came through one of the gaps recently made in the hedge they came to a shuddering halt and Garth and Mark Archer crashed into them and those behind crashed into those two. In front of them was a butcher's scene as men were dragging over the stripped bodies of the French ready for others to behead the corpses. Other men, with their shirt sleeves rolled up above their elbows, were tossing the heads into the bed of a horse drawn wagon.

'That,' said Thomas, over his shoulder.

'Is not very nice,' Godfrey completed.

The twins looked at each other; 'So glad we didn't let young Will talk us into letting him come along,' they said to each other.

Willikin rode over and stopped his pony short to allow the two hundred plus archers enter the butt's green. Once he was happy all but a few stragglers had arrived, he dismounted and climbed up onto a nearby wagon. Scathlock joined him on the wagon and blew his horn to get everyone's attention. Willikin lifted his smart hunting cap, wiped sweat from his brow with a square of linen and looked over the ranks of green, brown, red and yellow clad men before him. 'I know many of you do not like what you see but we need to terrify the French and rebel English and this is one of the ways we will do it. I will not force you to do the same but every time I run an operation this,' he indicated to the men gathering and beheading the dead bodies, 'is what will happen. This is the task of my own men. You,' he swept his hand over the newly arrived archers, 'will now be given cheese, bread and ale from the captured wagons.' William saw some calculating going on amongst the archers. 'Don't get envious: these wagons and draught animals belong to their English drivers who were, some would say foolishly, hired by the French,' he waited till the laugher died down. 'This is the back section of the supply train. We have a middle guard to take care of before we can get the front section of the convoy. I have arranged for a diversion to slow the middle guard down, but I can't let you rest here for too long. So, eat, drink, but don't get too merry for there are yet more Frenchies who have to die.'

Thomas looked to his twin, 'Thank God we are being given bread and cheese, I don't think I could face any meat at the moment.'

Bands of archers were met by Willikin's guides as they arrived in Blacknest Wood between the villages of Upper Froyle and Bently.

Godfrey took the bundle of a dozen arrows handed to him and joined his brother and the other men of Iping, Trottingham and Wulfbearding who had already been re-armed. 'Where next?' he asked Thomas, who was talking to John Little. The Forester's clothes were covered in dust and horse foam. John turned as he saw the other twin arrive shewing the top of his face to be as dusty brown as his clothes but the bottom of his face that was not covered by his beard was a contrasting white, having been protected by his cloth visor. The tall man coughed and spat out some phlegm, shewing that the visor had not been totally effective. 'You are to make haste down to Blacknest Park.'

'We know that park,' Thomas said with a smile.

'Good for roe deer,' Godfrey agreed.

Little screwed his cheek up and gave a disparaging look to the twins. 'You are not after deer, you are after Frenchies. Join the others already there. It will be much the same as earlier except the middle guard have already been halted. The last four wagons in the train are driven by our own men and the have managed to get them locked up, blocking the road. The Frenchies are trying to get the wagons untangled as we speak, so there is not much time. Before we can start the killing we need more archers there. If there are too few there is a risk of us being overrun and we don't have the men-at-arms to counter a charge. So,' John gave a glance to ensure all the members of the twin's band had arrows, 'get a move on. The signal to shoot will be the usual hunting horn call.'

Thomas looked at Godfrey tilted his head and indicated they should move off.

'Oh,' John Little called after them, 'and keep the noise down, we don't want our garlic eating friends to know they are being surrounded.'

'Surrounded?' Thomas called back as the band started to move off.

The Forester stopped walking towards the next group of men he wanted to talk to, turned and cupped his hands to carry his voice back to Thomas. 'Yes, so don't over shoot!' he yelled.

The twins' band slipped into position. They and their men were in the front line, behind them more archers came and formed a second and third line, using the slight slope down to the road to allow them to shoot over the heads to the archers in the rows in front of them. Below on the road was a mass of French men-at-arms, mostly dismounted. Although there were three men trying to direct operations to free the four ox carts that were jammed together little was resolving itself.

Godfrey lent over and elbowed his brother, 'Listen to them, the drivers are yelling at the French in English and the French are yelling back in French and nothing is getting done!'

'We must make sure we don't shoot the drivers; they are our men.'

'I know, I know.'

Mark the Reeve of Cassingham, judging his time to avoid observation made his way to Godfrey and Thomas.

'Sssssssshhhhhh. Do you make so much noise when poaching deer?'

Garth, who was next man over muttered to himself, 'Poach deer? : the warrant just hasn't arrived yet.'

'You can keep quiet too young man,' Mark hissed.

Erik Black, the son of Wulfbearding's blacksmith gave a snigger.

Mark the Reeve gave up and carefully edged his way up the slope through the nest two ranks to join Will Scathlock at the back of the ranks. They waited, ears a prick. Time passed and the French seemed at last to have got themselves organised and Mark looked worried. Scathlock placed a reassuring hand on Mark's shoulder. 'Patience Mark, patience.'

A distant sound of a tree crashing to the ground was quickly followed by more trees falling, closer this time. Mark Reeve turned to the freckled scarlet clad man, who was in the process of raising his long hunting horn to his lips. 'NOW!'

At the sound of the horn's blast the English archers stepped from behind their tree cover and drew their bow strings back to their ears.

'DON'T OVER SHOOT!' Mark cried out as an afterthought. 'DON'T OVER SHOOT!'

The arrows hissed, the ox cart drivers dived under their vehicles, the French turned to the sound and staggered as the shafts hit home.

'In your own time, mark your targets,' Mark instructed. 'And don't overshoot.'

'Don't over shoot,' Thomas mimicked as he loosed another arrow.

'Don't over shoot,' Godfrey's voice had a more mocking tone.

'Don't over shoot,' Garth's voice was even more mocking as he sent another arrow into the milling mass of French.'

'Don't over shoot!' cried out all the archers within earshot as they loosed.

'Don't over shoot!' This time every archer joined in the call.

Mark the Reeve shook his head and blew out his breath between pursed lips.

'They won't,' Scathlock assured him. 'They know their own men are the other side of the road.'

'I hope so.' Mark summonsed John of the Clear Sight to his side. 'Now?'

'Not yet; soon.'

Mark looked worriedly at the archers trying to judge how many arrows the archers has left. He looked again to the man of long sight. 'Now?'

'Yes; now.'

Scathlock gave another blast on his horn then, in unison with Mark cried out; 'HOLD! HOLD! HOLD!'

Mark watched. Happy the arrow barrage had stopped he gave another command. 'Bows down, swords and daggers – stop anyone who runs this way.'

The archers complied, drawing their blades, though some muttered and grizzled as they still had arrows left.

From the other side of the road and to the rear of the French troops men, some of Willikin's men in mael brinies and all with shields, formed a solid wall and then smashed into the surviving French and those of the horses still standing.

'*Form on me!*' a Frenchman in good quality war gear cried before being smashed down by a pole axe and trampled on as the shield wall from the woods moved on.

'*On me!*' another voice cried, before it, too, was silenced and the shield wall from the south advanced up the road to join with that from the woods.

'*Run! Run!*' cried a third voice as its owner started to climb the slope where the archers stood.

'Bugger this,' said Thomas as he dropped his sword, grabbed his bow, nocked an arrow, drew the bow and silenced the Frenchman with an arrow to the chest.

'Yes, sod this waiting to let them get close.' Godfrey copied his twin and picked off another running Frenchman.

'The further away they die the safer it is,' agreed Wulfbearding's Mark Archer lining up a target.

'NO! NO!" cried out Cassingham's reeve.

Will Scathlock, sword in his right hand, hunting horn in his left assessed the situation. 'Leave them be Mark, they do know what they are doing.'

'I suppose,' Mark Reeve conceded, waving his own sword around in an ineffectual manner. 'We did involve them because they knew how to shoot.' He took another look at what was happening below him on the road where the remaining French had been trapped against the ox carts. 'DON'T SHOOT THE OXEN!' he yelled.

'And?' Scathlock asked him.

'AND DON'T SHOOT THE DRIVERS!' Mark added.

'Do you lot ever do as you are told?' Mark Reeve asked the gathered archers. He was met with silence, though many could not resist a smirk. 'I thought not.' He took a deep breath before continuing. 'Well, as they say, no peace for the wicked. You must now, again at the trot, get to the next fight. This time Cotton's Copse the other side of Bently. Again arrows will be waiting for you.' He shooed them off with his hands. 'Off you go then; at the trot.'

The weary archers complied, too tired to complain.

'The need,' said William of Cassingham, 'is for the kill to be before Farnham because there have been French probing parties around there and we don't know exactly where they are.'

'The castle?' John Little patted dust from his travel stained over shirt.

'Yes, they are interested in the castle.' Cassingham turned to Midge the Miller. 'Midge, get your woodsmen to part chop trees north of River Lane and string the ropes to pull them down. There is a place there where the trees arch over and form a tunnel.'

'The local Lord has been lazy,' Midge commented. 'Not one hundred yards tree free there then.'

'Or,' added John the Forester, 'in most places in the Sussex and Surrey Weald these days.'

'Civil disturbances between king and barons does that,' William agreed. 'But back to the matter in hand.' He knelt and, using the point of his dagger, drew a crude map in the dirt of the path. 'Here is the road to Guildford and then London. Here,' he drew another line, 'is River Lane. Whilst here,' another line, 'is the Wrecclesham Road.' The squire of Cassingham tapped his shoulder with his dagger, thinking. 'The London Road curves before it is met by the Wrecclesham Road so we can fully fell trees to block it there as the French won't see the road block until it is too late.' He looked to Midge. 'You have enough men? For there is little time.'

'As long as we get going now and there are enough spare ponies and horses to get us there.'

John Little gave a brittle laugh. 'Not all the French mounts ended up as next week's meat, take as many as you need. They are back there, up the path.'

William stood. 'Then go Midge and hurry, just make sure you are not caught by the French vanguard part felling the trees we need to the rear.'

'They didn't catch us last time Willikin,' the miller assured him.

'Yes but you had more time for that trap; now go! Take as many of my own men with you as there are mounts for. They can help you till I get there with the others and the special wagon.'

'*Halt!*' Anne de Toulouse, the leader of the vanguard held up his right hand.

'*Halt!*' his Captains and Sergeants repeated in various French accents.

The vanguard leader and his two most trusted men edged their horses forward to examine the strange sight that met their eyes.

'*Heads?*' Anne questioned.

'*Heads!*' his companions confirmed.

'*Don't I know some of them?*' Anne asked.

'*I think you do – that one looks like Gaspard, the fat cook.*'

'*Such a cook,*' the other companion chipped in.

The first companion dismounted to examine the head. '*But he is looking so very dead.*'

'*My God!*' Anne exclaimed. '*What does this mean?*'

Three figures emerged round the bend in the road in front of the Frenchmen. The middle figure proved to be a man in humble and worn hunting green clothes but wearing a sporting cap with a pheasant's feather in it. The man's face was handsome and he sported a neat muzzle beard. On either side of him was a man in forest coloured clothes, hoods pulled low over their eyes and cloth visors covering the lower parts of their faces. The behated man pulled his hat off and gave a low bow. '*What does it mean my friend? Well it means your cook got carried away and lost his head.*'

Anne of Toulouse, whose first language was the Occitan spoken in Provence, looked to the companion who was still mounted for translation. The man thought, mentally working old Norman French into the French of the Isle de Paris before speaking. '*He is being rude and just saying the cook lost his head.*'

'*And the other heads?*' Anne asked.

'*The other heads,*' the man in the road explained, '*are to let you know what happens to you French when you enter my kingdom.*'

'*Kingdom?*' the Frenchman on foot asked. '*You are King John? I think not, for I have met him and he looks nothing like you!*'

105

The man replaced his hat, gave a winning smile, and gestured around him with his hand. *'This is the great Weald of England and I am Willikin of the Weald. I am looking after the Weald for his Grace, King John.'* With that he turned and walked into the woods that abutted the road and was followed by the two hooded men. The last man turned and gave a sharp whistle.

The whistle was answered by the sounding of more than one hunting horn, the sound of trees falling and the hum of arrows.

Anne de Toulouse drew his sword, pointed up the road shouted *'Go, as fast as you can'*, spurred his horse and led his arrow hassled cavalry in a mad gallop towards Farnham only to have to pull up short when they rounded the bend and found the road well and truly blocked by felled oak trees. The horses of the riders in the front reared; the horses behind crashed and bumped into them. Archers climbed onto the top of the fallen trees and shot arrow after arrow into the packed chaotic mess in front of them. Some of the horsemen at the back turned round and spurred back towards Alton only to find the road had been blocked by decrepit ox carts jammed together. Behind the carts were archers waiting to shoot the French riders down. The massacre was soon over and Willikin and his own men set about despatching the prisoners and starting the process of stripping the dead of weapons, armour and even clothes prior to beheading the corpses.

John Little called over and addressed the Hampshire and Sussex archers. 'Herla and Robin Boxholt?' the twins indicated that they were there. 'You are to get the road near River Lane cleared of carts. Use the local villagers, Tell them I will pay them. Then get the wagons of the convoy down there and away to Wrecclesham

106

where you will guard them.' The Forester held up his hand to silence any temptation to ask questions. 'Don't worry the French wagoners and their foot escort have all fled. The rest of you,' he looked over the others, 'are to hunt down the wagoners and French foot sloggers and kill them. Remember what Willikin told you: no survivors.'

'And their heads?' asked Cross Eyed Deer.

'Your call. Now go and happy hunting.'

The Boxholt men watched the others depart and then started to traipse away muttering about being left with the heavy work. Godfrey went back to speak with John Little. 'Uncle Bill? The Highway Patrol? What of them?'

John Little's face split in a wide smile, his white teeth shining in his brown beard. 'We want him to come back and see just what his incompetence has done! Willikin is paying the locals to put the collection of heads on stakes all along the road just to remind him.'

'So you will leave him alone?'

'Today. Tomorrow, after he has reported back to his masters, he and his men are yours, if you want them.'

'I think,' Godfrey said as he started to follow the others, 'he should be put out of his misery.'

'Well?' Scathlock asked William of Cassingham. 'Happy with the day's work?'

'Yes, but the day is not over yet.'

'No?'

'No. I have had word from my London source that around noon today a small lightly escorted group of French are due to leave for

London along the Winchester, Bassingstoke, London Road and I intend to use my own men of Kent to intercept it.'

Scathlock didn't look impressed. 'The men are very weary; they have been jogging between one fight and another with little rest. Why the need?'

'They are carrying gold and silver to pay the French army in London.'

'Ah,' Will Scathlock smiled. 'I see.'

'You may see why I must try and intercept it but you will not see it done. You will find Midge and get him to arrange for locals to fell trees all along this road after they have staked the French heads. He is to tell them that I will pay them more good money to do it: I need this route to London sealed and later I will do the same to the other road, provided I can get the other group and their money.' William put his arm around Scathlock's shoulder. 'Now, once you have done that get down to Wrecclesham and take a tally of what we have won from the supply train. I will get the war gear put onto pack horses and brought to you also. I don't want any unofficial plundering.'

Scathlock gave a cynical grunt.

'No Will; no plundering – I have a use for those wagons and their contents as well as the war gear.'

Chapter 7: It's An Ill Wind

The warmth of an early summer's day had encouraged the villagers to stay outside long after the day's tasks had been completed. Will Scathlock, dressed as always in red, mopped his cropped copper red hair and freckled face with a square of red cloth and watched as the young boys and girls of Iping took care of watering his pack horses with their cargo of wool packs. 'Best quality wool in the south that,' he said, the Yorkshire accent only hinted. 'I'm taking it on Portsmouth-London Road down to the port for export to Flanders.' He smiled as he accepted a pot of beer from Thomas Wulfson. 'I hope this ale is from your cousin Godwin.'

'It is – this time though it is a beer!' Godfrey informed him.

Scathlock sat down on a stool, being very careful not to spill any of the precious liquid before setting the pot on the round of wood by his feet. 'Excellent. I am glad you put me in touch with him: good ale, clean accommodation, and friendly people. I used to stay at Southwark with a Norman called Bates but I never felt comfortable there – he was friendly one moment and a bit scary the next, as for his mother …'

'Even more scary?' Thomas placed a wooden bowl filled with onion, leek and turnip pottage in front of the brother's guest.

'Only in her silence; she never spoke at all, as for her wizened looks well …' Scathlock tucked the red cloth up his sleeve and picked up the earthenware pot and breathed in the beer's aroma. 'Ah; wonderful.' He took a sip and then another before placing it alongside the pottage. 'I'm on way back up north after this trip.'

'More wool trading?' Thomas took his own sip of beer and gave an appreciative noise that was half sigh and half groan of pleasure as the bitter horehound beer assaulted his taste buds.

The wool merchant didn't reply straight away, taking another mouthful of beer first. 'Partly that but,' he rummaged in his script and produced a horn spoon, 'mainly to take word to Willikin's contacts in Sherwood, Barnsleydale and the forest around Carlisle. I have to give them some disturbing news.'

'Disturbing news?' Godfrey placed his leathern jack of beer at his feet.

'Well, that last action you took part in has stopped the French using Southampton for landing their supplies and then taking them by road to London. The result is they have switched to using Dover instead as they can then barge it up the Thames via the Wantsum Channel to London.'

Thomas joined his brother and Scathlock in seating himself on a stool. 'That is not good news.'

'That,' the red clad man explained, 'is not the worst of it. A fleet, captained by Eustace the Monk no less, has landed Louis the Dauphin and a claimed twelve hundred knights with their support there too.'

'Twelve hundred knights?' Thomas shook his head. 'I didn't think there are that many knights in the whole of England!'

'And,' Godfrey interrupted, 'I thought Eustace was working for our King John?'

Scathlock gave a grunt. 'Not any more it seems. It appears he has taken over the King's islands that sit to the north of Normandy, the Duchy he let fall from his fingers some ten years back. It is Eustace's base now, which means that evil pirate can choke off most of our trade with the continent as well as ferry the French in and out of England. This lot,' he indicated his pack train, is having to be sent to Flanders in a French ship at a price almost twice what I would normally pay.' The wool man lifted the wooden bowl of pottage to his chin and dipped his spoon in. 'But what choice do I have?' He blew on the spoons contents to cool it before putting it into his mouth.

The twins waited for their guest to eat several mouthfuls. As the red clothed man put down the bowl to return to his beer they looked at each other. 'What now?' they both asked at the same time.

'What now, indeed,' Scathlock replied. 'It seems King John, rather than risk a pitched battle, has pulled back his army of Brabanter and Flemish mercenaries towards East Anglia.'

'That,' started Thomas.

'Is not good news,' Godfrey completed.

'That,' Scathlock picked up the bowl and spoon again, 'is not all the bad news.' He pointed with his spoon in the general direction of north. 'Rumour has it that the Scots are planning to join with the rebel barons and the French and cross the border. Getting some more "on the ground" information for Willikin whilst I am up north is another reason for me heading back up that way.'

Thomas nursed his jack of beer against his chest. 'So, what does that mean for us?'

Scathlock finished off his pottage, keeping the brothers waiting for a reply. He mopped the bowl round with some bread, which he then ate. Eventually he replied. 'It means many things. Willikin says that the roads the French have been using are to remain closed; trees felled, foraging and exploring parties taken out. In particular he wants you and the men of the Boxholt to stop the

111

patrols on the Portsmouth-Guildford Road and to do it in such a way as the French, who still have some supplies in Portsmouth, won't want to risk using it.'

'We have ploughing and sowing to do,' Thomas informed him

'There is also our time rent to pay, looking after sheep on the South Downs,' Godfrey added.

'They,' Will Scathlock said, with great emphasis, 'will have to be sorted out another way.'

'How?' the twins asked.

'Firstly, that wagon of wheat and barley from the raid on the Southampton road – the one you were asked to look after.'

'Yes?'

'It, its oxen and its contents, are yours to keep. The grains are more than you would harvest I think.'

Thomas gave the Yorkshire man a sideways look. 'Willikin says?'

'He does. He also gave me this,' Scathlock undid a coin purse that hung from his belt and passed it to Thomas. 'Silver coin from the French. Use it to pay others to plough the land of you and your band and pay for others to mind the sheep.'

Godfrey took the purse from his brother hefted it in his hand then opened it to look at the coins it contained. 'There is a lot of money here.' He gave Will Scathlock a long look. 'How long is this sort of thing likely to go on for?'

'God alone knows, but Willikin suspects for quite a while.'

Godfrey Wulfson settled his back into the trunk of an ancient oak in Hunter's Chase and looked at his brother Thomas who was taking deep breaths to get his wind back. 'Are you ready to talk yet?' he asked, holding a piece of dried grass up before starting to use it to pick his teeth.

Thomas gave his elder twin an evil look and continued deep breathing. Eventually he gave a big out breath and reached for the leather water bottle alongside his brother's leg. 'The Haslemere boys are in place,' he sneaked a swig of water, 'the bridge over the Wey is fixed. Edward Black has done his usual perfect job but he isn't happy seeing as it might involve people being killed.'

'He is such a pacifist.'

'Indeed, everyone to his own.'

'Till things go wrong.' Godfrey tossed away his bent tooth pick. 'If his wife or son were threatened it would be interesting to see just how much of a pacifist he really is.'

'When do you want Mark Archer and Sam Samuelson, Gilbert Green and Cedric Steadham to get into the river?'

'Not yet, we don't want them developing webbed feet do we. We can wait until little Will Greenleaf comes and lets us know that the highway patrol and Uncle Bill are getting near.'

The grey skies left off the rain, but it still threatened. The riders huddled in their thick wool cloaks to keep out the chill of a typical English summer's day. Mostly they had pulled the cloaks over their helmeted heads, reducing their vision, leaving their sodden mounts to ensure they stayed in the formation. They had been riding the road from Petersfield to Guildford and back all day and they were tired, bored, saddle stiffened, and all they wanted to do was to get back to the barn in Weston where they were billeted. For the past week they had made the twice daily patrol and nothing ever broke the monotony now that war had stifled travel for all but military patrols. A horse belonging to one of the men-at-arms in the middle of the group stumbled. Men broke out of their stupor but, as soon as they realised what had happened, they settled back into their thoughts of home, whores, drinking, gambling, warmth and sleep. The two riders who were riding advance guard had slowly dropped back and the two rear guard moved forward as they all instinctively desired to huddle together to keep warm.

The lead riders came to the wooden bridge over the Wey and nudged their reluctant horses on to the rickety structure. The other riders held back watching their companions make it successfully across. The horses, seeing their fellows had safely made it to the other side were now less reluctant to venture onto the planking of the bridge. The rear guard turned their mounts to enable them to look back down the way they had come. The main body, four abreast, plodded over the Wey.

With a sudden painful groan the front and back of the bridge gave way as Mark Archer and Sam Samuelson, Gilbert Green and Cedric Steadham pulled the ropes that broke the bridge supports just as Edward Black had designed them to do. Sixteen riders in the patrol shuddered to a halt with their mounts whinnying their disapproval of what was going on, two in the middle started to rear, their hooves striking the horses in front of them causing the patrol to collapse into a muddle of milling horseflesh and yelling men who had started to realise that they were now isolated on the wooden bridge with no way on or off.

Archers stepped from the trees and onto the road north and south of the bridge and shot down the advance and rear guards.

'Steady, steady, control those horses.' cried William Atkins, Captain of the patrol, in his Old Norman French.

There was a muddled mix of French from his men as they called to each other asking just what Atkins had actually said.

The archers who had shot and killed the advance guard walked toward the damaged bridge, arrows nocked, bows at the ready. One of the patrol, who had confidence in his horse, nudged it forward and tried to get it to jump the gap to the road on the other side. Garth Robertson lifted his bow, drew and released bringing the rider down with an arrow through the throat. The horses on the bridge jostled each other, smelling blood, starting to panic.

Atkins, his horse under better control than most of his companions edged through the thrashing and milling mess of his patrol and stopped at the broken edge of the bridge. *'What is going on? You bastards will answer for this, God damn you.'*

'How do,' called out Thomas.

'How is life with you Uncle Bill?' ask Godfrey with a smile.

'I asked,' Uncle Bill replied in an English accent that shewed he came from Middlesex, 'What is going on!'

'Death,' Thomas advised him, loosing an arrow that whizzed past the Captain's ear and hit one of his patrol.

'Death all around you,' added Godfrey picking off another of the Frenchmen.

'Bastards: God damn you!' Atkins tried to turn his horse around but the chaos behind him prevented the manoeuvre.

'Ah,' Thomas shot another of the patrol.

'That was completely in English. I understood that.' Godfrey's arrow took down another mounted man.

Garth elbowed his two uncles out of the way for a decent shot. 'He has a funny accent mind.' Another shot and another dead man.

Thomas looked behind him and saw that the rest of the men of the Boxholt had joined him, Mark and Sam dripping water from their sodden hosen. 'Take them down, but leave Uncle Bill.'

The Boxholt band slowly and methodically started shooting down the French.

'I trust,' Godfrey asked his brother, 'that the men of Haselmere know to leave Uncle Bill?'

'So do I,' his brother agreed as he took a tricky shot at a dismounted Frenchman who was trying to hide amongst the horses.

Arrows flew, Frenchmen fell whilst horses milled about and shouldered each other trampling on fallen men.

Thomas watched then, satisfied that, apart from the Captain, there were not any active members of the patrol left he pulled up his hunting horn and gave three short high notes. The shooting stopped.

Seeing Atkins was now in the middle of the bridge fighting frightened horses, Godfrey called his men forward and they threw planking across the gulf and then they ran across, grasping the bridles of the horses, speaking quiet words of comfort to the creatures whilst others cut the throats of any Frenchman still alive.

Mark the Archer jumped up behind Atkins and smote him a blow across his collar bone causing the man to drop his sword. Mark then pushed the Captain's steel helmet off his head and stunned him with a whack to the head from the pommel of the dagger the forester had taken long before from a dead Frenchman.

Godfrey gave a purse of silver to Hi Ho, leader of the Haselmere men. 'Destroy the bridge, pay the local folk of Bramsholt, Liphook and Lynchmere compensation for the damage to their bridge and the inconvenience it will cause and get them to fell trees all along this road. We shall get folk further down to do the same.'

Thomas joined his brother, 'Tell them Willikin of the Weald says to do it and that he will send them grain and other supplies later if they need it.'

Hi Ho nodded and left to organise his men in order to start the demolition.

Thomas watched them go. 'So,' he said to his brother, 'now we talk to Uncle Bill?'

'Now we talk to Uncle Bill.'

The brothers walked past the men of the Boxholt who were busy about their tasks, tending horses, stripping armour from corpses and beheading the same.

'I still don't like Willikin's practice of taking off heads and staking them out on the road.' Thomas kicked at a thistle that dared to grow amongst the violets.

'Nor do I, but that is what he wants and I suppose it does act as a frightener to those who would oppose his hold on the Weald.'

'I still don't like it.'

The twins came and stood in front of William Atkins, Captain of the now extinct highway patrol. He was trussed up like a hog for slaughter and lying in front of the oak where Godfrey had sat earlier.

Thomas gave him a prod with his toe. Atkins gave a start and then gave his captors a baleful stare.

'Now, now,' Thomas said.

'Uncle Bill,' Godfrey added. 'No need to look like that.'

The trussed Captain spat inaccurately in the twin's direction. 'You two.'

'Uncle Bill,' the twins responded together.

'You are going to take a message to your masters,' Thomas informed him.

'French and rebel English barons,' Godfrey added.

'English?' questioned Thomas.

'Well Norman English,' Godfrey conceded.

'Them what are pissed off about having to give up the lands they hold in Normandy if they want to hang on to their English lands?'

'The very same.'

Atkins started to struggle against his bonds. The twins, now joined by their nephew Garth, watched with amusement as the Captain started to go red in the face with his efforts.

Garth cocked his head and sniggered. 'He is dreaming if he thinks he can get out of those.'

'Well,' said Thomas as the three walked back to the others leaving Uncle Bill to his writhing and wriggling, 'I hope all this tires him out as we will have to untie his legs if we are going to get him onto a horse and then secure him on it.'

'I think brother, nephew, that we should ask Mark to give our Uncle something to get to sleep again.'

The men manning the road block at Cosham where the Guildford-London Road met the coast road looked up. Coming towards them was the highway patrol; nineteen of the horses bore a headless rider. Bringing up the rear was the twentieth horse bearing the patrol's Captain, a bareheaded William Atkins. The men opened the barrier and the lead nineteen horses passed through. Atkins was last, his mount seemingly reluctant to move.

The Captain, seeing the road guards lifted his head. *'Thank God, my friends. We were ambushed. We put up such a fight. We must have killed hundreds but in the end they overwhelmed us.'* He turned his head to look behind him, the road was clear. *'Get me down and untie me.'*

The men looked at each other. *'I think,'* ventured a man from the Vexin, whose dialect was close to the Norman one. *'I think he said they had been ambushed, but his words and accent are rather strange.'*

It was then that a dozen arrows flew from the woods. Eleven hit Uncle Bill in the back, the last hit the rump of his horse. The animal reared in shock and the mortally wounded Atkins slid from his saddle and hung under the horse's belly.

'You silly sod Thomas,' Godfrey chided his brother as they moved through the thick woods. 'You missed and hit his horse.'

'Who said I missed? I thought it would be funny.'

'Uncle Bill wasn't laughing.'

Chapter 8: To Be A Pilgrim

Godfrey gave his brother a look that was part amused and part annoyed. 'Do you have to do that?' he asked.

Thomas his twin put a finger to his lips to quieten his brother. 'Yes,' he whispered, 'I'm bored.'

Godfrey watched as Thomas gently tossed another piece of dried horse meat to the fox that watched them from a gap in the brambles. 'Being bored is one thing, encouraging a fox to have no fear of man is another; it could come and raid our geese.'

Thomas gave his brother a disdaining look, 'We are miles from home. If it does raid a flock of geese, it won't be ours will it.'

'I suppose not.' Godfrey watched as the wild creature edged its way to the food. The fox locked eyes with Thomas before making a lunge at the meat, picked it up and then trotted back to its cover, taking a couple of quick looks over its shoulder to make sure it wasn't being followed. 'It certainly is getting tamer. How long have you been feeding it little brother?'

'All this week, days before you first saw me doing it.' Thomas glanced at his twin. 'I like foxes. They are not quite a wolf .....'

'Which our family are named after?'

'Indeed, but they are similar. It is just that they are not a pack animal and therefore have to be much more cunning.'

'Cunning? Like training a fool man to feed it his lunch?'

Thomas grinned. 'It is fun.'

'Well our time of watching this bit of road is almost up. What will your fox do for food then?'

120

'Hush!' Thomas moved forward slightly. 'Look; it is not a fox at all – it is a vixen and she has brought out two cubs to see us.'

'Oh joy; more mouths to feed.'

'I'm getting fed up with dried horse meat anyway.'

'Well, there is still plenty of it back at the village and being Willikin of the Weald's watchers means we can't go looking for deer in other Lord's parks.'

'Hare?'

'I like hares, just like you seem to like foxes. Now rabbits …'

Thomas smiled; 'Oh yes rabbits. It is funny how they keep escaping from their guarded warrens isn't it.'

'How the netting keeps getting broken is beyond me.'

'Must be getting done by one of my fox friends.'

Godfrey gave a laugh, causing the vixen and her cubs to dive back into the brambles. 'Or a wolf?'

'Brother; you frightened my friend and her youngsters.'

'Sorry Thomas. Here, give her this.' Godfrey pulled a strip of fluff covered dried meat from his script and passed it to his brother.

Thomas made clucking sounds and as soon as the vixen put out her inquisitive nose he made a slow underhand throw of the meat to her. The creature watched the twins moving her eyes from one to the other, and then slowly crawled on her belly towards the meat. She had just snared it when her two cubs came bustling out of cover and cavorted around her head, licking her face. Another sound quickly made the three animals dive back into cover.

Garth Robertson came and stood by his uncles. 'You still feeding that old fox Thomas?' he asked, reaching into his own script for food to offer the creature.

'You made so much noise you frightened her and her cubs.'

'She has cubs?'

'She has cubs,' Godfrey confirmed as he eased himself up off the ground. 'Our turn to watch the road then? Where is Mark?'

'Mark is waiting for you to relieve him or,' Garth gave a giggle, 'did he say he was going to relieve himself?'

Thomas got up and stood by his slightly taller brother. 'Just look after my foxes Garth.'

Garth sat down and started to use his eating knife to shred his dried meat into smaller strips to make it easier for the cubs to eat. 'Your vixen Thomas? I don't think wild animals actually belong to anyone.'

'Only to God I suppose.'

Thomas and Godfrey left the small clearing and made their way to where Mark Archer was waiting for them in a dense clump of ash trees that over looked the road.

Mark unstrung his bow and walked towards them, 'I would find a place a bit further along if I were you two; the ground is a bit damp here.'

The vixen carefully approached the sleeping Thomas and commenced to lick his face. Somewhat confused at the sensation Thomas opened an eye. Once she was aware that the man was awake the vixen left him and slunk back into her bramble bush. Thomas sat up and cocked his ear towards a slight rustling sound.

He nudged his twin brother who was dozing alongside him. 'Someone is coming.'

'At last!' Godfrey whispered as he eased himself up, taking his bow with him. 'Action.'

'What of Garth and Mark?' Thomas braced his bow.

'If it is trouble, they will soon hear and come to our help.'

The twins melted into cover behind an old oak tree, one either side of the massive gnarled trunk. Nothing at first happened. Eventually shadows moved through the trees in front of them so the twins nocked arrows. The rustling sound stopped.

A cuckoo called.

'A cuckoo? This time of year?' Thomas called out.

Ganger Greenwood and three of his forester comrades emerged from the trees and entered the clearing. 'It is the only bird call Gilbert here can do! Anyway it had to be something unusual didn't it, or you wouldn't have known it was us approaching.'

'True,' Godfrey came out from behind the tree.

'We knew someone was coming,' Thomas advised the foresters. 'You are lucky you didn't get shot.'

'We didn't make that much noise,' Gilbert dumped on the ground the pack he had been carrying on his back. 'I'm surprised though you knew we were coming.'

'We are foresters and know how to move with stealth,' Ganger added.

'We have a spy in the woods.' Thomas removed the arrow from his bow string and pushed it back into the rear of his belt to join the five others that resided there.

'You do?' asked Ganger, looking warily around.

123

'We do,' Thomas confirmed, wiping away the vixen's lick on his face.

Ganger touched Gilbert on the shoulder, 'You and Henry go and take over from Garth and Mark – just don't get yourselves shot.'

The two Midhurst foresters moved off, deliberately making their progress noisy.

Thomas started to gather the cloaks and other gear belonging to the Boxholt men together. 'It will be good to get back home and some normal life again.'

'I never thought I would find the prospect of farm work so inviting,' Godfrey laughed.

'Oh,' Ganger tilted his head and smiled. 'You aren't going back to farm work. Willikin has sent that entertainer on his round singing his funny songs. You and the other Boxholt men are to join him and his men of Kent at Shadoxhurst.'

'Do you know what for?' Godfrey asked him.

Ganger Greenwood laughed; 'You think that old fox would say why he wants to gather a war band of archers?'

'Talking of foxes.'

'Yes Thomas?'

'Don't harm my vixen; keep her well fed.'

The four archers went along the back road at a brisk walk, the quicker to get back home. Garth Robertson was on point with his uncles in the middle and Mark the Archer on rear. At irregular times Mark and the twins would take it in turn to swing round and take ten paces walking backwards. All had their bows strung and an arrow on the string. Wheel tracks told them that there was

traffic on the road and that it was not too far ahead. Suddenly
Garth went down on one knee and held his left arm high. As soon
as they saw his actions the other three followed suit before going
to join the young man at the crouch.

Godfrey was the first to come alongside Edith's son. 'Well?'

'Round the bend, just ahead, four wagons, two crossbowmen on
each wagon.'

Thomas and Mark joined the others. 'Well?' Thomas asked.

His twin looked at him and indicated for Thomas to keep his
voice down. Emphasising his whispered words with hand signals
Godfrey gave out a plan. 'Four wagons, two bowmen on each. You
and Mark take to the trees on the left of the road; Garth and I the
right. Get twenty paces ahead of the lead wagon. Take the bowmen
down. Wait till I shoot. Go.'

The pairs slid into the trees and quickly but stealthily they made
their way ahead of the slow plodding ox wagons. Once well in
front Godfrey held up his hand for his nephew to stop and silently
indicated where he wanted him to stand. The young man eased
against a tree trunk and waited. Godfrey let the lead wagon get just
ahead of him before he loosed his arrow and took out the
crossbowman sitting alongside the wagoner; Garth shot and hit the
crossbowman sitting on the wagon's load of heaped sacks – the
man gave a screech as he fell from the wagon and thrashed around
on the road. Thomas and Mark shot and took out the bowmen on
the rear wagon, though one man had only been hit in the arm.
Without any hesitation all four English archers loosed their next
shots and then their next and their next, hitting both new targets
and those who had only been injured with an earlier shot. One

125

crossbowman had a charmed life with the arrows meant to kill him hanging harmlessly from flaps on his padded jack which, being too big for him had ample spaces where there was no human flesh to hit. The man took careful aim at Godfrey and loosed. The bolt clipped Godfrey's head near his right ear and he went down. Thomas' next arrow took the crossbowman in the back of his neck, severing his jugular and making the man's life blood spray high.

'Uncle!' Garth knelt down to examine Godfrey.

'I'm fine, just fine except I have a ringing in my ear. I still have an ear?'

'Yes Uncle, you have an ear, it is just a bit mangled and hanging down.'

Godfrey took his nephew's proffered hand and allowed himself to be pulled up. 'The wagoners, see who they are.'

'No need Thomas is on to it.'

Thomas walked slowly towards the terrified wagoners. 'Where are you from? Are these your own wagons? Where are the goods from?'

'*Pardon? I can't understand you. Don't you speak French? Any kind of French will do.*'

'French?' Mark asked.

'French,' Thomas confirmed as he drew his bow and shot the wagoner down.

The other three drivers, seeing what had happened to their colleague, jumped down from the driving boards and started to run down the road, back from whence they had come.

Godfrey cautiously walked to the lead wagon and calmed down the oxen who were getting agitated with a twitching critically injured crossbowman rolling under their rear legs.

The other three archers walked down the road watching the French wagoners running in front of them.

'One each and a farthing bet on it.'

'Done,' Garth agreed.

'Make it a penny?' Mark asked.

'No. A farthing is enough as our Garth is just a boy and can't afford to lose more than a ha'penny.'

'Lose? Me?' Garth stopped walking looked at his target, rolled slightly forward then pulled his body back and drew his bowstring back to his ear before loosing his arrow. The shaft flew, sunlight catching the white fletching. The arrow struck the victim dead centre in the back and the man fell, his legs kicking up road dust.

'All right you hit him and saved your farthing but he wasn't far away. Give the other two another 20 yards Mark? Shew the boy what men can do?'

'Make it twenty five,' the Wulfbearding Forester replied.

'Twenty five it is.' Thomas took his stand. 'The one on the left is mine.' He drew and loosed bringing a wagoner down.

'If I do a head shot, do I get a penny?' Mark asked with a grin.

'A farthing was the agreement,' Garth insisted.

'A farthing then, even though the last one is now thirty yards further than your one.' Mark loosed his arrow and hit his target in the back of the head.

'Lucky shot,' Thomas insisted as the three of them sauntered up to the fallen wagoners to put them out of their misery and retrieve the arrows.

Garth stood over his man who was still giving an occasional gasp through blood foamed lips. 'I cant get my arrow out!' he whined.

Thomas walked back, his own blood tipped arrow in his hand. 'Just pull the shaft out and forget the head.'

Garth mumbled to himself, 'They cost money.'

Mark, now standing at the youth's elbow, spoke quietly in his ear. 'Time Garth, we don't have the time to go cutting up this body,' he kicked the now dead Frenchman. 'Pull the shaft out and stick a spare head on it. You should have used a leaf head not a barbed swallow head.'

Thomas tugged his nephew's elbow, 'Come on, we need to get back to Godfrey just in case any of those bowmen have some life left in them.'

Garth reluctantly pulled on his arrow and gave it a twist freeing the shaft from the bee's wax that held the head to the shaft and jogged to catch up with the others as they reached Godfrey.

Thomas examined his brother's head and face. 'You will need a few stitches to get your ear back on straight, but otherwise you should be alright.'

'My head rings,' Godfrey complained.

Mark patted Godfrey on the back, 'You are lucky you are not dead.' He looked over the ox wagons. 'What now?'

Godfrey took a deep breath and closed his eyes. He shook his head to clear it, the part severed ear leaving a bloody smear as it flopped around. 'Mark, you come with me and take the lead

128

wagons back to Wulfbearding. Thomas, take Garth and get the rear two wagons to Hill Brow using the Woodsmans Green Road.'

Thomas nodded his head in acknowledgement. 'That hamlet lost two men to the French recently.'

'Exactly,' Godfrey swayed and grabbed hold of the wagon he was alongside to steady himself. 'Now go.'

'Do we tell Willikin of this?' Thomas watched as Garth started the difficult task of turning the rear ox wagon round.

Godfrey gave his brother a sly look. 'Only if he asks.'

The population of Hill Brow stood in a chain from the two ox wagons to the hamlet's barn.

As he pulled the last sack of grain from the bed of the rearmost wagon the old bent backed man called to the next man along, 'Who was it gave us this?'

'Don't rightly know,' yelled the only slightly less bent and profoundly deaf man who took the sack from him.

'Him with the hood?' asked the next man along.

'Robin. I heard the other one call him Robin,' the short plump woman alongside him said.

'You are late!' Rather than being his normal benign self, William of Cassingham was rather irate.

Godfrey's damaged ear, stitched back in place by his sister Edith, was covered in a thick pad and held in place by a bandage that wound round his head. He turned his good, but bandaged ear, to his brother Thomas. 'What did Willikin say?'

'He said we are late.'

Godfrey turned back to the squire of Cassingham. 'We got delayed.' He patted his bandaged head. 'A little bit of grief from our French friends.'

William grunted and strode away. 'See me at noon. Eat and drink and be ready to move,' he called over his shoulder.

The twins and their men of the Boxholt watched him go. John Little, Willikin's tall forester waited till his master was out of earshot before putting an arm on the shoulder of each twin and walking them towards the area where women, under the control of William's wife, Mary, were distributing food and drink from the tail gates of two carts. 'A little bit of grief from the French you say?'

'A little bit,' Thomas agreed, unsure of where the conversation was going.

'Four supply wagons near Woodsmans Green?' Little asked.

'I heard about that. I'm surprised you have though.'

Little gave his head a slight nod, 'I listen to the birds singing; it is amazing what they say at times.'

Godfrey struggled to hear what was being said. 'What did he say?'

'Go back to sleep big brother, leave this one to me.'

John Little squeezed Thomas' shoulder. 'I would like to think that the wagons and their contents went to help the poor.'

'Oh, I would hope so too,' Thomas gave the tall man what he hoped was a reassuring smile.

'And not all to the poor of Iping and Wulfbearding either.'

'That,' said Thomas, 'is assuming men from there were involved.'

130

'Indeed,' Little agreed. 'Willikin would be happy for the perpetrators of an action like that to make some sort of gain for their efforts but keeping more than a wagon load of plunder could be considered by him to be greed. He works on the principle that if it is stolen it goes back to its owner. If it is French or rebel baron's goods then half of what has been taken goes to the poor, for we need the help of the local folk, so we are good to them. A quarter taken goes to those who do the work and a quarter to Willikin to look after for emergencies.'

'Oh I agree, and I'm sure my brother does as well,' Thomas leant forward to look over the bulk of the Forester. 'Don't you brother?'

'Eh?' Godfrey tried to catch what had been said. 'What?'

'He said "yes",' Thomas assured Little. 'Now, master John Little, I don't suppose you know anyone who might be interested in buying some second hand crossbows do you?'

'I might, but I would want a fifth of the price I got for them.'

'Agreed.' Thomas gave a satisfied smile.

'What?' asked Godfrey.

William of Cassingham climbed onto the bed of the cart that earlier had been used to bring barrels of ale and cider to the meeting. He looked at the men gathered before him, assessing their worth, remembering faces, putting names to them, recalling how they had acted under pressure, recalling their ability to fight, bringing to mind those that had held back. He turned to John Little. 'Sound your horn, get their attention. This won't take long, but we need to make the right decisions. While I talk, you and

131

Mark the Reeve watch the men; it will help when deciding who does what tasks as I value your opinions.'

John Little brought his hunting horn up to his lips and the action brought silence even before he blew as all the men gathered in front of the cart had been watching Willikin and his closest henchmen, waiting for something to happen. 'Silence for Willikin of the Weald,' the Forester called quite unnecessarily.

William of Cassingham cleared his throat, stuck his thumbs into the worn and scuffed brown leather belt that held his dagger and eating knife. 'I wish I had called you all here to say that the war is over and the French have gone home. Instead, I must tell you that things are not good and that our struggle will have to continue through the coming autumn and likely into the winter. Louis, the French Dauphin, has an army occupying Dover, though not the castle - yet. Alexander, King of Scots, has brought an army all the way down through England to Dover so that he, and most of England's barons, can give fealty to Louis the Dauphin as King of England.' He paused as the anticipated pandemonium broke out as the gathered archers shouted their disapproval of such treason. Willikin nodded to John Little and again the Forester blew his hunting horn but this time to little effect. Willikin nodded to John Little a second time and this time the horn's blast brought a gradual easing of verbal protest.

Mark the Reeve cupped his hands, 'Shut the hell up you rabble!' he yelled with a voice that was known to have sent deer in the surrounding woods running for cover with their ears turned backwards.

Willikin stamped his right foot on the cart's floor and at last got the silence he was waiting for. 'All this means is that we have work to do, especially as the French have just established bases on the South Coast at Rye and Sandwich. I will talk with John and Mark here and we will work out who is to do what. We will have to keep our stranglehold on the roads through the Weald, try and cut off the coast road ...'

'And French heads?' Gilbert of the White hand called out.

'And French heads,' William agreed. 'And we must see if we can do something about the siege of Dover castle.'

'No peace for the wicked then?' Thomas yelled.

'What did you say?' Godfrey asked.

'Who is next?' William of Cassingham sat behind a table made of two planks across two battered wooden crates. He looked to Mark the Reeve as John Little escorted Michael the Mouse back to his men.

'The terrible twins.'

William pulled on his beard and thought. He watched as Little headed off in the direction of the men of the Boxholt. 'We agree they work with us on the Dover problem?'

'Good men, not afraid to mix it, willing to use their initiative.'

William looked and gave a smile as his wife, Mary, brought him a replacement jug of cider. 'Thank you...?' he asked teasingly.

'Marion of the Freshwater my Lord,' Mary gave him a curtsey and a dimpled smile before making her way back to the other women who were packing the ox carts ready to return to Cassingham.

'Maid Marion,' William chuckled. 'I hope my wife never finds out about you,' he called out to her before he poured some of the golden liquid into a pottery cup. 'Now, where were we?'

'Initiative,' his reeve reminded him, leaning across and pouring himself some of the cider.

'Too much can be as dangerous as too little.'

'True Master, but the twins and their men have never proved rash.'

William screwed up his eyes after a sip of his drink. 'Ow, that is sharp – I think it needs some honey in it to smooth things down.'

Mark shrugged as he downed his own cupful in one gulp.

The squire pushed his cup away and looked towards the approaching twins. 'Well, let's see how they react to what I am about to say to them.'

Thomas and Godfrey stood in front of the squire; Godfrey had eased the bandage up on the uninjured side of his head in order to use his undamaged ear to listen with. 'Willikin,' they said together.

William gestured to the cider jug and some cups on the table and the twins helped themselves.

'Not bad,' said Thomas.

'Though a bit sweet,' Godfrey added. 'We don't get much cider our way.'

'So,' Thomas held his cup to Willikin in a toast, 'this is much appreciated.'

'As I am sure the people of Hill Brow appreciated the gift of two wagons and their contents.'

The twins looked at each other; 'Ahh.'

'A certain "Robin in the hood"?'

134

Thomas looked abashed: 'I have given up on Robin Goodfellow. I prefer Robin of the Boxholt to Robin in the hood.'

'Robin Hood is a silly name, so you are right – stick to Robin Boxholt.' William watched the twin's faces. 'Of the two wagons you brought back to your villages one is mine.'

'It,' started Thomas.

'Would have slowed us down getting here so we left it at Iping,' Godfrey completed.

Cassingham turned to his Reeve and Forester and whispered, 'I think I preferred it when yonder Godfrey had both his ears covered and only Thomas could hear and reply.' The two men sniggered.

'What did he say?' Thomas asked Godfrey.

'You are asking me? I can only hear with one ear!'

The squire turned his attention back to the twins. 'Leave the wagon where you have it, just don't sell the oxen and the wagon or consume its contents; we may well have need of all of it. One thing though; you should have some padded jacks from the backs of the dead escort in your care. They are mine so get them mended and sent to me here. If we are going to interfere with the siege of Dover castle we will need to be more than just archers. For you and your men,' William stared at the twins, 'a training programme in the use of sword and shield will be given. You have but a month to become competent because if you are not, in a month and a day you will be dead.'

John Little came and with a shooing motion of his hands indicated the twins should leave and go back to their men. As the tall Forester went off in search for the next band leader to be interviewed William of Cassingham looked to Mark his Reeve and asked him; 'How much is Little getting for selling on the crossbows those two young thieves got from that incident?'

'A fifth.'

William smoothed down his neat beard. 'Remind that big man that a quarter of that is mine.'

Thomas slumped down on the straw palliasse nearest the entrance to the four man tent he shared with his brother, nephew and Mark the Archer. 'Man I am knackered! I think my arms are going to drop off with all this sword and buckler practice.'

Godfrey in the middle of the tent continued re-lacing together two of the four tanned deer skins that made up the roof of the tent. 'At least we only use a buckler not a full war shield; they weigh a ton. I don't know how the men-at-arms manage to fight using them.'

'Bears,' Garth commented from the back of the tent where he was lazing on his own paillasse.

'What?' Godfrey now had his damaged ear unpadded but his hearing was far from normal in that ear.

'Bears,' his nephew repeated. 'They have arms like bears.'

Mark the Archer tossed his sword and buckler into the tent, just missing Godfrey and Garth, and sat himself down on the ground outside. 'What do you know of bears young man?'

'I saw a dancing one once; it was at Midhurst when the lordly ones came for the autumn cull. It was a bit threadbare and it smelt but it did dance in a shuffling way.'

Mark pulled off his turn shoes and started massaging his feet. 'Was that the first time you came to help as a beater what, three years back?'

'Yes.'

'I thought I remembered seeing you there.' Mark unbound his right foot in order to improve the massage. 'An uncoordinated shuffling dance complete with grunting sounds?'

'Yes,' the youth answered.

'That wasn't a bear; that was just one of our Norman masters!'

Thomas moved back to a rear paillasse. 'It may well have been a Norman, but at least he didn't smell as bad as your feet Mark.'

'Healthy smell that,' Mark insisted as he proceeded to unbind his other foot. 'You eat cheese don't you?'

Thomas looked uncertainly at the Wulfbearding Forester; 'Yes; and?'

'Cheese is healthy?'

'Yes; and?'

'If cheese is healthy and my feet smell like cheese,' Mark instructed, 'then it stands to reason that my feet are giving off a healthy smell!'

Godfrey slumped down on the paillasse next to his brother. 'There is no answer to that.'

'Are they ready?' William of Cassingham asked Ganger Greenwood who had been acting as his men's weapons tutor.

'As ready as they will ever be, though training and practice is one thing and facing a man who is going to try and kill you is another.'

137

'True.' Cassingham's squire watched as two more men faced up to each other with wooden waster swords and daggers. 'We had to send a few of the less able swordsmen down to the coast to help our parties there try and stop supplies getting along that road. I just hope the ones we have left will be up to the job I have in mind.'

'Well, Willikin, we will soon find out.' Ganger strode forward towards the combatants. 'You big girls; is that the way I taught you to fight? Jack in the Green you should have tripped him and then made to stomp on his throat not cuddle him as if you were going to kiss him!'

'I thought,' said Thomas as he crouched down in the bracken, 'that we were going to be attacking the French siege camp outside Dover Castle.'

Godfrey ran finger and thumb over his damaged right ear to ease the itching. 'We were not ready quickly enough I think. I overheard Mark Reeve talking to Ganger and he said that the French had undermined a castle tower and attacked through the breach but the garrison repelled them causing the French to lose a lot of men.'

'So,' asked Sam Samuelson, ploughman of Wulfbearding, 'why are we here, waiting along the road to Rochester?'

Young Eric Black shrugged; 'Don't ask us, ask Willikin. At least we are back as archers rather than men-at-arms.' He lovingly stroked his ash bow, braced it then pulled out a lump of bees' wax and ran it along the bowstring, settling the string's hempen fibres.

Thomas eased himself down and cradled his own bow close to his body. He and Godfrey exchanged questioning looks. 'Do you think the French are sending reinforcements down from London?'

138

'Could be,' Godfrey said. 'It seems the Scots have gone back home without helping out.'

Mark Archer, overhearing the twins, came and sprawled near them. 'Dear God I wouldn't like to be a town or village in the Scots' way; they can be worse than the mercenaries when it comes to mayhem and plunder.'

'The trouble with mercenaries is that they owe loyalty only to those that pay them and even then it is only as long as they get paid. They don't care who they take from, murder or rape. No villager is safe from them on either side of a conflict.' Ganger Greenwood, the only man in the group of archers hidden in a holt of trees near the Rochester Road with military experience spat, narrowly missing Eric's feet. 'Animals, all of them,' he added ignoring Eric's black looks.

'They say,' Sam added, 'that King John's army is mainly made up of mercenaries, because they are the only ones he trusts.'

Thomas brought himself up on an elbow and looked up. 'Steady lads, here comes that John Little followed by a bunch of youngsters carrying sheaves of arrows.'

The big Forester strode up to the men of the Boxholt and Midhurst and directed the young men with him to hand each archer a dozen arrows. 'Right you horrible lot; there are a bunch of Frenchies on their way. We are after the mounted vanguard. Caltrops will later be spread further up the road to slow them down. Your job is to stay hidden behind trees and wait for the horn to blow once they run into the caltrops. Shoot as many arrows as you can, aim for the horses, then on the second blow of the horn and,' he looked to Godfrey, 'keep your ears open for it,' he checked

139

the twin had heard him, 'and then you are to get out of here as quickly as possible before their foot soldiers catch up; horsemen won't risk the woods but foot sloggers will. Run rather than jog. Get back to the clearing near the stream and form a line. There will be more arrows there if you need them. We don't expect any of the garlic eaters to have made it that far, but just in case they do, be ready to shoot, but only on command – we don't want any of our own men taken down by mistake.'

Thomas checked the heads of his arrows and saw that they were exclusively big barbed swallow heads. 'Lots of Frenchies master Forester?'

'Too many for us young Robin Boxholt; all we can do is slow them down and get them worried. Willikin and his Kentish men will later take on their rearguard before high tailing it. As I say, there are too many for us to try and take out, but we might induce a bit of panic.'

'Best we find better cover then,' Godfrey made his way closer to the roadside.

'Don't get too close Herla,' Little called after him. 'They have a sweep of crossbowmen ahead of the mounted vanguard checking the edge of the road.'

The screen of crossbowmen in padded jacks and hardened leather helmets moved along the rutted road that ran between Rochester and Canterbury before ending at Dover. The sweat soaked men were alert to danger and fearful of what may be lurking in the green trees that stood the required hundred paces back from the roadside. Occasionally a pair of them would break off and get closer to the tree line and peer into the darkness trying to determine if all was safe. The English archers in their woodland colours pushed themselves closer to a tree or sunk lower into bracken, furze or brambles. The crossbowmen walked on, unaware of the watchers in the green wood.

'They should have had hounds with them.' Thomas whispered into Godfrey's good ear. 'They would have sniffed something.'

'With Mark around, only if they liked cheese,' his twin whispered back.

The archers watched and listened. The sound of a woodpecker tapping for its food sounded to the twins left. It was repeated and repeated, closer and closer, then the cry of an out of season cuckoo. 'Bloody Granfer Gilbert,' Thomas hissed. 'It's the only call he can do!'

Godfrey made his best woodpecker sound and heard it passed further down the tree line.

The archers stood, braced their bows, pulled arrows from their belts and nocked them on their bowstrings. A pall of dust preceded the clopping sound of the mounted vanguard as it proceeded four abreast. At a slow walk the horsemen passed the men of the Boxholt and Midhurst and the dust rose higher. The further down the column the more dust there was and the more the riders squinted to see and the more their horses snorted and sneezed. The dust muffled the sound of the horses' hooves and the occasional cough of a rider. Rank after rank passed the twins, Ganger Greenwood and their men.

Suddenly they heard a loud French cry that was repeated down the line: '*HALT!*'

The hunting horn sounded, the archers broke cover and the arrows flew. Horse after horse was hit, those on the flanks taking most of the shots and as the injured animals turned to avoid the stinging cutting pain of the hunting arrows they hit into the side of the horses on the inside of them. The arrows did not stop as horses reared, horses stumbled, and horses fell with their riders losing control, often losing their seats also.

The horn sounded again. 'Come on brother,' Thomas yelled in case Godfrey had not heard.

The archers turned back into the woods and ran. They ran and ran as behind them they could hear some of the dismounted French cavalry giving chase. Dodging trees, leaping ditches, avoiding uneven ground, the archers ran. Ahead, in front of the clearing by the river was a skirmishing line of other archers which they ran through. As the last archer formed into line the skirmishers ran back to join them.

The archers found, scattered along the line, handfuls of arrows with long bodkin heads. They grabbed them, nocked them, and waited.

As a handful of French broke into the clearing John Little cried out; 'DRAW; LOOSE!' and the French fell with arrows sprouting from them. 'Skirmishers give chase!'

Those who had formed the skirmish line grabbed more arrows and set off to hunt down any late coming French, giving the deer beaters' cry: 'He, he, he, he.'

'I have a special job for you two.' William of Cassingham studied the twins. 'The French caught Ganger Greenwood and John Forest yesterday.'

'I thought,' said Thomas.

'I hadn't seen them afterwards,' Godfrey completed. 'What happened Willikin?'

The squire of Cassingham sighed. 'It seems Ganger put his foot down a hole when running to the river clearing and did his ankle: his mate Forest stopped to help him. The French have them both at Canterbury.'

'And our job is?' Thomas asked.

'You have worked with Harold Harefoot before?'

'Yes,' Godfrey agreed. 'We have.'

'Take your nephew, Mark Archer and two others of your men; the most trustworthy and best swordsmen. We are going to try and get Ganger and Forest out of trouble. Go now and wait for Harold to join you – we must move quickly.'

The twins left to gather their party together. 'I don't know why Willikin chose us, we have only been to Canterbury a couple of times and then there is the matter of Harold Harefoot.' Thomas rubbed the cropped fair hair on his head.

'I don't like the sound of it Thomas, I don't like the sound of it at all,'

John Little watched the twins go. 'They are not men of Kent so why them Master?'

William of Cassingham ran his fingers through his short neat beard. 'Let us see just how good they are,' he replied.

143

John Shoemaker led the party of Sussex men through the narrow streets of Canterbury to a safe house in Beer Cart Lane. He looked around, waved to a neighbour who appeared to be on watch for him and ushered the men inside. 'I wish you had come in pairs not all seven of you together.'

It took a long pause for Godfrey to answer on behalf of the others due to him having to work his way through the man's thick Kent accent. 'Only Thomas and I have been here before. Even finding you was hard enough.'

'Canterbury; pilgrims; I want pewter token.' Harold mumbled.

The Canterbury man grunted then set off to find his apprentices and maids who were supposed to have had food and drink ready for his guests.

'You are not a pilgrim Harold,' Thomas advised.

'You have not worshipped at Thomas Becket's tomb,' Godfrey added.

'Canterbury; pilgrim,' Harold insisted. 'Want token.'

Thomas pulled off the long cloak he had been wearing to disguise the sword at his side. 'I'm not sure this will work brother.'

'Willikin has set us a difficult task,' Godfrey agreed as he, too, removed his cloak.

The others followed suit then removed the bucklers that hung over the hilt of their swords before removing the swords themselves from their belts. Harold Harefoot, who had no sword or buckler, lovingly placed his yew bow that was cunningly disguised as a staff against a wall; he caressed it with gentle strokes of his calloused hands.

144

John Shoemaker reappeared followed by three scruffy boys and two slightly dishevelled girls all bearing food and drink which they placed on a plain wooden trestle along the end wall. Once they had performed their tasks Shoemaker encouraged them to leave with none too gentle shoves in their backs; 'Back to your work you lazy bones; I have a living to make and it won't get made with you all hanging around gawking 'cos I have visitors. Now shoo.' He turned to the Sussex men; 'Kids of today eh? Not like when we were young. They don't know the meaning of work.'

There was a knock at the door, the Sussex men retrieved their swords but Shoemaker ignored them, peered through a knot hole in the door and then opened it. The previously noticed neighbour and two others entered. 'Fellow cordwainers,' the man explained. 'We have all moved on from making just work shoes you see.'

'Not that others see it that way,' one of the new comers grumbled.

'Now, now,' John the Shoemaker shook his head. 'It is not something our friends here want to discuss. What they want is information on where their friends are and what is happening to them.'

'Ah.' The grumbler walked over and helped himself to a cup of cider. He sipped it before continuing; 'We have found out that they are being held in the Baggeberi,' he inclined his head towards Godfrey, Thomas and the others. 'That is a fortified earthworks without the city wall, up by the North Gate,' he explained.

'It's where all the fancy French have camped,' the neighbour added as he, too, poured himself a drink.

The grumbler nudged the neighbour and took the cup of drink from him. 'Most of the Frenchies are camped between the River Stour and the South Gate, off the Wine Cheap Road.'

'The rough sorts,' Shoemaker clarified. 'Mercenaries I would think.'

'As far as we can tell the fancy French have been trying to get information from your two friends but without much success.' The grumbler swilled the remains of his drink around his cup before tipping it down his gullet. 'Word is they will be taking them to the Castle by the South Gate where they have better means of persuasion.'

'The Room of Little Ease,' the previously quiet other cordwainer added.

'Room of Little Ease?' Thomas asked.

'Too low to stand, too narrow to sit. Black as night and as dank and smelly as a privy,' the grumbler explained, looking for more drink.

'That's what I heard too Grumpy,' Shoemaker walked to the trestle. 'Oh, I forgot – help yourselves,' he picked up a thick piece of ham on the end of his eating knife as an example.

'Not many men can last more than a day in that place they say,' Grumpy the grumbler advised, refilling his cup and blocking the way to the jug that held it and frustrating Mark the Archer's attempts to get refreshment in the process.

'Do we know when the transfer will happen?' Godfrey called from the back of the queue that had formed behind the three large jugs of cider.

'Not yet, but hopefully within the hour,' John Shoemaker said as he walked to the shuttered window of the parlour with thick slices of ham on his knife and a flowing cup of cider in his left hand. He peered out through the crack between the shutters. He watched as a brewers' dray came along the lane. It stopped and one of the two men on the driving board climbed down before waving the dray on. The man looked both ways down the lane before sauntering across to talk to one of Shoemaker's apprentices manning the shop front next to the parlour. Shoemaker leaned to watch the brewer's progress, nibbling on the ham as he did so. The man said something, the apprentice laughed. 'Come on, come on,' Shoemaker mumbled between chewing. 'Ah, at last.' The brewer came to the door and Shoemaker placed his cider on the floor and opened the door before the man could even knock.

'Afternoon all,' the man said, walking from the street's sunshine into the darkened parlour. A waft of stale ale hung around him.

'Albert Brewer,' Shoemaker said, by way of introduction to the heavily bearded man. 'He has just come from the French camp at the Baggeberi.'

Albert ignored all in the room and headed straight for the trestle. 'Sitting behind them oxen that pulls the dray on a hot day like this creates a great thirst in a man,' he declared in an extraordinarily deep voice. The Sussex men all looked at each other for, if anything, this man's Kent accent was even thicker than Shoemaker's. The brewer picked up each of the jugs, giving them a sniff before putting them down again. 'What's this John the Shoemaker who would rather be called John the Cordwainer?

Cider? Do you think I am an apprentice? Where is the ale? Where is the beer? I'd even settle for wine!'

'Oh get on with it Albert,' Grumpy called out. 'We all know you – if it gets you drunk you will drink it.'

'True,' Albert agreed and swigged straight from the nearest jug. Having emptied it he gave a very impressive belch. 'But I am a brewer and it never hurts to advertise.'

'I agree with Grumpy,' Shoemaker walked over and examined the level of cider in the two remaining jugs. 'Just get on with it: tell these men what you know of the two prisoners held by the French while I arrange for these jugs to be refilled.'

'With ale or beer I trust?' Albert Brewer called after Shoemakers back. 'Food!' Brewer headed back to the trestle and took bread, cut it and used it to encompass a wedge of cheese and a whole boiled onion.

'Leave some.'

The brewer looked at the hulking bulk of Harold Harefoot. 'There is plenty there.'

'Leave some.' Harold repeated his cold eyes angry.

'I will indeed leave some friend,' Albert bit into his food. He continued to slowly eat his way through the bread, cheese and onion until John Shoemaker reappeared with two maids and an apprentice in tow with a full jug of cider each. The brewer confiscated one jug for himself then wiped the crumbs of food from his beard with his free hand before emptying the contents of the jug in one go, his Adam's apple moving rhythmically with each swallow.

148

'The news Albert,' Shoemaker asked once the brewer had put down the jug and given another impressive belch.

The brewer smiled and looked at the Sussex men and decided that the twins were the most interesting of the group, other than Harold who had descended on the food and was systematically eating his way through it. 'Well it seems, from gossip that I heard, that your friends are to be moved this evening, straight after the sounding of the curfew bell; it seems the French do not want to attract too much attention to what they are doing – them being French and the prisoners English. This city may be in the hands of the rebel barons, but that does not make the French popular. It would be a small party. From those we heard moaning and whining about being stuck with the job of escort no more than eight or ten. Of course, I may have it wrong as my French and their French is not quite the same, but my drayman was once a sailor and he knows several types of French as a result and that is what he agrees was said.' He smiled and belched again, this time the cider fumes were accompanied by the taint of onion.

The curfew bell sounded as Godfrey, Thomas and their party slipped along Stour Street. Coming to Hospital Lane Thomas, Mark and Eric peeled off and made their way to where the lane met Castle Street. Godfrey, Garth, Sam and Harold Harefoot continued on towards St Mildred's Church before ducking down Shit Alley towards Castle Street.

Godfrey and his companions watched the guard on the castle wall then, as he started his walk along the wall, went one at a time across the road and hid at the mouth of Little Wine Cheap Lane.

The Sussex men looked longingly at Harold's yew bow, which the big man had unwrapped from its camouflage and had braced up.

'I wish we had our bows with us,' Garth sighed.

'So do I,' his uncle agreed. 'But it was hard enough getting one bow in without us all having them.'

Sam Samuelson, slumped against the wall of one of the vintner shops and looked up Castle Road. 'This sword stuff isn't our way and them Frenchies are bound to know what they are doing, far more than we.'

Godfrey joined the ploughman, 'Ah Sam, but do they know we are here? At least we have surprise on our side.'

'No we won't uncle,' Garth hissed. 'Not if you shout rather than whisper. Ever since you got that whack on the ear from that crossbow bolt your voice has got louder.'

'What did you say?' Godfrey asked.

Garth gave an exasperated sigh and put an index finger to his lips.

'Oh, right.' Godfrey gave a somewhat embarrassed grin. 'Shush!'

Sam nudged Godfrey. Once he had his attention he inclined his head towards the end of Castle Street. 'Three in front, one either side of our men.'

'More at the back?' Garth asked.

'I would think so, but I can't see.'

Garth moved to the other side of Little Wine Cheap, slipped the lanyard of his buckler over his left hand and then gripped the small shield's handle before drawing his sword. He looked across and saw Godfrey and Sam do the same. Harold pulled an arrow through his belt and nocked it. They waited and Sam, who had very sharp eyes, watched the prisoners and their escort make slow and guarded progress down Castle Street. The lead Frenchman looked to the castle walls but, seeing no one in sight, shook his head and called something back to the rest of the party which made the other French laugh. The group went past Hospital Lane and, although the men on the right flank glanced down it, they saw nothing suspicious. They went past St Mary Street and the men on the left flank looked and saw nothing. They were getting close to the castle and started to relax and think of the warm guard room and the refreshments they expected to be awaiting them there. Before they reached Little Wine Cheap Lane Thomas and his men ran from their cover in Hospital Land and crashed into the three Frenchmen at the rear of the escort. The party halted. The lead French turned and looked back to see what was happening. Harold Harefoot stepped into the middle of Castle Road, shot the lead Frenchman, nocked another arrow and took down the second man and again the third, his movements slick and swift, the whole action over in seconds.

'GO!' Godfrey called and he, Garth and Sam ran out to help tackle the remaining French.

The castle guard, on his return walk from the tower where he had stopped to swig from a wine skin saw what was happening but, before he could cry a warning, one of Harold's arrows took him in the throat and he tumbled into the castle bailey.

Thomas had downed his man and turned to help Mark. Together the Englishmen took another Frenchman out by attacking him on two sides. By then Eric's Frenchman had run away but not before yelling out an alarum at full voice.

The Frenchman in front of Godfrey brought his spear up in a defensive guard so Godfrey pushed his buckler forward in a bind, pushing the spear downwards against the man's chest before slamming the pommel of his sword into the Frenchman's temple below the helmet. The fallen man groaned as he fell, his noise cut short when Godfrey stuck his sword in the man's throat and pushed down hard.

Garth and Sam had managed to drop the last French guard with Sam smacking him in the face with his buckler whilst Garth chopped down with his sword, smashing through the man's collar bone.

'RUN!' cried Harold as men appeared from the castle gate in response to their colleague's cry.

'RUN,' repeated Godfrey and Thomas together, grabbing the bound Ganger Greenwood and John Forest and pushing them towards Shit Alley.

The Englishmen ran pursued by angry French. As they reached Stour Street Harold stayed back and shot arrow after arrow at the French before taking off, like a hare, after the others. Unsure whether the arrow rain had finished the French moved past the bodies of their dead, dying and injured comrades, before cautiously gaining the end of the alley, and looked just in time to see the English pass Beer Cart Lane and disappear down a runnel between houses in the direction of the river. Seeing there was no obvious danger the French ran on.

Sam Samuelson was of heavy build, in fact he was rather fat. His love of food caused him to run slower than the others. Godfrey and

Thomas looked back together only to see him caught by the leading French.

'They have him!' the twins cried out together.

Harold Harefoot stopped and ran back. He pulled out his last arrow, nocked it, drew, and shot Sam through the heart.

'He knew too much,' he said, as way of explanation. 'Now RUN!'

They ran. They ran through the runnel. They ran to the banks of the Stour. They ran over the decks of the punts that someone had left sideways-on across the river. They ran through the gate of the Grey Friars convent. They ran through the grounds. They ran out the gate the other side of the convent. They ran over the sideways placed punts over the mill leet. They ran to a garden wall where someone had placed an upright barrel to help them leg it over the wall. They ran through the garden. They edged through the house and out the open front door. They ran across St Peter's Grove. They went through the open door of a house opposite. They pushed through the house and through its formally pathed and edged herb garden before climbing the end wall, helped by a parked wheel barrow and then they ran through the overgrown grounds of another house, though its back door and wheezingly made their way out the front door into Black Griffin Lane. Stopping to catch their breath they saw an open front door three houses up and made their way through it and out across the garden and over another wall, through another house and emerged into St Peter's Lane.

John Shoemaker flashed a lantern from further down the lane and the exhausted men staggered into the house where Shoemaker stood. He took them down into the cellar whilst an unseen person

153

closed the cellar trap door and dragged furniture over it. The cordwainer lit more lanterns and observed the panting men before him. 'I bet you had fun getting those two,' he indicated Ganger and John Forest who were getting their bindings cut off, 'over the walls seeing as they couldn't use their arms especially that one,' he indicated Ganger who was in a state of near collapse. 'Him with the hobbling gate.'

'We lost a man,' Godfrey gasped between dragging air into his punished lungs.

'He,' Thomas glared at Harold Harefoot, 'shot him.'

Harefoot cross his arms across his chest. 'Willikin said to not let anyone be a prisoner.'

'You would have shot us all?'

'I had arrows enough.' Harold, who seemed as fresh as he had been at the very start, looked around. 'Drink?'

John Shoemaker shook his head. 'Cruel necessity I suppose.'

'He knew too much.' Harold looked around. 'Drink?'

'Yes,' Shoemaker took them further into the dark cellar. 'Here; drink for all. But do keep quiet. Although there are people removing the "aids" such as the punts and barrels you used to get here, they will only do it if it is safe; if the French are not close enough and that,' he took a deep breath, 'is something we don't know. People have risked their lives in this venture so please keep your voices down and don't put them at any more at risk than needs be.'

Godfrey took a cup of watered ale from his brother Thomas. 'What now Master Shoemaker?'

The cordwainer waited till both the twins had had something to drink. 'You stay here till tomorrow night then we use a hidden tunnel to get you to the main branch of the Stour and then hidden in boats away from Canterbury.'

'You have a hidden tunnel?' Thomas asked after wiping his lips on the back of his hand.

'It is useful in bringing in high value goods without them having to pass through a city gate and attracting city taxes.' John Shoemaker indicated baskets of bread and cheese. 'Food for the day. Make it last as there will not be any more, the same goes for the drink. I am going now via the tunnel to make sure the French are not hanging around in the wrong places.'

'Our thanks to you and your people John.'

Shoemaker nodded his head in acknowledgement. 'Let us just hope there are no reprisals. I will be back tomorrow afternoon.' With that he made his way even deeper into the cellar and vanished from sight.

Thomas slumped to the ground. 'I didn't like Harold killing Sam.'

His twin joined him. 'Nor I. We should have turned back and tried to rescue him.' Godfrey looked over to where Harold Harefoot was helping himself to food and drink. 'Was there no other option to shooting Sam, Harold?'

'I was only obeying orders,' the cold eyed archer called back.

Godfrey looked to his twin. 'Someone will have to tell his brother Jack what has happened.'

'True.'

'And his now widow, her with the three childer.'

Thomas chinked his earthenware cup against his brother's. 'That is always the duty of the eldest, big brother.'

William, squire of Cassingham, pulled off his dust covered boots and slumped back into the high backed chair in his great hall. He took a deep breath which he let out slowly. His wife Mary entered and gave him a goblet of cooled white wine and then left. He looked to his two most trusted henchmen. 'Mark, John, this war will be the end of me. Overseeing the Sussex and Hampshire men to make sure they have the Weald sealed up. Running skirmishes along the south coast road to try and stop supplies moving along there. Ambushing troop movements to reinforce Dover, and,' he waved his hand in the air, 'we still have to do something to help break the siege of Dover Castle.'

'At least we got our two men out of Canterbury,' Mark the Reeve reminded his master.

'So we did.'

John Little looked towards a stool and William nodded his head for the tall man to bring it over and sit on it. The Forester sat. 'They did well those Boxholt men. They worked well with the locals and used common sense in making their plan work.'

William took a sip of his wine. 'How did they react when Harold Harefoot had to put the emergency plan into force?'

'They didn't like it,' John Little informed him.

'But they did accept it was the only thing to do,' Mark Reeve confirmed.

'The problem is,' Cassingham continued, 'Harefoot was only supposed to shoot Ganger or Forest if they got caught. They did

156

know too much, especially Ganger, but that poor Samuel Samuelson knew very little.'

'But even that "little" could have been too much.' John tucked his thumbs into his belt.

William took a deeper sip of wine before toying with his goblet, deep in thought. 'So, it seems we can trust the twins and put them to good use.'

'It would pay to talk to the twins though, before they start to spread word of what happened; make sure they know it was just Harold and his rigid interpretation of orders.'

'Hmmm.' William continued to play with the goblet.

Chapter 9: Surprise, Surprise

'Well?' Mark the Reeve of Cassingham stood before his squire. 'What do we do Master?'

William of Cassingham sat slumped in his seat of honour in his high hall. An early autumn fog hung in the far corners of the hall and servants, overseen by the Lady Mary, were rushing to get the fire in the central hearth lit and the damp air driven out. William continued to stare into space, caressing his neat beard, not answering his man. The servants had managed to get a small fire going and were feeding it kindling that gave out more smoke than flame. Still William said nothing. Suddenly a bright flame broke though the kindling twigs much to the relief of Mary who could see her husband's dark mood. The kindling was complemented now with small branches and gradually the fire took serious hold and logs were added. The squire waited for the fire to be truly established and the servants ushered out by his wife before responding to his Reeve. 'The French outside Dover are now too strong for us to even try a raid. We still can't do more than hassle the French using the coast road and, although our folk have parts of the Weald sealed up tight, there are still back roads they are using to get supplies through to London and their troops in the surrounding area.'

Mark indicated the seat alongside William, the one usually occupied by the squire's wife. Cassingham's lord nodded his head and the Reeve came and sat alongside his master. 'We still have the men gathered for the Dover attack tucked up in the woods around here; what of them?'

'We will have to let them go home. They have already missed the harvest and the hay making. Besides, we are running out of food to feed them; we have not taken enough French supply trains recently. One thing I don't want is them scattering everywhere hunting. Archers are too vulnerable unless either well hid or in large numbers – if they scatter to get deer there is a chance the French will get to know, track them down and pick them off.'

'They have foresters too, the French that is.'

'Correct Mark. Our advantage is that we know this forest and they don't but all it would take is one rebel or traitorous Englishman to lead them and ...'

'We lose a lot of our best men.'

'Precisely. No,' Cassingham stretched his legs with a slight groan,' we must let them go back to their homes until such time as we need them again.'

'Home?' Thomas Wulfson rubbed his hands with glee.

'Home,' Godfrey, his twin brother confirmed. 'I never thought the prospect of gathering the swine and the spare kine in for the blood month would ever be an attractive prospect.'

'But it is,' his brother agreed.

'We've got to decide on which sheep to cull,' Garth, the twin's nephew, called up from where he was unlacing the four cured deer skins that made up the crude four man tent they, and Mark Archer, occupied. 'It is never a job I like; one can get quite attached to them silly animals.'

'But they can taste so good in a stew,' Mark reminded him. 'Boiled up with some onions, hazel nuts, and neeps all with a bit of butter and sweet herbs.' Wulfbearding's Forester smacked his lips at the thought. 'Mind,' he added, 'with no lordships doing any hunting due to the war there will be plenty of venison available.'

'As long as it is not from your woods?' Thomas asked.

'Goes without saying does that. One always goes poaching in someone else's woods and they in yours. Which is not seen, of course, as a courtesy to them for turning a blind eye to your own poaching.'

Thomas came over, took his deer skin and started to place his cloak and spare clothing on it, ready to make into a roll for carrying. 'A gentleman's agreement between foresters? You poach on my land and I poach on yours.'

'Works a treat,' Mark confirmed as he took his own deerskin from Garth. 'It is only outsiders we try and catch and even then only if they forget to leave a decent haunch behind for us.'

159

'If only their lordships knew what went on,' Godfrey shook out his spare over shirt and brushed off the leaves and bits of fern leaf that clung to the tightly woven linen garment.

'Them that thinks themselves so clever are always going to be made fools of.' Mark tightened his roll in the middle with a spare belt and then used two lengths of leather thong to secure the ends leaving enough over to make a shoulder strap for carrying it.

Godfrey sniffed a pair of braies before deciding that he ought, in all honesty, wash them before packing them. 'I hope young Will Greenleaf has looked after the oxen. I know he is normally so trustworthy, but we have been away for so long.'

'He will be alright; good lad is that.' Thomas sniffed his own spare braies but, despite the smell, decided their washing could wait till they were back at Iping where hot water would be available as opposed to the cold in the stream at hand.

'I bet he hasn't patched the daub in the wall between the living space and the byre though.' Godfrey, having seen his brother place his dirty braies in his roll, decided he would do the same as they would be leaving that night and home in three days time.

'The West Sussex men are ready to leave Master.' John Little, Cassingham's Forester, joined his squire and Mark Reeve standing around the high table where William had placed various items in a seemingly random manner.

'Change of plan,' William of Cassingham informed him. "Leave to go home is cancelled.'

'Change of plan?'

William and Mark nodded.

'News has just come in from Dover,' Mark advised, contemplating a knife on the table that sat at right angles to two spoons and an apple.

William added two more spoons and another apple to the line. 'Hubert de Burgh and Stephen de Sotteghem, who hold the castle for King John, have just made a truce with Dauphin Louis.'

'But if there is a truce, then the men can go home. Can't they?' John moved slightly so he could watch the squire add more cutlery and fruit to the pattern he was making on the table.

'De Burgh and Sotteghem may have made a truce, but we haven't.' William of Cassingham gave his Forester a cunning look. 'The Dauphin has gone to London, taking many of his top men with him and quite a few of his troops too; the King has relieved the sieges of Lincoln and Windsor and, so I am informed, is now burning his way through rebel baron's territory in East Anglia. This means that there are few French still in the siege camp at Dover. Those that are there will be off their guard. The last thing they will expect is to be attacked from the rear.' Cassingham moved three small cups towards some stale bread rolls. 'So, leave is cancelled and we plan an attack.'

'I've just seen that Harold Harefoot going off with a bunch of Kentish archers.' Garth came and sat with the other Boxholt men sitting in the woods by Crabble Hill on the outskirts of Dover town. 'He has an oversized Canterbury pilgrims badge on his chest!'

Mark Archer grunted. 'I did hear that Willikin gave it to him as a reward for what he did in getting Ganger and Forest out.'

'Not for shooting Sam Samuelson dead?'

'No need to be bitter young man.' Mark sunk deeper into his thick woollen cloak whose colour reflected the many shades of the brown and grey sheep whose fleece has contributed to its make up.

'He was a friend, and his younger brother, Jack, is an even better friend.'

Mark slunk even deeper into the warmth of his cloak, pulling the back of it up to make a second hood over his head. 'War is cruel. Things get done that are deemed necessary that normally we would abhor.'

'Quite the philosopher aren't you Mark.' The young shepherd of Wulfbearding pulled his own cloak tighter around his body. 'I will talk to our priest, John of Chichester, when we get back home and see what he says.'

'When we get back home,' Eric Black chipped in.

'When are we going home uncle?' Gareth called out to his twin uncles as they came to join the others.

'Not yet,' the twins replied.

'We have a job to do here in Dover,' Thomas explained.

'When?' Eric called out from the depths of his cloak.

'Tonight as long as the fog does not return.' Godfrey pulled his sword from his belt and held it to his chest before enwrapping himself in his cloak and sitting down.

John of Dumpford and his brothers Albert and Arnold moved closer to where the Iping and Wulfbearding men sat and joined the huddle in the hopes of keeping the October chill out. John trapped the bottom of his grey wool cloak under his feet and rubbed his hands together in the space that had been made. 'Willikin can't wait too much longer before acting.'

'Half of Kent sitting in this and the other woods,' Albert contributed after wiping a dew drop from the end of his nose.

'Pardon my brother's exaggeration.' Arnold, taller and balder than his brothers had his cloak over his hood and a hat over the cloak to help keep his naked pate warm. 'But it does seem as if this wood alone has everyone in this part of Kent between the ages of eight and eighty gathered in it.'

'They have been pouring in all day.' John the woodsman looked over to where groups of people, young, old and in-between, male and female, were sitting together in hushed and whispering huddles, all trying to keep warm without the benefit of a fire.

Thomas looked to his twin for approval, having got it when Godfrey raised his eyebrows, he signalled for all the men of the Boxholt to gather round. 'We have just come from Willikin with tonight's plan of action.'

'Provided the fog does not return,' Godfrey added.

'Yes, thank you for that brother. As I was saying, Willikin has now firmed up his plan of action. We will move, as soon as it gets dark, to woods that are closer to the castle.'

'Archers will start an attack to the north of the French siege camp on the northern plain. We are to wait until the French try a counter attack and then raid their stores.'

'No glory for us then?' Garth murmured.

'No glory but, hopefully, supplies to see us through the winter, seeing as we have neglected the harvest this year.' Thomas produced, as if my magic, an onion and bit into it.

'Is anything happening yet?' young Garth struggled to stop his teeth chattering, all cloaks having been discarded to free arms for fighting.

'Not yet; go back to sleep.' The twins smirked to each other, enjoying the warmth the padded jacks they were wearing gave them.

'Is anything happening yet?'

'No Eric, nothing is happening yet.' Thomas stared towards the north.

'Go back to sleep,' Godfrey encouraged.

'Too cold for that,' Garth complained.

'Youth of today,' John of Dumpsford muttered as he slapped his arms against his thin body.

'Are you sure nothing is happening yet?'

'Did the others nominate you to be spokesman nephew?' Thomas asked Garth.

'Maybe.'

'You family connection is being exploited boy,' Godfrey called back from where he was scanning the horizon to the north. 'Nothing yet; your uncle Thomas will tell you soon as there is something happening.'

'Is anything happening yet?'

Thomas turned from where he was watching.; 'You drew the short straw this time Eric?'

The blacksmith's son shrugged his shoulder and sighed. 'We are all getting so cold Good Fellow Thomas.'

'Nothing is happening yet,' Godfrey confirmed.

The youth started to walk back to where the other Boxholt men sat in a huddle.

'No – wait,' Thomas called out.

'What's up little brother?' Godfrey joined his twin at the edge of the woods.

'I can hear something.'

'More than I can Thomas, these days a lot of the time all I can hear is a sound like the sea on the shingle at Brighthelmstone.'

'No, I can definitely hear something. Ah – look.' A fire arrow flew in the sky. 'It is all on.'

More fire arrows, apparently shot in volleys, lit the distant sky to the north.

'Right little brother, the attack on the siege camp has started; we need to get into place and ready to move.'

'Eric,' Thomas grabbed the boy's elbow and dragged him away from watching the spectacle. 'Go back to our men and get them to run to the village elders they were introduced to. The elders are to get their people to follow us at a distance.'

'And tell our men to hurry up about it and get back to us as they are to be in the skirmish line in front of the common folk.' Godfrey looked to his brother; 'Half archers; half swordsmen?'

'Just so.'

The line of archers, with the twins and others armed with swords and bucklers, cautiously advanced out of the woods and into the cleared ground that surrounded Dover Castle. The line advanced to where the castle's curtain wall started to turn to the north east then, following an owl call, halted. The men knelt and waited. The storm of fire arrows had long stopped though the sound from the clash of arms and the shouts of men had increased and carried clearly across the plain. Still the skirmishers waited. Then it came; a single fire arrow flew on a high trajectory with a green flame. The English line stood and slowly advanced in a north-westerly direction. Thomas was at one end of the line and Godfrey at the other. As the line advanced the twins kept its dressing. At a signal Garth and Eric broke from the formation to run back to the woods to instruct the village elders to get their folk moving. Slowly the line moved forward; archers with arrows nocked, the others with swords drawn. Ahead of them the siege camp came into view backlit by burning shacks, tents and crude bivouacs. Silhouetted against the camp by the firelight stood three sentries, their backs turned to the approaching line, the men's attention being all on the fight at the north end of the camp. An owl called, one sentry, more alert than the others, half turned to the sound. He and his comrades fell to the shafts of the archers in the skirmish line. Another owl call and the line continued its advance. As it reached the ramshackle shanty town Garth and Eric caught up with the others.

Thomas came down the line to where the two youths had joined Godfrey. 'Do you know where the storehouses are Brother?'

Godfrey turned his good ear to his twin. 'I think so. You stay here with the archers and hold the villagers till I get word back to you. Watch both the plain behind and the camp.'

'Yes, yes big brother. The French can come from any direction.'

Godfrey smiled at his brother's words. 'I know, I know.' He patted Thomas on the shoulder. 'Just be careful eh?'

'I will Godfrey; you just be careful yourself.'

Godfrey gave a shrill whistle that caused the other swordsmen to join him and, together, they slowly moved into the camp ever watchful. The camp gradually improved in the quality of its buildings and crude bivouacs gave way to sheds made of wattle walls, these in turn gave way to small houses of wattle and daub, complete with proper thatched roofs. Godfrey continued on, following in his head the map he had been shewn by Willikin, a map based on information provided by Cassingham's agents and contacts who had been in the camp. Coming to a narrow cross road Godfrey sent men along the side roads and waited for them to report.

A dark figure wearing a helmet with an iron frame and horn inserts that was too large for him came to Godfrey. 'All clear my side. They must all have gone to reinforce their mates fighting our lot to the north.'

Godfrey nodded and indicated that the man should now investigate further up the path to their front.

Another dark figure came, this one with no helmet, only a coif of mael. 'No one to be seen, not even a camp whore.'

'Good.' Godfrey gathered his men. 'Once Albert comes back with an all clear from our front we find the stores and secure them.

Once we have them in our hands Arnold here can go back and bring the villagers in to empty the stores and get them back to our base in the woods.'

Albert returned, slightly out of breath. 'All clear Herla; the store is just ahead and there are no guards.'

'Then we go.' Godfrey set off at a loping pace that set the hardened leather helmet on his head bouncing against the padded linen coif beneath it. Rounding a slight curve in the path he called a halt for there, in front of him, was a large building made of split planks. 'John, James and Jem break down the doors. Arnold – get the folk in; we all have work to do.'

Thomas stood with his brother watching the last of the villagers, a boy child of no more than ten summers, staggered away with a sack of grain across his thin shoulders. 'What now big brother?'

Godfrey looked to the flames that had increased ahead of them. 'Let Mark Archer get the folk back to the woods and guard them there. He can take half the archers. The other half can remain on watch till we come back but I want Garth and Eric here with their bows.'

You have a plan?'

'No; just a desire to cause some mischief.' He turned to his brother. 'An attack in the French rear wouldn't go amiss.'

'As long as it doesn't turn into a battle big brother.'

The twins, with their swordsmen and the two archers, moved through the southern part of the siege camp stealthily. As each man at the front made ten paces they stopped and let others pass them with the new front men doing the same once they were ten paces ahead. In this fashion they advanced with care along the path. Then the front men both held out an arm. The group stopped and the twins made their way forward to the front. Once there they saw why there had been a need to stop. In front of them, twenty paces ahead where the path they were on opened up into a road, was a group of French. One, a rather fat man with a small moustache, was flapping his arms around seemingly giving orders only to cancel them and start again after talking to one of his companions.

'He looks important,' Thomas whispered to his brother.

'Mischief rather than a battle?'

'Indeed big brother. Let's take him as a present for Willikin if we can.'

Godfrey signalled Garth and Eric forward. 'Take out the ones on the end. You should get in another shot each before we get in your way.'

'I'll tell the men to charge after the first arrow. I'll tell them to make sure they don't kill the fat one.' Thomas edged his way back down the line whispering instructions to the men.

Godfrey waited till his brother returned, constantly watching the Frenchmen. 'All ready Thomas?'

'All ready big brother.'

Godfrey stepped into the middle of the path, looked at the two archers, turned and pointed to the French with his sword. Two arrows flew towards their targets. Godfrey took a deep breath then screamed 'OUT! OUT! OUT!' and charged followed by all the others. Two more arrows flew and then the young archers joined in the back of the charge adding their yells to those of the other English.

Three French were already down with arrows in them, two coughing blood the other sitting and trying to stem the blood spurting from his neck. The rest of the French party, still not seeming to comprehend what was going on, turned in stunned silence to watch the English charge towards them and then falling to the impact as they were hit.

'Don't kill the fat one,' Godfrey yelled.

'What?' Albert called out as he was just about to fillet the moustachioed man.

'Don't kill him!' Thomas insisted as he pulled Albert's sword away from the flabby white flesh of the Frenchman's throat.

'All right Good Fellow Robin; no need to shout – I am not your deaf brother.'

Having seen the French party slaughtered to a man Godfrey came to where Thomas, Albert and the trembling Frenchmen stood. 'Get him out of here now, before the French realise what has happened.'

'With pleasure.' Thomas bent, undid a belt from a dead French knight and secured the fat man's hands. 'Right fatty; move.'

'I do not understand what you are saying.'

Thomas prodded the prisoner with the point of his sword. 'We go walkies. Savey?'

'Well done Robin & Herla.' William of Cassingham placed an arm on the shoulders of the twins.

'Thank you Willikin,' the twins responded.

'We couldn't have done it on our own,' Thomas told the squire.

'Our men did well, but so did the local folk Willikin.' Godfrey added.

'We all need each other.' William steered the twins away from the fire in the woods where they and the Boxholt men had been warming themselves. 'I have something of great importance to tell you. A courier has just arrived with some startling news: King John took ill and died two days ago. '

Thomas stopped dead, causing William and Godfrey to swing round and face him. 'What does that mean to us and what we are doing?'

Cassingham sighed. 'I honestly don't know. So, until we do know exactly what is happening and what this will mean to the struggle, you can go home and take your men of the Boxholt with you. But, the thing is – the King is dead.'

'You are sure the King is dead?' the twins asked in unison.

'He is. His only legitimate son, Henry, is but nine years old so, just who will lead the fight against the French, if there is to continue to be a fight, we don't know. Things are complicated by the fact that King John lost the treasury when the tide came in unexpectedly as he crossed the Wash. There is now no money to pay his mercenaries. If the war is to continue, someone will have to organise finding the money to pay them or there will be no royal army. I have sent agents out to see what is happening and who, if anyone, is taking charge. Until I can get some good information we hold what we have and wait to see what happens.'

'We will not accept Louis as king,' the twins insisted vehemently.

171

'As I say: we will wait and see what happens and who, if anyone, steps forward to take on the French. Meantime there are some tasks I need you to do.'

Thomas gave a groan and rolled his eyes.

William gave a gentle laugh. 'It is not all hard work. No, what I want you to do is take that wagon you took near Hill Brow, distribute its contents to the people of Iping, Cassingham and Wulfbearding then get it back here for more supplies. I can allow you three more loads from what we have taken from the siege camp. Once done the wagon and oxen are yours to dispose of as you see best.'

Thomas nudged Godfrey in the ribs and gave a gentle smile.

The squire seemed not to notice the action. 'Then, young men, I want you to organise and oversee the ongoing blocking of the West Sussex Weald to the French and their allies. As you know that old soldier Ganger Greenwood is dead, killed in last night's fight. He shouldn't have been in it given he had problems just holding a sword, let alone swing it. He was a pig headed and bloody minded man and insisted on a chance to get some revenge on the French. He and his friend suffered a lot at the hands of the French when they put them to the question and I am letting John Forest go. He can no longer draw a bow after what they did to him. This leaves the men of the area without a leader; you two will combine them with your own men. John Forest will, however, be your contact in the Midhurst area; you will lead the men and lay the plans whilst he will make sure you have enough men to do whatever needs to be done. He will also gather information for you.'

The twins waited, but William of Cassingham had finished saying all he had to say and was looking unseeing into the distance, stroking his beard. The brothers dipped their heads and went off to arrange the departure for home.

'Godfrey,' Thomas said to his brother, making sure he was on the left and therefore alongside his twin's good ear. 'I was thinking about the wagon and oxen, after we have brought back the supplies Willikin has promised us.'

'Yes?'

'Well, with Sam Samuelson dead his younger brother will step up as the village's main ploughman.'

'Most likely.'

'Well, that means Sam's widow will have to rely on her brother-in-law's charity to survive and her with three youngsters to feed.'

'And?'

'Well,' Thomas put his arm around Godfrey's shoulder and pulled him closer. 'I thought it would be the right thing to do to give her the oxen and wagon so she had a means of income.'

'You coseying her up?'

Thomas just smiled and gave his brother's shoulder a squeeze. 'With no lord around at present I wouldn't have to pay merchet scot, at least not until the war is well and truly over and the Lady Maud eventually finds out that Lucy has a new husband, if she ever does that is.'

'You are serious. You'd better let her have a period of mourning before you pay court mind.'

'True, but I have always admired her. She is hard working, pleasant to talk to and nice looking as well.'

'Sounds like my Rosie.'

'True, but Lucy doesn't smell of fish.' Thomas let go of his brother and ran before Godfrey could grab him.

William looked at the huddle of trussed up French prisoners. He turned to John Little, his Forester. 'Get them on the road between Rochester and London, use the back roads where you can. Take carts if you think it best. I want them strung up by their necks one at a time from any convenient tree on the main road. You would be wise to take the last man in the line and wait till the others are out of sight before you do it; you won't want a panic. I can't afford you any more men than you already have under your command and even men whose arms are bound can be dangerous when they think their life is in danger.'

John Little continued to use an oiled rag to wipe clean his sword blade. 'I've thought of that. I will take the victim into a house and use my rough French to say that we are billeting him on a villager. Once the others are out of sight we will emerge from the cottage and teach our French friend how to dance and kick on the end of a short rope.'

'Excellent idea. Now, how close can you get to Southwark?'

'Fairly close. Why?' Little held his blade to the light in order to ensure he had got all the blood, brain and flesh off it.

'I want him,' Cassingham indicated with his head towards the man who had been left in charge of the French camp and taken prisoner by the twins. 'I want him strung up on a public gibbet as near to Southwark as you can make it. I want the French and the rebels in London to know just how far our reach is.'

'If that is what you want.'

'It is.' The squire walked over to his high ranking prisoner. *'Your men will be taken care of between Rochester and Southwark. You will be taken to London.'*

The Frenchman mentally worked his way through what William had said in his antiquated Norman French, the squire's Kent accent not helping. Finally, having grasped what he had been told, the man nodded that he had understood. *'I am Rene Artois, Lord of Nouvion; my wife, Edith, will organise my people and they will pay a good ransom to get me back.'* The plump French lord gave an ingratiating smile. *'I am highly thought of as a hero of France.'*

'Oh, don't worry,' Cassingham turned to John Little and gave a wink, *'we will ensure you get a high place of honour when we turn you off.'*

'Off?' The Frenchman creased his brow, shrugged, then put the English squire's choice of word down to his not speaking correct French.

Chapter 10: The Guardian

As the lead horsemen progressed along the muddy road they held their spears at the ready, using them from time to time to prod and poke the small bushes that ran along the roadside. In normal times the road would have had a clearway on either side but the troubled times had brought about neglect and now broom, bramble and sapling oak had started to creep from the woods towards the road. Fifty paces behind rode the main party of knights and their sergeants. In the middle of the group, riding a fine silver grey courser, rode a man whose own flowing hair matched the colour of his horse. Straight backed and stern of eye, the man watched his advance riders checking the road ahead whilst he, himself, regularly scanned the woods to the side of the road. Like the rest of his party he wore a mael hauberk covered by a surcoat half green, half yellow, emblazoned with a scarlet lion. Suddenly his advance riders pulled their horses to a halt and held up their right hands and cried '*HOLD!*'

'*See what is going on Phillip,*' the silver haired rider said to the knight at his side.

Phillip, an elegant young man with carefully maintained light brown hair that had a curl to it that did not look natural, did as his lord commanded him. As he reached the advance guard he saw the problem. In front of them, at fifty paces, stood three archers, hooded with a cloth visor covering their faces and with arrows nocked on their bowstrings, the bows held ready to be drawn.

Phillip edged his horse ahead of the guard but did not go too far ahead of them as he saw the archers take some slack out of the bowstrings as they prepared to draw and shoot. '*Who is it that dares to prevent the King's Representative from travelling the King's highway?*'

Will Greenleaf lent his head towards Godfrey, who stood in the middle of the road with his nephew Garth on his other side. 'Good Fellow Godfrey, he is speaking in Old Norman and he said "Who is it that dares to prevent the King's Representative from travelling the King's highway?", at least I think that is what he said, because Old Norman is not my own dialect you see.'

'Ask him "Which King".'

'Which King?'

The haughty young knight was losing his temper and shouted;

'King Henry of England, the third of that name, now answer me – who dares to prevent the King's Representative from travelling the King's highway?'

Godfrey spoke to the slim boy at his side 'I got that; tell him Herla of the Boxholt and I will only talk to the alpha wolf, not one of the fleas that infest his hide.'

Will cleared his throat. *'You are talking to Herla of the Boxholt and he will only speak to your leader.'*

Phillip laughed; *'He will talk to me or we will ride him down!'*

Hearing a noise behind him the young knight turned and saw the silver headed man riding his horse towards him. Coming alongside the man leant over; *'Did he say "Herla?"'* the elder man asked. *'Then I will talk to him myself.'* The man dismounted. Two of his household knights, who had ridden at his heel, started to dismount as well, but he waved them to remain in their saddles. He strode forward fearlessly towards the archers and stood not five yards in front of them and placed his hands on his hips.

Will looked to Godfrey. 'Shall I ask him who he is?'

'I think I know, but ask him anyway.'

Will coughed then addressed the tall silver haired man, *'My Lord, my master, Herla of the Boxholt, asks who you are. I am Green Leaf who will translate your French into English for him.'*

The man in the green and yellow surcoat with its red rampant lion threw back his head and laughed.

'My Lord?'

'I need no translator young Green Leaf.' The man's English carried a slight French accent. He turned his attention to Godfrey. 'Herla of the Boxholt; I am William Marshal, Earl of Pembroke, Guardian and Regent to King Henry of England!'

Godfrey un-nocked his arrow and went down on one knee, Will and Garth did the same. 'My Lord.'

The Earl of Pembroke signalled for them to rise. The archers did so then pulled down their cloth visors and pulled back their hoods. 'You speak good English my Lord,' Godfrey commented.

Marshal laughed again. 'So I should think. My grandmother was English and she made sure we learnt proper English and not the sort we might be taught by the stable boys. Now, Herla, is this it, just the three of you?'

Godfrey passed his bow and arrow to Garth, pulled up the hunting horn that hung from the green baldrick over his shoulder and blew a short tune. Archers emerged from the trees along the roadside flanking the Earl's party.

'So,' Marshal gave an appreciative nod of his head.

'Just so my Lord. One never knows just whose armed parties are travelling the King's highways these days.'

The Earl creased his brow; 'I thought we were supposed to meet you at Michaeldiver and that is another five miles or so away. From there to go to Chichester to meet with your leader, Willikin.'

'Too many spies around my Lord; one never sticks to plans that others may know about.'

'Good thinking. So, Herla, now what?'

'My Lord, we travel to Midhurst via the back paths where you are to meet Willikin of the Weald.'

'With you on foot?'

Godfrey smiled, placed the horn on his lips again and gave another short tune. Green and brown clad men came along the road from behind him with short legged ponies and gave the three archers the animals' bridles.

William Marshal, the King's Guardian and Regent, looked the horses over. 'You think those short shanked things will keep up with me and my men mounted as we are on our coursers?'

Godfrey handed his bow to a waiting woodsman and swung into the saddle of his pony. 'My Lord, on the paths and tracks we shall be travelling over it is you and yours who will have problems keeping up!'

Thomas watched Godfrey lead the party away and down a narrow track. 'Well,' he commented to Mark the Archer, 'that leaves us in charge.'

'What fun Thomas.'

'Depends on what the French are up to Mark.'

'And what that Lucy is up to?'

'Mind your own.'

'Oh I do; I mind my woman very well.'

The pair laughed and walked to where the rest of the Boxholt archers were gathered.

William Marshal, Earl of Pembroke, Guardian of King Henry III and Regent of England by the late King John's will, sat at a long table set up in the body of the Angel Inn in Midhurst. On either side of him sat his two most senior knights and advisers. Opposite him sat William, squire of Cassingham, flanked by his Reeve, Mark, and his Head Forester, John Little. Neither party said anything whilst servitors placed out plates of cold meats, jugs of ale and wine and pewter goblets. Once the table had been set the servants left, passing through doors guarded by armed men; half being Willikin's archers and half Pembroke's knights and sergeants.

William Marshal watched the departure. Once happy that they were now alone he faced the Cassingham squire. 'Willikin?'

'My Lord.'

'Willikin, I understand, and am grateful for, your full support of our young king. As you know I have been appointed Regent of England until such time as the king is old enough to reign in his own right.' Marshal gave a tired smile. 'I am now almost seventy and do not want this war to go on until I am eighty. I will see the French expelled. I will see King Henry firmly established on the throne that is his by rights. If all the world deserted the young boy, except me, do you know what I would do? I would carry him on my shoulders and walk with him thus, with legs astride, and I would be with him and never let him down from island to island and from land to land.' The old man's eyes burnt bright. 'In the King's name I have re-issued the Magna Carta. In the King's name I have offered pardons to the rebel barons and their followers. In the King's name I will restore any land that has been confiscated from them. As a result barons are returning to us, seeking to acknowledge King Henry as their liege lord. The King and his men hold the west, they hold the north, with you we hold much of the south east. Together we shall win, we shall overcome and we shall see our young king in possession of what is his.'

One of the Marshal's knights leant forward; 'Midhurst Castle?'

William of Cassingham played with the empty goblet he held in his hand. 'Is still held by men loyal to the rebel baron, Henry de Bohun, Earl of Hereford.'

'And we are sitting but a mile away from them?' the knight persisted, his English heavily accented with the nasal roundness of French.

Cassingham smiled; 'They leave us alone and we leave them alone. As long as they are able to get food and drink brought in they don't venture out far.'

John Little grunted. 'They know what will happen to them if they do!'

The Marshal put a hand on his knight's arm to prevent him from continuing the line of conversation. 'Willikin, you obviously know what is happening in the Weald, who you can trust, who you can ignore, who you must watch. You are a man who commands respect in the Weald. Word is that you command a thousand archers.'

'A thousand? Dreams are free,' John Little muttered under his breath. Cassingham kicked him under the table whilst all the time maintaining eye contact with the Regent.

The Marshal leant forward, placed his elbows on the table and steepled his hands. 'So, commander of a thousand men, let us talk about how we can help each other.'

'Help each other?' Mark Reeve spluttered when he, William and John were alone in their own lodgings at The Spread Eagle inn. 'He is the one who needs help, not us!'

William of Cassingham just sat and stroked his beard which had started to acquire silver strands in it. There was a knock at the door and he signalled John Little to open it. In came Gamble Gold, Alan of the Slaed, Will Scathlock and Godwin Wulf. 'Seats; pray be seated.' The men all found somewhere to sit and looked to the squire. 'John here would have briefed you on what Pembroke has said and what he proposes.' The four nodded agreement. 'So, what I now want to hear is what is actually happening, not what the King's Regent wants us to think is happening. Scathlock; you first.'

The red haired and clad man inclined his head. 'Well,' he began, 'The King's men may hold the north, but the Scots are still raiding across the border and holding English land. The Earl of Pembroke may hold his part of Wales but there is trouble in the Marches and the North Welsh keep poking their noses over the border. The Midlands are mainly in royalist hands and some barons are said to be switching allegiance but nothing is certain.' The scarlet man reached out to the small table in from of Cassingham and pulled a jug and cup towards himself and started to pour wine.

'That's it Will?' William asked.

'That's it.' Scathlock started to sip his drink.

Cassingham looked to Gamble Gold. The pedlar shrugged; 'I haven't been north of Watford, but I agree with Will about the Midlands. The Thames Valley is similar; I think everyone in those areas is waiting to see what the main players do before making any sort of commitment one way or the other.'

'Alan?'

'Nothing extra to add except that the King's men do seem to have the West Country firmly in their hands.'

William of Cassingham turned to Godwin Wulf, the brewer of Battersea. 'I have brought you here at great risk to yourself and not a little expense to myself. I hope you have something useful to tell me.'

Godwin's eyes smiled and he pursed his lips, 'I wouldn't have come if I hadn't.' He got up and took the jug and looked in it. 'Wine? Don't you have any decent ale or beer?'

'The only decent ale or beers come from you Godwin,' John Little said. 'So, unless you brought some of your own; no there is only wine.'

'Wine? Sheep's piss more like.'

Cassingham tapped is fingers on the table, obviously losing patience. 'Godwin – the news?'

The brewer creased his face with a big smile, knowing he had everyone's attention. 'The word in London is that almost three quarters of the English barons are still siding with Dauphin Louis. However, it is true that many are thinking seriously about the offers Pembroke is making them. Rumour, and it is only rumour mind, is that King John's bastard brother, William Longsword and his close friend the Marshal's own son, William the Younger, are set to leave the French side. It seems Louis has been too generous to his own countrymen with the spoils of war; castles, land and plunder, and not generous enough to the rebel barons.' Godwin sniffed the jug of wine and turned his nose up. 'Interestingly I did hear that your good friend, Hubert de Burgh, over at Dover Castle,

183

was advised by others on the Regency Council, and Pembroke is only one of four Regents King John nominated despite what he may have said to you, de Burgh was advised to surrender said castle as the royalists couldn't help him anymore. I also picked up word that Louis had offered de Burgh a decent backhander to do just that.'

William of Cassingham's eyes opened wide; 'News to me. Did your contact say if he had accepted the advice and offer?'

Godwin took another disparaging sniff of the wine and shoved the jug to Scathlock. 'It seems he took the offer to the garrison, but they all turned it down; at least that's what I was told. There is more: at the last meeting of the Brewer's Guild two members were saying that they had been told to cancel deliveries to Dover and rather send the drays to Hertford. Now all this is a long way from London, so the size of the army heading that way must be more than the locals can supply with drink. My guess is that the bulk of the French will be outside Hertford castle afore long.'

'Thank you Godwin – I shall see if we can find you some ale to drink. John?'

The tall man left to search for ale.

Cassingham leant towards his Reeve, 'Gamble; find the Regent and let him know about Hertford. Mark, find out what is happening at Dover. If the French army is leaving Dover alone and moving to Hertford, de Burgh might like a hand from our men of Kent to see what new supplies the French camp has after we raided it. He may need a hand to burn the remains of the camp to the ground so that if they return they will have to start from scratch.'

Mark started to get up; 'It wouldn't hurt Master if we pulled all the English folk out of Dover and its surrounds and destroyed anything and everything for miles around so any returning French would have to bring all their supplies in in order to set up another siege.'

'Good thinking Mark. Get word to de Burgh. We can find homes for the refugees of Dover in the villages in the Kentish Weald and feed them on some of our own plunder from the French camp.'

'A truce?'

'Yes Robin,' Gamble confirmed as he took a mug of mulled ale from Godfrey. 'A truce from St Thomas' day till The Conversion of St Paul.'

'Time for ploughing.' Godfrey chinked his pottery mug against that of his brother's.

'Time for courting!' Thomas winked at his twin.

Chapter 11: Crusade

'Just as I like a church service,' Thomas blinked as he emerged from Iping's small church of St Mary.

'Short and to the point?' his brother Godfrey asked.

'Exactly. The sermon in English is fine but all that Latin?'

'It's all foreign.'

'Just as well we have great granfer's new testament glosses.'

'True, at least we can check to see if what the priest says is gospel.'

Godfrey gave a short barking laugh then his lop sided grin. 'Even having that is not such a blessing these days.'

'The English is very old; so many words we never use these days and often the words are in a back to front manner.' Thomas shook his head.

'Apparently it originally came from the Archbishop of Canterbury's library at Croydon at the time of the first King Henry. It is said that our ancestor, old Godfrew of Garrett, otherwise known as Wulf the Norman slayer, was a monk there.'

The twins stopped at the gate to the church yard and nodded and smiled at other villagers as they passed by.

Thomas picked some lichen off the wooden frame of the gate. 'I suppose our family have always been a bit light handed.'

'Ah; there you two are.' The twins turned to see Rose the wife of John of Chichester, the priest of Trottingham. 'My husband would like a word with you two before he moves on to take a service at Steadham's St James'.'

'How many churches is he looking after these days Rose,' Thomas gave the priest's wife a beguiling smile.

'Too many,' she replied, ignoring the inviting eyes Thomas was making at her. 'All this trouble and strife and then all the priests disappearing to act as chaplains to their lords and their war bands.'

'Or just clearing off,' Godfrey added caustically.

'Or just clearing off,' Rose agreed as she set off back to the stone church expecting the twins to follow her. Thomas looked to his brother, shrugged and followed at a distance that allowed him to appreciate Rose's swaying hips. Godfrey gave his brother a disapproving look and a nudge in the ribs; Thomas just changed his smile into a leer.

'I hope he doesn't want us to move the weapons we have hidden in that sarcophagus at his own church at Trottingham,' Godfrey whispered. 'We don't have anywhere in our own village to hide them.' Thomas ignored his brother and continued to watch the attractive plump body of the priest's wife as she walked ahead of them.

Inside the small Saxon stone church John of Chichester was clearing away the holy vessels from the altar with the help of Will Greenleaf, who had acted as altar boy that day, and Elfwyn the blacksmith's wife. As he worked John quietly chanted a psalm and Will added a descant to it. Rather than disturb them the twins held back, but the priest's wife had no such qualms.

'John, I have the Wulfson twins here.'

'Ah, thank you Rose,' John turned and sketched a blessing over the brothers. 'News cousins, news.' The priest looked to see if Will and Elfwyn had finished their tasks, smiled, blessed them and indicated to the door for them to leave. 'Rose, can you make sure they don't linger?' he asked once the pair were out of earshot. 'I doubt Elfwyn would but that young Will is a curious boy and it would be best if he heard the news from the Wulfsons with all the others of their band rather than half hear and start rumours.'

'If you say so husband,' Rose left and the twins and the priest heard her give a clucking sound as she shooed Will out into the church yard away from the door.

'That boy,' John of Chichester, shook his head.

'Is very useful to us.' Thomas folded his arms across his chest.

'We would have problems managing without him.' Godfrey mimicked his brother's action.

'It is no criticism, but his cat like curiosity may get him into trouble one day.' The priest took his gaze away from the door where his wife now stood guard. 'Right, Godfrey and Thomas, or should I say Herla and Robin?'

'We have given up the cover names Father. The French don't venture this way these days and we are no longer worried about informers,' Thomas advised.

'Though brother,' Godfrey glanced at Thomas, 'you do rather like being "Robin" don't you.'

'Only outside our own patch.'

'Now, now, boys,' John said with an exasperated voice, knowing how quickly the twins could start a teasing that quickly descended into bickering. 'The news.' He cleared his voice. 'I have had news from the Bishop of Chichester, Richard Poore, one of the late King John's supporters. He has advised that Pope Innocent, on the recommendation of his Legate, Cardinal Guala Bicchieri, has declared the Dauphin Louis excommunicate and thus all who fight against him are crusaders.'

'Oh great: that will win the war for us,' Thomas' voice had a very sceptical edge to it.

'Well,' John hastily threw in, 'eleven of the Bishops who supported the rebel barons have come back to the King's grace.'

This time it was Godfrey's turn to speak and he did so with a voice that dripped sarcasm. 'Right eleven bishops have changed side, I don't suppose they brought eleven thousand men over with them? We are getting a mite short of fighters.'

188

'Brothers, please,' John the priest pleaded. 'It is a crusade, which means that if you die you will go straight to heaven with all your sins forgiven.'

'Can't say I have read that in the gospels' Thomas examined his finger nails.

'Hush Thomas,' the priest put his finger to his lips. 'Many would take the fact that you have holy writ, albeit in Old English, makes you a heretic.'

'If they can read it, let alone understand it!' Godfrey laughed.

'Actually,' John's brow furrowed, 'I did hear that Cardinal Bicchieri can read Old English and has set about collecting manuscripts in that language, but I digress.' He turned his full attention back to the twins. 'As crusaders you, and your men, are to wear a white cross on your breast. Isn't that wonderful?'

'A white cross?' Thomas asked.

'On our breast?' Godfrey added.

'Yes; isn't it wonderful boys?'

'I don't suppose you know the French for "Crossbowmen: Shoot Here" do you?' Thomas laughed and his twin joined in, much to the consternation of the priest.

'The truce is over. Willikin says for you to gather as many men as you can and get them down to Plumpton Green.' Alan atte Slaed walked alongside Godfrey as he ploughed behind his team of six oxen.

'Aren't you supposed to sing that in a clever song that we then have to work out the meaning of?'

189

'No time, besides the need for subterfuge has gone.' The jongleur stumbled over a clod of earth in the furrow he was walking in. 'Can you get word out so I can move to the next band leader?'

'I suppose so; I assume you have let John Forest at Midhurst know?'

'Yes.'

'Then move on.' Godfrey gave his attention to his plough boy leading the team. 'Will? Get over to Wulfbearding quick and ask old Limp Leg if he and his boy can finish this ploughing for me. I'll let him borrow our team for free in exchange.'

'Well?' William of Cassingham was for once at his home manor and dressed in decent clothes, unlike the drab coloured hunting gear he wore when in the field.

John Little in his road dusty clothes came and stood by the fire in the central hearth of the great hall. 'That Battersea brewer's man has just confirmed that Louis the Frenchman is definitely on the move and heading, in force on the road down towards Brighthelmestone.'

'So,' William went and joined his Forester. 'It seems the rumour that Godwin told us about the Dauphin running out of men and money might be true.'

'So also may the rumour that he is having to go back to France to raise the extra troops and funds in order to continue.' Little held out his chilled hands to the fire's warmth.

'The rebel barons won't like that.'

'God willing he won't even come back.'

The heavy wool hanging that covered the door into the hall blew inwards as Mark, Cassingham's Reeve, entered bringing cold air in with him. 'Have you heard? Louis is heading to the coast through the Weald.'

'Yes Mark,' William assured him, 'the brewer's man told you, as he seems to have told everyone else in the place. The question is, just where is the Dauphin headed? It can't be Rye as that sea dog Philip d'Albabini has taken it for the King and his fleet is blockading the coast. Besides, why take the road to Brighthelmeston? We know he can't be headed anywhere other than the south coast as Hubert de Burgh has left Dover Castle and is sailing another fleet off the Kent and Essex coasts.'

'Ah,' Mark threw back his cloak and held his own hands to the fire. 'But are either of the fleets capable of tackling Eustace the Monk?'

William turned his back to the fire and lifted his over shirt to warm his buttocks. 'The more relevant question is: "are we capable of stopping Louis from reaching the coast"? If my spies are correct the Frenchy Prince has gathered most of his force together to force his way through the Weald. William Marshal, the King's Regent, may think we have a thousand archers but three to four hundred is the better figure, and even that depends on whether word can be got to them all in time.'

'You have already sent word though, haven't you?' Little, having decided his hands were now warm enough, had joined his master in toasting his nether regions.

William smiled. 'Just because you have been out and about John does not mean I have spent my entire time sitting around warming my body by the fire.' He dropped his over shirt down and stepped away from the heat. 'Word has been sent. It will take some days to get folk where I want them. You and the men of Kent will come over into Surrey and start attacking the French rearguard as soon as they leave Reigate. Take as many men as you can get, strip our lookouts; I need numbers. Just be careful about exposing our forces though; I don't want a battle out in the open – that is not what you do with archers, not unless you have more than enough men-at-arms to support them. Start the attacks from Reigate but only harass the French. No big operations till they get into the Weald. After they have passed through an area recruit locals and fell trees and break bridges behind them.' The squire turned to his Reeve. 'Mark? Leave the fire and come here. Right, now, you will take the Kentish men and the men of East Sussex and get into Winchelsea. My guess is that Louis will head there with Rye taken and hopefully us blocking his way to Southampton and Portsmouth. Get the folk out. I have sent word via Gamble Gold to d'Albabini asking him to take the town's folk on board his ships and move them down the coast to safety. Before they go get them to strip the place of food and supplies. See Midge Miller and get him to come with you as I want the Winchelsea mills destroyed and he will know how best to do that. I will give you enough money to compensate the mill owners.'

'French gold and silver?' Mark asked him.

'Not much of it left, but I will spend it where I think it will get the best result.'

'What are the West Sussex men going to be doing? I don't want to clash with them; there is nothing worse than to shoot your own men.'

William gave Mark a hard look.

The Reeve of Cassingham cast his eyes down; 'I wasn't referring to Harold Harefoot's action in Canterbury.'

'Good: cruel necessity, even the twins understood that. Which brings me to the West Sussex men; the twins will lead them and use nuisance tactics to keep the French on their toes. Lewes Castle is held for the rebels and it would be nice to get the French bottled up there for a while whilst we regroup.'

'They won't stay there long,' John Little, his woollen clothes starting to smell of wood smoke and beginning to scorch, moved away from the hearth. 'We have made sure that place isn't getting much fresh food and, if the French army is as big as we think, they will soon eat the place clean. Besides there isn't that much space for an army to camp.'

'That,' William advised him, 'is what I am expecting, but if we can get enough men in place we can deny the French the road to Southampton and Portsmouth and force them to move on to Winchelsea which, if Mark has done his job, will be bare and we may have a good chance to starve them into submission.'

'Brilliant if it happens Master,' Mark looked to John Little. 'Wouldn't you say?'

'If we can make it happen and to do that we need men, wouldn't you agree Master?'

William, squire of Cassingham, nodded his agreement. 'Men and luck. Everything we do needs both: men and luck.'

'I'm getting tired of this big brother,' Thomas prodded the ground with a pointed twig turning the earth's hard crust into dust. 'I mean, we are getting more and more like soldiers and less and less like farmers and woodsmen.'

Godfrey grunted and rolled over on the hard ground to face his twin. 'You want the same to happen now as happened in Willie the Bastard's time? All our lands to be given to foreigners?'

'Of course not.'

'Then, little brother, we have to fight and kick the buggers out.'

'If only there wasn't all this waiting around, killing time, waiting for orders, waiting for them to change, waiting, waiting, waiting.'

'Keep your voice down,' Godfrey looked over the rows of bivouacs made of deer skins, four skins to a tent, four men to a tent. 'Most of the camp are sleeping and maybe we should turn in too.'

'Ah, yes, we are true soldiers now; "at every opportunity a soldier should eat, sleep and shit for he never knows when the next chance to do so will come".'

'Shut up Thomas and get in the tent for a sleep.'

'I think I will have a shit first.' Thomas loosened his hunting knife and set off to find a place to dig a hole and relieve himself.

Thomas came back wiping his knife blade on some dock leaves. 'You will never guess who was digging a shit hole next me; that bloody Harold Harefoot, that's who.'

'You don't like him much do you brother.' Godfrey, keeping his voice low, was trying to use his cloak to act as a curtain to the

194

small tent he and Thomas shared with Mark Archer and Garth Robertson.

'No I don't'

Godfrey examined his rude attempt to provide a means of keeping the chill winter wind out. 'I suppose none of us will really get over Harold shooting Sam Samuelson in Canterbury.'

'I think we all knew we were disposable on that raid to rescue Ganger and John.'

'Which is why I wasn't happy about having Garth with us. I mean, he is our sister Edith's only son. I still feel that we should have tried to save Sam even if it meant putting more of us at risk.'

'Oh I don't know.' Thomas, who was far better at knots than his brother, took over securing the cloak to the staves that acted as the poles of the deer skin tent. 'Given how many of them there were and how few of us, I doubt we could have saved him. In fact, Harold shooting him was what had to be done. I think we all knew it was for the best. Anyone the French caught would be tortured to get information from them. After that they would string you up by the neck to dance on a short rope, so Sam getting killed with a clean arrow shot was something of a mercy. Besides, it has had another advantage.'

'Lucy?'

'Lucy.'

'So, if you don't dislike him for killing Sam, and are happy that he has created a situation where you can court Sam's widow. So why do you dislike him?'

'That pilgrim's medal. He never did pray at St Thomas' shrine so he isn't entitled to wear it.'

William of Cassingham back in his dowdy and worn hunting clothes, though with a jaunty hunting cap complete with a peacock feather in the fancy brightly coloured chequered hat band, stood at the entrance to the Wulfson's tent holding back the cloak that had sealed its opening. 'If I were a Frenchman you would all be dead by now.'

Thomas opened a sleep blocked eye. 'Willikin if you were French we would have smelt you long before you got to our tent.'

'Garlic and stale urine; gives them away every time.' Godfrey raised his head from under the cloak he had been sharing with his twin.

'Cheap perfume,' Mark contributed from the rear of the tent. 'They stink of that too.'

'A rebel Englishman would have had a better chance Good Fellow Willikin,' Garth contributed, his voice muffled by the fact that he had a second hood on his head that was reversed to cover his face.

Cassingham started to dismantle the tent over the heads of its occupants, unlacing the centre seam that held the pairs of deer skin, exposing the four longbows that made up the structure's central ridge. 'No time for sleep I need you and all your men to get on the move. I want you to annoy the French vanguard. We need to stop them heading for Southampton or Portsmouth. As an alternative they may head for Newhaven. I want them driven east towards Winchelsea. Harass them but don't get involved in any pitched battles. Send men down towards Beddingham and get the road blocked; drive them to the downs.'

'We have folk tending sheep on that part of the downs.' Thomas, having pulled himself together, had taken over the dismantling of the tent whilst Mark and Garth had left to rouse the other men.

'Part of our rent Willikin.' Godfrey had taken to trying to undo the knots his cloak still had in it after having been cast aside by his leader.

'Word has been sent for them to get the sheep off the downs and into the marshes near Romney.' The squire stood with folded arms watching the twins complete the breakdown of their bivouac. 'The last thing I want for the French, or their rebel English friends, is to get food on the move. Which brings me to another point; as well as making a nuisance of yourselves with the French vanguard see if you can appropriate some of their supply wagons- the less food they have available to them, the better it suits our plans.'

'Are you going to be leading us on this Willikin?' Thomas had started to roll his gear into his deer skin before securing it with leather thongs.

'No. You two will oversee this part of our operation. I am on my way to meet the Regent. One can only do so much by messenger and this game of ours is too critical to risk any misunderstandings or lack of co-ordination.' With that William of Cassingham inclined his head to the twins and set off to gain his horse.

'In charge!' Thomas stood tall, with his hands on his hips.

'Yes, but don't forget I am the eldest so that means I am in charge of you little brother.'

'As always,' Thomas muttered to himself.

'Always the wait,' Thomas eased his buttocks on the hard ground.

197

'Nothing new,' Godfrey agreed. 'And now it seems we will have high wind to contend with,' he looked across the roadway at the bending trees on the other side.

'That and the fact that some bright spark has been assiduous with his duties and, despite the recent and current wars, has keep the road clear of trees fifty paces either side.'

Mark Archer wandered over and sat with the twins 'Probably has his name down for being the next Sheriff.'

'If he has picked the right side,' Thomas commented as he massaged his left cheek.

'Well,' Godfrey, who was lying on his side, eased his own body into a more comfortable position, 'he can always change sides.'

'Like so many others,' Mark agreed.

Thomas returned to his original sitting position and pulled his cloak closer, trapping the front edge under his feet. 'Which is something we won't be doing; we know where we stand in this fight.'

'Hang on,'

'What Godfrey?' Thomas had a concerned look on his face. 'You are not thinking of blowing in the wind like yonder tree?'

'No, I thought I heard someone coming.'

Thomas shook his head in wonder; 'You? Heard something? With your hearing? I don't think ….'

'They are coming.' Slim young Will Greenleaf appeared from behind the group.

'One day young man you will get shot creeping up on folk,' Thomas warned.

Will gave a gentle smile and ran his hand over his black newly cropped hair. 'I am good aren't I! No, Good Fellows, the French are coming. A screen of crossbowmen on foot then about twenty horsemen. After them come about a dozen ox wagons.'

Godfrey eased himself into a sitting position. 'How far away?'

'Oh,' Will stepped forward towards the road, waiting for the others to follow him. Once he had his audience the lad peered north up the road. 'About five hundred yards away I think. You won't see them for a while given the bends in the road.'

Godfrey followed the youth's gaze. 'How much distance between the footmen and the horses?'

'About a hundred and twenty yards. After the horsemen are the wagons with supplies on, all with men-at-arms alongside them, then more horsemen followed by a huge number of infantry.'

Godfrey turned to his brother; ' What do you think Thomas? Let the first lot through then cut them off from the rest? Or take the first lot on to block the road?'

Thomas stroked his chin, thinking. 'Will; how much space between the wagons and the second lot of horsemen?'

'A fairly big gap; I think the wind is blowing too much dust from the road at them for them to want to get too close.'

Thomas thought some more. 'In that case big brother we can do both. Let the screen and the horsemen through, block the road behind the wagons. Leave the rest of the column to clear the road whilst we sort out the horsemen.'

Godfrey screwed up his face. 'Hmm, but the crossbowmen; they can get into the woods after us. What do we do about them?'

199

'Easy.' Thomas started to lead the party back into the cover of the trees. 'We don't need, or want, the horses so drive them up the road into the crossbowmen.'

'It could work little brother.'

'It has to because if we spend too much time trying to take them out before the horsemen we will have no element of surprise and I suspect the cavalry will fall back and try and get more of their infantry forward to take us on.'

'It has to be worth a try I guess.' Godfrey turned to Will; 'Where is Garth?'

'Still tracking the lead French Good Fellow.'

'Get him to drop back with a handful of men and find a way of blocking the road after the wagons have passed. I don't know how he can do it with the roadside having been cleared, but he has to think of something.'

The dark youth gave a chuckle, 'Oh I have an idea. I saw something that may be of use.'

'Then get going. Thomas you take half our men and get to the other side of the road a hundred yards ahead of me.'

'Right; Mark with me and get the lads sorted.'

Garth looked at Will Greenleaf with a frown on his face. 'Are you sure? Normally bee skeps are on the ground.'

'Honestly, I saw them just back over there in the clearing - half a dozen of them and they are on what looks like stools. I think the lack of flowers around here means that they can't leave their bees in one place for too long so they have to move the skeps around.'

200

'Well, even so, we will have to be very careful moving them: I hate getting stung.'

The ox wagons rolled past the watchers hidden in the trees and fern. One of the footmen walking alongside the last wagon glanced at the straw skeps on their unusual stands. He shrugged his shoulders at the English peculiarity, spat out some dust infused phlegm and trudged on his footsore way.

The watchers waited as the road dust settled leaving just a few dust motes hanging in the air. Still they waited then, at last, they heard the jingle of horse harness and then the snort and iron shod clomp of the horses themselves. As the first rank of three horsemen came level with the first skep Will stood, whirled his sling around his head and then let fly a stone; across the road Garth hurled a lump of mud. Both stone and mud hit the eke off the top of the skeps that had been aimed at; bees flew from the open tops of the skeps. Other hidden archers stood and threw mud and stones at the remaining skeps, knocking them over and causing angry bees to swarm from them.

The lead French horsemen and their mounts were soon encased with angry bees and they turned trying to find an escape route, but they were all blocked by the following riders who, having seen what had happened in front of them, were also trying to get out of the way of the angry bees whose homes had been broken or knocked over.

Garth watched the chaos. 'Time to get out of here Will.'

'Not just yet,' the youth declaimed as he and the other archers picked up their braced bows and loosed arrows into the rear riders of the milling mass of cavalry on the road.

'Now I said.' Garth went along grabbing archers and shoving them towards the almost unmarked path that lead southwards towards the rest of the band. 'We may be needed to help my uncles take care of the lead Frenchies.'

A cuckoo called.

'Bloody Granfer Gilbert,' hidden archers muttered along the line commanded by Godfrey. They watched as a dozen crossbowmen approached round the tight bend in the road. The Frenchmen stopped and redressed their line whilst one man on each side stepped ahead and looked into the trees at the edge of the cleared roadside. The Frenchmen continued along the road cautiously, constantly looking into the trees. Still the hidden archers watched, arrows nocked on bowstring, faces hidden by low pulled hoods and high pulled cloth visors leaving only their eyes and weathered cheekbones visible. Again a cuckoo called, this time followed by a closer woodpecker "knock" and then another even closer. Godfrey looked down at the arrow with its specially cut fletching that sat on his bowstring. The horsemen rode by unaware they were being watched. Further down the column were more riders who had their heads down trying to keep the road dust from their eyes. Godfrey waited till there was only three rows of three riders left to pass him before he lent forward, pushed his left arm forward and then pulled his bowstring back with three fingers on his right hand then pulled himself upright using the muscles of his back whilst using his shoulder blade muscles to take the load as he pulled the bowstring back to his ear and then rolled the string off his fingers. The arrow sped forward making a loud buzzing sound as it flew and arched towards its target of the nearside rider in front of him. Hearing the sound of the buzzing arrow the other archers nocked and loosed their own arrows, targeting the riders rather than the horses, which is what they would normally have done. More arrows flew and soon the rearmost riders had all been hit with most now on the ground. The front ranks broke into a gallop, clearing a hundred yards before, on command from their Captain, they started to turn in order to charge back down from whence they had come. It was then that the archers on the other side of the road, under Thomas stepped clear of their cover and loosed volleys into them, spilling riders into the dust.

The crossbowmen walking ahead as a screen were round a bend in the road when they heard the cries and screams behind them. They turned and started to run back to help rescue their comrades.

Godfrey and his men ran up the road from the opposite direction, they changed arrows from those with a bodkin head to those with a hunting swallow head and started shooting at the horses causing them to charge down the road and crash into and run down the crossbowmen.

'Jack, Albert, Charlie, Richard,' Thomas called out. 'Get into the woods – I saw a couple of them run into the trees the other side of the road, hunt them down. Remember: no survivors!'

Godfrey came up to his brother; 'All down?'

'I hope so. We have the wagon escort and drivers to sort out next.'

The brothers called their men together, with the exception of the hunters and jogged down either side of the road. Ahead of them stood the ox wagons, deserted.

'Bugger,' muttered Thomas at the head of his line of archers.

'They got away,' his twin called across from the other side of the road.

'No they didn't,' came a distant cry.

'Garth?'

'Yes, it's me and we got them all.' The twins' nephew, followed by his handful of men walked up the road towards them with the thin, cloud shaded winter sun, reflecting off their newly acquired swords, some of the archers with two. 'Are we supposed to lop heads Uncles?'

'I think Willikin would like it but we haven't time. We only have enough time to take swords and spears from the fallen.' Godfrey turned and started examining the contents of the wagons. 'Wheat and barley: good. Garth, you and your men get these wagons off the next side turning and hidden in the nearest hamlet or village. Then get you down to us.'

'Where will that be uncle?'

'Patcham.'

Godfrey and Thomas stood alongside John Forest of Midhurst and watched as Patcham's villagers finished pushing carts and wagons together in a double row to block the full one hundred yards of road and clearway. The front row of wagons had been turned on their sides. 'It has taken some effort to find enough wagons to do this, let alone persuade the owners to part with them.'

204

Godfrey turned to the old Forester, 'It is much appreciated John.'

'Much appreciated,' Thomas confirmed.

'I can no longer draw a bow, but I do have my uses.'

Godfrey gave his lopsided smile. 'You certainly have John: excellent organisation.'

'Are the French close behind you?'

Godfrey looked to Thomas and they both shrugged.

'We broke some bridges and spread some brambles across sections of the road,' Godfrey advised.

'Enough to slow them but not enough to stop them; we were told not to stop them,' Thomas contributed before taking the stopper from his costrel and drinking some of the now luke warm water it contained.

'Willikin did say that others would completely destroy the bridges and fell trees to close the road after the last of the French had passed; using local folk rather than archers.' Godfrey rubbed a tired hand over his face.

Forest pointed to the left hand side of the road in front of them. 'Willikin sent us a load of caltrop so I have heavily sown them along there, partly to protect us from a cavalry charge, but mainly to stop them trying to use the tracks on that side. Also,' he indicated to the right, 'some over that side but I have done it in such a way as they will take the Lewes road as the sensible option.'

'They are French,' Thomas reminded him.

'So sensibility doesn't always come into it.'

'True,' John agreed. 'But with the wagons and carts blocking this road they have little choice. The spears you have brought in, some of which we have laced the wagons with, will help discourage them from using horses against us and, hopefully, your archers will keep their infantry off us. Willikin wants them in Lewes, so to Lewes they will be encouraged to go. Once they settle there we will have to get to Beddingham to stop them going down to Newhaven. I have already set the villagers there to making hazel hurdles to use in blocking the road. We have to do that given their lack of wagons – it is a poor place.'

'Well, with about a hundred archers we can't stop them if they are really determined to smash their way through. Thomas?'

'Agreed, even with the bundles of arrows Willikin has sent us. It all depends on how many men do they want to lose when Lewes offers a safe haven and the chance of gaining a better sea port at Winchelsea?'

'Hopefully, they will not want to lose too many.' John left the twins to find food and drink for their men whilst he double checked the work the local villagers had been doing.

Thomas was about to put the last piece of hard cheese into his mouth when the cry went up that the French could be seen. He stood up from behind the tipped up wagon that had been his shelter and peered through the gap between it and its adjacent upturned wagon. At extreme arrow shot stood an extended row of crossbowmen being dressed by an officer. 'It looks like we have visitors big brother.'

'They took their time.' Godfrey pushed himself upright and joined Thomas. 'Let's see what they do.'

'I'll send word along the line to make sure everyone has their bow braced.'

'While you are at it get Garth to get the locals to walk up and down between the overturned wagons and the next row. If they hold the spears high; it might make it look as if we are much stronger than we are as all the French will see are the spear points.'

Ahead the crossbowmen, now accompanied by others holding a pavise each, slowly and cautiously advanced towards the barricade.

'I don't like the look of those big shields big brother, those buggers can hide behind them and then pop up and shoot and then drop back behind whilst they re-load.'

'I don't like that Harold Harefoot, but I do wish he were here now Thomas, I just wish he were here now.'

'We do have Henry the Hunter of Crowhurst – he's a good shot.'

'Get Will to go find him; him and Mark Archer.'

'Right.' Thomas ran off to find Will.

'Trouble Uncle?' Garth Wulfson walked up tucking arrows into his belt.

'Those big shields.'

'Pavise.'

'That's it parvies.'

Garth rolled his eyes and shook his head at his uncle's perverse determination to mispronounce any word not English. 'How to get arrows into the men behind them?'

'Exactly nephew.'

'Drop shots.'

'Tried it once and failed.'

'The men over Lingfield know how to do it: it is their village game for May Day. You know: drop shot the arrow and the one nearest the nosegay gets to kiss the May Queen.'

'Lingfield's May games? Yes: I'd forgotten that the Surrey men play strange games. Find Michael the Mouse and Gasper the Ghost, get them to bring their village men over – Gasper is not from Lingfield, but he is from Dorman's Land, the next village and I bet they know how to do a drop shot, if only to best the Lingfield men at their own game.'

A volley of crossbow bolts hammered into the upturned wagons causing men to duck, even though the wagons were higher than even the tallest amongst the archers. Godfrey peered through the gap between two wagons and judged the distance between him and the French who had dodged behind their pavise to reload their crossbows. He nocked an arrow and waited. The crossbowmen, on a shouted order stepped to the side of their covering pavise and aimed. Godfrey drew, loosed and instantly pulled back behind the wagon bed. His arrow bounced off the helmet of one of the Frenchmen just as another salvo of bolts slammed into the upturned wagons. Other arrows from the English landed near the crossbowmen or struck pavise, but no Frenchman was killed or even injured.

Garth ran up and skidded to a dusty halt. 'Michael and Gasper and their boys are on the way.'

'Right, now get a handful of men from the Boxholt band and work into the woods over the far left. There is a road there. It has been sprinkled with caltrops but, even so, the French may try to take that route rather than go to Lewes. Pick off any that try.' The youth started off. 'Oh,' Godfrey called after him. 'Find Thomas and see if he has found the marksmen yet – it is urgent as those bastards are creeping forward.' As he spoke another volley hit home and the depth the bolts had penetrated the wooden floor of the upturned wagon was markedly deeper than the ones from the earlier salvoes.

'You looking for me brother.' Thomas with two men in tow came from the opposite direction to that Godfrey was looking.

'About time little brother.' Godfrey grabbed the tunics of Mark and Henry and pushed them to the gaps between the nearest wagons.

'Hmm,' Henry watched as the pavise holders with the crossbowmen crouched behind them advanced five yards and then knelt holding the big shields in front of them. 'What do you think Mark?'

'A farthing I can get one of the bowmen and you can't.'

'You are on.'

Both the men pulled a bodkin headed arrow out from their belt, nocked it, took some of the strain on the string and waited. The crossbowmen, obviously now nervous about being shot, stood up from behind their pavise and aimed. Henry and Mark moved to get a clear shot through the gap in the wagons, drew to the ear and loosed. Nocked another arrow and loosed again before getting back into cover as crossbow bolts hammered home.

'One each,' Henry observed. 'A draw. Same again next time?'

'Did you notice though, infantry are coming forward.'

Godfrey moved Mark out of the way. 'Bugger. I wondered what they were up too.'

Thomas joined his brother. 'Oh yes, the crossbowmen are just out there to make us keep our heads down whilst they get infantry ready to charge and force the barricade.'

'Clever, Godfrey, clever.' Mark took over the gap and stood ready to shoot again.

Will tugged at Thomas' sleeve,' I can't find – oh, there they are.'

'Yes Will there they are. Now, go chase up Gasper and Michael the Mouse, FAST!'

The slim dark youth shot off and called out for the Surrey men as he ran.

The crossbowmen, having advanced, stood and aimed. Henry and Mark drew and loosed two arrows off, but only Mark pulled back under cover. Henry, with two bolts in his chest, staggered back and collapsed on the ground making mewling sounds, his legs twitching and jerking.

'Oh God,' Godfrey pulled the fallen archer clear and behind a wagon. The Crowhurst man looked at Godfrey, his eyes widening as red froth ringed his lips. Henry gave a final twitch and then fell limp.

'Leave him big brother, the Surrey men are here.'

Godfrey lowered Henry to the ground and went to meet Michael and Gasper who led a band of twenty men. 'You can all do drop shots?'

'Clout shooting we calls it,' Michael, a small rodent looking man with sharp pointed features was looking at Henry whilst talking to Godfrey.

'Local sport in Surrey, about time you Sussex men learnt eh Michael?' Gasper added in his deep voice.

Thomas watched as the pavise and crossbowmen started to make another advance, 'Well you can teach us. Have a look at these and tell us if you can drop arrows down on them – you will have to do it blind from behind the wagons as we can't risk you exposing yourselves.'

'Exposing ourselves?' Michael looked at the crossbow teams as the pavise were jammed into the ground. 'We don't do that in Surrey, we leave that sort of rudeness to Sussex men.'

'Get taken before the Hundred Moot for that sort of behaviour in Surrey.' Gasper called back as he, too judged the distance to the targets.

'Mind Gasper, I do hear that Sussex women don't mind that sort of thing: eighty yards.'

'That's 'cos Sussex men are of such small build they can't see what is being shewn them! Eighty yards it is.'

The two Surrey men stood back as another shower of crossbow bolts flew towards the English.

Michael turned to Godfrey; 'They reload before advancing?'

'Yes.'

'Right lads, spread out eighty yards range, clout shots it is, look sharp now.'

The men of Surrey spread out, and nocked arrows. Gasper looked to Michael who quickly checked that the French had not moved forward yet. Michael nodded. Gasper pushed his bow forward took the strain on his string. 'Eighty yards, DRAW,' the men pulled back on the bowstrings and using their back muscles pulled the strings back to their ears as they lifted their bows up at a high angle. 'LOOSE!' Twenty one arrows soared up, reached similar heights and then plunged down onto the French below.

Michael peered at the targets. 'Again, quickly and Alan and Tingle you are shooting short it is eighty not seventy five yards.'

'NOCK, DRAW, LOOSE!'

Michael took another look. 'They are moving forward again so hold. We want them stationary.'

Thomas found Godfrey's good ear. 'Brother, I will get some of our men together; if they can see what angle the Surries are holding their bows at they can copy them and learn this "clout" shooting.'

'Go Thomas; good idea.'

Michael clucked his tongue. 'Come on little Frenchies, come on. Get into position so we can kill you. Ah,' he smiled. 'That's better. Even numbers seventy yards, odd numbers seventy three.'

'That's precise,' Godfrey commented.

'We,' the Mouse insisted, 'are precise men in Surrey.'

Gasper looked to Michael and got the nod.

'NOCK, DRAW, LOOSE.'

'Nigel,' Michael called. 'You are an "odd" not an "even".'

'Sorry.'

'Yes, well, you still managed to hit one,' the Mouse conceded. 'Ah, they run, the few left, they run.' Three arrows in your own time, increasing range: GO'

Arrows flew and although the twins saw few hit anyone, the shafts created a satisfying confusion. The French infantry started an advance, allowing the fleeing crossbow teams that remained through their ranks. Godfrey turned to Thomas; 'Get one of our

212

Sussex men alongside each Surrey man and get them to match the
bow angle when they draw.'

'You heard that, get into the line!' Thomas shouted.

'Hundred and fifty yards,' Michael called, sitting on top of one of
the over turned wagons the better to see now that the threat of
being shot by a crossbow had gone.

'On my command,' Gilbert called. 'One on the string.'

'One and forty.'

'One and forty; DRAW.' The Sussex men watched their Surrey
counterparts and mimicked them. 'LOOSE!'

'One and thirty five.'

'NOCK, DRAW, LOOSE.'

'One and thirty.'

'NOCK, DRAW, LOOSE.'

'They are now starting to run at us; one and ten.'

'NOCK, DRAW, LOOSE.'

'They have stopped; again.'

'NOCK, DRAW, LOOSE.'

'They fall back.'

'In your own time three arrows, ranges over one ten.'

Godfrey and Thomas joined Michael the Mouse on the top of the
wagon and watched as the French, encouraged by the random fall
of arrows, pulled back to their start point in good order and then
halted out of arrow range. Pushing their way through the foot
soldiers came three horsemen who, even at two hundred yards,
looked impressive in highly polished armour and brightly coloured
surcoats. The riders looked towards the English lines, the central
rider standing in his stirrups.

'Again, I wish that Harefoot was here,' Godfrey conceded.

'I think he's the only man who could hit that fancy French cockerel at that range.' Thomas agreed.

Mark eased his way between the wagons and looked at the French horsemen.

'A groat if you hit him Mark.'

'Thomas, I would want a shilling if I did.'

'Are you going to try Mark?'

'No Godfrey, I would only be wasting an arrow.'

The French horsemen, after a short discussion, turned and rode back through the infantry. Slowly the French re-organised themselves and started to progress down the Lewes road.

'Ah, Garth.' Godfrey jumped down. 'Any problems?'

'No Uncle, a small patrol of horsemen did try a probe, but we soon discouraged them.'

'Good.'

John Forest joined Mark watching the French move on their way to Lewes. 'Good, they are going where Willikin wants them to be.' He looked up at Thomas. 'I'll get the locals to hand back their spears and then set to blocking the road back into the Weald. Then I'm off to Beddingham to get the road block there set up. And you and your men? Off to Lewes I suppose?'

'Yes, once we have collected arrows, Lewes,' Thomas jumped down and stood by his twin.

'To help keep the French where Willikin wants them and to practice clout shooting.'

Michael the Mouse, with Gasper the Ghost at his side, grunted. 'Just as long as you don't get good enough to steal the May Queen's kiss.'

William of Cassingham sat at table in the well furbished pavilion his men of Kent had taken from a French supply train. Partly eaten fresh baked bread rolls with butter and slices of warm meat sat on their wooden platters. William patted his stomach and gave a discrete belch. 'I bet our French friends across the way have not had such a pleasant repast.'

'The Dauphin and his lords might have, for the Earl of Surrey has, until recently, been able to keep Lewes castle reasonably stocked with food and drink, despite our efforts, but the rank and file in their camp of tents and bivouacs will have rumbling tums.' John Little took another bite of his food.

Mark Reeve, undid a notch on his belt and pushed his own platter away. He picked up a gilt goblet of good French wine that had been part of the pavilion's original provender and sipped the contents. 'The castle's supplies won't last much longer; their guests have been there three days already and troops being troops, they would have been out helping themselves to things they are not supposed to have, and thus depleting the stores.'

William nodded his agreement. 'They will have to move soon, I think they have stayed put in the hope that the wind and rain will stop before their supplies run out.'

John pulled Mark's abandoned platter towards himself. 'The delay has allowed us to get all the folk of Winchelsea away from the town and to put all the mills out of action.' He picked at the food on the newly acquired platter and selected some of it for his consumption. 'Thank you for that Mark – handling Winchelsea I mean, not the food,' he winked at the Reeve.

William refilled his own goblet but then, rather than drink from it rolled it around in his hand, watching the red wine glint in the lamp light. 'The Boxholt boys?'

John stopped selecting food for a moment. 'Have brought their men of West Sussex, together with the South Surrey men. They have had to let some go though to attend to their farm work. Others will come to replace them they say. I think we should also let them have the Hampshire men when they get here, just to keep their numbers up.'

Mark, having emptied his goblet reached for the wine jug. 'Odiham Castle?'

The Cassingham squire looked up from his wine. 'Still in French hands. I sent word for the Hampshire men watching it to come down and join us. They have spent the past six months putting the fear of God into Odiham's garrison, picking off any that ventured too far when foraging. It will take a while for the garrison to realise that they are not currently being watched'

'So they have picked off foragers but didn't the French send out bigger parties to counter this?' Mark poured himself a generous measure of wine.

Cassingham inclined his head in acknowledgement. 'Oh yes, but always they lost one or two dead and others wounded. Even when you know that the size of your raiding party is such that you won't all get killed, the fact that some of you always do is often enough to dishearten men.'

John snorted, allowing some of his food to escape his mouth. 'Who knows if the next arrow won't have your name upon it?' he spluttered.

Mark flicked off some of the bread roll that John had sprayed onto his sleeve. 'Thank you for sharing that John.'

The big man smirked as he continued chewing.

'Well,' William at last brought his goblet to his mouth, 'at least we and our men have plenty of food to share around.'

The men of the Boxholt and their friends stood under a large awning made up of the canvas coverings taken from captured French wagons. They listened to the sound of the rain as the high wind drove it home. The fire in the pit outside had been doused by the rain and now merely gave off sullen smoke which, fortunately, was driven by the wind away from them. Thomas worked at a crude table on which a pig's carcass lay, cutting thick slices of meat from it and laying them on a large silver dish which had been found in a wrecked ox cart after a French supply train had been ambushed by another band of archers.

Godfrey joined his brother. 'If the other archers left this dish behind it makes you wonder what other plunder there was in that convoy.'

Thomas just shrugged and then turned and called over his shoulder; 'More meat anyone?'

'Is it pork again?' Jack Samuelson, who had just arrived as a replacement archer, asked.

'Yes.'

'No venison?'

'Just pork young Jack. If you don't want it I am sure there are many in the French camp who would take it off your hands.' Godfrey picked some of the crackling off the outside of the pig and popped it into his mouth, crunching it so loudly others turned and came to help themselves to the delicacy.

Jack elbowed his way to the pork, 'I didn't say I didn't want any, just that I fancied something different.'

Thomas went back to slicing meat. 'Well it seems all we find when we take stuff from the French is pork. Live pork, cooked pork, smoked pork, salted pork. They do like their swine flesh the French.'

'I've been to France.' Edwin Fish of Bosham pulled out a slice of particularly fatty meat from near the top of the pile. 'When you see what their women look like over there you know why they like pork.'

'Oh ah?' Jon Fish, his cousin and Rosie Fish's brother helped himself to a hunk of crackling. 'You saying they Frenchwomen look like swine?'

'Oink!' Edwin replied causing the rest of the men under the awning to laugh. 'Not that they can't taste good mind.'

'Not that I want to know that cousin.'

'Just you get on with your bit of crackling.'

'Ow, I likes a bit a crackling.' Jon bit into the treat with noisy enthusiasm.

Thomas stood back and looked at the depleted pig's carcase. 'Well that's that and if you want more you can pick over the bones.'

Godfrey wiped his greasy hands down his faded green hose. 'Looks like luck is on our way lads, the rain has eased just as we go out looking for French stragglers.' He turned to Jack Samuelson, the young ploughman of Wulfbearding, 'Any supply carts we take will help keep us in food and, you never know Jack, they may have meat other than pork on them.'

A throstle bird called. Thomas looked up and Godfrey gave him a hand signal that caused his twin to carefully make his way through the trees to where half a dozen Boxholt men waited. Thomas braced his bow, which he then covered with his cloak to keep the light drizzle of rain off the string; the others followed suit. The bird called again and the hidden archers threw back their cloaks and nocked arrows. Six small ox carts, each with a driver and a man-at-arms, trundled down the road, the occupants keeping their heads down and tucked deep inside their cloaks to avoid the rain.

As the carts passed Godfrey and Will Greenleaf stepped into the road behind them. Will called out, in his pleasant high voice; '*Hey, where are you going?*' in the nearest to Old Norman French as he could manage.

The man-at-arms on the last cart stood and turned to face them. 'Can't you speak English?'

'Whose man are you?' Will replied.

'Warenne's. Why? Are you here to escort us to Lewes Castle?'

'The Earl of Surrey's man?' Will shouted to the disappearing cart.

'Yes,' came the distant reply.

'Is he with the King or Louis?' Will asked Godfrey.

The throstle bird called again, this time it gave its distress call.

219

Arrows flew and then flew again from Thomas and his men until the drivers and men-at-arms were all dead.

'Louis.' Godfrey answered as they walked to the shambles that was the supply train.

'Heads?' Thomas asked.

'It's what Willikin wants,' Godfrey replied as he and Will sauntered past the carts.

'Pork again?'

'Yes Jack, pork again, though we do have some salt fish to go with it this time.' Thomas carried on cutting meat.

'Master William?'

'Yes John.'

'The Frenchies are on the move.'

'Right, get our men moving. You take command of roving bands to harass the French columns; just harass mind, no pitched battles. I know that there is not so much cover to hide in near the Downs but do the best you can: no risks. Tell Mark Reeve to get his lot to block any side roads that prevent us from driving the Dauphin to Winchelsea.'

'The terrible twins?'

'Send them to Beddingham as arranged just so our French friends don't get tempted to divert to Newhaven.'

The West Sussex men and their Surrey comrades stood and sat behind the wattle hurdles that had been erected to block the road to Newhaven and the coast. The gap was only twenty yards wide as the roadsides had not been cleared for years but Beddingham was a poor village and had few carts or wagons, and hurdles were the first line in the road block with but three carts and one wagon in reserve.

Thomas prodded the woven hazel of the hurdle he stood behind. 'I hope they don't send crossbowmen against us as these hurdles won't stop anything.'

'No, they won't; the bolts will go straight through.' Godfrey looked round at the carts and wagon. 'We can turn them over and stand behind them to do Surrey clout shots but it is all a poor defence.'

Garth gave a hacking cough and then spat phlegm onto the road. 'Uncle?' he gasped.

'Nephew?' Godfrey sat huddled with others in the shelter of a half collapsed wayside chapel that only partially kept the cold wind out.

'The French.' Garth went into another spasm of coughing.

'The French what?' Thomas asked as he came back adjusting his hosen after empting his bladder, having been careful to do it downwind.

'The French are here.'

'And after this young man,' Godfrey pulled himself up with a hand from his brother. 'You are gone from here.'

'Back home to recover.' Thomas found his bow and started to walk to the barricade.

'There is no way we can hide in the woods with you barking like a dog every few moments.'

'Yes Uncle Godfrey.'

'Is Will any better yet?' Thomas asked as he climbed onto the bed of one of the carts in order to look over the hurdles.

'Still coughing,' Garth managed before himself coughing again.

Godfrey joined his twin. 'Take him with you.'

'But Uncle, I will miss all the fun.'

'Fun he says.' Thomas shielded his eyes with his right hand.

'I suppose he enjoys chopping heads off dead Frenchmen and sticking them on stakes along the roadside.' Godfrey passed Thomas both his own and his brother's bow before climbing onto the cart.

'No,' Garth insisted before sneezing. 'I mean,' he sneezed again, 'I just enjoy hanging out with you all.' The youth gave a combined cough and sneeze before slouching against the cart's side gasping for breath.

'Shush,' the twins said together.

Up the road, just out of ordinary bow shot, sat a patrol of a dozen or more horsemen. One, accompanied by a standard bearer rode forward to get a closer view of the village defences.

'Come back Harold Harefoot,' Thomas intoned.

'All is forgiven,' Godfrey added.

'I'll give it a go.' Mark the Archer joined the twins on the cart.

Thomas continued watching the slowly approaching French horsemen. 'What are you going to do Mark? Take off your shoes and stink them to death?'

'No, not this time.' Mark felt behind his back and fingered his arrows before pulling out a very light flighting arrow. 'I thought I might try and get our flash friend there.'

'A groat if you hit him,' Thomas offered.

'Tuppence if you only get his horse,' Godfrey qualified.

Mark wet his finger to get wind direction, held his arrow flight end up to help judge wind strength then, once happy, nocked his arrow, drew and shot. The wind gave a gust and blew the arrow off course and it pierced the standard. It was enough for the Frenchmen who turned and rode back at the trot to their comrades before the whole party went back from whence they came.

'A penny?' Mark asked.

'A farthing,' Thomas offered.

Mark climbed down, 'Tight wad, that's what you are young Thomas who would be Robin of the Boxholt.'

'Alright a halfpenny,' Godfrey called after him.

'A better offer than your brother's.'

'We will pay you later,' the twins called out.

'Winchelsea?'

'Winchelsea!' the twins replied.

'Winchelsea?' Garth asked before coughing.

'Not for you young nephew,' Godfrey jumped down off the cart.

'Wulfbearding for you young man.' Thomas passed down the bows before getting down himself. 'It is a safe place for you and Will to recover.'

Chapter 12: Beside the Seaside

'Well?' William of Cassingham stood and watched as men started to pitch his pavilion on the only bit of decent flat ground without the walls of Winchelsea.

'It is not as tight a net as we would like Master William, but it is the best we can do with the numbers we have got.' Mark Reeve folded his arms and looked on as the centre poles were inserted into the pavilion, lifting the roof. 'Oh and John Little has a couple of prisoners for you after one of his little ambushes.'

William turned with his brow creased and a look of anger on his face. 'I have always said "no prisoners". Kill them in a fight, shoot them in the back as they run, hunt them down, hang or behead them if you capture them, but never, never, never take prisoners!'

'These two are the Count of Nevers' cousins – or so they say.'

William let out his breath, mollified. 'Well in that case get them to The Regent. They may be useful bargaining tools.'

'And if they aren't?'

'Get them back here and we will take their heads off in front of Winchelsea's walls.'

'Anything happening?' Godfrey peered up from the bed he had made for himself using his own cloak and three others no longer needed by their dead French owners. His head was larger than normal as it was covered with his own hood and three others donated by the same dead Frenchmen.

'Only the wind getting stronger and it has started to rain.' Thomas joined his brother in the booth they and others from the Boxholt band had made. They had used scraps of timber and canvas coverings from wagons that had been damaged when French supply trains had been captured. The structure was mostly water and wind proof and to prevent flooding a trench had been dug around its perimeter; something that had caught out the incautious in the dead of night.

'No Frenchies sneaking out looking for food?'

Thomas pulled off the oiled linen cape that covered his thick woollen cloak and hung it from one of the crude pegs jammed into knot holes in the wall of the booth. The cape dripped into a small puddle that had formed on the dirt floor where the booth's roofing was least effective. 'No. The last lot that tried using nightfall as a cover for reaching that old walnut tree in the hopes we had left any nuts there didn't make it back and the others don't seem keen on trying themselves.'

Godfrey reluctantly eased himself out of his warm bed keeping his own cloak wrapped round himself and went over to gain his oiled cape that was hanging next to his brothers. 'I suppose old Willikin sticking their heads on poles in front of the tree would have discouraged them from getting too cheeky.'

Thomas availed himself of the spare warm cloaks and rolled himself in them before finding the space between two other men on the dry floor. 'Enjoy your patrol: your boys are getting themselves ready in the next booth over. Jack Samuelson is one of them and he is still moaning about the lack of variety in the food he is being given out.'

William of Cassingham gazed across at Winchelsea and watched the banners of its French occupiers flapping furiously in the strong wind. He turned to his visitor; 'Well Gamble Gold, is it tonight that the men of the fleet are due to launch another raid against the French outposts?'

'It is Master. We are asked to pull our men back and only guard the roads out; they don't want their men being shot by mistake.'

'I hope it is more successful than their last raid; a lot of noise and confusion but not many French dead.'

'Noise and confusion may be enough; that and starvation.'

'I doubt it.' William turned back towards his pavilion, head bowed down against the wind.

'There is a problem Master.' Will Scathlock, dressed as always in maroon and scarlet woollen clothes, look tired as he slumped into the folding chair inside Cassingham's wind swept pavilion. He pulled down his hood and ran his fingers through his coarse red hair. 'A problem on more than one front.'

The squire went to the low table set against the wall of the pavilion and selected a goblet, checked that it was clean and then poured some red wine into it. 'I know that a small relief force from London is coming down the coast road from Canterbury, our brewer friend sent word days ago and local folk have been keeping me up-to-date on its progress. Some of our folk have roughed it up a mite but, with most of our strength here at Winchelsea, they could not do that much damage. I understand the French are almost at Romney. We should be able to stop them getting any further towards Winchelsea, though it is a distraction.' William gave the filled goblet to Scathlock. 'What is the other front? We have most of the Weald sealed. Well,' he returned to the table and started to refill his own gilt goblet, 'I say "sealed" but the odd messenger seems to be getting through to London else they would not have sent reinforcements.' William came and sat down on a

226

chair opposite Scathlock. 'I suppose the ones we catch are the French and the ones that get through are the Earl of Surrey's men from Lewes castle – they would know the back tracks and paths as well as our own men. Give them woodsmen's clothes and we might not know them from our own. So, my man in scarlet, what other front is there, than the two we already have?'

Scathlock looked up from lowered brows. 'Winchester; my lord the Regent has, at least for the moment, chased the French garrison out of the city and they are now on their way here. I came across them at Petersfield where they are making a nuisance of themselves gathering supplies, which included my train of pack horses. I rushed here almost killing my own poor old horse in the process. I'd say that they would be back on the move in a couple of days.'

William of Cassingham put down his goblet on the floor and stroked his now greying beard. 'That is not good news. I will let the terrible twins know as the road from there to here runs right through their home villages. I had better see them myself to make sure they don't send all their force there as we still need to keep the French penned in at Winchelsea.'

Godfrey looked to his brother; 'How many men do we have in camp at present?'

Thomas pursed his lips and did a mental count. 'Just under a hundred I think if we include the Surrey men we seem to have inherited. I can't say exactly, but about that number.'

Godfrey looked at William of Cassingham; 'How many can we take to fight the Winchester garrison?'

227

The squire sucked in between his teeth; 'Fifty at best, but I can let you have the seventeen Hampshire men who have turned up. See my man guarding our horse lines and he will let you have mounts – the short legged things that look more like overgrown dogs; and you call them horses.' He wagged his head and smiled at his own joke, 'But ...' The twins looked at him. 'But, only one of you can go – I need the other to stay here and keep our trap tight.'

Thomas lent his head towards his twin's good ear; 'Lucy,' he whispered.

'Thomas will go and I will stay.'

'No!' Lucy, Sam Samueleson's widow, pulled sharply away from Thomas and faced the open door of her cottage.

'Please, don't refuse me.'

'No Thomas, no – I won't.'

'But what harm is there in you saying yes?' Thomas came and stood behind her, his breath stirring the strands of golden hair that had escaped her wimple.

'My conscience won't let me.'

'But Lucy ...'

'But nothing Thomas.' Lucy turned her head towards her would be suitor's face. 'The answer is "NO", so get over it.'

A shadow crossed the threshold and Cedric att Steadham, ploughman, charcoal burner and currently one of the Boxholt archers looked in, his face almost as dark as his shadow from the ingrained soot and charcoal. He gave a discreet cough that was full of the fluid his lungs always seemed to contain. 'Err, Thomas; safe to come in?'

228

'Yes Cedric, it is safe.'

Lucy pulled away from the man who wanted to be her lover and went to lean against the door portal and looked out on the road that ran through Wulfbearding. 'Safe is it Thomas?' she called back.

Cedric gave her a quick smile, bent round and grabbed at a person holding back outside. He dragged his reluctant victim into the cottage. 'Old Limp Leg here is also saying "NO"!'

Osbert Limp Leg smiled shyly and shook his head; 'No I won't young Thomas, and I am not the only one either. Cedric here has been asking anyone he can accost and they all told him the same.'

Thomas sighed, rubbed his hands over his face and took a deep breath before replying to the charcoal burner. 'Well Cedric, it seems the whole damned village is of the same mind and saying a very loud "NO!"'

'Gilbert were right then when he guessed they wouldn't run into the woods to keep out of the way of the French coming from Winchester.'

'Yes, but fighting the French. I mean, they are trained men-at-arms they would be taking on. This will not be a village football game.'

'Oh, I don't know,' Osbert Limp Leg hobbled over to a chair and sat himself down with his stiff leg poking out straight in front of him. 'Last time we took on Chithurst there was one dead, two broken arms and a broken leg.'

'Ah,' Cedric interrupted. 'But old Alby had a heart that kept thumping when he exerted himself, not that he did that very often. He used to go blue in the face. Put his humours all out of balance that did and I'm sure that's what killed him.'

'That and being under about a dozen men,' Osbert reminded him. 'He were pressed to death.'

'Look you two,' Thomas said, his voice edged with exasperation. 'That was an accident.'

'That's not what the Chithurst men said afterwards.' Osbert nodded his head knowingly.

'He weren't popular mind,' Cedric chipped in.

Thomas stamped his foot. 'Look all this reminiscing is not helping us get over the fact that sixty odd Frenchies are coming this way soon and these stubborn villagers won't leave their homes.'

'Had enough of they foreigners we have,' Limp Leg eased his position, using his hands to manually move his stiff leg to a more comfortable position. 'Eh Lucy.'

Lucy just grunted and folded her arms.

'Right then; tell me what to do.' Thomas started to rub his fingers together as his nerves started to get the better of him.

'Well,' Limp Leg scratched at a flea bite on his arm. 'We fight that's what we do and, unlike the village football, we do it with weapons.'

'Weapons?' Thomas asked. 'What weapons?'

Lucy stomped back into the cottage. 'Don't say stupid things Thomas. What sort of man are you? You are a country man aren't you? We've got mattocks, we've got bills, we've got axes, we've got mauls. Everyone, even the childer, knows how to handle a staff and that can be as good a weapon as a spear. God help us, we even have frying pans and they hurt when you get hit by them.'

Limp Leg rubbed his hand over an imaginary bump on his head. 'Oh they do that all right. My late wife had a way with a frying pan, especially if she thought I'd been on the ale.'

Lucy snorted her disgust. 'Thought? She knew you had been on the ale you old fool. Right, Thomas, so now you know that we are armed, what plan do you have to lead us into battle?'

Thomas stopped his compulsive finger massaging. 'I do have an idea. At least I think I have.' He strode to the door, cast his eyes around. Seeing Will Greenleaf and Garth standing together laughing about some private joke he called them over. 'Nothing to do? Right, get back to Iping and bring back the deer nets that are stored in the barn. I'm sure our lords and masters won't need them for some time. Oh; and see how many of our villagers will come to help in the fight. Now hurry.' The two youths set off down the road to Iping. Thomas now sought out Edward Black, carpenter and blacksmith.

'Are you after me Thomas?' Edward's red gold hair stood in marked contrast to his smoke smudged face.

'There you are; yes.' Thomas pointed to one of the cottages. 'There are five cottages each side of the road opposite each other.'

'And another four on the south side only, heading east towards the village green.'

'Yes Edward, but I am only interested in the ones that have another cottage opposite them. Can you rig a post or something from the eves of the cottages nearest the road? Also find a way of pegging nets across the alleyways between the cottages?'

Edward looked at the cottage nearest and examined its construction. 'Quite possibly.'

'Good, please set about it straight away. And your son is in my band; does he know how to sharpen tools?'

'Of course; he has been brought up properly.'

'Then set him to work on anything the villagers have that he can set an edge on. While you are doing that I will get the folk together and tell them just how we might be able to deal with the French. We have a day, two at the most before they arrive.'

Mildred Nearboxholt and Agnes Crosseye sat on three legged stools facing the road through the village. Draped across their knees were deer nets that they were cutting into widths marked by pieces of old linen rag. Their rough working knives flashed in the rare bright sunlight as they sawed their way through the tough hempen cords.

Mildred paused to wipe her brow on a sleeve. 'I suppose when this is all over we shall have to spend hours and hours mending them they nets and putting 'em back together again.'

'Just you keeping working Good Wife Nearboxholt,' Lucy called out as she passed by leading a horse with yet more netting carried on its back. 'Mind; if they French don't get stopped and killed off you won't have to worry about mending nets 'cos you will be dead yourself!'

The two older women waited till Lucky had gone out of earshot. Agnes peered after the younger woman, 'She's got a lot bolder with her tongue since that young Thomas Wulfson took a fancy to her.'

'Since he's been away fighting he sees himself as a man with prospects he does. I still remember him running round snotty nosed and bare arsed.'

'Wasn't that long ago, only a couple of years ago I think when that strange illness took down so many of us.'

Mildred snorted a laugh. 'You silly old thing, I was talking 'bout when he was a kid!'

'Oh, I know that,' Agnes gave a smile that shewed she had lost many of her teeth. 'Still, Thomas would be a fine catch for a widow with childer to worry about. Mind he would have to take on the children, many a man wouldn't.'

'Three children plus a fine pair of oxen and a wagon!' Mildred went back to cutting the net.

'That Thomas is a better man than Lucy's Sam was.'

'Wouldn't take much to be better than that ale sodden fat lump.'

'Oh yes, that Thomas has nice long legs, slim but powerful body and a glint in his eye.'

'Sounds like you fancy him yourself Agnes, you being a widow woman and all that.'

Agnes gave a dreamy smile and sighed. 'Years back maybe but I'm too old for such fancies now.'

'Well years back you may have been willing, but Thomas would have been a snotty nosed bare arse little knave and no good to you at all.'

The women cackled and bent back to their work.

Edward Black, helped by his son Erik, adjusted the rope over a pulley system that was crude, but far more sophisticated than that which Thomas had envisaged. The system protruded from under the eve of the cottage on the south side of the road and was secured by rope and nail to the buildings side beam. Edward fiddled with the setting some more, making sure it was fully secured and the rope that went through the pulley ran freely. Once happy he and his son climbed down their ladders and stood by the side of Thomas.

'It is ready for testing Thomas.'

'Good.'

Edward and his son stood by the cottage wall, picked up the rope and took up the slack. The blacksmith looked across the road where his wife Elfwyn and Lucy stood alongside the cottage on the other side of the road. 'NOW!'

All four pulled on their ropes and the deer net quickly rose from the road and formed a net wall across the thoroughfare.

Thomas nodded. 'Yes, very good. All we have to do now is get the rest of the preparations in hand and practice at getting the nets up faster.'

Thomas gathered his archers in front of the fire that burnt bright on the green at the end of the village. Ale, meat and bread were passed round by Wulfbearding's villagers.

'Venison!' Garth said appreciatively between chews. 'I bet Jack Samuelson wished he were here.'

'I bet Thomas is glad he isn't.' Will Greenleaf licked the meat juice from his fingers. 'He might get in the way of Thomas courting Lucy the widow. Jack might be worried about losing the family's inheritance.'

'True, though Jack has already taken the land, seeing as Sam's eldest is just a little boy and isn't even big enough to do anything other than bird scaring; certainly not ploughing, not even as a plough boy.'

Garth washed his meat down with a decent swig of ale. 'Best keep quite as it looks as if Thomas is about to speak.'

Thomas strode into the firelight, lifted his hunting horn to his lips and gave a high pitched strident blast.

Garth screwed up his face at the sound. 'I wish he wouldn't do that.'

'Or at least warn us beforehand,' Will shook his head as if trying to get the sound out of his ears.

'Shut up and listen you lot,' Thomas looked round at the gathered band. 'I said "SHUT UP AND LISTEN!"'

The hum of talk quietened down and then eventually stopped as men poked talkative neighbours or put fingers to lips.

'Right,' Thomas continued. 'The plan; the Hampshire men will base themselves about three miles down the road towards Winchester. Jake here,' he indicated an elderly man at his side, 'will act as their guide so that they don't get lost.' The remark brought laughter and even some jibbing from the Boxholt men towards their visitors. Thomas waited for the noise to ease before talking again. 'I know, I know, but they must use the deer tracks and back paths and they will need local help in that. Their job will be to harass the rear of the French. I don't want an ambush, what I want is for them to know they have been spotted; I want them to think that it is just a couple of locals taking pot shots at them. I want then edgy and unsure but no more at that stage. We have a limited number of arrows, so easy does it. Archers should be strung out along the road on both sides, so make sure you don't over shoot and put your own men at risk. Shoot then drop back in pairs along the road towards Wulfbearding. It could all be done by two or three archers but, just in case the French do try and make a fight of it, I want all the Hampshire men involved. Once the French are within a couple of hundred yards of the village then all the archers can shoot, but only at the rear ranks of the French. Don't be afraid to come out and stand on the road; let the French see that they are now being attacked by more than just a few archers. Hard and fast shooting as I want them to start to panic. I want them to hurry. I want them close up on the ranks in front. I want them to see the village. I want them to see the clear ground of the green at the end of the village and get it into their minds that they can make a stand there. What I don't want is for them to have time to think clearly.' The Hampshire men started to talk amongst themselves. Thomas lifted his horn to his lips and it was enough to restore order and all fell silent rather than suffer another assault on their ears. 'You Hampshirers can move over there with Jake and discuss matters. I need time now to go over the rest of the plan with my men of the Boxholt.'

Thomas sat in the forked branches of the big oak tree and watched as the mounted French vanguard rode through, and sometimes over, the screen of crossbowmen in front of them in their haste to reach the village green they could spy ahead of them. Hurrying behind them came footmen at the run, many leading pack horses loaded with supplies and equipment. At the rear of the column were more horsemen pushing into the rear ranks of the foot, forcing them to go faster and pushing them into the back of the vanguard as it struggled through the broken ranks of the crossbowmen. As an encouragement for haste, arrows flew as the Hampshire men sealed the road back towards Petersfield and Winchester. Thomas waited till he saw the leading horsemen near the penultimate pair of cottages then gave a single blast of his horn. At the sound a deer net flew up across the road in front of the horsemen too late for the lead riders to stop their mounts plunging into the net. The following footmen slammed into the trapped vanguard and the rearguard crashed into them, shunting the infantry even more tightly against the horses of the vanguard. Thomas gave two blasts of his horn and villagers pulled on ropes and another deer net flew up across the road between the rearmost cottages ensuring that all the French were trapped on Wulfbearding's main road. The French were now packed tight as salt herrings in a barrel.

'*BETWEEN THE COTTAGES; BETWEEN THE COTTAGES,*' the garrison commander shouted.

Those who had the ability to try that avenue of escape saw that the alleys between the cottages were also blocked by deer netting. They drew swords to try and cut their way out.

Thomas gave three blasts on his horn and archers appeared in the alleys and on the road in front of the French and steadily and methodically started shooting, for once concentrating on the men and not the horses.

A few of the French cavalry found themselves alongside a cottage so left their mounts and climbed onto a cottage roof. Most were shot down, but those who were not and jumped down into an alley were met by angry villagers who mobbed them before

237

slaying them with whatever tools they had to hand. One though managed to break free and ran down his alley towards the beckoning freedom of the coppiced trees at the path's end. He looked back and saw that he had a good lead on the pack of young children who were pursuing him. He looked back to his front only to see Lucy standing there. She hit him in the face with her iron frying pan and it gave a satisfying crunch as the Frenchman's face came in contact with it. The man staggered back, his nose, jaw and teeth shattered before going down under a pile of boys egged on by their sisters.

Thomas climbed down from his tree and jogged towards the village, but once there he could see that the fight was over so he signalled that the nets could be let down. Villagers quickly rushed in, some to finish off any injured Frenchmen, others to secure the horses. Archers joined them, retrieving arrows, cursing when arrow heads had to be left behind in a corpse or a shaft had been broken.

Jake Jackson, Osbert Limp Leg and old Egbert the Toothless came and stood by Thomas' side. Osbert coughed to get Thomas' attention. 'Err, Thomas.'

'Yes?'

'What now?'

'What now? Yes, what now.' Thomas ran his hand over his cropped fair hair and thought, all the while watching the clear up of the fight. He came to a decision; 'What now? You get the carts and wagons of the village. You strip the French, cut off their heads, then stick the bodies and heads in the wagons. At every hundred yards or so on the way back to Petersfield stick a head on a stake and drop a body on the road so that anyone travelling along the road knows what happens to any French or rebel that travels along it. If there are still bodies and heads left over dump them all outside Petersfield in a heap: don't risk going any further towards Winchester.'

'Do we get to keep any of the plunder?' Egbert hissed through his unsupported lips.

Thomas gave a short laugh. 'You mean in addition from what folk have already secreted away?'

Egbert, Jake and Osbert had the grace to go red and look away.

Thomas gave another short laugh. 'You get to keep a quarter, but that does not include the chestnut pack horses, for I know their owner. A half goes to the fighting men and a quarter to Willikin.' He gave the three men a strong eye. 'And that includes anything already taken. Willikin has a way of finding out about how much was taken in plunder and you wouldn't want to incur his displeasure now would you?'

The three elderly men looked at the carnage that still clogged the main road. 'No.' they all echoed.

'Come here young Thomas,' Lucy caught hold of the young man's arm and pulled him towards herself. 'Where's my reward?'

'Your reward? Talk to Osbert Limp Leg – he seems to be in charge of village things these days?'

'Not that sort of reward, silly man.'

'Pardon?'

'I want what I need!'

'Need?'

'A woman has needs you know,' Lucy said as she manoeuvred Thomas towards the door of her cottage.

'You have?'

'Oh I have and that fat dolt of a late husband of mine never met them, whereas a fit, strong, handsome man like yourself with your long legs and full head of fair hair; well .....'

'Oh,' said Thomas in a fluster. 'That sort of need?'

'That sort of need Thomas.' Lucy pushed her victim through the cottage door and secured it with a block of wood.

'The children?'

'Playing football.'

'Football?'

'Them using a Frenchies head.'

'A Frenchman's head Lucy?'

'Yes, I'm sure Willikin won't begrudge them just one head will he?'

'No, err, I suppose he won't,' Thomas gave a weak smile.

'I'm only teasing – it is a sheep's head they be kicking.'

'Oh, right.'

'Being allowed to kick that old thing around is their reward for using their slings to take down that Frenchie what tried to escape over Old Mother Enid's roof.'

'Reward, yes,' Thomas managed to say as Lucy pushed him against the wall with her impressive strength.

'Same as you won't begrudge me my reward?'

'Err, no Lucy.'

'Good, now come closer and don't be so shy.'

Godfrey looked at his twin brother; 'Man, Thomas, you look knackered!'

Thomas slumped himself down inside the cabin out of the persistent wind. 'I am, I've come here for a rest.'

'How's things going between you and Lucy? No trouble I trust.'

'No trouble big brother. No trouble; we are now sort of betrothed.'

'What do you mean "sort of betrothed" Thomas?'

'Just that.' Thomas eased off a pair of riding boots he had gained from one of the French at Wulfbearding. 'Just that.' He looked at Godfrey. 'Seeing as I might be getting married soon and we always said we would do it together, hadn't you better get serious about courting your Rosie Long Legs?'

'Chance would be a good thing.'

'Go, I have access to a horse whenever I need one; William Scathlock has arranged it as a favour in gratitude for me getting his pack horses back.'

'My daily turn on guard duty?'

'I'll cover.'

'Thomas you will get tired out.'

'Trust me Godfrey; it will be very restful after Wulfbearding.'

'Right …' Godfrey looked at his brother to try and determine the actual meaning of the statement but his brother's mind seemed to have drifted off elsewhere. 'Thomas?'

Thomas gave a shudder and looked at his twin, 'Sorry?'

'I will be missed won't I.'

'No, we will just pull the trick we used to play when we were boys.'

'In that case, I am off to Bosham and Rosie.'

'Just don't come back smelling of fish,' Thomas whispered to himself as he set about making a bed to sleep on.

'Ah Thomas,' Mark Reeve stood alongside the Iping man as they both used the piss trench in the latrine.

'No, it's Godfrey.'

'Godfrey?'

Thomas shook himself and retied his braise. 'Yes?' Thomas pulled his hood further over his right ear to ensure that Willikin's man could not see the difference between him and his brother.

'Nothing, it is just that I never seem to see the two of you hanging around together in the normal way these days.'

'Busy, Mark, we are both so busy. I will give Thomas your regards when I see him,' and with that Thomas made a hasty retreat whilst reminding himself to put on a different hood as soon as he got back to the cabin in readiness for his own stint of picket duty.

'Much happen whilst I was away?'

Thomas gave his twin the hood he had been wearing each time he had impersonated him. 'A single French ship has made it past our own ships and got into harbour.'

'That's not too bad.'

'It was captained by Eustace the notorious monk.'

'That is bad. Anything else?'

'Well Eustace is a bright as well as a naughty pirate. Since arriving he has caused a bit of excitement and has got the Frenchies better organised. It seems our trapped Frenchies had some siege machinery with them when they came here. They now have it rigged and are hurling stones whenever any of our ships get too close to shore. I did hear, from a sailor I was swapping some pork with in exchange for fresh fish, that they are now adapting one of our ships they captured into a sort of barge to carry one of the stone throwers out to sea.'

'Ambitious.' Godfrey picked up the pair of riding boots Thomas had brought back from Wulfbearding. 'You didn't find any for me?'

'Sorry, no; these are the only ones that fit me.' Thomas claimed his treasured boots back from his brother. 'Ambitious? Well it is only rumour.'

The twins and a handful of their off duty men stood on the cliff and watched as the rumoured barge sailed into reality escorted by four much smaller vessels. As it came within fifty yards of an English ship the trebuchet mounted on its main deck loosed a stone, causing the craft to rock severely. The stone it had hurled splashed harmlessly yards from the English vessel, but it was close enough to frighten the English captain and cause him to put about and sail further from shore.

'Not just ambitious,' Thomas said.

'It is impressive,' Godfrey concluded.

Cedric of Steadham screwed his eyes up and watched the missile ship rocking as the trebuchet arm continued moving back and forth defying its crew's attempts to grab the rope that would enable them to pull it back down for reloaded. 'I wouldn't like to be on that there ship; not seaworthy is that.'

'Not seaworthy,' agreed Jon Fish, Rosie Long Leg's brother.

243

The strong wind blew the heavy clouds across the night sky and obscured what faint light the quarter moon provided. Godfrey held back against the dark body of the old oak and kept his fighting staff close to his body as he watched three men, stoop backed, make their way out of the tented camp and across the cleared area without Winchelsea's town walls. Every fifty yards the men dropped down and rested; even at this distance Godfrey could hear one of the men's wheezing breaths. Gradually the group got nearer the clump of trees that held Godfrey and his night patrol.

'Taking advantage of the distraction our fleet raiders are creating attacking the French camp along the town wall, they know we pull our pickets back when they raid,' hissed Mark Archer as he slipped alongside Godfrey. 'They also know our lot tend to go and watch the fight.'

'True, Mark, true. The French may be daft, but they are not stupid.'

'Shame it is too dark to shoot these creeping buggers. Well, too dark unless you are Harold the Harefoot.'

'Which we are not,' Godfrey whispered back, 'and it is why we brought sword and staff.'

'I'd still prefer to shoot them; the closer you get to any enemy the more chance of getting killed yourself.'

'I agree, but it is not always possible, now shush and just watch; they are getting too close for us to talk.' Godfrey concentrated harder in order to watch the shadowy figures. 'Mark,' he hissed. 'Get the lads ready.' Without waiting to see Mark move, Godfrey edged his way silently forward to where he estimated the three men would enter the woods knowing the others would follow. The two leading Frenchmen made it to the edge of the spinney and grabbed the third man by the elbows and forced him to join them. They looked around, but saw nothing. They moved along the edge of the woods till they found the animal track they were looking for and stealthily moved along it with the wheezing man in the middle. Godfrey let them pass him before he stepped out, swung his quarter held staff and smacked the rearmost man on the back of the neck. The man staggered into the wheezing man before collapsing on top of him. Mark and two others took on the lead Frenchman, landing multiple blows on him with half staff, forcing him to his knees before Mark slammed his staff up and under the Frenchman's chin, snapping his neck.

Godfrey pulled his own opponent off the wheezing man and checked he was dead. On finding it was so he lifted the survivor's head, exposing the man's throat. Godfrey dropped his staff and pulled out his hunting knife.

'Don't, please,' the wheezing man cried. 'I'm English.'

'So are the rebel Barons and their men.' Mark stood in front of the wheezer and drew his own knife.

'But I am not a rebel.'

'Easily said.' Godfrey pulled the man's head back further and placed his knife on the man's throat.

'But,' the man gurgled through gritted teeth, 'I was being forced to shew the Frenchmen the way through the woods, they had a message they wanted to get to London.'

Godfrey lowered the man's head to enable him to speak more clearly. 'And?'

'And I am a Winchelsea man. I got left behind. I can tell you what is happening in the town.'

Godfrey looked at Mark. 'That might be useful to Willikin.'

'Agreed. So, we had best remove these,' he kicked a dead Frenchman, 'rather than hang them from the tree so that way the French will think that they got through.'

'Drag them back to the camp we can bury them there. Jon, Jack, Alan, Grim; an arm each will lighten the load. Tom, Gilbert and Ralf – escort our wheezing friend here to Willikin. Mark and I will hang about and see if anything else is happening along here. All of you must get back here as soon as you can.'

Godfrey and Mark watched the Boxholt men go. Godfrey sheathed his knife and bent down to pick up his staff. 'I hope for the sake of our breathless friend he has some information of use.'

So do I 'cos if he hasn't ….'

'If he hasn't Willikin will chop his head off in front of the French lines as he has done with all the other messengers he has caught.'

John Little entered William of Cassingham's pavilion just as the wheezing man was taken out accompanied by two of William's most trusted archers. John watched the parties departure before dropping the pavilion's flap down and looking at Cassingham's squire. 'Well, did he give any good information?'

'A little.'

'Will you give him the chop?'

'No, I will send him to one of the villages in the Weald where the Winchelsea folk have been given refuge. If he is a traitor, seeing as he didn't leave with the rest of them, they will know and will do

246

what they think best with him. Henry our friar is keeping a list of who is where, so he will know where to send him once we find out just where in the town he lived.'

'So Master, what did you find out?'

'They are starving. They have grain but, thanks to our foresight, they have no mills to grind it with and, again because of our foresight, the folk have gone with their hand querns as well as all the food and animals. The French have been existing on the nuts from the trees and by eating the pack animals. Now the nobility have even started to eat their war horses.'

'The rank and file won't get any of that very expensive meat!'

'No they won't.' William picked up a thick slice of bread from a side table and thickly spread it with butter from a crock. 'Gamble Gold has just got back from seeing the Regent and his Lordship and an army are on their way here but it will be at least a week before we see them as they have to take some strong points along the way.' He bit into the food and looked thoughtful.

John Little joined his master in taking bread. 'Is that too long Master? We can't force the town as we have no siege machinery and I wouldn't like to even think about our lightly armed archers trying to take the camp let alone storm the walls.'

William finished his mouthful. 'God alone knows John, God alone knows. In the meantime we do our best to keep the place sealed off from the land whilst the King's Admiral, Philip d'Albabini, seals them off by sea.'

Garth burst into the rough cabin causing the wind that followed him to lift the canvas roof and threaten to remove it. 'Uncles come and see, uncles come and see!'

Godfrey looked up from the repair he was making to a torn shirt that belonged to Thomas. 'What now young Garth?'

'You found another badger's set you want us to sit in front of for hours in the hope we may actually see something move?' Thomas sat with his back to the wall, clad only in braies and linen undershirt.

'No Uncles, quick, get some clothes on, you must come and see; the fleet have captured the stone throwing ship. They have towed it as close as they can to Winchelsea harbour and are slowly dismantling it before the eyes of the French!'

'Might be worth the effort Thomas.'

'I suppose so big brother: tie off that thread and pass me my shirt.'

Will leapt up and down with joy as the English sailors on board the captured vessel took it apart and threw the pieces into the sea. He started to sing for the first time in months.

'Tis down to the sea in ships we go,
To brave the waves and heed the flow.
The seas they crash and seethe and foam,
As for other shores we set to roam.'

Godfrey tapped him on the shoulder. 'I wouldn't get too excited young Greenleaf for look,' he pointed out to the far sea. 'I think our boys will have other things to do soon than take captured ships apart.'

The youth turned and found the other archers staring at the dark smudge of shapes that spoilt the horizon.

William of Cassingham stood on the cliff overlooking the sea and watched the English fleet stagger in disarray away from the massed French fleet. 'Well John that is that. We had best get our men away from here and back to their homes. When things have settled and I have worked out what to do next we will call them in again.' He sighed and shook his head. 'Two hundred ships full of fighting Frenchmen. Where does that Louis get the money from?'

'Our sailors did try Master.'

'Yes they did try, but the English idiot who turned, rammed and sank one of our own ships started the rot and threw all into confusion. No, that is it; Louis will get to France. Whoever he leaves in charge will use the reinforcements to re-take Rye and other towns along the coast and our Regent will have to consider pulling his army back beyond Winchester.' William pulled his fingers through his grey beard. 'No, God didn't will us to win this one, but it is not over yet.'

Chapter 13: The White Cliffs of Dover

William Marshal, Earl of Pembroke, King's Guardian and Regent of England, smiled as he saw William of Cassingham, Cassingham's Reeve and his Forester out of the inn that was the Royalist's headquarters. He put a hand on the squire's shoulder and patted it. 'Well done William, I am sure you will continue to fight the king's war well.'

'Your Grace,' William replied as he lead his men towards the shack that had been their own quarters for the past two days.

'What will it mean Master?' John Little asked as he looked behind to watch the Marshal and his bodyguard go back indoors.

'John I have no idea.'

Mark Reeve hitched his sword belt and gave it a little jiggle. 'Warden of the Weald, Chief Man of the Seven Hundreds of the Weald.'

'But what does it mean?' John insisted.

'The only thing it really means is that I now have status when dealing with the French. Remember John, when we had them trapped in Winchelsea, they would not talk to me because I was just a squire. They would have talked to Philip d'Albabini, seeing as he was a noble, but he was always at sea. So the only one they could negotiate with was the Regent. If they had dealt with me we may yet have got them to surrender before that relief fleet arrived. Remember we let the emissaries through so they could see the Marshal in order to discuss surrender terms.'

'I recall the terms as "We will surrender if no relief arrives within five days",' Mark said. 'Or so I heard.'

'It was,' William confirmed. 'But it took two days for them to find Pembroke. If they had dealt with me they would have run out of time before that damned Eustace the Monk reached Winchelsea and chased off our fleet.'

The Boxholt men were on the way home. Near Hurstpierpoint they set up camp, pitching their bivouacs, setting out a horse line and guarding their accumulated plunder.

'Warden of the Weald?' Thomas stirred the fire under the cauldron that contained their horse meat and vegetable stew.

'Warden of the Weald.' Godfrey threw in some more sliced neeps he had traded for at the village.

'But what does that mean?'

'Don't ask me.'

'More taxes, more like.' Mark Archer, with gloved hands, carefully chopped up some fresh green nettles to add to the stew.

'Well,' Godfrey sat back on his heels and squinted his eyes against the wood smoke that a capricious wind had blown his way. 'You haven't paid any taxes since before this stouch started and I am sure there will be ways of avoiding taxes in the future for those who know their way round the system.'

'Good news Master William, or should I say "Warden of the Weald"?'

William sat at the high table of his manor house at Cassingham with his wife Mary by his side. 'We need some good news Gamble. Since the French fleet relieved Winchelsea it has all been bad news.'

Mary turned her head and spoke quietly to the man servant behind her. The man took the silver wine ewer from the table and walked to the side table where he filled a gilt goblet made in the French fashion.

Gamble Gold took the proffered goblet and made a toast to William: 'William Longsword, Earl of Salisbury, the old King's bastard brother and William Marshal's eldest son, William the Younger have deserted the rebel barons and joined the Royalist cause.'

William and Mary returned the toast. After a sip of wine William grunted. 'Hmm; interesting. Well, Thank God for that but I wonder just what they think is in it for them?'

'Isn't that being cynical beloved husband?'

'It is being realistic sweet wife.'

The couple entwined their drinking arms and supped from each other's goblet.

Cassingham's steward ran across the garth in a cloud of disturbed chickens and children. Seeing his master by the smithy he changed direction and skidded to a halt in front of William. 'Master,' the man gulped for air. 'Master, we have a,' another gulp of air, 'we have a visitor.'

'We have a visitor James? We often have visitors, so why the rush.'

'Master this one is ….'

'*Oliver Fitzroy*,' said a tall handsome man with dark wavy hair that hung to his shoulders. '*The "Roy" being King John.*'

William went down on one knee; '*Your Grace.*'

'*Up man, you are Warden of the Weald and I but one of King John's many bastards.*'

William got to his feet, '*But an illustrious one Your Grace.*'

'Call me Oliver if we are to work together in the field to drive the French out of our lands. I mean, we can't let formality get in the way of that task, now can we?'

'*Oliver,*' William stuttered, finding it hard to address a royal bastard so informally. *'Do you speak English at all? Our men only speak that language and I wouldn't want them thinking that you were French.*'

'Yes, a little – who doesn't these days?'

'Any news of Winchester – err – Oliver.'

The young man thought, mentally translating the English into Old Norman French. 'Winchester? Yes. Winchester is back in Royalist hands; what? That is the,' he thought again. 'Good news. Yes; good news.' He looked pleased with himself for being able to converse in what was not his native language. 'The dashed bad news old thing is that Louis the Dauphin is on his way back. Can you, how you say,' he crossed his brow in thought, 'gather your bands at Dover to welcome him back to England?'

'Again?' Godfrey stood behind his stationary pair of oxen with their harrowing sledge.

'Again big brother.' Thomas picked up a handful of heavy soil and rubbed it between his hands. 'It seems we have to gather what men we can and get over to Dover.'

'I suppose so.' Godfrey looked to the box holt at the end of the ploughland. 'We will have to get the old men out to finish the sowing.'

'And,' Thomas added as he came and stood by his twin's side and looked to the trees, 'we can't take all the fighting men with us if we are to continue to watch the roads and paths.'

'If only there were more men.'

Oliver Fitzroy stood shoulder to shoulder with the Warden of the Weald and looked at the siege camp before Dover Castle. '*There do not seem to be many French guarding the place. With my fifty men-at-arms and your thousand archers destroying this place should be easy.*'

'*A thousand archers? Well I won't have that many to command.*'

'*You won't?*'

'*They are yeomen and freemen; foresters and farmers; woodsmen and herdsmen. They fight to keep the French from taking their lands as happened once before. I can't force them to come and they have a living to make. They also have to keep the French and rebels from foraging in the Weald, and they stop the patrols and messengers from using the roads. The best I can hope is that three or four hundred will answer my summons. It is made all the more difficult by giving them such short notice.*'

'*Ah, I see. I forget they are not retainers or mercenaries.*'

'*Quite and Oliver?*'

'*Yes?*'

'*Do try to speak in English.*'

'Right oh old boy.'

Harold Harefoot and his chosen men stood on the edge of the treeline to the north of the French siege camp, watching, marking targets. Behind, deep in the woods and hidden by the trees, waited more archers in small bands each with five of Oliver's men-at-arms. Not all the archers carried their bows with many being armed with sword and buckler or fighting staff. Some of these archers wore padded jacks and a few a coat of mael. Other woodsmen hid nearer the tree line armed only with their hunting knives. All stood waiting. Their stillness and silence meant that the birdlife of the woods ignored them and gave no sign of alarum. From the French camp came a drift of sound as the camp came slowly to life. The night sentries stood with their replacements talking whilst camp followers and off duty soldiers emerged from huts and cabins ready to start their day. Harold stiffened as he smelt wood smoke from fires being lit for cooking and he smiled. The marksman archer gave a blackbird's mating call and his men reacted by bracing their bows and selecting an arrow from the half dozen stuck in the ground at their feet and the hidden woodsmen pushed deeper into their cover. From the French camp came a group of camp followers with an armed escort. As they passed the sentries the group exchanged banter with them and there was much laughter before the sentries carried on talking with each other and the group continued to the woods to gather fuel for the cooking fires. Harold nocked an arrow to the string of his beautiful yew bow and let the French party get closer. As they got to the woods the group scattered amongst the trees looking for firewood and their escort relaxed and lent against tree trunks looking back to the camp, watching the smoke from the cooking fires and thinking of the meal to come.

One by one the camp followers were taken care of silently by the woodsmen, the men killed, the women and children taken prisoner, gagged, bound and passed along to others deeper in the woods. The adults were stripped of their outer clothing which was passed to members of the waiting bands. The escort eventually grew inpatient and the sergeant in charge sent two of his men to find out why the wood collectors were taking so long. The men never returned, so he sent two more, who also never returned. Eventually he and his remaining four went to look for themselves. Arrows took them all down once they were out of sight of the camp. Still Harold and his chosen men waited, marking targets.

The camp followers and their escort left the woods with bundles of firewood and kindling and headed back to the camp though they seemed to have left the handful of children that had gone from the camp, behind in the woods. They were just twenty paces from the still gossiping sentries before an alert sentry noticed that the women in the group didn't look quite the right shape and at least two of them appeared to have whiskers. The sentry cried *'HALT!'* just before Harold's arrow took him in the throat. Harold's chosen men loosened their arrows and the other sentries fell.

'Run!' Oliver cried and the faux wood gathers dropped their firewood, drew swords from under their stolen garments and rushed the camp. Two of the men-at-arms tripped on their long skirts, which they hastily ripped off before continuing to rush the camp.

From the tree line Harold Harefoot, his chosen men and the mixed bands of archers and men-at-arms joined in the charge to the camp.

The slaughter was quickly started and the mostly unarmed Frenchmen were rapidly chopped down: the women and children were spared unless they decided to fight.

Godfrey emerged from a dilapidated cabin of woven withies and shook his head; 'No one in there.'

Granfer Gilbert took the burning brand in his hand and applied it to the thatch roof. 'I hope this thing catches due to the fact it's been raining on and off these pass two days.'

'Just stick it in and leave it old man.' Godfrey moved to the next cabin, which was in slightly better order. He kicked in part of the end wall and saw a woman crouching by the canvas screen that served for a door. 'Out – get out; NOW!' The woman looked at him confused. '*Get out; NOW!*' he repeated in his best French. The woman took seconds to grasp what he had said then nodded her head and scampered out of the cabin. Godfrey looked round for the rest of his band. 'Garth? Get over here and get this thing burning. Old Granfer is still trying to get that other place alight. And Garth?'

'Uncle?' the youth stood with a sword in one hand and a fire brand in the other.

'Watch that woman; she may yet decide to fight rather than run.'

'Uncle.' Garth kicked over more of the cabin before setting fire to a pile of broken wall. He watched the woman who had lived there; she eyed him back and looked to the way he held his sword at the ready before deciding that flight was better than fight.

257

A band of archers lead by the Kentishman Robert the Bear came down the crooked roadway. They were leading ox carts full of provisions, forcing Godfrey and his men to stand aside. 'Leave the huts man; get to the front of the camp and help destroy the siege machines: Willikin wants them burnt more than he does these shanties.'

Godfrey nodded acceptance and took his men towards the edge of the camp where it faced the castle. A man-at-arms stood in the middle of the road in front of them. Jon Fish, who had his bow with him, nocked an arrow.

'Don't shoot; I'm one of Oliver's men!'

Godfrey reached out and stayed Jon's arm as the archer started to bring his bow up. 'He's one of ours.'

'Don't sound like it to me,' Jon replied. 'Maybe he's lying. I think we should shoot him just in case.'

'Oliver Fitzroy! Long live King Henry!' the man cried out, seriously worried.

'Leave him be Jon; he may be a Norman, but at least he is one of our Normans.'

'All bloody foreigners if you ask me,' Jon grumbled as he took the strain out of his bow. 'I still think we should nail him.'

The man-at-arms smiled hesitantly and then turned his back on them and led the way to the siege machines.

Thomas and his men were already at work using axes and picks they had found in the camp. Bits and pieces of trebuchet, mangonel and petraria were thrown into a huge bonfire whose flames reached higher and higher. 'Just like midsummer's day big brother; you can't beat a decent bonfire.'

258

The English worked and worked breaking down the machines and feeding the fire. Eventually the job was done and they started back to the woods, burning huts, cabins and bivouacs as they went. Ahead of them was a swarm of female camp followers and children running in all directions, some to the woods, some to Dover town, others to the open fields. The returning men ignored them.

'How long before you can get your archers to the cliff top William old boy?' Oliver stood at the cliff edge and looked back to the burning camp.

'Soon. But first – can you get your men to learn some English? You are lucky only one got shot because he spoke in French.'

'They are all born here in England; what?'

'So get them to speak English!'

'Most do, it is only some who don't, don't you know? Well, they know how to swear in English, who doesn't?'

'Then tell them to swear if they are challenged.'

'I will. Now, William old chap, the archers on the cliff top – hmm?'

'They are on their way, though some of them have another task in hand.'

'But old thing, we need numbers up here so that Dauphin Louis and his fleet,' Oliver looked over his shoulder at the approaching ships and the wind blew his dark wavy hair back from his face. 'So Louis thinks we have the thousand archers you are supposed to have at your command, you being Warden of the Weald and all that.'

'There will be a thousand, but most of them local village folk.'

'Oh I think that should do; what? Louis don't know the difference between your yeomen and freemen and what he regards as peasants. To him anyone below the rank of knight is a peasant of some sort, don't you know.'

Two French galleys headed for Dover harbour whilst the rest of the fleet hove to. As the ships started to clear their decks ready for landing Harold Harfoot and his chosen men stepped out from the cover of the dock buildings and loosed controlled volleys of arrows, clearing the deck of the first ship. The second ship quickly went about with its oarsmen frantically pulling as the archers turned their attention to it. As the range increased so the archers turned to individual shots until only Harold, a Canterbury pilgrim badge on one breast and a white crusader's cross on the other, continued to shoot. His target each time was the steersman. As one steersman went down so another replaced him and Harold shot him too until the galley was over three hundred and fifty yards to sea. At last Harold unstrung his bow. He turned to his chosen men, 'I did well!' he cried.

'YOU DID WELL!' they shouted joyously back.

'Your men in the harbour William; they did well.' Oliver had returned from watching Harold Harefoot's triumph in Dover harbour and now stood at the Warden of the Weald's shoulder.

'No less than I demand Oliver; no less than I demand.' Cassingham's squire looked along the ranks of people manning the cliff top of Dover; over half of them were town's folk of Dover and the folk of the local villages and hamlets. Women in men's clothing stood alongside elderly men and young boys. Instead of real bows they held staffs or sticks with strings attached to them to look like unstrung bows. In front of everyone on the cliff were rows of arrows jammed into the thin soil that covered the chalk.

The French fleet sailed under the cliff just out of arrow shot and headed south towards a less hostile landing place.

'They are at Sandwich and heading this way Master.'

'Thank you Gamble.' William turned to Oliver and the noble's household knights. *'My Lord.'*

Oliver smiled to see that, with others present; the Warden became more formal in addressing him and was speaking in French too. *'Yes William?'*

'I suggest that we pull out of Dover and return to harassing the French rather than get involved in a battle we don't have the numbers to win.'

'I agree that that would be wise.'

Oliver's knights joined him in discussing their next move. John Little stood near them with a blank look on his face not betraying the fact that he understood everything they were saying.

William turned to Gamble Gold. 'Get back and see what the Dauphin is up to. I suspect that Dover will not be his only objective.'

'I will. I will also pray for the people of Sandwich – they swore loyalty to Louis then changed sides when the Regent came their way. Louis will not like that.'

'Changing sides is always fraught with danger Gamble, always fraught with danger.'

Chapter 14: Back and Forth

Godfrey sat on the bench outside the fisherman's cottage overlooking the jetty at Bosham. On one side sat the object of his desire, Rose of the Long Legs, on the other her brother Jon Fish. The sun was setting and the warmth of the spring day was leaching away. Godfrey bent down and picked up his cloak and put it around Rose's shoulders. She smiled at him and snuggled a bit closer. Jon watched and smiled. 'Don't offer me no cloak then Godfrey who would be Herla.'

'Ha, a big brave fisherman like you our Jon? What you need a cloak for? Tis us fair and delicate maids that needs comfort!' Rose turned and smiled at Godfrey. 'He's just a dumb lump him, don't you take no notice of Jon.' Her red hands, that still gave an occasional glisten from a fish scale despite having been washed, reached out and took those of her swain. 'I like that you looks after me Godfrey Wulfson.'

'I would like to look after you all the time Rosie. Would you be happy for me to ask your father for your hand?'

'Don't ask Godfrey, just take her. Our dad would be glad to get her off his hands.'

Rose Fish poked her tongue out at her brother then laid her head on Godfrey's shoulder. 'I would like that very much. When would we be wed then?'

'After all this fighting is done Rosie.' Godfrey risked putting an arm around his beloved's waist. Seeing as he wasn't pushed away Godfrey pulled Rose closer. 'I don't know when that will be. Last we heard the Marshal has pulled out of Winchester after slighting the castle and city walls. The French Prince is at Dover now after burning Sandwich down. Thomas has taken men towards Surrey to help them watch the roads down into the Weald as word is that the French are trying to bring an army south from London.'

Rose put a slightly fish perfumed hand to Godfrey's face. 'I hopes it all ends soon – my love.'

Godfrey blushed at the words and gave a deep happy sigh.

'Snipping.' Thomas slumped onto the bed in the cottage he and his twin shared. 'Too much open country so all we managed to do was pick off stragglers and anyone too stupid to wander off the main road between Reigate and Guildford.'

Godfrey helped his brother remove his fancy French riding boots. 'They were on the way to Winchester. The Regent has abandoned the place; Will the Scarlet told me on his way to inform Willikin.'

Thomas removed the cloths that wrapped his feet exposing toes that were wrinkled and very white. He bent forward and massaged them. 'It is so good to get them boots off it must be a fortnight since I last took them off.'

'Smells like it too.'

'Not as bad as Mark's though?'

Godfrey went and brought back a wooden bucket of water for his brother. 'Nothing is as bad as Mark's feet.'

'How's things with Rosie then?' Thomas got up and then stood in the bucket of water.

'Progressing slowly.'

'Get any fish?'

'Some smoked fish; we can have it tonight if you like.'

'It will make a change from dried meat and berries.' Thomas did a strange sort of dance causing the water in the bucket to slosh around. 'I wonder when Willikin will make another demand on us?'

William the Warden shook his head. 'Why would he do that without telling me? Why would de Burgh sally out from Dover Castle without telling me first?' he demanded of his Reeve.

Mark shrugged his shoulders, 'Saw an opportunity?' he suggested.

'He had a truce with the French. It is not like him to break a truce.'

'Something must have happened Master, but who knows what it was.'

'Well he has pulled a wasp nest around his ears hasn't he. The Dauphin has gone back to Dover, rebuilt his siege camp and brought more trebuchet over from France and started pounding the castle like it has never been pounded before.' William paced up and down. 'Get the word out Mark, we will have to go and sort out the Dover situation once again.'

William and his Reeve watched from the cliff as the French fleet fought against the rough seas to try and make Dover harbour. After a couple of hours only five made the haven and the other ships put back to France.

The pair stood and dusted down their clothes.

'That will buy us some time Master.'

'It will, but will it buy us enough time?'

'Word has been sent to Admiral Philip d'Albabini?'

'Yes,' William did his habitual beard stroke. 'But will he arrive in time to be of help?'

'Here we go again,' Godfrey loosened his cloak and let it drop to the ground.

'More waiting,' Thomas mirrored his twin.

'Well,' Mark the Archer sat himself down on the cliff top outside Dover and pulled his leathern costrel round from his back. 'It could be worse, at least these days we can ride a horse to get here rather than walk.' He pulled the cork from the stopper and took a swig. 'Ow, cider from Kent tastes good.'

'Pass it here when you have finished.' Will Greenleaf continued standing and watching the fleet of about forty French ships that were approaching Dover.

'You, young man,' Mark took another swig of cider. He shuddered with pleasure. 'You are too young to be drinking such powerful stuff as this.'

Godfrey pulled his leather bottle off his shoulder and passed it to the slim youth. 'Here, try this instead.'

Will looked askance. 'Cider?'

'Sorry, no, just watered ale.'

Mark grinned and handed over his costrel. 'All right young 'un. Get your laughing gear around this if you think you can handle it.'

Will took a swig, coughed and spluttered. Once he recovered he took a more cautious mouthful. 'Powerful alright Mark.'

'Don't drink too much Will.' Thomas sat down alongside Mark. 'You may still have to draw a bow if the French make it to land and try to move out along the coast road.'

'If they make it Good Fellow Thomas for, look, here come the English ships.'

'Aye,' Godfrey shaded his eyes. 'And twice as many of them as there are French and it looks as if many of the English are big ships too.'

'Big or small ships big brother, it is skill in handling that will determine the outcome. Remember what happened at Winchelsea when the lead English ship turned and sank one of its own?'

The band of archers from the Boxholt all nodded their heads.

'Are they close to the French yet Will?'
'Not yet Good Fellow Thomas.'
'Wake me when they are.'

'Well Will?'
'Almost there Good Fellow Godfrey.'
'Wake me when they are.'

Will Greenleaf eased the leathern costrel from the sleeping Mark Archer's hands and took a sip of the cider within it. He smiled, took another sip, replaced the stopper and put it back into Mark's

266

hand. He nudged the sleeping man until he awoke. 'Mark, the English ships are coming up fast on the French ones.'

'Eh? What? Oh!' Mark pulled himself up on an elbow and rubbed his eyes. 'Best wake the twins.'

'We,' Thomas assured him, 'have been awake for some time.'

'You have had too much cider Mark,' Godfrey tapped the costrel with his toe. 'That stuff is too powerful for you I think.'

Mark grunted and stood with the rest of the Boxholt men to watch the coming clash of fleets.

As the English ships drew within bowshot almost half the French made about and fled back towards France. The English let them be and concentrated on cutting off the rest of the French from Dover. The remaining French ships closed on each other in a tight formation with the English ships snapping at them like wolves attacking a flock of sheep. The French tactics allowed nineteen of them to make harbour, battered but secure, whilst the English ships towed away eight as prizes.

The men of the Boxholt sat back in the familiar setting of the woods facing the south of Dover Castle. Sitting on a round of wood sat a wooden hogshead of ale already half empty.

Godfrey stood and refilled his leather jack from the spigot. 'They would have had more success if they had had proper archers like us on the ships, not crossbowmen.'

'Shorter range, slower loading they are,' Thomas agreed as he held out his own jack for more ale.

Garth joined his uncle Godfrey at the hogshead and took Thomas' jack and held it under the spigot whilst the golden ale gushed into it. 'They still took eight ships though.'

'And let nineteen get in!' Godfrey sat carefully down next to his twin.

'More work for us soon I guess,' Mark Archer commented as he chewed on some dried meat.

'They did for the French crews I heard Mark.'

'Oh they did young Jack Samuelson, they surely did. Threw them all overboard to drown.'

'Not the knights!'

'True Jack, true. That's chivalry for you that is.' Mark ripped another shred of meat off into his mouth.

'Knights will save knights Jack,' Godfrey explained.

'That, young man, is because you can ransom a knight or above. Sailors though, are not worth anything.' Thomas took a mouthful of ale and swallowed. 'That's how chivalry works: you act generously to a captured foe – but only if you can make money out of it!'

Garth half filled his battered pewter tankard with ale. 'They would not have thrown any clergy overboard to drown would they? I know the Pope has excommunicated any who side with the rebels or the Dauphin, but surely they would have spared priests or monks if they were aboard.'

Thomas chortled and almost started to choke on his ale. Eventually he got himself under control. 'Well nephew, I'm sure they would, being chivalrous knights and all that, but not if the clergyman was Eustace the Monk.'

'Even the Pope would have chucked that pirate overboard.'
Godfrey downed his ale whilst the others of the Boxholt nodded in
agreement with his statement.

'Well?' The Warden looked up with a furrowed brow.
'The English fleet have started to blockade Dover harbour
stopping any more French ships getting in or those in there from
getting out.'
'And? What is happening with the large number of
reinforcements from those ships that got in?'
'Well Master, some of the French troops are rebuilding their
siege camp but a lot of them are heading down the coast road
towards Hythe and Romney.'
William of Cassingham looked at Mark Reeve then stood up
from his camp stool and strode purposefully into his pavilion. He
went to his bed, picked up his sword and came back out. 'I am
guessing they are on their way to punish those towns for swapping
sides and sending ships to join our fleet; the fleet that has just
given the French a bloody nose.' The Warden of the Weald looked
towards the woods where his men were gathered, awaiting
instructions. 'Get the Boxholt men to horse and head on the back
road to Hythe; they are to take on the vanguard in the hope that
they can stall the French long enough for the folk of Hythe to get
out of the place first. The men of Kent we will lead and attack the
rear guard in the hopes the others will turn round to help them.'
'I am not sure how this will work out Master; there is not much
cover on the coast road for archers to work, and them trying to
take on cavalry on open ground is just asking for disaster.'

'I know Mark, but we must try.'

Godfrey and Thomas sat on their short legged horses ahead of the men of the Boxholt and looked at the long column of French progressing down the coastal road towards Hythe.

Godfrey took a deep breath and let it out slowly. 'I don't like this Thomas; I don't like it at all.'

'How on earth are a hundred or so archers, unarmoured, expected to take on and beat two, three thousand armoured troops? I mean, they have more heavy cavalry than we have arrows, let alone men to shoot them.'

Thomas stared at the view in front of him. 'We can't. We can cause them some grief, but that is all.'

'And it will cost us just to do that!'

'Agreed big brother. We must do what we can, but stop them we can't.'

'Willikin did say he had sent word to Hythe and Romney to evacuate and for the folk to get into the Weald didn't he?'

'He did Godfrey, he did.'

'But, we all know what folk are like ….'

'Don't like to leave things behind.'

'They always hope for the best Thomas, despite what stares them in their face.'

'Let's send Will Greenleaf with a couple of the youngsters to chase them along.'

'Good idea brother but will they take notice of a youth?'

'Then I will write letters for him to take to the burgesses.'

'Don't sign them in our names; sign them in Willikin's, they will take more notice then.'

With that the twins turned their mounts around and made their way back to their men.

The archers waited for the French army just over two miles before Hythe - just after the road from the small hamlet of Sandgate started its gentle climb to the heights that led to the Cinque Port's walls. The men were distributed in four rows one behind the other, each row being one hundred yards apart from the one in front. Behind each row stood five of their number holding the horses. The rear row was made up of men from Surrey and Hampshire under Michael the Mouse, the next was a mixture of Surrey and some East Sussex men under Gasper the Ghost. The front rows were the men of the Boxholt under the twins.

Godfrey turned in the saddle and looked back at the fighting formation he and Thomas had set out. 'I hope we have this right Thomas.'

Thomas followed his brother's line of sight. 'So do I, though it is very risky but then …'

'We can't think of any other way to fight this skirmish.'

Godfrey eased himself off his short legged mount and took it to young Seb to hold. He nodded his thanks before resuming his talk with his brother. 'Give them what? Two hundred yards? It's extreme range.'

Thomas rode to the side of his brother. 'No more nor less; two volleys and then off.'

'Not three?'

'No big brother, I don't think so.'

'Better safe than sorry then.' Godfrey walked to the end of the line of his archers and collected his bow from his nephew Garth. Thomas rode back to the next line back and handed his horse to Granfer Gilbert before he also took a position at the end of the line of his men.

They waited.

It was the dust rising in the air that first warned of the French approaching along the road from Folkstone. After the warning from the dust came the sound - the jingling, tramping, creaking sound of an army on the march. Eventually the point guard horsemen appeared starkly outlined against the dust blurred ranks behind them. The horsemen halted then two peeled off and rode back to the body of the army whilst the rest carefully and suspiciously rode slowly towards the English.

'Come back Harold Harefoot,' Godfrey muttered under his breath. 'All is forgiven.'

The point guard halted again, this time only about two hundred and fifty yards away. Soon they were joined by five conroi of armoured horsemen. The horsemen formed into two ranks deep and started to trot towards the English.

Godfrey watched, noting the rate of approach as the French neared the marker he had set for two hundred yards. At two hundred and ten yards he cried; 'NOCK!' At two hundred 'DRAW' the archers of his line pushed their bows forward, pulled back on the string and raise their bows skyward 'LOOSE!'

The arrows flew. Thomas called to his men. 'NOCK!'

Without waiting to see the result of his men's volley Godfrey called 'NOCK – DRAW – LOOSE!'

The arrows again flew. Godfrey slipped his bow over his shoulder as he ran. 'To horse, to horse,' he cried and his men ran too and grabbed their mounts from the horse holders. As Godfrey's men mounted Thomas cried 'DRAW – LOOSE,' and his men's volley went flying towards the French cavalry which had now moved from trot to the canter. Godfrey's men rode through the gaps in Thomas' rank as those men loosed their second volley. As Thomas' men ran to their mounts the men under Gasper's command loosed their first volley just as Godfrey and his men went through their ranks and made for those of Michael's. As the second volley left the bows of Gasper's men, Thomas and his men rode through them and Godfrey's men passed Michael's ranks. As Michael's men made their first volley Godfrey's men had formed a rank behind them and stood ready with arrows nocked. By now the surviving French horsemen were at the gallop; in the distance more conroi were forming up.

The game started again; first Godfrey's men, then Thomas' men, then Gasper's men, then Michael's shot two volleys and then fell back through the other ranks. The first cavalry charge had floundered in a mess of fallen men and horses but the next wave was already on its way. Again the archers shot volleys and then fell back, rank by rank. This charge also petered out though more of the cavalry remained mounted as the English archers' hurried shooting became less accurate. The surviving French turned and waited to join the next wave of attackers. Godfrey stood in his stirrups; he pulled his hunting horn round, put it to his lips and gave two short and one very long blast. The archers looked to him and he pointed towards the Whitenbrook Woods before kicking his horse into the best gallop it could muster.

The others followed but Gasper's men were slow and got run down as they tried to mount. Whilst the front row of French finished off the men of Surrey and East Sussex the following ranks broke formation and set out to pursue the other English who were headed for the woods. The English made the woods first and slid from their horses and quickly drew bows and turned those French silly enough to enter the woods into feather covered hedgehogs, but it was all too late for Gasper's men and also too late for Granfer Gilbert who rode a horse as ancient as its rider and the poor beast had proved no match for the French destriers in the race for the trees.

Finding it too dangerous to hunt the English archers in the woods the French cavalry turned and re-joined the main body of the army and the whole moved on towards Hythe.

Godfrey and Thomas watched them go. At last Thomas spoke. 'I will miss not hearing old Granfer Gilbert's stupid cuckoo call.'

'So will I. Michael Mouse will miss his mate Gasper too, they were very close.'

'There will be much mourning in the villages of southern Surrey and East Sussex after this day's actions.'

Godfrey sighed and lowered his head over the neck of his horse. He stayed there for several heartbeats. Eventually he lifted himself up. 'The problem Thomas is that the French can lose as many men as they like and bring more in from over the sea to replace them. We? We have only a finite number of men, if you only want good

274

archers that is. It takes years of training. As it is we are already using men such as Jon Fish, who only shoots for sport. We can't go on like this – they will wear us down. What we need is a miracle.'

'Or the French to do something really, really stupid.' Thomas yanked on his horse's bit and turned the animal around. 'Romney? We make a stand there?'

'No; we can't risk losing any more men. We go there and make sure the folk know to get out and seek refuge in the Weald. Then we go home and lick our wounds.'

Rain rattled on the roof of the run-down hunting lodge in the wild woods south of Dover. Inside a damp Alan of the Slaed declined the offer of a seat that William of Cassingham had made. 'Too saddle sore to sit,' he said wryly, gently massaging his buttocks.

William gave a grimace; 'Yes, I have been doing a fair bit of riding myself, mostly trying to evade the French! Trying to attack them as they moved towards Hythe was a debacle. We got cut up until we managed to withdraw back to some woodland. If we had had more men-at-arms with us to supplement Oliver Fitzroy's few, maybe we could have made a stand but ...' He sighed. 'Too late now, one cannot rewrite the past and we cannot bring our dead comrades back to life.'

'The French have taken and burnt down Hythe and Romney.' Steam rose from the jongleur as his body heat started to dry out his clothes.

'That is what I assumed they would do.' William started pacing up and down.

'Now they march on Winchester.'

William stopped; 'No surprise there and, if he has any sense, the Regent won't try and hold it. We need something to happen; a miracle, a big change of luck, the rebel barons to realise that all they started this war for has been conceded by the Regent in the King's name. Something.'

'The French could always do something silly – they can be quite capricious and even woolly headed at times.'

The Warden of the Weald gave a short barking laugh. 'One can but pray that they do. I will get my priest to get on his calloused knees and start praying straight away.' William walked to the window and lifted the edge of the leather curtain. 'Well, I will once the rain eases off.'

Chapter 15: A Split Decision

William of Cassingham sat at high table with his wife, Reeve and Forester by his side. Facing them were his agents, Gamble Gold and William Scathlock; all of them were deep in thought and the cold meats, cheese and bread sat between them remained uneaten. Standing behind the squire in his black habit was Henry atte Trottingham, the Franciscan friar who acted as parish priest for Cassingham.

The deep silence was broken when the double doors eased open and James, Cassingham's Steward, came in and hurried to the high table. He bobbed his head in politeness; 'Master!'

William broke from his pondering and looked at the bald-headed servant. 'Yes James?'

'Your singer is here, Alan Slaed. He is taking his horse to the stables. Shall I bring him straight here?' James gave an ingratiating smile; 'I know you are expecting him.'

William gave a bored yawn. 'Yes James; bring him straight here.'

John Little snorted, 'Unless he first needs to use the …'

Mark Reeve kicked the tall forester under the table and indicated his head towards William's wife, Mary.

John looked abashed; 'Err, yes, it would be good if you could bring him straight here.'

Before the Steward could act the doors pushed open wider and Alan atte Slaed, jongleur and one of William's spies stepped in, his clothes splattered with horse foam and his hair windswept. James moved out of the way as Alan strode up to the table, a beaming smile on his face.

'They have done it!'

William gave his man a strong look; 'Who have done it Alan?'

'The French of course!'

'Done what?' the Lady Mary raised a single eyebrow.

'Something silly my Lady, something very questionable. Something,' he looked at the friar, 'something we have been praying for.'

William stared at the jongleur and impatiently tapped out a drum roll with his fingers on the waxed oak table. 'Alan, don't talk in riddles man; keep your word tricks for when you are entertaining. Just tell us what has happened!'

277

Alan, his eyes bright, was not discouraged in his enthusiasm; 'The Dauphin has split his forces!'

William abruptly stood up; 'What?'

'Yes, yes. I was playing my lute in the hall at Farnham, where he sat with his French nobles and the leading rebel barons, when he agreed to the Earl of Winchester's request to send a relief force to Mount Sorrel where his garrison is being besieged. Louis is sending half his force!'

'What of the rest?'

'Well Master, they continue on to try and retake Winchester.'

Gamble grunted. 'Easily done as the Regent has slighted the castle and city walls and pulled his men out.'

'And,' interrupted Will Scathlock, 'some of the French have gone back to continue the siege of Dover castle; I saw them on the coast road on my way here.'

'Well,' Alan continued, 'a lot of the French were not happy about going to Mount Sorrell. I think it may be because they may have to go through the Weald to get to London on the way.'

William sighed, 'Yes, well, those that live on their route may give them some grief as they make their way through the forest but after our mauling on the road from Dover to Hythe it will be hard to get the men of the Weald to muster in enough strength to stop them altogether.' He turned to his man in scarlet; 'Will – do we have any good contacts near Mount Sorrell that may be able to assist the Regent?'

'We have,' Scathlock replied. 'Robert of Loxley for one and I know he is spoiling for a fight.'

'He is an outlaw mind Will,' Gamble reminded him.

'Depends on who named him a wolfshead doesn't it.'

'True Will and if he can get his band of fellow outlaws to help thwart the rebels and their French friends I am sure there will be a pardon available.'

'Indeed Gamble.'

William, still standing, coughed. 'If you two have finished?' The Warden's men fell silent. 'Right, good.' William turned to Scathlock; 'Will, get word to this Robert and any others nearby. Gamble?'

'Master?'

'Find out what route the French are taking then see if our London contact knows if those garrisoned there are being used to boost the force. I need information to alert our own folk – I want them to annoy the rear guard of any army going through the Weald; I do not want the French blocked from moving north as it would stop them splitting their forces. The London information needs to be got to the Regent. We can do that?'

'Oh our London contact, Godwin Wulf, he has sons to spare and all of them only too willing to run errands, especially if there is a silver penny or more in it for them.'

'Good; see to it.' William turned to his Reeve. 'Mark try and get enough men of Kent together to remind the French besieging Dover that we are still around.'

'John get over to the Boxholt men and make sure they are still willing to fight.'

'Master.'

'Henry?'

'Master?'

'Back to the church and get on your knees to thank God for His mercy and French stupidity.'

The friar gave a resigned sigh; 'Yes Master.'

'Alan?'

'Master?'

'Get yourself cleaned up and then fed; I will have tasks for you too once you are refreshed.'

'Master.'

William turned at last to his wife as his men hurriedly left the hall. 'It seems, my love, that once more we have some hope.'

'My love.' Mary reached out and touched her husband's hand. 'Will you be staying here to organise things?'

'No; I must go and find the Regent and see what he plans to do. You, my sweet, must do the co-ordinating and, if necessary, get word to me. The men trust you as they trust me.' William lifted his wife's hand and kissed it.

Will Greenleaf carefully hoed between the lines of dark green cawel in the small fenced off garden behind the cottage he shared with the Wulfson twins. The late April sun dried the soil as he cut and turned it, exposing the roots of the grass and weeds that had grown there whilst they had all been away fighting the French. The gentle warmth of the sun and the quite babble of the women and children going about their daily tasks lulled the youth into a dreamlike state. His mind wandered until a song caught in his head and he started to quietly sing to himself:

'Summer is a coming in and winter's go away-o,

We shall start to dance and sing all the live long day-o,

Bessie Bright and Hodden Horse shall come and join the fun-o,
For summer is a coming in and winter's go away-o!'
'You won't have time for May celebrations and Hodden Horse
this year lad!'

Will stopped singing, came out of his revelry, lifted his hoe
across his chest and swung round, ready to strike.

John Little smiled at the slim youngster's warlike attitude. 'Only
me, youngster, only me.'

'Good Fellow John Little; you gave me such a shock.' Will
lowered the hoe and lent on it to observe the strongly built tall man
facing him. 'To what do we owe the honour?' Will said, his eyes
guarded.

John saw the look and spread his hands to indicate his presence
presented no threat. 'I was passing through this part of the Weald
and thought I come and see how the Wulfson twins and their
people were faring, that's all.'

'We are fine, though the widows to the east and north are not so
well in their feelings.'

'Ah, yes, war is hard, especially for those left behind.' John
glanced around; 'Are the twins about?'

Will considered the question, still leaning on his hoe; 'Hunting,'
he eventually said. 'With no nobles demanding a hunt there are too
many deer and they are entering our pastures and crops so most of
the men have gone out to cull the numbers down.'

'And provide free meat?' John asked, a twinkle in his eye.

'Yes, meat for the families of the village, seeing as many of the
men have been away fighting and therefore the grain harvest will
be poor again.'

The tall forester saw that his attempt to lighten the conversation had failed so he gave a grunt and had a quick look around, hoping to see one of the older men, but the only village folk he could see were women and children, Will being the eldest male in view. 'Is Mark Archer around, or is he out with the hunters?'

Will shifted his stance a mite. 'He is a Wulfbearding man not an Iping man. Besides, he is out with a handful of other men of the Boxholt watching the roads for French messengers and patrols.'

'Right young Greenleaf; it is Will Greenleaf isn't it?'

'Yes, that's me,' the finely built youth replied, still keeping a watchful eye on Little.

'Right Will, when you see the twins ask them to be ready to gather the bands together in the next week or two; things are stirring, big things.'

'Will it see the end of the fighting Good Fellow Little?'

'We live in hope, young Greenleaf, we live in hope, but nothing in life is certain and in war even less certain.' John Little walked back to his horse, which had hung its head over the garden fence in the futile hope it could reach the green plants growing within. He mounted the beast, gave a farewell wave to Will and rode off on the road north still looking around in the hope of seeing the twins.

Will left the vegetable patch, secured the gate, and stood by the cottage door. 'Did you hear all that Good Fellows?'

Godfrey opened the door a fraction. 'We heard it.'

'And,' Thomas added, 'we are glad you kept us out of it.'

Will nodded and returned to the garden and his hoeing.

Inside the cottage Godfrey and Thomas went back to preparing the venison stew for that evening's meal.

'What now little brother?' Godfrey asked as he scrapped the sliced mushrooms off his cutting board into the cauldron of water.

'I think you can still go to Bosham to court long legged Rosie Fish. I will cover for you and send word if we are called to action by Willikin.' Thomas continued to dice the meat on his own cutting board.

'I just wish this fighting would come to an end – I have more important things to do than keep on shooting Frenchmen.' He looked to his brother. 'It is alright for you as your Lucy lives in the next village.'

'True and that is why I am happy to cover for you whilst you go a courting big brother.'

Mary, the Lady of Cassingham, sat in the solar with two of her women mending linen shirts, enjoying the warm sunlight. One of the women started to hum a folk tune but she was interrupted by the sound of someone running up the stairs from the great hall beneath. The door flew open and William of Cassingham burst in holding a rolled parchment in his hand. 'Mary, Mary – news! Great news!'

His wife stood, put down her sewing and gently ushered her women out. Once they had left she turned to her husband and wagged a finger at him. 'You shouldn't do that William! In these times you don't know who you can trust – you use spies and agents yourself, so you should know better. Amice was one of the women who we took in from the siege camp at Dover, for all we know she may still side with the French.'

'My love,' William swept his wife up with his spare hand and spun her round in a dance. 'My love I can see the light!'

Mary glanced to the window and then back at William; 'Husband?'

'The storm may be passing as the sky is starting to shew some sunlight!'

Mary forcibly stopped the twirling dance. 'William, my love, husband; talk clearly for at the moment you speak in riddles like Alan Slaed!'

William stood there and just smiled. 'This,' he shook the parchment at her. 'This is from the Regent – his army trapped the rebels and the French between them and the castle garrison in the city of Lincoln.'

'Yes?'

'They crushed them – THEY CRUSHED THEM.'

Mary came and took her husband in an embrace. 'At last, there a chance of winning.'

'Indeed there is for the rebel barons are all but destroyed, the French leaders killed or captured, the French army, those that survived, are fleeing and being attacked by the local folk. CRUSHED!' William kissed his wife with a passion. 'Crushed,' he whispered in her ear.

Mary pulled back from her husband; 'But they always get more men in from France.'

'That is my worry too but, for now, let us celebrate!' He swirled her back into his improvised dance.

Thomas stood by the head of his brother Godfrey's short legged horse and stoked its neck. 'All well big brother? Long Legged Rose still loving you? I'm sure she does as you smell of fish!'

Godfrey slipped off the horse and started to untie the bulging cloth bags that hung from the back of the saddle. 'Don't start that one again. The smell comes from the bags; they are stuffed with dried fish from Bosham; I thought we might take it on campaign if we get called out again – it would stop Jack Samuelson moaning about a lack of variety in his diet.'

Thomas pushed against the horse's neck as if for support. He raised a rather bloodshot eye at Godfrey. 'You look tired.'

'Not as tired as you look. What are you getting up to?' Godfrey watched as Thomas' face went red. 'Oh, right; late nights of meaningful talks with Lucy.'

'Something like that big brother.'

Godfrey snorted. '"Something like that" - something like that indeed.'

'It's not just Lucy that is tiring me out. I mean, in order to make others think you are here, I have to change my clothes and then back into my own ones – I hardly know at times just who I am!'

Godfrey lent over his brother and sniffed; 'I don't think it is just being my double that is causing your confusion.'

'Ah, yes,' Thomas wiped his mouth on the back of his hand. 'Elderberry wine. Lucy gave me some, two years old – it is rather "heady".'

'Hmm, Thomas,' Godfrey ruffled his brother's cropped fair hair. 'Sometimes I worry about you.'

'Don't do that!' Thomas shook his brother's hand away and immediately regretted the action as his head swam. He looked about then shouted; 'Will Greenleaf: come and take this....' Thomas lowered his head. 'Dear God I wish I hadn't done that. Godfrey; can we go inside once Will has the horse in hand? I prefer the darkness at the moment.'

Will came bounding over, took control of the horse, winked at Godfrey, poked his tongue out at Thomas, who still had his head down, and lead the creature towards the village pond for a drink.

Godfrey, his bags over his shoulder, chest shoved his brother towards the cottage.

Thomas staggered inside and happily slumped onto a large sack of flour, sending up a fine white haze. 'I am so glad you are back.'

'To keep you from Lucy's arms or keep you from her elderberry wine?'

'Neither, for both are wonderful,' Thomas slurred. 'No, it is that we are summoned by Willikin. If you hadn't got back today I would have had to send word to bring you home.'

'I trust it is for a more sensible course of action than that last shambles.'

'Who knows big brother all I know is that Will, the red haired man in scarlet, was here this morning saying that the French had relieved somewhere, Mount of Sorrow, or something like that, and now were headed for Lincoln. It seems that a rebel baron has taken that town and wants the castle.'

Godfrey joined his brother and started to take off the French riding boots he had borrowed from Thomas without asking. 'Shew me a baron who does not want a castle – they all want castles.'

286

Thomas looked at the boots trying to remember if he had lent them to his brother or not. Eventually his fuddled brain gave up. He focused on what he had been saying before seeing his missing footwear. 'Mount of Squirrels, that's it, then Lincoln.' Thomas smiled, 'Got it. Lincoln is where the Regent hopes to bring the rebels and the French to battle, seeing as they only have half the Frenchies' army there.'

'What's that to us Thomas: and don't go to sleep!' Godfrey gave his brother a shake.

'I'm not going to sleep,' Thomas blinked his eyes open. 'No: "what is it to us"? No idea.' With that Thomas fell back on the sack and started snoring.

'He wasn't happy.'

William of Cassingham turned to his jongleur, Alan atte Slaed, 'I bet he wasn't.'

'The Dauphin was in fact very pissed off.'

'No surprise there. Having half his force and the rebel's main army destroyed; I'd be pissed off too if it was me. Did you hear what he planned to do next?'

'He is expecting replacement troops from France.'

'Word has been sent to Admiral Philip d'Albabini?'

'By fast pony; one of the stable boys I have been keeping sweet.'

William looked at the jongleur quizzically; 'Sweet?'

'He likes ribbons and little bells and things he thinks will get him into a girl's favour; Gamble Gold supplies me with them.'

'Right.' William ran his hand over his grey beard. 'You didn't think of going yourself?' he asked.

'Too obvious. If I am to keep getting into places I need to preserve my cover, besides my music is in demand with the French.'

William poked Alan in the ribs and whispered in his ear; 'I've always said the French had strange tastes!'

Godfrey, Thomas and the men of the Boxholt stood back on the cliffs of Dover overlooking the sea and once again looked at French and English ships coming together.

'You have good eyes Garth,' Thomas pointed to the converging fleets. 'How many Frenchies do you think?'

The youth squinted his eyes and his lips moved silently as he calculated. 'About a hundred and twenty, well thereabouts, I can't be precise,' he said eventually.

'More than us then,' Godfrey sipped from the stone crock of elderberry wine before passing it on to Surrey's Michael the Mouse whose men now stood with those of West Sussex.

Mark Archer pointed, 'What's that then? Oh no, French ships coming out of Dover harbour.' Michael passed him the crock of wine and then sat down to watch.

'Wake up uncles,' Garth bent between Thomas and Godfrey took hold of an elbow of each and shook them. 'Things are happening.'

Godfrey rubbed his eyes and sat up. He looked down at the sea. 'Bugger - the French from Dover are chasing our own ships away.'

Thomas edged himself up and leaned against his brother. 'But look; the English ships are going about!'

Godfrey looked at Thomas; 'You know nautical terms?'

'You are not the only one to go sniffing amongst the fishing boats of Bosham brother.'

The twins stood up, brushed grass from their clothes and joined the other watchers on the cliff.

'Well,' Thomas concluded as he put the now empty wine crock down. 'That was an unexpected surprise.'

Garth picked up the crock to check it was indeed empty. 'Eight French ships captured.' He gave the upturned crock a shake, but nothing came out.

'Eight captured? Seems that eight is a luck number for the English fleet!' Mark Archer took the empty cock and double checked it was indeed empty.

Godfrey pulled the crock from Mark and shoved it into Thomas' hands. 'A feigned retreat. They knew they couldn't take on the big French fleet but they tempted the Dover based ships to chase them till they were beyond help from the others then cut them off and took them.'

'Very clever,' Mark came and put his arm around Thomas' shoulder. 'Did you say you had some more of the stuff back in your bivouac?' he said as he looked at the empty crock.

A gentle breeze stirred the hooked up flap of Cassingham's pavilion.

'He wasn't happy.'

William of Cassingham looked up from his seat on the camp chair planted in the pavilion entrance and gave his full attention to his jongleur, Alan atte Slaed, 'What about this time? It seems the Dauphin is never happy these days so, what is it this time?'

'The number of men they sent him; lots of ships, few supplies and very few men.'

'Good – it will make our job easier. Any news on what he will do next?'

'He is sending the ships back to France in the hopes his wife and his supporters there can scrape the barrel some more and get him the extra men he needs to save his campaign. There was talk around the table of them all leaving Dover and moving to London as the garrison there was depleted to join the Mount Sorrel relief force, the one that got the chop at Lincoln.'

William played with his beard. 'Can you get back into their camp and find out more?'

'I will try and see what I can do.'

'Don't take too many risks Alan.' William smiled. 'You are too valuable a man to lose.'

John Little strode through the woods that Willikin's men were camped in blowing his hunting horn. Behind him strode Mark Reeve shouting again and again; 'UP, UP, UP the French have burnt the surplus boats, their army is on the move to London and we are going to go and burn the siege camp.'

'Again?' Thomas asked Godfrey who just shrugged his shoulders in response.

Godwin Wulf sat at the high table of Cassingham with William and Mary; between them on the table stood a half firkin of mead on a wooden cradle. The glow in the cheeks of all three of them shewed that the half firkin was no longer full.

William sighed contentedly. 'Wonderful stuff Godwin, and I thought you only brewed ale and beer.' His wife dabbed her lips with a napkin and also sighed with pleasure.

Godwin took the gilden goblets of his hosts and refilled them. William and Mary both went to protest but then, with a smile, accepted the vessels that were now filled with fragrant golden liquid.

William took a sip and then took an appreciative deep breath before turning to the Battersea brewer. 'It is true then? The Dauphin has sealed up London to keep the Royalists out and the citizens in?'

'Indeed Master William, or should that be Lord William seeing as you are Warden of the Weald?' Godwin lifted his own goblet in a toast and they all drank in response. 'Yes, London is all sealed up as tight as a barrel. I have no problems, being without the city and in Surrey, but even I, a supplier of provender, can't get into London.'

'Bad for business?' Mary placed her goblet down on the table with a slightly unsteady hand.

Godwin smiled. 'Not really my Lady. I may not be able to get my brews into London, but nor can travellers get into the city and they have to stay somewhere whilst they wait out events and "The Falcon" is as good a place as any.'

Mary looked at the brewer and tapped the lip of her goblet. 'With drink as good as this, no better place!'

'Thank you my Lady.'

William took another appreciative sip of the mead. 'Godwin, much as we like your company,'

'And information,' Mary added quickly lifting her goblet for another sip.

'And information,' her husband confirmed. 'As well as the superior ales, beer and now mead that you sell us, we do need you back near London to keep us informed of what is happening there.'

'You mean "how the Regent's negotiations for a French surrender" are going?'

'I don't believe that anything will come of them – the Dauphin is stalling for time, hoping for reinforcements to arrive so he can get back on the war trail.'

Mary giggled, took another sip of mead and looked at her husband 'With so many of the barons deserting the cause and going over to King Henry, Louis must know his only hope is from France.'

William looked at his wife, for whom giggling was something only to be done in the privacy of their bed. 'Err, yes my dear; the Regent has been very shrewd in re-issuing Magna Carta, handing out pardons to all who change sides and giving them back the lands they held before the war.' He gave his wife another look as she sipped more mead before merrily waving to him and giggling again.

Godwin gave a polite cough. 'My Lord I will leave now but is it right with you for me to see my cousins first?'

'Yes, I have sent them home now that the Dover siege camp is no more; just don't take too long in getting back to Battersea.'

Mary waved to Godwin as he left the room, giggled again, leaned across and laid her head on her husband's shoulder; 'Hi handsome,' she whispered in his ear before nibbling it.

Chapter 16: Down To The Sea In Ships

Wearing only thin linen shirts and straw hats the men and youths of Iping and Wulfbearding moved along the wheat crop with their sickles cutting the stalks whilst behind them followed the women, their skirts tied high into their belts, binding the cut wheat into sheaves. Behind the women came children, working in teams with an older child in charge, putting the sheaves into stooks of twelve sheaves to ensure the crop stayed dry. The day was hot and sunny and dust motes hung behind the reapers and the children following, despite wearing a cloth visor over nose and mouth, frequently had to break from their work to cough and sneeze. Ahead of the reapers hare and mice ran from the corn field seeking shelter in the woods that surrounded the leah land. As the sun rose so the reaping became harder and as the sun reached its zenith the workers headed for the shade of the trees where those too old or young to work had set out food and drink.

The day being hot eating was followed by sleeping by the adults. Whilst they dozed the young folk and children played club ball on the unploughed headland: Wulfbearding against Iping. The break from work was ended when Osbert Limp Leg brought a convoy of four ox wagons to the common field. Whilst the men went to fetch the club ball teams, the women stood, gossiped and laughed. The women's laughter increased when they heard the youngster's loud protests against the ending of their game before a result had been declared and the men's grumpy replies. The women called out support for their offspring and, eventually, after much catcalling, the men conceded and the club ball game was allowed to finish its final round of play with Wulfbearding's winning youngsters running back to the women and the wagons with yelps of glee followed by the smiling but less happy youth of Iping. The men trailed behind the players reminiscing about the games they had played together before the war came.

The folk clambered onto the wagons with women being given a helping hand, often in such a way that there was ribald laughter from those watching. Children were lifted up into the hands of the women before the men too embarked. The wagoners prodded their oxen with a goad and the wagons lumbered off from Iping to nearby Wulfbearding where the corn cut the day before stood waiting in stooks to be lifted onto the wagons and from there to the village barn from whence the church tithe of a tenth would be sorted and sent on to the Hundred tithe barn.

It was dark before all was gathered in and the folk of Iping made their way on foot back to their own village.

Godfrey trudged tiredly alongside his twin. 'It went well today Thomas, but I am looking forward to something to eat and drink and then bed.'

Thomas gave his brother a smile from a mouth edged with fatigue and brown dust. 'So am I. We have been blessed with five days of good weather; all we need now are another four.'

'That and not being needed by Willikin of the Weald.'

William of Cassingham, his Reeve and Head Forester all stood round a table in Dover castle's great hall. Facing them were the castle's commander, Hubert de Burgh, and his household knights of the Dover garrison.

De Burgh tapped the crude map on the table with a long slender finger; '*The rebels and French are gaining strength again Warden Willikin.*'

'*If only those at the battle of Lincoln had followed my practice of taking no prisoners this would not be a problem. Taking nobles and knights for ransom is gross stupidity, especially when it allows them to re-enter the fray.*'

'*Chivalry demands it, besides,*' de Burgh gave a wolfish grin. '*Besides it is very profitable – it makes money.*'

'*And,*' William re-joined, '*it could lose us the war.*'

The baron grunted then continued; '*Right, having got our differences out of the way, let's get on with working out a plan of action together.*'

'*I hear that you have been asked to lead the fleet.*'

Leaning over the map again De Burgh slowly nodded his head, the sunlight from an arrow slit reflected off the small bald patch that only those taller than the lanky baron normally saw, unless he bent over. '*Yes, I will sail from here with ships from East Anglia to meet up with Philip d'Aubigny and his fleet made up mostly of ships from the Cinque Ports.'*

'And Lord Philip will not be put out by you taking charge?'

'Not after all the winning and losing that has been going on in the Channel recently.' The baron straightened up. *'The Regent thinks we need a new leader at sea with fresh ideas and new tactics.'*

'How does this affect us?' William held out a hand, palm up, and indicated John Little and Mark Reeve.

'Archers.'

'Yes,' William agreed. *'We have archers. What of it?'*

'Your bows can outshoot crossbows?'

'They can. We are faster and our bows have a longer range.'

'Exactly. We need to outshoot the French before closing with them.' De Burgh hooked his thumbs into his belt. *'Can you get me archers, preferably ones who can also fight with spear, bill and sword?'*

William looked to his companions. 'Can we?' They nodded. William turned back to the baron. *'Yes we can.'*

'I hear you have a thousand archers.'

'I have heard that too my Lord, but I have always found that one should never believe all that one hears.'

John Little rode into Iping, this time with fifty or so mounted archers at his back. He rode straight up to the twin's cottage and threw his reigns at Garth Robertson who was lounging outside. 'Where are your uncles?' the tall and broad Forester demanded.

'On a deer cull,' the youth replied without reaching for the reins.

John Little gave the young man a hard brittle stare and eventually Garth stirred himself and took the horse's reins. 'Poaching then are they?' the Forester asked.

'I'm sure they have permission, it is just that, in these troubled times, it takes a long while for it to come back from our lord and master.'

The Forester dismounted and walked towards the cottage door. 'Boy if you only knew the number of times I've heard that excuse whilst in the execution of my duties.' Little pushed the door open, but saw no one within. 'So, they really are out after deer.'

Godfrey came round from the end of the cottage, brushing deer fur from his clothes with hands tinged with blood. 'Just back actually John Little.'

Thomas followed him, also brushing off fur. 'You have a task for us that Willikin wants done?'

John Little folded his arms across his chest and looked the pair over. 'Deer?'

'So many of them at present,' Godfrey advised him as he started to wash his dirty hands in the bucket of water by the cottage door.

'No parties of fancy folk wanting to hunt them these days,' Thomas explained.

'The war you see.' Godfrey moved out of the way to allow Thomas access to the water bucket.

'Eating our crops they are.' Thomas stood up and dried his hands on the hem of his shirt, which was rather the worse for wear and had many patches of mismatched colours.

'Something had to be done,' Godfrey shook his own hands to dry them.

297

'It does have an upside mind,' Thomas offered his shirt hem to his brother who declined the offer.

'We have plenty of venison.' Godfrey finished drying his hands with a quick wipe on the side of his shirt. 'Would you like some Head Forester Little?' he then asked with a smile.

'Cheeky buggers.' John Little unfolded his arms and winked at the twins. 'A carcass or two would not go astray; for the lad's evening meal.'

Thomas started to go back round the rear of the cottage but the Forester called out; 'No, stop. You can get the meat later. I need to talk to you first.' Little looked at the mounted archers, 'Right you lot, get your mounts some water at the pond and have something to eat yourselves – we have a long way to go today.' The men, led by Michael the Mouse of Surrey and Abe of Hampshire, turned their horses and made off for the village green and its pond. John Little watched them go before turning his attention back to the twins. 'How many men can you muster for what could be the final push?'

Godfrey looked to Thomas; 'Fifty? Sixty?'

'Probably more like forty seeing as not all the villages have brought in the wheat harvest as we have.'

The twins looked to John Little. The Forester gnawed at his thumb. 'Could you try and get it to the fifty at least?'

'If there was an incentive, perhaps,' Godfrey said.

'Like some share in decent plunder,' Thomas added putting an arm on his brother's shoulder.

Little pulled his thumb away. 'Plunder plus soldier's pay?' The twins said nothing, waiting for more information. 'Four pence a day?'

298

The twins looked at each other.

'Sounds fair,' Godfrey said to his brother.

'Must be a catch though,' Thomas cautioned.

The twins looked back at the Forester.

'Well,' the big man started. 'Not so much a catch as a risk.'

'Risk?' asked Godfrey.

'We don't like risks,' Thomas added. 'That's why we like being archers.'

'We kill at a distance.' Godfrey smiled and then put his own arm on his twin's shoulder.

'Ah.' John Little looked abashed. 'Well.' He gave a little cough. 'You will be acting as archers but you may have to act as men-at-arms too.'

'Risky that Godfrey.'

'Risky indeed Thomas.'

'You can wear mael.'

'John Little …' Godfrey started.

'You know full well we sold you all the coats of mael we have taken.' Thomas reminded the Forester.

'Less Willikin's fourth of course Little Brother.'

'True Big Brother.'

John waved his hand in front of him. 'Of course said coats of mael they would only be leased to you and your men. Though you may decide that wearing mael is not such a good idea, seeing as you will be at sea at the time.'

'Sea Little Brother? Did he say "sea"?'

'He did indeed Big Brother; he said "sea". Most definitely he said it.'

'Yes, yes, you comedians. I did say "sea". You have been on a ship before haven't you?'

'He has,' Thomas said, indicating his brother. 'He has been on a ship – he is courting a fisherman's daughter down in Bosham after all. Yes he knows all about ships does Godfrey.'

'What I have been on was more a boat actually: ships are bigger.'

'Have your men of the Boxholt been on boats or ships? Yes or no,' Little demanded.

'Yes and no, wouldn't you say Little Brother?'

'Those from the south yes, Head Forester, those from the north no. They might have paddled a bit on the River Rother, but I am sure that does not count.'

'Well my terrible twins get as many men as you can to Sandwich. We can sort them out there. We will need men based on land as well on ships.' John Little took his horse back from Garth. 'We are on our way there via Canterbury. I think you know that place. I think you used sword and buckler there – bring them with you this time too as you may need them. Willikin will meet you at Canterbury if you hurry or Sandwich if you don't. Hurrying would see Willikin in a better mood – bear that in mind.'

Garth watched the big man ride off to join the force of archers on the village green. 'So uncles we are now to be sailors.'

'So it seems sister's son, so it seems,' Godfrey set off to return to the slaughtered deer behind the cottage in order to select two for Little.

'As long as we don't end up smelling of fish!' Thomas whispered to his nephew as they went to join Godfrey.

'Ah, the perfume of Rosie Long Legs lingers long on my uncle.'

300

Jon Fish and his younger brothers Alf, Piers and Henry sat alongside the twins and Garth Robertson watching the English fleet as it gathered in Sandwich harbour. Jon Fish broke off some of the smoked herring in his hand and passed it to young Jack Samuelson who had been slowly edging closer in the hopes of varying his diet with produce from the sea. 'Here you are boy; now go leave us family in peace.' Jon looked knowingly at Godfrey. 'Well, soon to be family. That is if we aren't already family seeing as your'n mum came from Bosham too.'

Thomas choked back on a laugh and covered it by turning it into a cough.

Jon looked at him with concern; 'I hopes that cough ain't from fish bones.'

'They can be dangerous can fish bones,' Alf commented as he pulled a fragment of smoked fish from the near naked herring skeleton that sat in his lap, the oily ghost of the whole fish shewing on the salt stained linen of his shirt.

'That they can,' Piers confirmed whilst the youngest brother, Henry, nodded his agreement.

Godfrey, wanting to change the subject, pointed to the vessels in the harbour. 'Jon, they all look to be a lot bigger that the boats you sail in.'

'Oh they are that, that they are.'

'Ships, not boats see,' Alf clarified.

'That,' Jon said, indicating a ship with a single sail that was being manoeuvred towards a dock by oars, 'is what they now called a "nef" - French word is that.'

301

'At Bosham we always said they were a "karve",' Alf explained.

'Danish word is that,' Piers added. 'But then until Willie Bastard came, Countess of Wessex lived at Bosham a lot so I've heard, an' she were Danish see.' Henry nodded agreement.

Jon turned and saw that Jack had finished his bit of fish and threw the youth the remaining smoked herring he held. 'Fast they are, the nef,' he said as he turned back to the others. 'Good craft, but you can't overload them seeing as they sit fairly low in the water.'

Godfrey studied the nef and watched the crew as they shipped oars and let her glide into position against the wooden dock that protruded into the harbour. In front of her was a much larger ship that sat higher in the water. 'And that one?' he pointed.

'Ah,' Jon said. 'That be a cog.'

'Trader; lot slower than a nef but can carry a lot more.' Alf flicked the remains of herring off his lap. 'Used to call 'em knarr, but we are all Frenchified now.' He pulled the stopper from his leathern bottle out with his teeth. 'Well, 'cept our old dad – he do still call them a knarr.'

'Bit different is a cog from a knarr though Alf.'

'True Piers, true; higher in the water is a cog.'

'Them building fighting platforms on that 'un.' Henry suddenly looked embarrassed as his elder brothers looked at him, surprised that he had contributed to the conversation.

'Well, little 'un,' Jon said, with not a little condescension in his voice. 'That is because we are going to fight. Those platforms will be most useful for archers, especially if they are fighting against a nef. All that extra height makes even average archers like us useful.' The fisherman looked at Godfrey and then patted him on the shoulder. 'For we know that we are not as good a shot as an experienced forest man like you and,' he gave a cursory glance at Thomas and Garth, 'the others.'

Thomas, not liking the way he was being left out of things, shuffled himself forward a bit so that he could be seen better by the Fish brothers. 'What worries me is less archery and more the fact that we have been told that we will have to join any boarding party if we come alongside a French ship. I don't like close fighting.'

Jon chuckled. 'Well it is not so bad, we've done it a few times.'

'Taken French fishing boats we have,' Alf downed some of the watered ale from his bottle.

'Even taken a nef once,' Piers reminded him.

'With help from others of Bosham's fishing fleet mind,' Alf wiped his mouth with the back of his hand. Henry nodded his agreement.

Jon pulled a large canvas sack towards himself and rummaged inside before producing a selection of weapons. 'Now, I know you like the fact that you have swords now but when it comes to close fighting on a ship what you really need is one of these.' Jon laid the pile of weapons out in front of him. 'Often there is little room to weld a weapon like a sword. Now a nice hand axe is good.' Jon picked one out of the pile and checked it for balance before putting it down. He pointed to the next selection of weapons; 'A hand slasher works fine, or,' he picked up a long knife with a broken back profile, 'a good old fashioned saexe if you likes your tradition.'

303

'Our dad is very traditional.' Alf re-stoppered his bottle.

'True. Now,' Jon used the saexe to point to a lump of wood, 'this may look like just a piece of wood to you but it is in fact a specially designed club that we use on any big fish we catch.'

'Can't have big fish floundering around in your boat; might cause a capsize see.' Alf went to slip his arm through the bottle's long strap.

Piers took Alf's bottle from him and pulled the stopper out again. 'Just as good for stopping a French sailor from floundering around too as we have found.' Henry nodded agreement.

Jon put down the saexe with loving care before picking up the heavy club. 'I only brought one of these with us, so if you want one you will have to get or make your own; just make sure the club is made of a nice heavy wood; no point in it being soft is there.'

Piers screwed his mouth up after drinking from this elder brother's bottle. 'Terrible stuff this – I don't suppose, Godfrey, brother to be, that you have any of your Battersea cousin's beer left?'

Will Greenleaf came up quietly to the twins as they began getting ready for bed. 'Good Fellows?'

Inside the deerskin bivouac Godfrey looked up from the pile of straw he was shaping into a crude mattress. 'What's up young Will? You do not look at all happy.'

'About tomorrow.'

Thomas threw his cloak onto his own pile of straw before throwing himself down onto it. 'What about tomorrow? Worried about the battle? We all are. I am not sure about this sea thing.'

Will cast his eyes down. 'It is the sea thing.'

Godfrey continued to try and form a tidy bed from the straw. 'What about the sea thing Will?'

Will's voice went down to a whisper; 'I can swim.'

'You can swim?' the twins said together in amazement. 'We can't!'

'Yes, well I can swim and that is not a good thing.'

'Well,' Godfrey at last gave up his attempts with shaping the straw and imitated his brother by just throwing his cloak on the pile. 'Well I would have thought that was a good thing, being able to swim. If your ship goes down, or you fall overboard you can swim, whilst we,' he looked at Thomas and the already sleeping Garth and Mark Archer at the far end of the small tent. 'We drown.'

'But,' the swarthy youth insisted, 'that is the problem. If you can swim you would struggle for ages that far from shore before you drown; it is better not to be able to swim and then you drown quicker.'

Thomas looked up from his straw bed; 'He has a point – I know for a fact that none of the Bosham fishermen can swim and never want to either from what I have heard. All they can do is tread water, and you can't do that for long before you go under.'

Godfrey slowly eased himself onto his bed trying to have it maintain something of the shape he had moulded the straw into. 'So, Will, you want to stay on the land. Willikin did say there would need to be archers ready to counter any landings. I will have a word with him for you.'

'Oh I say, Willikin old chap,' Oliver Fitzroy walked up to the Warden of the Weald who was standing with John Little and Mark Reeve as they tried to work out which archers should go on what ships.

William left his henchmen to continue their deliberations and walked towards King John's bastard son. 'My Lord; you are sailing into battle too?'

'Oh no old boy; no sea legs me.'

The man who stood by Oliver's side guffawed. 'He goes as green as grass crossing the Thames on a wherry, what?'

Oliver smiled and grinned. 'Oh it is so true! I'm to command part of the land army, just in case the naughty Frenchies get ashore. Not that I think they will land here seeing as we hold the harbour. More likely to go on their way to London, don't ya think? By the way,' he inclined his head to the other man who was shorter than him by at least a head, but had the same dark wavy hair. 'This is my half-brother Richard.'

'I'm another of our late king's bastards!'

'In fact,' Oliver added with a laugh, 'we are a right pair of bastards!'

'Oh jolly good Oliver; what?' Roger held out a hand for William to shake. 'Nice to meet you old thing; Oliver here warned me that you prefer to speak English rather than French – bit rusty though, so please excuse the odd mistake; what?'

'Mistake? Richard your mother always told our father that you were a mistake.'

'And "odd" too no doubt! Ha, ha.' Richard laughed till tears appeared in his eyes.

'Anyway, Willikin old thing,' Oliver continued, turning his attention away from his half-brother who was now wiping his eyes with a piece of white silk that he had produced from his sleeve. 'It seems our Richard here has been given command of a fast nef and he wants to make a name for himself.'

William eyed up the other royal bastard, assessing just how good the man would be in battle. 'And, my Lord?'

'Oliver old boy, I've told you; call me Oliver. Anyway; archers. He wants some archers. I said you had the best in the land and over a thousand of them to boot; marksmen all. So, can you give him a handful of your best; what?'

'If you wish – Oliver.'

John Little watched the bastards leave and then came and stood at Willikin's side. 'Why do most of the nobles speak such funny English? It puzzles me.'

'Stable boys, John, stable boys.' The Warden smiled. 'If they bother to learn English at all our noble Normans tend to pick it up from their stable boys.'

'But?' Little's forehead creased. 'But stable boys don't speak in that funny way.'

'No they don't – they just find it amusing to teach their betters a form of English that will cause actual English folk to laugh at them behind their backs.'

The Head Forester's face cracked into a huge smile. 'Bloody brilliant – I hadn't thought of that.' He coughed before putting on a high pitched voice. 'Oh well, back to the jolly old work; what? What?'

It was Saint Bartholomew's day and ranks of priests lined the dock with their acolytes. Clouds of incense from swung thuribles hung high in the blue cloudless sky before the breeze caught the smoke and carried it over the departing ships. The English fleet set sail in pursuit of the much larger French fleet that had passed Sandwich and was now headed for the Isle of Thanet en-route to the Thames and London.

Godfrey, on board Hubert de Burgh's nef, looked across the gentle sea and waved to his brother Thomas who was on board Richard Fitzroy's nef. Thomas waved back and then pulled Mark Archer up alongside him so that he could wave too.

A crossbowman came and stood at Godfrey's side. He nudged Godfrey and once he had the Boxholt man's attention, he looked down at the two arrow bags at Godfrey's feet. 'What's that for? Not just you surely. Must be two dozen arrows in each of them bags.'

'Two dozen exactly,' Godfrey confirmed, his eyes still on the nef his brother was in.

'Who are you sharing them with? Him?' the man indicated Garth who was hanging onto the side of the ship with both hands, afraid to let go.

'He has his own four dozen.'

The crossbow archer patted the pouch at his side. 'A dozen bolts in there – it is all there will be time to use,' his English spoken with a Gascon French accent.

Godfrey gave a final wave to his brother before facing the man. 'I just wish we had been able to bring more arrows on board. This lot won't last long at the speed we can shoot.'

'Time will tell English, time will tell,' and with that the man made his way carefully past the four pairs of rowers to the ship's bow.

Godfrey looked at the French fleet that sailed ahead of them along the Kent coast and estimated that there were around a hundred ships. He looked over the English and knew them to be under a forty though all the English ships were filled with fighting men and he knew most of the French ones were full of supplies.

Hubert de Burgh was in his element with the sea breeze blowing his hair back and the smell of the sea in his nostrils. The nef sailed closer to the French. As soon as it was within crossbow shot de Burgh gave the order for them to heel away. The French jeered and some of those on the nearest ship loosed crossbow bolts at them, many of which hit the nef's hull. Encouraged by this the French warships broke from the convoy and turned away to chase de Burgh. The end ship was a large cog and it attempted to intercept the fast fleeing nef. Before it could do so another English nef came and cut off the French cog.

'Archers!' cried Richard Fitzroy. 'Do your thing.'

'Not easy Thomas,' Mark muttered. 'Not with us having to shoot up with that cog thing being higher than our nef whatsit.'

'Just do it: Surrey clout shots!' Thomas looked to see if his dozen archers were ready. 'SURREY CLOUT SHOTS – AIM THEM HIGH. IN YOUR OWN TIME.'

The arrows flew; some were caught in the French cog's sails, others studded the ship's wooden decks, others struck down men.

The nef rapidly closed on the French cog. As soon as she was close enough grappling hooks flew from the nef and hooked on the rails of the cog. The French quickly cut the ropes with axes though the archers managed to nail some of the axe swingers. To counter, French crossbowmen manned the rails and managed to loose off a telling volley that struck the rowers on the side nearest the French. The nef broke away as fresh oarsmen came, heaved overboard their dead shipmates, and manned the oars.

'Get the bowmen! Get the bowmen! What?' Richard called out.

Thomas nocked another arrow: 'You heard the man: "Get the bowmen"; What!'

An English cog, one of the ships from Winchelsea, came along the other side of the French cog, its archers in the fighting castles that had been built at each end shooting down onto the French ship which, because it was heavy laden, was lower in the water.

To avoid being shot many of the French crew and fighting men knelt behind the cog's top strake, held up shields or retreated under the fighting platforms. The English now threw grappling hooks and secured their own ship tight against the French one.

'Break away Ship's Master, old chap,' Richard Fitzroy called out. 'I know what comes next, don't yer know, and we don't want to be part of it seeing as the wind is blowing our way. Make about and come alongside the English Cog so we can add our men to theirs for the boarding.'

As Fitzroy's nef gained sea way the archers on the English cog put down their bows, all except Harold Harefoot and his two chosen men. The other archers bent down and picked up the clay pots at their feet and put them into the cloth pouches on the end of poles.

Jon Fish looked to his brother, Alf Fish; 'I do as hope this works, for we have hardly had any practice.'

Jon shook his head worriedly. 'So do I,' he said trying a gentle swing with his pole.

Michael the Mouse of Surrey stood up holding his pole in his hands. He looked to his men; 'Ready? Then let's do it.'

The archers swung the poles and hurled the pots down to break on the French deck. Harold and his chosen men picked up arrows with cloth pouches full of lime over the arrow heads and aimed the clumsy missiles at the stern of the French cog and the steersmen. The powdered lime contents of both clay pot and cloth pouch lifted in a blinding dust. Helped by the sea breeze it entered all parts of the ship. Frenchmen screamed at the burning pain in their eyes, mouths and noses and the English on the Winchelsea cog prepared to board as the remaining lime blew out to sea.

'We have the wind gauge!'

Hubert de Burgh took a deep breath. 'Thank you Ship's Master,' he said, his English flawless. De Burgh then cupped his hands; 'RAISE THE RED BANNER!' He turned to the household knight at his side. *'Now we have them, so let our wolves attack!'*

The English ships, seeing the red banner raised to the top of de Burgh's ship, turned to the attack, cutting the French fighting ships off from the rest of the convoy.

As his nef came within bow shot of the nearest of the French de Burgh lent forward and yelled at the top of his voice: 'MEN OF

THE WEALD – SHEW THESE FRENCH HOW REAL ARCHERS CAN SHOOT!'

Godfrey and his men already had an arrow on the string. 'SHOOT DOWN WHEN THE WAVE LIFTS US; VOLLEY SHOTS!'

The timing of the waves matched the ability of the archers to shoot and all the crossbowmen could do was wait until the range closed. The French ships were more heavily laden with men and supplies and thus lower in the water and less responsive to the helm. De Burgh's ship was the lead one and it passed along a line of French, the archers releasing volley after volley and it was not till they reached the last French ship that de Burgh allowed them to close. Now the crossbows were able to be brought into use, but their slower speed meant that they could only get one arrow off to every two of the archers using a longbow. The length of the action had taken a toll and now the arrows were almost spent.

'Take her in Ship's Master!' Hubert called and the nef turned to starboard, the oars went out and she gathered speed. 'Brace yourselves men!'

As the English ship rammed into the side of the French one, smashing in its hull Godfrey and Garth were jolted off their feet and into each other on the wet deck.

'Up Garth, get up quick.'

Garth struggled to his feet, only to go sprawling again as de Burgh's ship back rowed to extract itself from the wreck of the French nef. Finding greater stability low down the youth stayed where he was.

'Bring her about Ships Master; we have others to kill.' De Burgh looked to the French selecting his next victim. 'That one, I want to lay about that one,' the baron cried pointing at a French craft that had put out its oars in an attempt to disengage itself from an English adversary. 'He thinks he is going to get away. Lime pots at the ready – careful and throw only when I say – I don't want our own people blinded.' As the English ship came to windward the Ship's Master, without waiting to be told, swung her so that the lime would blow clear of the other English ship. 'LIME,' de Burgh cried and the pots were slung. 'WEAPONS!'

Godfrey pulled Garth to his feet. 'Take this,' he forced a wooden club enhanced with nails into his nephew's hand.

'Nice uncle.'

'It isn't pretty, but it should work.' Godfrey lifted the metal buckler off his sword and pulled out the crude and heavy vanned mace he had swapped for a mael coif with one of the men-at-arms. 'This is far from pretty too.' He hefted the weapon feeling its weight and noting its lack of balance, for it had obviously been made by a village blacksmith rather than a city weapons master.

De Burgh watched as the last of the lime floated overboard the French deck.

'GRAPPLE!'

The grappling irons flew and hooked on. Strong muscled sailors pulled on the ropes and drew the ships together.

'BOARD!' de Burgh led the boarding party, leaping down amongst the blinded French, laying about them with his hand axe.

'Over we go nephew.'

'Yes uncle.'

313

Godfrey found himself jammed between fellow archers and English men-at-arms, all keen to finish the job and take the ship. A wave, bigger than the others, sent them all staggering. Suddenly a Frenchman, obviously unblinded, rushed at him with a spear. Godfrey went down on one knee, shoved his buckler upwards, lifted the Frenchman's spear high, stood and smashed his mace into the man's ribs with a satisfying crunch. As the Frenchman doubled over Garth finished him off with a swift smack to the head with his club.

Godfrey looked around, now very aware, but the fight was already over and his fellow English were engaged in throwing blinded Frenchmen overboard.

'Well done men,' de Burgh called out before repeating it in French. '*Well done men.*'

'*All French overboard Sire,*' a household knight reported.

'Good. But do speak in English – I don't want those archers throwing you overboard by mistake.' The Baron went to the side of the French ship and looked for the Ship's Master of the English one. 'Can you nominate some of your sailors to crew this thing back to Sandwich?'

'Yes my Lord.'

'Good, pray do so and then we can seek more game.'

The fighting men on Richard Fitzroy's nef climbed the nets that had been lowered over the sides of the Winchelsea cog and waited ready to join the English already engaged in fighting on the big French cog. On the other side of the French cog were two other English nef sending their men into the struggle.

Richard went and stood by the side of Stephen, the owner of the Winchelsea cog. 'I say old boy,"

'*My lord?*'

'Oh French, how nice, best stick to English though – don't want an arrow or an axe aimed at me by mistake; what?'

'My Lord.'

'That ship, it is rather a splendid one.'

'It is Eustace the Monk's own.'

'Is it? Oh right oh. We must take it then; what?'

The French ship had a full fighting force, including many nobles and knights and, with much effort, they forced the English back to their own ships.

'LIME!' the cry came from somewhere.

More pots were thrown.

Harold Harefoot and his chosen men shot the last of their arrows at the men trying to cut the ropes that bound their ship to the English ones. 'All gone,' Harold declared then he and his chosen men picked up hand weapons. Harold pushed his way to the front of the boarding party waiting for the lime to clear over the French stern.

'BOARD!'

Over the sides went the boarders.

'I AM ENGLISH!' Harold Harefoot yelled as he jumped down on the French deck, a war axe in each hand and started laying about with them on the choking and blinded French, sending up a spray of blood and bone fragments.

'He is English!' repeated his two chosen men as they joined him in the slaughter.

Frenchmen emerged from the lower decks and charged towards the English invaders. Two had crossbows and they loosed them at Harold. One bolt pierced his chest where he wore a white cross and the other bolt smashed into the shiny pewter Canterbury pilgrim's badge he wore on the other side. Harold looked at the bolts protruding from him with dismay. 'I am dead!' he whispered as his knees gave way.

'They are dead!' his chosen men yelled as they ran down the crossbowmen, who were in the act of pulling on the goats' foot on their belt to cock their bows, and smashed the Frenchmen to the ground with repeated blows from their hand axes.

'Save the knights and nobles.'

'Who said that?' Thomas asked Mark Archer.

'Not one of us: "no prisoners" was Willikin's rule and that still stands as far as I am concerned.'

'TAKE THE NOBILITY PRISONERS CHAPS,' Richard Fitzroy called out. 'LOTS OF SILVER FROM RANSOMS DONT YER KNOW – SHARES ALL ROUND.'

'Oh well,' Thomas pulled back from cutting a French knight's throat. 'Money, well that changes things doesn't it.'

'Yes it does,' Mark agreed as he clubbed the knight unconscious.

'I say; has anyone seen Eustace the monk; what?'

The English forced the French of value they had taken on board the nefs and then forced those of no value overboard. They then started a systematic search of the ship for Eustace.

Suddenly a black bearded figure burst from a hatchway, grabbed an oar and attacked all in his way.

'I say,' Richard Fitzroy exclaimed. 'It's Eustace! After him chaps.'

Thomas tried to get out of the way of the black bearded and clad man with the swinging oar but received a blow to the back that sent him flying overboard. He hit the water with a resounding splash and found himself floundering in the water surrounded by drowning Frenchmen. He remembered being told to tread water when as a child he had been on his maternal grandfather's fishing boat and fallen into Bosham harbour. He trod, but with each wave he swallowed more sea water and began to get tired. He stopped treading and his head went below the waves. He looked up at the green walls of water above him and was spurred to start treading again. More waves and more water; he went down again. With extra effort of mind over matter he began wearily treading and managed to just get his head above the waves. He moved his befuddled head and saw he had drifted round the Winchelsea cog. A figure appeared on the ship and looked down at him. Thomas lifted a tired arm and started to sink again. With a splash the figure dived into the water and swam out to where Thomas had sunk then went deep to find him. Grabbing the drowning man by the neck the slim swimmer pulled him to the surface. Thomas spluttered and coughed as arms came under his, laying him backwards in the water and the pair slowly made it back to the cog. A net was dropped and willing hands pulled the pair out of the water.

Thomas propped himself up on the deck on one elbow and looked at his rescuer. 'Will? Will Greenleaf?' he spluttered.

'I knew it was you Thomas; no one else would wear a yellow hood with a red shirt. Well a red shirt with green and brown patches.' Will smiled as he stood dripping water. 'I couldn't let your drown could I?'

317

'I thought.' Thomas stopped to cough up more water. 'I thought you were going to stay on the land?'

Will laughed. 'Well I changed my mind: I couldn't let you and the others get all the glory could I. Or all the plunder come to that.'

The Master of de Burgh's ship left the side of the steersman and approached the baron. 'My Lord, the French fighting ships have turned and started to run back towards France. Do you want us to try and run them down?'

Hubert de Burgh thought for a moment, looking from the fleeing fighting ships to the rest of the French fleet, which was now in disarray with some ships turning to join the run back to France, whilst others continued along the Kent coast towards Thanet. 'No,' he decided. 'Let them run, our job is to capture those heading for London – we can't let the Dauphin get any supplies or reinforcements.'

'As you wish my Lord.' The Master returned to the steering board, and set about changing course.

Seeing de Burgh's ship change direction those English not engaged in fighting French warships also changed direction to pursue the heavily laden French supply ships. The English ships carried no cargo and were thus much faster and it did not take long to run the fleeing French down. This time few arrows flew as most had already been shot. Instead the dreadful lime pots were slung before boarding.

'Here we go again nephew.' Godfrey let his buckler dangle from its lanyard and gripped the thwart at his side and waited for the jolt of the nef jamming alongside the French ship. He turned and saw

Garth doing the same, except with both hands, his club held between his knees.

The nef bumped alongside the Frenchman and was quickly secured. Godfrey joined the rear ranks of fighting men as they jumped down onto the French deck. He lifted himself onto the top strake and leapt. The deck was slippery with blood where the English boarders had already hacked their way along the ship towards the stern and Godfrey went down with Garth stumbling over him.

'Sorry uncle!' Garth exclaimed as he got himself up and went off in pursuit of the French crew, many of whom decided to dive into the sea of their own accord rather than be assaulted with a weapon before being thrown overboard.

Godfrey tried to stand, but the searing pain in his right ankle caused him to slump against the French ship's hull and hold to the top strake for support. He nudged the mace he had dropped with his good foot until it was out of the way and waited for Garth's return. The throbbing in his ankle seemed to match the lapping of the waves against the ship's side and he closed his eyes to help master the pain.

'Are you alright uncle?'

Godfrey opened his eyes to mere slits and looked at his nephew. 'No. Help me?'

'Get back on our own ship? Why bother. We have taken this one and I am sure his nibs de Burgh will send her back to Sandwich as he did the other he captured.'

'Then help me to get to that rowing bench and sit down; all this ship fighting is too much for me.'

William Marshal, Earl of Pembroke, Regent of England, Guardian of King Henry III, stood alongside Hubert de Burgh and Philip d'Aubigny watching the unloading of the captured ships.

'*My Lords, we have a veritable fortune here.*'

'*And, your Grace, there are more captured French ships to bring alongside the docks yet.*' Hubert's eyes glistened with joy.

Philip d'Aubigny turned to the Regent; '*I assume you will claim the French nobles and knights for ransom Your Grace.*'

'*Yes: the royal treasury needs the funds, besides; it will give me more leverage when the Dauphin begs a peace treaty with us.*' He gave an amused snort. '*Louis has little option now – he cannot carry on the war with few men and no supplies or money and the rebel barons have lost their taste for defiance.*'

'*Well Your Grace,*' de Burgh looked down to the dock where another captured ship was being warped in. '*You have offered generous terms to the rebels; only a fool would continue to side with Louis.*'

The Regent acknowledged the baron's comments with a slight nod. '*And we would be fools to not offer good terms to the rebels and will offer sensible terms to the French; this war has almost ruined the kingdom of England – our job now is to heal the wounds and rebuild the land.*'

Philip watched another heavy chest being hauled out of the hold of a damaged French nef. '*There is a lot of treasure taken today, enough money and goods to have kept Louis in the field for a year at least.*'

'*Yes,*' the Regent agreed. '*But we will be fair to those who fought for us today and brought this victory with their strength, effort, blood and sometimes their lives. Seeing as this is Saint Bartholomew's day I have it in mind to build a hospital here in Sandwich dedicated to him and that it will treat the poor. But, the rest of the booty should be divided up, not only amongst the survivors of today's conflict, but also to the families of those who died. If we do that I am sure God will continue to bless us and our enterprise. Don't you think so Hubert?*'

'*Indeed, if you think it best. There is another matter your Grace, what should we do with Eustace the Monk's head?*'

'*Ah yes; the great pirate's head. I did hear that Eustace offered Sir Richard Fitzroy ten thousand marks of silver to spare his life.*'

'*Money isn't everything your Grace.*'

'*That, Hubert, is not like you?*'

De Burgh gave a short amused laugh. '*Not true your Grace,*' he protested. '*I did turn down French offers of money in exchange for me surrendering Dover castle to them.*'

'*I know. Without the loyalty of men like you, Philip here and others ...*'

'*Such as Willikin of the Weald?*' d'Aubigny suggested.

'*Yes; such as Willikin of the Weald. Without men like you the kingdom of England would by now be just another French fiefdom. Loyalty will not be forgotten – it will be rewarded.*'

Hubert de Burgh rubbed his hands together as yet more laden chests were brought ashore. '*Willikin deserves a reward, and so do his chief men. I know how much they contributed. Without them I could never have held Dover castle.*'

321

'*Yes*,' William Marshal watched the Dover castle's commander with amusement. '*I will make sure the honourable thing is done. In addition to closing the great Wealden forest and its roads to both French and rebels, Willikin has shewn us much that can be put to use when it comes to warfare, especially the value of good archers. The only thing that worries me is that he seems to have taught Sir Richard Fitzroy that the only good Frenchman is one without his head – that ten thousand marks could have been most useful.*'

Chapter 17: Land Ho

Godfrey, with his new wife Rose on his arm, limped from the doorway of St Mary's church in Iping where the union had been blessed by the priest John of Chichester. Alongside him strode his twin brother, Thomas, who had his arm around his obviously pregnant wife, Lucy. Behind them came the villagers of Iping, those of Wulfbearding, family from Bosham, Trottingham and Steadham. They all headed for the Iping village green where Rose, the wife of John the priest, Elfwyn Black and the leading women of the local villages had set out a feast of suitable proportions.

Standing in front of the trestle tables that groaned with food and drink stood Willikin of the Weald and at his right hand his wife Mary, sometimes known as Marion Freshwater. They were flanked by Willikin's Head Forester, John Little, and his Reeve, Mark. As the wedding party made its way forward, its speed dictated by Godfrey's sprained ankle, William of Cassingham and his wife advanced to meet them.

The party stopped and waited in front of the squire and his wife. William smiled at the newly married couples. 'I bring blessings to you from our King Henry and his Regent, the Earl of Pembroke.'

William's wife, Mary, nudged him, smiling brightly all the while. 'Tell them husband, don't be a tease.'

'My wife has been a great blessing to me, as I hope yours will be to you, Godfrey and Thomas, but she can be a bit impatient at times.'

Mary gave William a gentle kick in the foot.

The Warden of the Weald gave a loving look to his wife before resuming. 'The blessing I bring from the King is more than just words. His Grace has followed the advice of the Regent and has granted each of you his own holding.'

'You will no longer be yeomen,' Mary explained. 'You will be Esquires.'

'Thank you my dear. As I was saying you have been granted your own holdings. Seeing that you led the men of the Boxholt it seemed appropriate that the land you will have and hold of the crown will be Boxholt and Rotherbridge near Salehurst in Sussex. You will live side by side.'

Thomas looked to his twin; 'You can have Boxholt I want Rotherbridge.' Thomas gave a smirk; 'I will change its name to Robin's Bridge!'

Thomas, slightly the worse for downing too much bog myrtle beer that his cousin Godwin had sent down from Battersea, leant on his brother Godfrey's shoulder. 'Means moving from here Big Brother. What,' he slurred, 'shall we do with our rights in Iping?'

'We could keep them,' Godfrey responded, his head clearer as he had only been imbibing Godwin's honey ale. 'Or we could pass it on, subject to the Lord of the manor's approval.'

'And scot brother.'

'And scot, though what we got from the battle off Sandwich will not make that an issue.'

'Who to pass it to?' Thomas had problems with the "ss" and made it sound like "shh".

'We could leave them to our nephew, Garth, our sister Edith's son, but he already holds in Wulfbearding following his father Robert's death.'

'I want to pass it on to Will Greenleaf.'

'A good idea Thomas for he did save your life.'

'And life ...' Thomas didn't finish the sentence as he suddenly fell asleep.

'Is worth the living,' Godfrey completed for his now snoring twin. 'Especially as England is now free of foreign invaders.'

***

A certain youth, William by name, a fighter and a loyalist [to King John] who despised those who were not, gathered a vast number of archers in the forests and waste places of the Kent and Sussex Weald, all of them men of the region, and all the time they attacked and disrupted the enemy, and as a result of their intense resistance many thousands of Frenchmen were slain. Roger of Wendover, Flores Historiarum, II. 182 (Rolls Series, London, 1887).

***

Assize of Arms 1252 Henry III: All freemen with property worth 40 -100 shillings must have a bow, arrows, sword and dagger.

***

Author's Notes

The genesis of this novel goes back many years. I had heard of Willikin of the Weald as a young boy when reading about King Richard and King John in a text book: it was just a single line but the name stuck. In 1995 I wrote a novel, 'Woden's Wolf', about the English resistance to the Norman Conquest though the eyes of Godfrew of Garrett, a displaced Thane who takes the nom de guerre of Wulf. Many who read it asked for a follow up, which was a hard ask as, not only had I changed jobs and had less time, but also I had killed Wulf off at the end of the book.

In recent years I have taken up re-enactment, heading a Household of 14thC English archers. Being who I am, I have written several short stories that create background to the persona the Household members have assumed. The key to the Household is a real historical figure, Sir Alan de Buxhall of Salehurst (Buxhall is one of at least eight spellings of his name), Knight of the Garter, King's Counsellor and Constable of the Tower of London to both Edward III and Richard II. The fiction is that my persona, Geffrey de Wulf, is descended from Godfrew of Garrett's middle son and Sir Alan from Godfrew's eldest son.

I recently had my interest in King John and the Baron's war revived by reading some of Elizabeth Chadwick's excellent novels of the period. This, in turn, led me to buy Sean McGlynn's excellent book on the French invasion of 1215-17 "Blood Cries Afar". Nils Vissar's entertaining and lightly written Web sites on the topic that start at http://nilsvisser.hubpages.com/hub/Archers-Quest-4-A-Nasty-Piece-of-Work also gave me food for thought.

Again Willikin came up, but again, there is little to know about the man despite recent claims that he was one of the origins of the Robin Hood legends.

This novel is not about Willikin himself but that of some of his band of archers. I have made the main men the twins Godfrey and Thomas of Iping, near Woolbedding and Trotton, where my family originates from. They are the descendants of Godfrew's eldest son and that Godfrey is the ancestor of Sir Alan, who was born at Bugzell, near Salehurst, East Sussex. I have thus tried to provide a bridge between Godfrew of Garrett and Geffrey đe Wulf, and Sir Alan de Buxhall whilst at the same time give those who enjoyed Woden's Wolf the follow up novel they craved. It also gives a fictional, but reasonable, explanation for the Boxall/Boxell/Boxill family being originally from the Woolbedding area yet the most famous of that name coming from Salehurst (for those not from Sussex, Bugzell is how Boxell is said there and Bosham is spoken as Bozem).

One reviewer of Woden's Wolf criticised it for being "a series of 'boy's own' adventure tales". Well, that's the way it was at the time and, indeed, it is very true for the over two years covered by this novel. Just remember that I am only covering the Wealden activity too: the amount of military action packed into the period of the French invasion of 1215-17 is amazing.

I have tried to keep the story as close as I can to that undertaken by Willikin and his archers. I do confess though that the assassination of Mark Strongman and his lover is fictional but the way it was done is based on an actual recorded event. With regards to the amount of poaching at the times read Stenton's 'English Society in the Early Middle Ages' which shews that it was on a massive scale through the whole Mediaeval period. The methods of sending lime dust onto the French ships during the Battle of Sandwich are taken from an illustration in Matthew of Paris' description of the battle.

The Weald was important as it lay between England's South East Coast and London, which was the main base of the rebel Barons and the French. Getting supplies to London would have been easier and safer if they went through the Weald, rather than via the River Thames, except Willikin and his archers lived and operated in the Weald, and they had no intentions of allowing safe travel to the French.

I have called Prince Louis of France "The Dauphin": in fact this title was not in use for the heir apparent to the French Crown till 1315.

Thanks must be given to Google whose access to maps, both ancient and modern, proved so helpful.

Of course, when it comes to thanks, there is my mate Mark Tustian, a fellow member of the Wulfing Household who kept me honest when it came to historical accuracy and fellow re-enactor, Ann Dugmore for finding my grammar and spelling mistakes.

Geoff Boxell

aka Geffrey de Wulf

***

Notes:

Wulfbearding: the old name of Woolbeding, West Sussex.

Trottingham: Trotton, West Sussex.

Hurst: a trap for deer. Normally it consisted of a run enclosed by wicker hurdles or scrim that had places for those hunting to stand and shoot with either a bow or a cross bow. The Weald is full of towns and villages that end in "hurst" which indicates the location not only of the site of such a trap but, usually, the site of a noble's hunting lodge.

Script: pouch or purse.

Murthrum Fine: Due to the habit of the English of killing off any of his supporters who wandered away from the beaten track, William the Conqueror introduced a law that said any dead body that could not be proved to be English was to be assumed to be French and thus under his personal protection. The man's lord was then obliged to produce the killer within a short period of time or pay a fine of 46 marks. The lord could then demand from the Hundred where the body was found to reimburse him. Dead English would be dealt with in the normal way without a fine being involved for not handing over the killer.

Throstle bird: thrush.

Ox teams: oxen always work in pairs. The number of pairs used depends on the load they have to pull or the heaviness of the soil if they are being used for ploughing. The names of the pair are usually associated and one has a name with one syllable whilst the other two syllables.

Cassingham: the old name for Kensham, Kent.

Holt: a small wood or spinney

Robin Goodfellow: a woodland spirit

Herla: a Saxon king known for his hunting, possibly the origins of Herne the Hunter

Lute: in this tale more likely to be its predecessor the oud but I have used "lute" as this is what most readers would know and the difference is small.

Pender: dialect word for a village pound keeper where the pound is a walled or fenced area used for restraining straying animals until they are claimed and a fine paid.

Costrel: a leather drinking bottle, normally cylindrical in shape with its opening central in the body of the cylinder.

Buckler: a small round shield that can also be used as a knuckle duster.

Longbow: Literally a "long bow". The term is a much later one than the period covered by the book. We know from findings in sunken ships in Roskilda Fjord and from Otzi the Iceman who had a yew longbow and died around 5,000 years ago between the end of the Stone Age and start of the Bronze Age, that such bows existed years before the 100 Years War where their use became so famous. The ideal bow was made of yew, but ash, elm or hazel were commonly used. For more information read "Archery in Medieval England" by Richard Wadge.

Garth: enclosed yard.

Manchet Bread: the best quality white wheat bread normally reserved for the top table.

Rouncy: a general purpose riding horse suitable for warfare when needed. 14-15 hands high it was sometimes also used as a pack horse.

Caltrop: an anti-personnel/horse weapon made up of two or more sharp nails or spines arranged in such a manner that one of them always points upward from a stable base (for example, a tetrahedron).

Cordwainer: shoemaker who makes fine soft leather shoes.

Curfew bell: a bell rung in the evening as the signal for everyone to put out the fire and go to bed.

Leet: small artificial stream often connected with mill pond overflow or supplying water to a:-linen tenter field: where the cloth was laid on tenter hooks to bleach after being soaked in water.

Braies: under pants.

Merchet scot: a fine to be paid to one's lord when a woman was married.

St Thomas' day: 21 December.

The Feast of the Conversion of St Paul: 25 January.

Brighthelmeston: original name for Brighton.

Skep: a traditional straw beehive.

Eke: the removable top of a skep.

Hurdle: a woven section of fence or wall usually made of hazel, willow or wicker.

Pavise: a large oblong shield behind which a crossbowman can hide whilst he reloads his weapon.

Bill: an agricultural slashing tool. For normal use it has a haft thigh high, but the head can be mounted on a staff. In later years it became a standard military pole arm.

Groat: a coin worth four pennies.

Maul: a long handled wooden mallet used for hammering in stakes and poles.

Deer net: whilst "noble sport" meant either hunting deer on horseback or shooting them in a hurst, taking deer for bulk slaughtering was normally done by driving them towards nets that were hung at the end of a chase or hurst.

Coppice: trees that have been cut down to a stump once they had produced new growth to a required height. The trees are then allowed to regrow, thus giving a continual source of straight wood.

Trebuchet: a stone throwing siege machine that works using a counter weight.

Mangonel and petraria: siege machines that work using torsion ropes.

Quern: stone tool for hand-grinding grains.

Cinque Ports: five ports in Kent and Sussex that by a Royal Charter of 1155 gave maintenance to ships ready for the Crown in case of need. The chief obligation laid upon the ports, as a corporate duty, was to provide 57 ships for 15 days' service to the king annually, each port fulfilling a proportion of the whole duty. In return the towns received many privileges and exemptions.

Conroi: a cavalry combat group of about ten mounted men who fought as a combined unit.

Destrier: a war horse.

Cawel: a non-headed cabbage. The headed cabbage is only known in England from the 14thC onwards.

Solar: a room in a manor house or similar generally situated on an upper storey, designed as the family's private living and sleeping quarters. In such houses, the main ground-floor room was known as the great hall and there all members of the household, including tenants, employees and servants, would eat and meet. Access to a solar was often by an external staircase from the garth.

Leah land: an area of woodland that has been cleared for cropping.

Saint Bartholomew's day: 24 August.

Thurible: incense holder that is swung on a chain.

Thwart: a structural crosspiece forming a seat for a rower in a boat or ship.

Useful Web Sites:

http://www.ask.com/wiki/Open_field_system?o=2802&qsrc=999&ad=double Down&an=apn&ap=ask.com

http://www.foxearth.org.uk/oxen.html

www.bahs.org.uk/AGHR/ARTICLES/20n1a2.pdf

https://www.english-heritage.org.uk/publications/turning-the-plough-loss-of-a-landscape-legacy/turningplough.pdf

http://www.ace.hu/am/2013_3/AM-13-03-NM.pdf

http://lucasshipsides.com/blog/research-and-essays/traditional-folk-music-jongleurs-and-troubadours-in-the-middle-ages/

http://en.wikipedia.org/wiki/Lute

http://edithsstreets.blogspot.com/2010/08/thames-tributary-falcon-falcon-turns.html

http://www.british-history.ac.uk/vch/sussex/vol4/pp182-188

http://en.wikipedia.org/wiki/Horses_in_the_Middle_Ages

http://en.wikipedia.org/wiki/Curfew_bell
http://en.wikipedia.org/wiki/Guala_Bicchieri
http://en.wikipedia.org/wiki/Beehive
http://plantagenesta.livejournal.com/30673.html

www.ingramcontent.com/pod-product-compliance
Lightning Source LLC
Chambersburg PA
CBHW070212260626
47160CB00002B/527